LITKE THE AIR AFTER RAIN

THE HILTON LEGACY, BOOK 2

a novel by Kellyn Roth

Published by Kellyn Roth, Author

Wild Blue Wonder Press

ISBN: 978-1-962222-05-1

Scripture quotations are taken from the King James Version (KJV).

Cover design by Carpe Librum Book Design

Developmental Editor: Grace A. Johnson

Copy Editor: Andrea Renee Cox

admin@wildbluewonderpress.com

www.wildbluewonderpress.com

Dedication

To Kara.
Thank you for all you've done for me and for so many other young authors.
You bring so much light—and fire—to this sometimes cold world.
There are far, far better things ahead.

TABLE OF CONTENTS

The Characters

The Americans

Lorelei "Lore" Hilton — a young woman who lives to face the storm. Lorelei hails from the Hilton family of Boston, who own the Hilton Shipping Co.

The Hiltons of Boston — Clarence and Dorothy-Lynn "Lynnie" Hilton and their children: Patrick "Trick," Lorelei "Lore," Gwendolyn "Winnie" Hilton. Clarence Hilton is Philip Knight's oldest friend.

Harriet — Lorelei's faithful maid.

Mr. Patrick and Mrs. Cassie Hilton — Lorelei's older brother and his bride. Patrick is banished from the Hilton family and lives in Philadelphia where he works for their rival company, Baldwin & Sons.

The Baldwins of Philadelphia — owners of Baldwin & Sons, a rival shipping company to the Hilton Shipping Co. Mr. and Mrs. John Baldwin and their sons: John Jr. and Rupert.

The Strausses — a family from Philadelphia, Pennsylvania. The eldest son,

Peter, is married to Cassie Hilton's dearest friend, the former Miss Alice Knight.

THE ENGLISH

Aubrey Montgomery — a gentleman who just wants to go home to his country estate and rest. Formerly Cassie Hilton's suitor.

Francesca "Fran" and Constance "Connie" Montgomery — Aubrey's younger sisters.

Mr. Anthony and Mrs. Aimée Burton — the local doctor and his somewhat eccentric wife.

Gibson Ashfield — a most unsuitable man; dearest friend of Aubrey Montgomery.

The Knights of Pearlbelle Park — owners of an estate located in Kent, England. Mr. Philip and Mrs. Claire Knight and their children: Alice, Ivy, Ned, Caleb, Jack, and Rebecca.

Content Warning

Some readers are uncomfortable with certain types of content in the books they read. Though my novels are all closed-door romances with no gratuitous content, contain no swearing, and handle all topics discussed biblically, I have a brief list of content warnings for each of my books below. Some of these may contain minor spoilers. Read at your own risk! kellynrothauthor.com/content-warnings

CHAPTER ONE

April 1884
Boston, Massachusetts

B IRTHDAYS WERE SUPPOSED TO be happy occasions, but Lorelei Anne Hilton had never had a happy birthday. With the nineteenth one being even more unpleasant than the eighteen before it, she believed this would never change.

This year, the *expectations* had been raised, which heightened the normal pain of her disinterested parents and the lavish parties created to distract from the increasingly obvious dysfunction of her family.

Oh, the expectations weren't so terrible. After all, it wasn't that she didn't *want* to be married or that she didn't *want* the Hilton Shipping Company to keep running. No, it was more that the *reason* she must marry, and must marry someone her father could easily manipulate, was because her brother was no longer a part of her life.

It had been less than a year, so she supposed she must allow herself some time to grieve both Patrick's absence and the life that left when he did. At the same time, it had been long enough that she knew better than to pout. She did—truly.

It was just that this was her first birthday without Patrick at her side. She was so used to his affection—his gifts—the way he made even the most extravagant ritual on her parents' part feel small and intimate and about her ... and not about the Hilton legacy.

Patrick was a married man now, and she had been one of the biggest proponents of his leaving their family forever. He had gotten out. And she had said she'd be fine. And she had meant it. And she had cried herself to sleep that night for the first time since she was a baby.

It meant more to her, perhaps, that Patrick had gotten away from the company, the house, and their parents than that she be afforded some slight freedoms.

Now she stood in her room, staring into the mirror and playing with her pearl necklace while her maid arranged her dark hair into an elaborate crown about her head.

Behind her, scurrying paws and barking preceded a girlish giggle as the door flew open.

Lorelei closed her eyes briefly. "Winnie." She hoped the one word contained all of her exhaustion. "Please put both dogs in the kennel, as I asked you to *hours* ago."

"Mars was crying, and Potato looked so disgusted with me." Lorelei heard rather than saw the pout on her younger sister's face. "I had to bring them up. Let them stay in my room during the party, Lore—if you don't tell Mama, no one will care."

"Whatever. Just get them out of my room."

Mars—a large sable shepherd that her brother had left with them—jumped up, his gangly legs flailing on her lap as he realized he had miscalculated the leap. She jerked to her feet as Mars and Winnie's grouchy black-and-white spaniel, Potato, began scurrying about her feet. They were clearly intent upon murdering each other. "*Now.*"

Winnie sighed and flopped across the room in disdain. She scooped up Potato and called Mars, and the entire company frolicked out of the room.

Lorelei took a moment to compose herself before lowering onto the seat in front of her vanity once more. "Continue, Harriet."

Her maid resumed the preparations of her hair. "I should have locked the door." A soft chuckle followed her words.

"Talk about something else, will you? Winnie has been so utterly impulsive lately, and I don't want it on my mind throughout the party." It was Lorelei's fault. Patrick had always been able to manage Winnie. Yes, Lorelei could manage adults to a certain degree—but at seventeen, Winnie still clung to childhood like one might cling to a warm blanket on a cold night.

Understandable, but hardly acceptable. Lorelei didn't know how to talk to Winnie about this without alienating her further.

Patrick would've known what to say, but Patrick was not here.

Harriet removed a pin from between her teeth. "Are you excited for this party, assuming your sister doesn't cause any … incidents?"

"Oh, I suppose so."

"I believe your parents have certain expectations about the evening." Harriet was always good at prodding Lorelei right toward the point of the matter.

She met Harriet's soft brown eyes in the mirror. "American royalty. That's what Patrick always called us. Don't tell Mother I mentioned his name." She sighed.

"True." Harriet tucked one final pin in place and stepped back. "What do you think?"

Lorelei tilted her head from side to side, taking in the arrangement her maid had devised. A tiara perched atop her hair, and Harriet had managed to turn the straightness into delicate curls with a mix of overnight rags and cautious arrangement. "Perfect. Thank you."

"You're welcome." Harriet stepped around Lorelei to begin gathering combs, brushes, and boxes of pins and ribbons. "I hope you have a nice time at the party."

"I hope I do, too." She rather doubted it. It would be yet another opportunity for her parents to hammer home the idea that Lorelei was "practically engaged," whatever that meant, to William Pent.

There was nothing particularly wrong with Billy, but he wasn't husband material. Oh, he might be someday, but he was Lorelei's age—barely nineteen—and had always seemed like a younger brother to her despite being a few months older than she. Besides, he was so young, more interested in shooting guns than he was in her, which was never a pleasant position for a woman to be in.

Yet he pursued her because, perhaps, he had nothing better to do—and because his parents wanted him to—and because his brother was now married and would soon take a larger part in the Pents' company, leaving Billy with no business to go with his business degree—once he got it, that was. He was finishing up his second year at a prestigious university. Mr. Hilton talked constantly about how bright Billy was, and he was, but it wasn't hard to get ahead in school with private tutors and a family pushing you to move faster, mature faster.

She understood why it was important to her father that Billy be academic, and in truth, one of the few things Lorelei liked about him was how academic he was. It showed that he wasn't like the other boys she'd grown up with, the ones who took tours of Europe after college and wasted time. Lorelei couldn't stand wasted time.

Yes, Billy was studious. Unlike her brother, who had chosen to forego college, as her father had called it a ridiculous waste of time. Of course, that was pre-Billy. Now Mr. Hilton had reason to insist that college wasn't so bad. The man who would end up in charge of the Hilton legacy attended a university, after all.

So no, it wasn't Billy that Lorelei resented. He was nice enough. It was the fact that her inheritance was contingent on her marriage when she could have been the heiress in her own right. She was more than capable of managing the Hilton Shipping Co. with or without a husband—so why must she marry? Her father had had an opportunity to rewrite the will in any way he wanted. His choice was to involve another man rather than rely on his elder daughter.

It shouldn't have surprised her as much as it did. It was the natural choice. Yet Lorelei couldn't help but think that he could've used her as he'd always used Patrick. She didn't mind. It wasn't like she'd be much of a housewife—maybe a half-decent society wife, but she wasn't naive enough to think that simply being a society wife was really enough to make a marriage and family work even if her parents seemed to think it was.

No, she would do far better simply obtaining an occupation rather than a relationship, but that was no longer an option. Her father had not made it an option.

There was a knock at the door.

"Come in."

Her mother entered the room, herself pristinely prepared for the evening's revelries. She looked a lot like Winnie—auburn hair, gray eyes—but Lorelei could trace hints of herself in her mother's face and bearing. "Ah, you're ready."

"Yes." Lorelei waved her hand slightly to dismiss Harriet. "Guests will be arriving soon."

Mrs. Hilton nodded, stepped forward, and, without a word, placed a small package wrapped in brown paper on the vanity.

Lorelei looked up. "I thought we were saving gifts for later."

"This one is different."

"Oh?" She picked up the package. It was clearly some piece of jewelry, but that was hardly an unusual present from her parents.

"It's from your brother."

She stilled. Since he'd walked out of the Hilton house and out of their lives last July, there had been nothing from Patrick—or if there had been, her parents had not seen fit to share it with her. She knew based on a brief announcement in the paper that he had married Cassie and that he now worked for Father's primary competitor, Baldwin & Sons.

Now she was receiving a birthday present? How strange.

She raised questioning eyes to her mother's face.

Apparently uncomfortable under her scrutiny, her mother squirmed. "There is no note, I don't think, so I saw no harm in it. Your father needn't know."

Ah. So her mother's fury over Patrick being disinherited without so much as an intelligent conversation had finally taken a physical form. Yet to say that to her mother was probably unwise, so she simply replied, "Thank you."

"You're welcome. Please come down in five minutes." With that, Mother turned and left.

Lorelei swiftly unwrapped the paper to find a small, black velvet box. She lifted the lid—within was a compass attached to a chain and with a cross engraved on the outside.

Hmm. What an interesting choice, Trick.

She withdrew the compass, turned it over, and then flipped the lid open. An engraving read, "*Und das hat mit ihrem Singen Die* Lorelei *getan.*"

She blinked, recognizing the line from a German poem—with only the original name, "Lore-Ley," edited to her own. It was like Patrick to pick that—and to know that she'd recognize it. She seldom forgot something she read, and this poem by Heinrich Heine had contained her name and the intriguing legend of an enchanting mermaid.

The line he had had engraved was roughly translated to: "And this by her song's sheer power, fair Lorelei has done." Hardly accurate, as she wasn't a musical person, but she suspected her name had been the primary motivator—and the memory of those days in Germany when Patrick had attempted to get her to learn the language.

She had. Not that she could speak it, but she could read it. Winnie was another matter entirely. She doubted Winnie would survive five minutes if forced to encounter any language but her native English.

Lorelei snapped the compass closed and turned it over a few times. Her mind wandered back to those slow days in Berlin—wandering the streets, sipping hot chocolate at a cafe while Winnie sampled every kind of pastry available, and talking to Patrick about this and that.

He'd been distracted then—mind filled, she believed, with thoughts of Cassie and of how his growing attraction to her conflicted with their parents' mandate: that he would marry, without love, to the woman of their choice.

That was no longer happening, which was good. It would have bothered Patrick, Lorelei felt, to marry without love. He'd spent his whole life deriding their parents' marriage, which was more one of hatred than affection, and it was better that he had found a woman he loved—a good woman, at that—and settled down with her.

The Lord had had such a plan for Patrick, for he deserved it—and he needed it. Lorelei, on the other hand?

She had been built for the task at hand.

So why the spiraling nerves?

This was the best option. The *only* option.

She set the compass on the vanity. Yes, she remembered those days in Germany. The words he had said to her—trying to prepare her to run the company. He had known, perhaps, in his heart of hearts that there might come a time when he was not there ... and that Lorelei was his natural replacement.

Of course, that was part of the reason she felt restless. She was not going to be his natural replacement. There was no place for her in the Hilton Shipping Co. While she remained in Boston, married to a man of her father's choosing, that could never change.

She didn't feel she was making the step forward she had hoped.

At last, she straightened the skirt of her silver dress and made her way to the top of the stairs. Her father met her there, extended his arm, and allowed her to take it. His hand pressed over hers must look affectionate and fatherly to the outside observer, but it was all for show.

In some ways, that made Lorelei more comfortable. She wasn't always sure there was much to her beyond the surface, and it was far better that the relationships in her life conformed to this lack of depth within her. It would be a shame to be stuck in the shallows while her family explored the depths.

Lord, show me how to live this life as myself. Show me how to find my place here—with my family or in my own family. I can't be a piece of driftwood anymore, reliant on the strength of a mightier wave to force me to whatever beach it sees fit. Make me like an albatross, mistress of my own fate.

She descended the stairs, then walked into the ballroom. The arched ceiling was hung with fairy lanterns—the floor was full of elegantly-dressed personages—and music was already drifting from somewhere.

The evening progressed as it ought to. Dancing, a dinner near midnight, and more dancing. Conversations with her old friends ... and being dragged away from those conversations by Billy Pent.

He talked of his studies. Of what he was learning about the world of business. That, Lorelei could appreciate, but she couldn't help but realize that he knew these things so she would not have to. So that she would not be allowed to.

That thought was a difficult one, turning the glass of punch in her hand bitter despite the overall sweetness of the concoction.

"Are you all right, Lorelei?" Billy's eager voice broke through her inner thoughts, forcing her once more to the present. "You look a thousand miles away."

If only she were a thousand miles away, off in San Francisco or Italy or Africa, pursuing her father's interests for the Hilton Shipping Co. That would be the life.

The captain of her own ship. In charge. Looked to for guidance and order, which she could surely provide.

Yet if she could not run the empire, she could influence it. Perhaps her hold on Billy would strengthen after their marriage. Perhaps he would no longer turn first to her father for everything—perhaps he would realize the value of heeding his wife's opinion.

Not that it was likely.

Frustration invaded again, and she took another sip of her punch before replying to Billy. "I'm fine. A little tired. These sorts of parties are hardly to my taste." She'd frankly have preferred something a little more intimate; unlike her brother, she was not suited for the social element of making connections. She'd rather be calculating than polite.

If only toughness was a valued element and not another thing that had made her father decide he needed someone a little easier to influence at the helm.

What did he think would happen when he died, though? She wanted to growl with exasperation. He was not thinking of the long-term—simply of protecting his interests now. Everyone had to die, even Mr. Clarence Hilton, and when that happened, his company would fall apart if he didn't first entrust it to someone who could manage it in his absence.

Then what would happen to the Hiltons? Surely they would be no more!

The hours ticked on toward dawn, and at last, the guests trickled home. Billy was one of the last to leave. He'd managed to gain a promise from her to meet in a few days, which was more initiative than he'd taken in the last several months combined.

Perhaps Father was pressuring him to act swiftly. After all, there were certainly other men interested in Lorelei—the party that evening had proven this—and her father couldn't want her to think of anyone but Billy.

Sweet, gentle, kind, easily manipulated Billy.

Her steps were slow as she ascended the stairs. Winnie had been sent off to bed earlier, and her parents were settling last-minute details with those they had hired to serve at the party, so fortunately, Lorelei was able to make this trek on her own.

Back in her room, her maid came to divest her of her gown, undo her hair, and put away her jewelry—and of course, draw her a bath. It was a painstaking process, and the sun was beginning to peek over the horizon when the water grew cold and Lorelei was forced to slip into her nightdress ... and take coffee next to the window, for she wouldn't be able to settle her mind until she'd had a few hours of silence.

"What's this?"

Lorelei glanced over her shoulder to find Harriet holding the compass from Patrick.

"Where shall I put this?"

"Oh, give it to me. It's a trinket—I'll find a spot for it."

The compass was placed in her hand, and Lorelei sipped her plain black coffee and held the trinket.

Harriet left, and in the stillness, Lorelei discerned a soft rustling sound. *Wait.*

She popped the compass open. It was broken. He'd given her a broken compass? She squinted at the engraving, then turned the compass over. Where the chain was attached, a small musical note was engraved—right next to what looked like a small lever. She wiggled it, and the compass unfurled. A slip of paper fell onto her lap.

A happy giggle escaped before she could stop it, a reminder that she had once been a small thing with far too many curls and a wide grin, chasing Patrick around everywhere and delighting in the secret passages at her grandfather's former plantation in Virginia.

She set the hollow compass on the table in front of her and picked up the note. Patrick's handwriting—his sensible, cautious, familiar handwriting—scrawled across the wrinkled bit of paper.

> *Dear Lore,*
>
> *Happy birthday! I love you so much, sweetheart. Cassie sends her love, too. I hope we can see you again soon because we shall soon have someone for you to meet.*
>
> *Nineteen is the year of 'why aren't you married?' in our family, or so I learned. Rather young to make such a permanent and meaningful choice, I think, so make sure you choose wisely. I know you may not have much autonomy here, but Father isn't going to be quite as quick to disinherit an unruly child given that he's running out of options. Winnie is always going to be unmanageable, and he knows that. Use it to your advantage.*
>
> *What would allow you to stand at the helm?*
>
> *I know you have the gumption to do whatever you need to.*
>
> *Praying for you always. Give this to God—but don't be afraid to act, too.*
>
> *Sincerely,*
> *Patrick Hilton*

She set the paper down. Despite her exhaustion, her mind had perked at his words. Patrick knew that her father would probably default to Billy Pent as her husband—did that mean her brother was then encouraging her not to marry him?

Why else would he say it if he wasn't sure this was not the right choice, as Lorelei rather suspected?

Patrick was not the most logical person in the world, in Lorelei's opinion. Yet if even he was encouraging her, as far as she could see, to take the logical path in life—to fight for a future that would allow her some influence—then who was she to say no to that?

Besides, if she were to secure her stake in the company, she wouldn't have to worry about Winnie. Not that she did much anyway, but she wanted her sister to be safe even if she did find her frustrating at times.

How she longed to run the company in the way she wanted to run it: profitably and with a mind toward passing it on to children and grandchildren and even the generations after that. Both of those were in danger if her father continued on his current path. Without Patrick's stabilizing influence, Father had been making increasingly risky decisions.

Lorelei wanted to stop that in its tracks.

What option did she have, then? Her father would not place her in control. No, he wanted a man who he could manipulate.

Yet there was nothing stopping Lorelei from choosing a man of her liking, practically, and getting married to him without her father's consent. There was nothing stopping her from marrying someone who could view a marriage in a similar way to how she wanted to—as a business arrangement allowing them both the freedom to pursue their own interests.

Surely if she married someone with enough money and interests of his own, he would give her free rein to do as she wanted.

If she could then convince her father that the man, not herself, was really the one pulling the strings ...

Oh, but that would never work. She took another sip of her coffee and pondered her options. In Boston—or New York or Philadelphia, for that matter—her father would be able to easily keep tabs on her.

What if she left the country?

Her greatest days of freedom had certainly been that year touring Europe with Patrick and Winnie. During that time, despite being far too young to wed, she'd run into any number of diplomats and men with titles looking to marry a woman because they had to marry at some point—and presumably beget an heir.

There had been interest then. If she were to return to Europe, would there still be interest in an American heiress who wasn't necessarily un-attractive and was certainly young enough to furnish a son or two if the circumstances were right?

There was no chance that a man who already had a title and an estate and all of those sorts of things would care about an American shipping company.

So what then? Could she manage the company, or branches of it, from Europe while also being a serviceable enough wife to a man who probably wouldn't care about her except that she was female and fairly decent at a polite conversation in a parlor on the occasions that it was needed?

She thought so, and if she could convince a man, just one, that it was so, that would be enough. Men were easy to convince, or Patrick always had been.

Lorelei closed her eyes and leaned her elbows against the table. What were the rules for a woman marrying a man in various European countries, though?

The only rules she knew for certain were those of England. In England, a wife became "one with her husband," legally speaking, and anything that was hers became his. A nice concept, but Lorelei wasn't about to attach herself to any member of the male sex. Further, it meant that unless her father completely withdrew any inheritance or control from her, her husband would be the one with true swaying power.

With the right man ... Yes, with the right man, that'd be all right. Someone like Patrick—decently malleable. It would actually give her more protection from her father, as another party would be involved. A male party.

Yes, she could bear that. She could, and she would.

With this decided, she finished the last drops of her coffee and returned the slip of paper to the interior of the compass, then snapped it shut.

Lord, help this work because I can't do it on my own. Bring the right man to me—or help me get to him in the first place. I trust You to make this happen.

Perhaps not a prayer her brother would have approved of, but she couldn't help it. After all, it was the only way. Wasn't it God's job to accomplish what seemed impossible?

CHAPTER TWO

July 1884
London, England

THE KNIGHTS' HOME WAS beautiful for a town house, though that wasn't saying much. Lorelei had never liked London—never imagined staying there for long, never much cared about whether or not she visited again—but there was something charming about the tall, grand houses crushed together on the narrow cobbled streets.

The charm was doubtless a short-lived one, for who could truly appreciate a life in such a crowded place? Yet she reminded herself that the Knights had a large, luxurious estate in Kent where they spent most of their time.

That was what Lorelei wanted, she decided—a man who owned property in the country. A title was preferable, but not a necessity, as she believed marrying a gentleman of leisure would also indicate a lack of interest in business procedures. As far as she was concerned, every man with some amount of money in England was practically useless—and she was looking for someone practically useless ... but every so slightly intimidating, so she need never worry as long as he was on her side.

So now she sat, preparing for the day in one of the bedrooms at the Knights' home, with Winnie moaning about how bored she was on the bed behind her.

Lorelei didn't know how to stop her, how to make her feel better, or how to be her friend so she would not be bored, so she ignored her.

Her mother had instantly seized on the idea of a trip to England, to see the sights and visit old friends. Her father, fortunately, had been unable to come—Lorelei wouldn't have wanted to go if he'd been able to come along, but he was terribly busy without Patrick's help.

All the more reason his insistence that Lorelei couldn't help him was ridiculous.

The fact that Mother was along for the trip didn't bother her. Her mother could be abrasive at times, but she had been kinder to Lorelei since Patrick left. Lorelei had an idea that her mother missed Patrick more than she'd let on. It seemed to have rekindled her parents' hatred for each other, too, as they had been far more quarrelsome.

That was probably an additional reason why neither of her parents had objected to this sudden trip. Of course, the Knights were always willing to receive them—Mr. Knight and Father had been old war buddies, and that sort of bond between men seemed a difficult one to break, even after nearly twenty years.

"Now, we're going down to take tea with Mrs. Knight." Lorelei tilted her head from side to side, taking in the hair Harriet had touched up, but not quite redone, since their arrival. Yes, it would do. "She opened the house for us, so I hope you're going to be polite and on your best behavior."

Winnie sat up. "I am *always* on my best behavior."

"Really? Your best resembles a three-year-old who's gotten into the sugar bin."

"That's not fair!" Winnie slouched her way over to the mirror and double-checked her own reflection—for no reason, truly, as despite her flopping around, her running about where she oughtn't to be, and her general wild-fairy-child approach to life, her auburn hair always stayed in place. "I am becoming quite respectable. Mother says I'm almost a lady."

"She says that because you seldom act like one." Lorelei whirled on the fabric seat of the bench she sat on and pinned Winnie with a glare. "A lot rests on this trip. For you and for me."

Winnie laughed. "Your face is so serious! You look about forty—or, I don't know, some other *old person* age. Whatever do you mean?"

"Never you mind that." Lorelei glanced back at the mirror once more and rose, her hands making small, useless adjustments to her dress, a simple blue-and-white affair that reminded her of a naval outfit—but feminine. "Just behave yourself."

"I always do," Winnie insisted.

Lying through her teeth, the little monster.

Nevertheless, Lorelei ignored this glaring falsehood and led the way out of the bedroom she was staying in and down the hall and stairs to the parlor where Mrs. Knight had bid them come for tea.

Mrs. Knight was about Mother's age—blonde, blue-eyed, taller than any of the Hilton women, and otherwise rather uninteresting. She was straightforward—more so than most women of her rank and nationality—but there was sometimes a subtle bite to her words.

Lorelei frankly wasn't sure how this meeting would go. Mother must know that Mrs. Knight's daughter was close friends with Cassie, Patrick's wife. It might come up—and Mother might realize that she'd have to address Patrick's disinheritance in some manner.

Instead, Mrs. Knight and Mother chatted about light things. The weather. The London Season. How things were in both of their families. Patrick was avoided entirely, somehow, despite being, in Lorelei's mind, a rather big piece of the Hilton family.

Yet the subject could not be avoided forever, especially given how many flavorless pastries were passed around and bland cups of tea drank. Lorelei was focused on trying to quietly indicate with facial expressions that Winnie must *not* put six lumps of sugar in her tiny teacup, but this stopped immediately at Cassie's name.

"Of course, Alice is blessed to have Cassie as a friend." Mrs. Knight took the tiniest sip of tea. "I'm sure they are a great comfort to each other. I believe both of them are traveling to England with their husbands, to see Cassie's family and to visit us. We'll all enjoy that, especially since we've yet to meet Cassie and Patrick's little one."

Mother's teacup rattled on the saucer, but she said nothing.

Mrs. Knight proved far too keen. "Yes, they have a son now. His name is Aidan Frederick—which is interesting, I think. Aidan is not a name I'd prefer, but I cannot fault Cassie for choosing an Irish name, even if I do find it rather a funny one. Alice says they're both terribly pleased."

"Of course," Mother stuttered out. "I've heard he's healthy." Yet there was a tremble to her voice, a way that her eyes flicked about as if looking for purchase, that told Lorelei the full story.

Mother had not known. None of them had known. Though Lorelei was only mildly interested in meeting "Aidan Frederick," it was clear that Mother was greatly affected by the news of him.

Mother wished she could meet her first grandchild.

If only Father hadn't been quite so harsh, all their problems would have been solved!

"Yes," Mrs. Knight said. Her voice was softer now. "I've heard he is healthy and strong—and the most charming little fellow, too. Alice was unusually wordy in her descriptions. Perhaps my letters from her would be more recent than what you've received, what with your traveling, and you would care to see them?"

Mother hesitated, and Lorelei's eyes flew to her face. Pride wouldn't overcome even the desire to hear about Patrick's son, would it? Thankfully, Mother nodded, and Lorelei breathed a silent sigh of relief.

Mrs. Knight instantly rose and went to a small table in the corner, the sort with a drawer in it, then withdrew a letter, which she handed over. "On the second page, she speaks of him. The rest is not private—though it would be rather dull to you, I'm sure. Just details about domestic life."

Mother scanned the letter swiftly while Winnie rose and came around to read over her shoulder, mouth half-open, eyes wide. Lorelei, for her part, was careful to restrain her reactions. The letter would be passed to her at leisure and then she would know. The most important facts were that Cassie had safely delivered and the child was all right. The rest was detail—and Lorelei had never been one for babies. She supposed she liked them from a distance and recognized their importance and value, but she was not the motherly sort. She was hardly even the sisterly sort.

Mother finished reading, blinked away the telling dampness in her eyes, and passed the letter to Lorelei.

The paragraphs concerning Patrick, Cassie, and the child, written in an unfamiliar hand and voice, outlined a picturesque story.

Of course we are glad to be coming your way to show off Aidan, who is growing by leaps and bounds. He has become round and chubby, and he red, curly hair, though if Cassie asks, tell her I think it's auburn. He's got a lot for such a little thing, though I'm told it'll fall out. We're still all seeing different things when it comes to his eye color, and that will last for some time. Patrick says they will darken to look more like Cassie's, but we'll see. In terms of his face—ears to nose to mouth—he is his father's son.

As for how they are doing, they are well. You asked if Cassie is adapting well to motherhood—I say yes. She is thrilled with Aidan, and I've not heard a word except that he is the new center of her world. She seems convinced he's the sweetest, cleverest little fellow, and nobody dares contradict her.

Yes, I did come to Philadelphia for the birth. Patrick was able to leave work for a day or so, but those first few weeks are difficult, so we stayed on to help. I'm beginning to realize what a great deal of work one baby can create. Some of it cannot be taken away from the mother, but we did our best to help wherever we were needed.

As I mentioned, Patrick is the most devoted father I have ever seen. Cassie told me that when he is home, she seldom gets to hold Aidan, for Patrick must have him from the moment he walks in the door. He can't even allow her to get up with the baby in the night—and she must be the primary carer then, so his interference is dreadfully unneeded. Yet you met him; he simply cannot bear to think that he's not an active participant in anything he considers to be his own. He's very protective of Aidan—Cassie finds it silly, but she certainly smiled when she said it.

There. That's wordy enough for you, and I will repeat that I'll be there in person. So why the request for a lengthy reply on this subject? Not that

I believe you shall tell me.

Love you and everyone else there. I'll send further details about arrival time later.

Alice

Ah. So Mrs. Knight had requested more information probably knowing that a mail ship would arrive before they had a chance to … and anticipating that information about Cassie, Patrick, and the baby would be appreciated by Mother.

That was far more thoughtful than Lorelei believed a woman like Mrs. Knight could be.

Lorelei passed the letter back without a word and forced herself to take another sip of the vaguely-flavored water.

Mother chatted for another five minutes before excusing herself and Winnie, claiming a headache. Lorelei started to follow her, then hesitated.

It would be good to get Mrs. Knight on her side. But how?

"What of you?" Keen blue eyes turned to her, perhaps kind but certainly piercing. "What are your plans while in London, Miss Hilton? Your mother seems convinced you'll get some attention while you're here."

Lorelei raised her eyebrows slightly. "She's likely not wrong. I don't know if my mother ever mentioned it—or if you heard the gossip at all—but I am now the heiress of a significant bit of my father's fortune and properties, not to mention my portion of his company. I am also unengaged, and I would like to change that—on my own terms. I know a lady wouldn't mention such things, much less anything monetary, but I am American, and I presume everyone here, yourself included, expects me to be a little crude. I'm not that, but I do think I live in a harsher world—and yet also, a world where I can make a future for myself if I try." She smiled and took another determined sip of the bitter leaf-water. "I hope you're not too taken aback by my honesty, but as my host, I couldn't help but feel you deserved it."

Mrs. Knight simply regarded her with half-closed eyes, a rather pensive expression on her face. "It's not money you're looking for in a match, then, as you have plenty of that. What are you looking for?"

Lorelei pressed her lips together. How to describe her desires succinctly? "Security. Honesty. Freedom."

A trace of humor played around Mrs. Knight's lips. "Some would say those cannot be found in a marriage."

"Hence my desire to be selective. Yet security can be found in the marriage itself. When I am married, I know I go from my father to my husband, but I would be more secure with my husband than with my father—trust me."

If there was a slight softening in the older woman's eyes, it was subtle. "I understand that sentiment. In truth, you should expect honesty. I am not sure about freedom, though. I have heard that is seldom reflected in a marriage—in fact, that's rather the source of the security: the lack of freedom."

"You're perhaps right. However, I believe I could find a man who didn't care too much about my whereabouts. Simply put, I can probably be involved with my father's business if I have a husband working as my face while I'm the true hands and feet. I think my father would like to establish himself in England, too, given that his key competitor is trying to do the same."

Mrs. Knight inclined her head. "You realize that may not be easy in England."

"It would be impossible in America, with Father ever between us. I couldn't have a marriage there, Mrs. Knight—I would always take second place to my father. That's not a life I'm willing to enter. And yes, I should marry a man strong enough to stand up against him ... but this is simpler. It's a guarantee—Father can't *always* be in England."

"That may be true." The tight line of Mrs. Knight's lips indicated that she didn't quite believe Lorelei, but that didn't matter. There was no cause to gain her approval—Lorelei hardly knew the woman, after all. "I have received an invitation to a ball at Lord and Lady Dalbury's home. Their daughter debuted at the same time as Alice—and your sister-in-law. Do you wish to attend?"

Lorelei kept her hands and eyes steady as she regarded Mrs. Knight. "Yes. Yes, I would."

CHAPTER THREE

AUBREY MONTGOMERY STOOD ALONE at the edge of the ballroom, watching his friend Gibson Ashfield dance with a woman he'd met five minutes ago. More accurately, Aubrey had met her and spoken to her briefly and then Ashfield had strolled on over and flashed a charming grin—and that was the end of that.

Of course, Aubrey could tell Ashfield to back off, but he never did. Not anymore. There had been a time when Aubrey was actively seeking a wife—and until he'd settled on the lady he thought he was going to marry, he'd not been shy about informing Ashfield that he'd better let him get a word in edgewise.

Now? He took a sip of his punch and sighed. He ought to try again ... for his sisters, if nothing else, now without any female guidance given the recent passing of his mother. However, Francesca and Constance would have to survive a little while longer, for no woman had seemed *quite* right after ... well, *after*.

Ashfield escorted the young lady back to her parents and returned to Aubrey's side. "Lovely woman," Ashfield commented. "Are you pursuing her?"

"No." Not that Aubrey knew whether he wanted to or not, but it was hard to be interested in any woman whose head was so easily turned by Gibson Ashfield, a known rake. Not that Aubrey could judge the young lady solely based on that, but again, he lacked the desire to truly test her character. He was content, for now, in the role of casual observer.

It was better that way. *After.*

"I honestly don't know why I let you drag me to these parties," Ashfield grouched, though his tone was light and cheerful as ever. He was the type of man who found little entertainment in the London Upper Ten Thousand—rather, he preferred a less appropriate social circle. The type Aubrey could never participate in.

"I didn't say you had to come with me—only that I would be going." Aubrey found himself shuffling behind a pillar in the corner; he didn't want to be here either. "I think it best to continue my acquaintance with Lord and Lady Dalbury, especially with Fran debuting next year."

Ashfield shook his head with a soft chuckle. "Fran can't be debuting. She's all of six years old."

"She's seventeen." Nearly a lady. Yet Aubrey was thankful his friend only saw Aubrey's younger sister as a child. Gibson Ashfield was a womanizer, and Aubrey was fiercely protective of his sisters.

"Hmm. I choose to ignore that." Ashfield smirked. "What of it, Montgomery? Will you marry to provide Fran a sponsor? Or will she be passed off to some graying aunt who smells of mildew?"

Aubrey shrugged. "I haven't a 'graying aunt who smells of mildew.'"

"Then?"

"I'm not sure." He'd not been sure of anything for a long time, in fact—over two years. Every time his mind was almost made up—every time he determined he was soon to be on the hunt for Mrs. Montgomery—something stopped him, an unseen force or a vague inclination. He wanted to say it was God Who stayed his hand, or rather his heart, but that might be too easy, an escape from the truth.

If Aubrey were perfectly honest with himself, he'd admit that he was frightened.

This was a ridiculous state to be in as a twenty-seven-year-old man. He ought to have perfect control over every aspect of his life, but if the Lord *had* led him to this point, He would have to lead him right out again.

The music began again, and Aubrey's eyes trailed across the ballroom. Couples swayed about in an intimate waltz to the strings of the musicians Lady Dalbury had hired for the occasion. There were a number of handsome women here tonight, certainly, and some of them would make perfectly suitable brides. Many of them were seeking exactly that thing.

What was he supposed to do, choose a random one and start courting her?

Lord, what am I supposed to be doing? If You would convict me ... make it easy on me ... not allow me to back away, cowardly at the last second. It would be so much simpler if I didn't have to make this decision on my own.

Yet no magical fairy dust spelled out the name of the woman who was to be Mrs. Aubrey Montgomery, and no booming voice from Heaven indicated her identity either.

There was little to do, therefore, but to wait patiently in the corner.

Across the room, he saw a small group enter. He instantly recognized a tall, dark-haired man and the blonde beauty on his arm as Mr. and Mrs. Philip Knight, a couple he'd come to know well during his courtship of Lady Mary O'Connell. Their eldest daughter was Lady Mary's dearest friend.

Ashfield had been courting Miss Alice Knight, actually—she was the first woman Ashfield had ever taken an interest in, for reasons Aubrey couldn't fathom. Ashfield never made much sense to Aubrey. He remained his friend for old time's sake, despite some of the stories concerning his friend's poor behavior he'd heard floated about. Yet he knew what Ashfield's family was like—his cruel father, his battered mother—and he couldn't help but feel some sympathy. Aubrey had been gifted with loving parents and a safe home; much of his boyhood from Eton on had been spent trying to gift Ashfield little bits of that.

It hadn't worked. If anything, Ashfield was less interested in a wholesome life than he ever had been.

Aubrey sighed and shook himself back to reality. Despite his break with Lady Mary, he didn't dare ignore the Knights, if only because he feared alienating himself and therefore the Montgomerys and Fran from anyone with any real social standing.

"You can leave, if you like," he told Ashfield. "The Knights are here, and I probably need to greet them. They're with a young lady and her mother, so it's likely I'll have to speak with her." He didn't know either of the Knights' guests, but since they had just arrived and he had not seen her before, it was likely she would need a dance partner. It would be rude not to offer.

Ashfield nodded and disappeared into the shadows, as usual, and Aubrey made his way around the dance floor to greet the Knights.

Mrs. Knight was gracious but stiff. Aubrey had a suspicion that no one in the Knight family was entirely certain why Aubrey and Lady Mary had broken things off—only that they had, and that their loyalty belonged completely to Lady Mary.

Mrs. Knight made the introductions as her husband had already wandered off toward the card room. "Mr. Montgomery, this is Mrs. Clarence Hilton, and her daughter Miss Hilton."

Aubrey stilled, wishing he'd disappeared along with Ashfield rather than coming over to her. The Hiltons. Patrick Hilton's family. The man Aubrey suspected Lady Mary had refused to marry him because of.

Of course, Patrick Hilton was presumably cut off from his family. Aubrey wasn't sure of the details, but it sounded like there had been some issue with him breaking an engagement to a woman he was promised to—all for Lady Mary's benefit.

Aubrey understood the impulse. Lady Mary O'Connell was a beautiful woman with a cheerful outlook on life. She wasn't overly exuberant or overwhelmingly noisy like some women—Aubrey didn't know how he'd handle that—but she had a quiet charm about her that he'd liked. So much so that he'd decided almost instantly upon meeting her that she was the woman he wanted.

None of that mattered now. He collected himself and bowed and said polite, kind things to Mrs. and Miss Hilton, who both seemed unaware of his internal struggle.

Miss Hilton was less than interested in his presence. In fact, from the moment he'd appeared, the girl had been looking over his shoulder and about them in a clear attempt to involve herself in anything but him.

It irritated him when he was the only person thus far who had cared enough to approach her, but he shouldn't judge her. He was a particularly boring person—and what girl, perhaps twenty years old, wanted to involve herself with a particularly boring person?

He asked her to dance, for politeness's sake. For politeness's sake, she accepted, in a soft accent that dragged out the word "delighted." He wondered if that was a natural inflection of Boston or if she'd done it for the benefit of her mother, who spoke with the barest hints of a Southern American drawl—something he recognized from a trip to the United States Ashfield and he had taken many years ago.

For a moment or two, Miss Hilton and he danced in silence while he scrambled to remember some fragment of small talk that might interest her. Nothing came to mind, and it was Miss Hilton who spoke first.

"You were engaged to my sister-in-law, weren't you?" Her voice was quiet but cutting. It held a forcefulness, an abruptness, that most women didn't possess—or didn't wish to show, if they did possess it.

Aubrey narrowly avoided stumbling over his own feet. "Excuse me?"

Her head dipped in acknowledgement, as if this were the most average conversation subject on earth, but her gray eyes, light and dancing, held what looked like amusement, as if his being flustered was a matter of hilarity. "My sister-in-law. Cassie—Lady Mary O'Connell. You were her fiancé, weren't you?"

"No, I was not." He steered her around another couple before he spoke again. "I asked her to marry me, and she refused."

"Ah." Another slight inclination of her head. "I see."

Then she said nothing. Absolutely nothing. Did she want an explanation? Did she want to humiliate him? What a frustrating situation. If it were not for the fact that he was loath to cause damage to a young lady's reputation, he would return her to her mother and leave.

Yet that was not an option. Instead, he began to talk, not sure what he was saying or why—only knowing that he couldn't bear the silence, the potential judgment.

"We had courted for several years," he said, then paused to clear his throat. "I had been quite sure of her. I knew there was something standing between us—but I believed it was my reluctance to commit. I have never been one to move quickly, not when I can measure my steps and make intelligent decisions. I made her feel as if I didn't care—and that's a fact for which I am eternally sorry. She shouldn't have had to doubt me, if she did. Perhaps you know more of this than I do, or perhaps you do not. As for me, I was not given an explanation, nor do I need one. Her decision was final enough. I don't begrudge her that. I wish I had loved her well enough to make her stay, but I don't want you or anyone else to believe that I wished to hold her against her will."

Miss Hilton was silent for a moment, then slowly nodded. "I don't think I ever believed anything about you at all. I think my brother made the right decision in marrying her—and I think she was made for him, in all honesty. I don't care what you do. I don't think I ever did. I think Cassie should have left you sooner, but that's not personal." Her chin rose as her eyes met his. "You could find any number of women here who would serve your purpose."

His brow furrowed. "Whatever do you mean?"

Unblinking, she stared at him as if what she said was the most logical thing on earth. "I mean, there are dozens of women in this room alone who, I'm sure, would make you a perfectly decent wife. I doubt you want anything special, and the kind of woman you're looking for is bred here. I suspect you're overthinking it." Her tone was casual.

How old was she, anyway? Maybe eighteen? Why did she feel she had the right to speak to him so openly?

Yet he curbed his offense—he'd been learning more and more that the natural prickling of his pride was not an emotion he wanted to cultivate. Certainly, with two young sisters tempting him to frustration every day, he had to adjust—or suffer the loss of their affections, which he could not bear. No, anything but *that*, regardless of how tempestuous their emotions.

So he replied calmly, with the same voice he used when Constance was being particularly irrational. "I'm overthinking *marriage*? As in, the life-long decision? As in, ''til death do we part'?" Perhaps the logical statement of matters would call the girl back to reality.

Apparently not, for her eyebrows arched, and what could only be called a grin appeared on her face. "Oh, *that* marriage. Sorry, I was talking about the union of Minneapolis and St. Paul." She rolled her eyes. "No, 'that' marriage."

"Why would you 'suspect' that I am 'overthinking' it?" She didn't know him, and she felt qualified to make such broad judgments?

"Because I saw enough of you at Alice Strauss's wedding to know you do not take risks and because when a man is ready to get married, he marries. You proposed to Cassie; therefore, you are ready to be married; therefore, you are delaying unnecessarily from seizing what you ought." She said this as if it were the most practical thing in the world rather than wild speculation. "It's a simple matter."

He frowned. "Who would you recommend?"

"As a wife?" She laughed. "Surely you can make that decision yourself."

"As you seem to know everything, I am hardly foolish enough to neglect your keen advice." Aubrey couldn't keep the sarcasm out of his tone. "What should I be looking for?"

Small tendrils of nut-brown hair bounced about her head as she laughed. "What do you want?"

He moved his shoulders in the slightest of shrugs. "Someone who will stay, primarily."

She shook her head, another grin dancing about her pink lips. "Not a jab that hits its mark with me, but I get your point. Here's how you do it: propose to someone. If you marry them, they'll have to stay."

"Ah, so you're suggesting kidnapping?"

"If that's what it takes." She turned from him as the music ended, tossing "A real man would do it" over her shoulder.

He didn't know why he followed her. He could've escaped, exited stage right, never had to speak to her again.

Instead, he trailed her back to the Knights like an obedient pup on a leash.

Chapter Four

The Knights and Mrs. Hilton almost immediately introduced the young lady to another gentleman who led her out onto the dance floor. Aubrey knew him somewhat—knew he would make a perfectly acceptable match for Miss Hilton—and for some reason, that filled Aubrey with consternation.

He hoped it wasn't jealousy, for that emotion had never helped anyone. Every time he'd allowed even a hint of it to color his relationship with Lady Mary, she'd reacted in the negative. She probably didn't think he knew how badly it upset her when he'd acted possessive. Aubrey didn't understand why she didn't *want* to be possessed. After all, Aubrey would have been happy to belong to Lady Mary.

A part of him had always known she did not care for him. She had a restless soul—dancing into his life, charming him immediately, but hard to grasp. It wasn't faithlessness, no—it was more a desire for something more than what Aubrey could offer. He hadn't known what to do with that.

When Aubrey didn't immediately take his leave, Mrs. Knight turned to him. She had cool blue eyes, and he disliked how effortlessly they pierced him—much as Miss Hilton's gray eyes had seemed to do. Only Mrs. Knight was English, not American, and she didn't say anything about whatever it was that she saw in him.

When she did speak, it was brief and polite. "How have you been, Mr. Montgomery?"

"Well. Quite well. And you? How is your family?"

"We are all well. You know my eldest daughters are married, and two of my sons are in school now, so it is quiet. I confess I don't mind. I was sorry to hear about your mother. She was a good woman."

"Yes." Aubrey inclined his head. "She was." She'd been such a calming force in his life, though he had seldom acknowledged it, not wanting to be seen as weak by his friends. He wished he'd told her, even once, what it meant to have her stand by him even if she didn't agree with his decisions.

"How are your sisters?"

It was kind of her to remember them. "They are thriving as much as can be expected given the loss of their mother. Francesca is seventeen. We expect her to debut next year."

"I see. I wish her all the best." Then Mrs. Knight scanned him, as if weighing him in the balance. Whether she found him wanting or not was not shown on her face. "You will marry for your sisters."

Was every woman in London suddenly struck with a strange mental illness that forced them to question his marital status? "We shall see what God brings my way." Even if God's will was becoming more of an excuse than a legitimate expression of his devotion, he still found it hindered some of the worst suggestions.

"Indeed. We shall see."

Did that mean she intended to do something to influence the Lord one way or another? As if one could, but certainly it could be said that sometimes God used people for His purposes, and if Mrs. Philip Knight decided she was willing to be used, there was little chance of Aubrey escaping this season without a bride of her choosing.

Lovely.

Why did she even care about him? She was far from a bored dowager. Her youngest child, a girl whose name he couldn't remember, was all of five or six years old. Mrs. Knight was still relatively young, had a full life ahead of her, though she was older than him by ten or fifteen years. In every way, Mrs. Knight had the right to ignore him, and further, she'd enough in her life to keep her from taking an interest in his potential future wife.

There must be something in the air tonight that led to an abundance of curiosity and impertinence.

Miss Hilton returned to Mrs. Knight—Mrs. Hilton having disappeared into a conversation with a group of women. The young woman's eyes found his as Mrs. Knight's had.

"You're still here?" Miss Hilton commented cheerfully. "I thought you had a woman to find."

There was a slight stiffening in Mrs. Knight, but he ignored it, much as Miss Hilton apparently did.

"I told you—I'm waiting for your advice." He raised his shoulders in a half-hearted shrug. "You know very well I've no idea how to make this decision on my own."

"I do?" Her brow pinched. "See, this is the problem. I give men advice and then they fail to simply take what I so generously bestow on them. Rather, they either ignore it completely or find a way to make me responsible for what ought to be their duty. Please don't tell me you can't take care of this on your own."

"*Lorelei*." There was a firm emphasis in the way Mrs. Knight said the name.

"Lorelei's" eyes flickered over to her chaperone for a brief moment. "I know my place with Mr. Montgomery, Mrs. Knight. I trust him not to spoil my reputation—as he could, I know, if he shared how impertinent I have been with him."

He nodded. "It's all in good humor, Mrs. Knight, I'm sure. She's not that much older than Francesca, so I'm not offended. I understand it's an age of questioning—even what one ought not to question." He fastidiously kept a straight face despite the glare Miss Hilton sent him—that had touched a nerve. *Not so pleasant to be belittled yourself, is it?* "Shall I introduce you to my friends, Miss Hilton? I know the character of most of the men here. I would not steer you wrong." As much because he had an idea Lady Mary would value this young woman, and she had the look of someone who might go crashing toward earth in a hurry if she were not offered a proper set of wings.

"I *am* a bit older than 'your Francesca,' but I shall ignore that comment if you are willing to help me." She glanced at Mrs. Knight. "Surely it is no different than if my own brother were to help me."

"It is *quite* different." There was a warning in the woman's tone that Miss Hilton might not heed—Aubrey would. "But yes, Mr. Montgomery may introduce you to gentlemen that he knows."

Mr. Montgomery nodded and glanced about. "Mrs. Knight, I leave this up to your wisdom—if I were to dance again with Miss Hilton, to discuss who I should and should not introduce her to, would that be appropriate?"

A slight inclination of her head. "But no more than that, as you well know."

Indeed, he knew how swiftly a couple could become 'a couple' in the eyes of society if they danced too often, spoke too much, or looked in each other's direction more than was considered proper.

Then Miss Hilton was in his arms again, and it was a waltz—slower, more intimate, but easier to talk.

Her gray eyes met his through dark lashes that practically fanned her cheeks with every blink. She certainly wasn't unattractive—no, not in the least—and no, she wasn't Fran's age. Oh, she might only be two or three years older, but there was nothing girlish about Miss Lorelei Hilton. She might not be as wise as a woman with a few more years to her name might be, but not *unwise*. Impulsive, perhaps, but there were many women far older than her who remained so.

"Who do you recommend?" Of course she couldn't fail but arrive straight to the point, but Aubrey was beginning to accept and even appreciate that. There was little guessing with her—and Aubrey was so tired of guessing, especially since he wasn't particularly good at it. "Is there anyone you have in mind for me?"

He glanced about, suddenly tempted to say there was no one—but that would be a lie, and he wouldn't lie to her. "Charles Harriot is a decent enough fellow. You'd do well together—I'm happy to introduce you. Then there's Oliver Hawke and Johannes Lindner. There are others I would recommend, but they are not here tonight. As for those to avoid, I could name half a dozen. Gibson Ashfield is the primary one—honestly, come to think of it, he might ..." He hesitated, not sure if he should tell her. "You're not an unattractive woman. I'd advise you to steer clear of him."

"Oh?" Lorelei grinned. "Is he one of your unsuitable friends? Cassie mentioned them."

"She did?"

"She did. I don't judge you too harshly as I have a number of unsuitable friends. Of course, you're not anything to me—not like Cassie was to you—so it affects me less." This was said with a barely discernible lift of her shoulders, a clear indication of her lack of botheration.

For some reason, he found himself irritated by this. Yet he couldn't let her know, for what a silly thought that was. She had no reason to care about whom he was friends with. "He is my 'unsuitable friend.' My *only* unsuitable friend, in my opinion." Being the only person Aubrey had let close since he was a boy, Ashfield was therefore the only one who could be counted as such.

"Hmm." She drummed her fingers lightly along his shoulder. "Then why? I am not someone well-suited to making intimate friendships with anyone—I would say that my acquaintances truly are *acquaintances*. Unsuitable or not, they have little impact on me. I don't let them—I wouldn't even let someone if they might have a *good* impact. I should far rather set my own sails. However, it would seem that you are quite *close* with Mr. Ashfield. Why would you waste yourself on him?"

Aubrey blinked. No one had put it that way before—it had not occurred to him that he was "wasting himself," that there was any impermanent element of his being that could be "wasted." "I don't know," he answered honestly, for that was clearly the only answer this woman would accept. "We have been friends since childhood. He has always been present in difficult moments—and I, for him. I am not a particularly sociable man, nor do I find it easy to make new acquaintances."

A brief dip of her chin, but her eyes were sharp. "You are a Christian?"

"Yes."

"Then there are two approaches you may take—one is to attempt to influence him toward growth, and the other is to step back and allow him to finally plummet toward the bottom until he hits those rocks we always hear about. Stagnation is never an option, Mr. Montgomery." A soft laugh bubbled from her lips. "See, I find it difficult to make friendships, too. Perhaps I should try harder, but I am, in general, more comfortable with a solitary life. That said, I believe even the strongest Christian can be influenced by evil companions—and if we must have friends, let them be good ones."

"You are perhaps right." She was *certainly* annoying, but least she came out and said it, unlike Lady Mary, who had hinted for years and then offered only vague reasoning when she'd actually spoken on the subject in straightforward terms. "I should evaluate my friendship with Mr. Ashfield. If I tell my sisters they cannot associate with him, and I tell *you* not to associate with him, there is a touch of hypocrisy in my responses." He wasn't sure he meant it, but if that was what Miss Hilton thought best ...

Then he stopped his thoughts, halting them in their traitorous tracks. *No.* He wouldn't let her truly influence him—that would be wildly unwise.

"There is a touch—but just a *touch*, mind you—of hypocrisy in my insistence that you must abandon your friendship with Mr. Ashfield when I haven't any friends at all, much less an experience with a lifelong friendship. The closest I have come to true friendship is with my siblings—and I can't get rid of them." She laughed again—merry, careless, not sad at all at her own proclamations of what sounded, to Aubrey, like a lonely existence.

At least, he was lonely, and his existence was not too different.

"But back to the subject we were speaking on. I am in search of a man who is independent, who could use some funds, and who would allow me a degree of independence to gain them. He would have to be honest, and he would have to respect me, despite my sex and age, enough to make promises to me, and it would then follow that he would need to be honorable enough to keep those promises."

Aubrey's brow furrowed. "What promises?"

"I know I won't be a legal person if I marry an English gentleman—oh, don't protest; I understand how the law works, and that's fine; I don't need to worry about that at all if I am married to the right man—but I would still like to, for the purposes of blunt communication and personal contentedness, establish a sort of contract between myself and my husband. It would be a list of what we both expect from the marriage, sealed with a promise, and as sacred, in my mind, as our vows. That way, even though I don't expect to add *love* as a factor, we can still hope to get along in a way that pleases us both. I think it's a *splendid* idea."

Aubrey blinked, opening his mouth to protest, but it occurred to him that it wasn't just a splendid idea.

It was brilliant.

It cut out all the frustrating parts of relationships in general and romantic relationships in particular. A simple list of tasks and duties, set out in proper legal terms, would simplify marriage to a business deal. There would be no guessing, no missed signals, no wishing for more. All would be practically addressed within the bounds of a contract—or, because of the lack of legal protection married women received, a set of *promises*, as Miss Hilton put it.

"Well," Miss Hilton said, plainly not bothered by his silence, "that is what I am looking for." Her fingers drummed on his shoulder as if sharing her plan had given her a burst of energy that even the dance steps couldn't negate. "Have you any idea who would suit?"

He swallowed uncomfortably. Was he insane, or did it make sense to …? But no. He'd met her less than an hour ago. For all he knew, she was a candidate for Bedlam. Yet something in him wanted to delay rather than immediately point her in the direction of a man who might be amiable to her unique situation and plan.

Scheme, more like, but she was a lady, and a lady didn't deserve to be accused of scheming. Not when her options were so limited as it was. "I might need some time to think about that." *Liar.* Immediately, sweat beaded on his forehead; he hated to lie. "That is, I have a few ideas, but I don't know if it would be best for me to share that information in public."

Yet truth with an underlying motive might as well be a lie. "I'd like to talk to you again." There. He'd said it. She could do with that what she would.

Her eyes flew to his face, sharp and unyielding. "Truly?"

"Yes." He swallowed. "I, um—perhaps—maybe you would like to meet my sisters?"

At that, her face broke from skeptical to amused, and she laughed, a soft, rhythmic sound.

His face was surely bright red. "You have a younger sister of their age," he said defensively. It wasn't such a strange thought, that she might care to know Francesca and Constance. Though he supposed Miss Hilton couldn't know what sweet girls they were.

"No, no, it's ... *oh*." She freed her hand from his to dab at the tears that had gathered at the corner of her eye. "Heavens. All right. Let's be honest with each other. You owe me that—as a fellow human being, as a woman, as a Christian—so exercise your courage. You'd like to see me again, and you're using your sisters as an excuse. Yes?"

Baffled, he hastened to say, "We should discuss what you're looking for in private."

"Oh, I see." She rolled her eyes. "Right. It's all about *me* and *my* needs. Goodness, I've heard that before. What is it with the men in my life and using their younger sisters as an excuse to talk to whomever they want to talk to? Just come out and say it. It's simpler. You know, though, I've nothing better to do, and it might be good to give Winnie someone else to ramble to besides me. There's been far too much of her babbling lately, and she'll talk the ears off anyone who has them. But, Mr. Montgomery, remember who I am. My brother stole your fiancée."

"Your sister-in-law was never my fiancée."

"*Semantics*. Potential fiancée. Fiancée-to-be. Pre-fiancée."

The music ended.

"I see your point. It could be awkward." He extended his arm to her. "Let's get punch. I suddenly have a headache."

"Yes, let's." She obligingly placed her hand on his forearm. "Right. It might be awkward, especially as that may or may not have been—and, in fact, certainly was—why my dear brother and I are no longer on speaking terms."

"So we are allies, then, in truth." His tone was edging on far too sardonic. "Both of us have lost someone due to her."

She laughed again. "Oh, but I didn't say that I didn't *want* to be on speaking terms with him. I miss him dearly, every day." There was a solemn note in her voice, one that reminded him of how close she had seemed to her brother in those few glimpses he'd had of her at Peter and Alice Strauss's wedding.

He inclined his head as he plucked two glasses of punch from the refreshment table and handed one to her. "You did say you valued her as a sister."

"Theoretically. I admit, I've had little actual experience with her being my sister, but I know she will be a good one whenever circumstances change. Which I hope they do. And again, this all makes our relationship quite awkward indeed, for all parties. Assuming things change and I am able to see them again, would you like every family visit to be in Cassie's presence?" She took a sip of her punch. "This is too sweet," she declared, but took another drink nonetheless.

Aubrey paused, imbibing from his own glass and considering what she'd said. Yes, it would be awkward to see Lady Mary—or "Cassie"—again ... at first. But already, the sting was beginning to fade. Were it not for the fact that he was absolutely certain he did not know how to love a woman, he would have contentedly moved on rather swiftly from her absence in his life.

Oh, he had loved her, in his own way. Devotedly, in fact. But when they had parted, and when he stood in front of God, honest and barefaced in the aftermath, considering his options and wondering about what had gone wrong, he had admitted his faults in the relationship including the fact that he had not moved nearly as quickly as he ought. He *had* strung her along—she *had* had cause to wonder if he cared for her. Not to mention that, whenever she finally got around to saying whatever he'd done that had annoyed her, he hadn't always reacted well.

He'd allowed irritation at *her* delay to change his manner toward her, when he knew very well it was a fault they both shared. They'd avoided conflict until his desire to keep her to himself and her desire to run had at last proved an insurmountable obstacle.

He cleared his throat. "I would still like to see you again."

Miss Hilton's eyebrows quirked. "Very well then. You know we are staying with the Knights. Perhaps we could go for a walk tomorrow—with our sisters." She smirked. "Since that appears to be so important to you."

"It is." If only because it would be a nice distraction. Perhaps with his sisters there, with the knowledge of his duty to them, he would be more in control of his rioting thoughts.

Theoretically, anyway.

CHAPTER FIVE

THE NEXT MORNING DAWNED bright—or as bright as a gray city like London could manage—and Lorelei found herself quite looking forward to her outing with the hilarious Mr. Aubrey Montgomery and his excuse-sisters.

Oh, he hadn't meant to be hilarious, and Lorelei ought not to laugh at a man who hadn't meant to be hilarious. Men hated being laughed at—she knew that, and she'd tried to be respectful of it, despite the fact that it was among the least attractive of their qualities.

Yet how was she to think of him as anything but funny when he so obviously had taken an immediate interest in her and then used his sisters—as her brother had often done, if she were honest with herself—as an excuse to see her again?

Oh, she didn't begrudge either of those self-deceived men that. After all, a man generally only had a few sisters, and why shouldn't he use them to his benefit? Lorelei liked being useful as she liked little else. Besides, sisters weren't, like wives, to be cherished. No, siblings, as a general rule, were meant to harass each other.

At least, that was how it worked in her family, and certainly there was no love lost between them. Mostly. She gritted her teeth at some of Winnie's antics, but that didn't mean she loved her less. If anything, a fierce protectiveness rose at the hint of any recklessness in her sister, and she was bound and determined to save her from said recklessness. If that wasn't love, what was? Lorelei wasn't sure she'd ever experienced anything else, and she was quite sure she never would, especially if she went through with her plan.

Mr. Aubrey Montgomery's carriage pulled in front of Mr. Philip Knight's London town house at the appointed time, and out stepped Mr. Montgomery and two young women of about Winnie's age. With her hand brushing the lace curtain aside and her body angled parallel to the wall, Lorelei observed their progress up the steps from her window. Winnie was next to her—less discreet, of course. She pressed her face to the window, and if any member of the Montgomery family had looked up, they would have witnessed her stub nose.

A maid in an adorable little mobcap knocked and then entered Lorelei's bedroom. "Miss Hilton, Miss Gwendolyn, the Montgomerys are here to see you. Mrs. Knight has received them but hoped you might join them."

"Ah, indeed." Lorelei, already obviously prepared, turned to her sister. "What say you, Winnie?" She affected the slightest hint of an accent, lowering her voice so the maid might not catch her soft, jocular words. "Are we at home?"

"Yes!" Winnie squealed. She made friends rapidly—but this did not stop her from seeking out new ones wherever she went. As Winnie danced ahead, Lorelei followed at a more sedate pace.

She only hoped Mrs. Knight had finally procured some coffee, or Lorelei would be "sedate" in even the matters she didn't want to be sedate in. She was *not* drinking more of that tea, nor did it have the same effect at all.

The parlor was far too light even for this hour of the late morning, yet Lorelei managed what she hoped resembled a smile at the Montgomerys. Like their older brother, both the girls had blonde hair and blue eyes and were moderately attractive in that specific English way that Lorelei didn't find intriguing. Though perhaps she was too harsh. She never was one for great beauty, anyway.

At least Mr. Montgomery bore his bland looks nobly. She'd hardly noticed, in fact, as she stood with him and danced with him, that he was bland at all. But without a cup of coffee to tide her over, she was reluctant to admit him to be handsome. No, let him work for the title. She didn't believe in people simply coming into things, even their own good looks. All favorable opinions must be earned. How else could she know if someone had any worth?

Mr. Montgomery rose upon her entrance and bowed. She didn't curtsy—she wasn't sure why, as she had been taught how to behave, certainly, but she felt like doing whatever she wanted with him. It was as if, all of a sudden, he was as familiar to her as Patrick or one of the Pent boys or Herbert Jackson, and she felt she could run all over him as she pleased.

She made a big show of adjusting her skirts as she sat, murmuring polite nonsense so she could hide her wince at these absent thoughts. Perhaps that was not the noblest way to treat someone one was unfamiliar with. In fact, it was entirely possible that she had strong convictions regarding how a marriage ought to be run, and if she continued on this current path—

Then she paused. She wasn't thinking of Mr. Montgomery as a marriage prospect, was she? Even if she suspected he was considering her as such, she wasn't one to rush into anything. There were actual reasons, serious reasons, why they could never be anything but acquaintances. She must remember that.

"Lorelei, Gwendolyn, these young ladies are Francesca and Constance Montgomery, Mr. Montgomery's younger sisters." Mrs. Knight gestured to the two young ladies as she spoke. "Mr. Montgomery was saying that he would like to take you both on a brief walk with his sisters."

Mr. Montgomery met Lorelei's eyes across the length of the parlor. His expression said "as promised." At least he wasn't a liar. She could respect that in a man, certainly.

"I think that would be lovely," Lorelei said. "Let's fetch our hats, and we can go." As if she didn't have them laid out on her bed, ready to be swiftly pinned on.

Mrs. Knight cast Lorelei a "this is against my better judgment" look, but she made no further protest, and soon they were walking down the pavement that rolled along the street between houses exactly like the Knights'. Despite their initial shyness, the Montgomery girls were in fits of giggles within minutes of their acquaintance with Winnie, and this noise making took up the first dozen or so yards, allowing Lorelei and Mr. Montgomery to remain silent.

Winnie had a Montgomery girl on either side of her, arms linked, and they stepped slightly ahead ...

Mr. Montgomery and Lorelei would have to speak now. Which, she supposed, was what they'd come for, but suddenly she had no idea whatsoever what she wanted to say.

"How old are they?" Lorelei asked, gesturing ahead to the gaggle of geese—oh, she meant *girls*.

"Fran is seventeen, and Connie is fifteen." Mr. Montgomery extended his arm, and it would've been rude not to accept it.

Sliding her gloved hand around his arm and *very* lightly grasping his bent elbow, she nodded. "My sister—Winnie, we call her, not Gwendolyn; she scarcely responds to it anymore—is seventeen. Hard to believe. I think of her as twelve, at most. It's her exuberance. It's blindingly immature."

To her surprise, he chuckled. "Do you think of all cheerful individuals as immature, Miss Hilton?"

"No, only *most* of them," she countered. "A few are simply blessed with ideal circumstances."

"What a sad view of the world that is." He didn't press the subject further. "I know it isn't polite, but may I ask how old you are?"

"So you're not eager to take a child bride? I had wondered," she said, not so much avoiding the question as testing how far she could provoke him. Always a good thing to do, she'd found, when faced with a new man. Find one's boundaries rapidly—and avoid becoming injured by surprise later on.

He sighed heavily. "Are you never serious?"

"Oh, and now you're trying to discern whether *I* am immature? What an excellent game this is." Yet she smiled, even though she did it with her head toward the house they were passing, as if it were the most interesting thing in the world. "I am nineteen. How old are you?" She turned her head suddenly to find him examining her with a pensive expression on his face.

"I am twenty-seven," he replied. "Far into my dotage and ridiculously serious."

"Aren't we a matched set? Hardly old enough to walk and almost too old to walk," she murmured, but she didn't mean it. Twenty-seven was a spring chicken, in terms of men. They matured slower than women, she'd found.

"It's important that I be ridiculously serious, you know," he said, clearly choosing the easy path, which was not addressing her comment. "Those two girls are my world. When our mother died last year, everything fell to me. I am glad to be old enough to deal with them—but I admit, at times I feel that I have delayed too long in seeking a wife. They should have a woman around the house. I haven't the foggiest idea what I'm doing half the time."

Ah, so they were getting right to the point, were they? "The idea that women necessarily need a female influence is outdated, in my opinion. A decent brother is worth his weight in gold." Oh, there had been a few awkward moments, but Patrick was made of sterner stuff than most men, and he had an intelligent mind. Her brother had adapted swiftly to whatever Winnie and she needed him to help out with. Though she did admit that her first monthly had been painfully awkward given that it had taken more than the one month for Patrick to be entirely comfortable with the concept, which included obtaining certain garments and providing all the chocolate she requested without question.

These wonderings aside, Constance and Francesca should be well past that by now.

"That may be true," Mr. Montgomery said, "but I cannot offer the same level of care a mother or elder sister could. Next year, Fran will debut. I want her to feel free to marry as she chooses, not be held back by what I do and do not know about the marriage mart."

Lorelei nodded. "I understand." He didn't seem like he just wanted to foist his sister off on the first man that offered, yet what man could really know what a woman needed in a husband? He must be helpless in this concern, especially as he hadn't found a wife. "What you're saying is, if you were to marry, it would be to provide your sisters with female influence and ease their connections."

"Well ... I mean ..." His arm twitched under her hand. Despite his outward insistence upon sensibility, he plainly didn't like the idea of only marrying for practical reasons. Strange. "I would also want a *wife*. My sisters may marry and be gone, but I would still be married. I'd want someone who would undertake social events with me and for me, who I could trust to make the right decisions—and of course, forgive if she did not, but some civil instincts would not be unwelcome. There's the matter of children. I've no one to leave what my father and grandfather built if I don't have a son someday. I'm in no rush, but someday, I wouldn't be opposed to the idea of having a child or children simply for the fact of them. I think I might learn to like them. I've little experience outside my sisters, but from a distance, I've always thought parenthood must be ... rewarding."

He was rambling again, apparently nervous at these admissions, but Lorelei nodded along, as this all made sense. Yes, yes, she'd expected this. An English gentleman would want an heir or heirs—though the "eventually" and the additional detail of his desiring them because they were "rewarding" was welcome, too. Perhaps he would not simply impregnate his wife and leave her, as well as the child, to starve for his affection. Lorelei wanted that, even if she had no idea of herself being a decent mother. She simply knew that if children were to be conceived of in the mind, and therefore conceived in the body, it ought to be done with some respect for the fact that they would be little humans, and little humans wished their fathers would love them.

Sometimes. Just sometimes.

The social calendar was also expected, and Lorelei had always known that would be a part of her life. It was unavoidable, if pressing. The main concerns there would be simply setting and maintaining healthy boundaries, and—

Stop it. She had to cease planning a whole life around him. She'd known him less than twenty-four hours, and there were significant reasons why he might not be suitable.

That said, how long did one have to know a man before entering into a gentleman and gentlewoman's agreement with him?

Of course, the most important consideration was one she could continue poking at until she was satisfied. Not that she couldn't do that about any subject, but this one concerned her intimately, and she had no qualms about doing this poking.

"As for my sister-in-law, Mr. Montgomery, you must tell me more about what passed between you. I know she rejected your proposal of marriage, and from what I understand, you did not attempt to convince her to change her mind. But I would like to understand more about that and why it took you so long to make that proposal. I know the fault does not lie with Cassie—but I'm not necessarily blaming you. Such things happen, after all. Maybe," she said with great charity, "it would take a lot of a man to be worthy of Cassie."

He inclined his head. "Perhaps that was true. I came to care for her a great deal—not that I believe it was a particularly abiding affection. She didn't manage to break my heart." Mr. Montgomery smiled. "I believe our marriage could have been a success, if she had stayed. But she didn't stay—and I am not the type of person who would keep a woman where she did not want to be." He chuckled to himself as another thought seemed to strike him. "After all, the whole purpose of marriage is to represent the union of God and the Church, and the Bride of Christ was never one to enter into an arranged marriage."

"Perhaps you're right, though I'm inclined to think you're wrong. But we can debate theology at a later date. Any marriage can be a success, if you are determined it should be, but do you truly believe Cassie would have rejected you if you were suited?"

He shook his head, a wry expression on his face. "I don't know. I don't understand her motivations much—only that, from what I can gather, she had determined that it was not God's will to marry me. Or that she felt God had somehow forbidden her to do so. I admit, that's kept me awake a few nights. I don't begrudge her doing whatever she thought was best—truly.

And as I said, there was no abiding affection between us. When I first met her, I thought her everything a woman should be ... and perhaps I still think it, to a degree. But I do not think she was all a woman should be for me. I needed something different. Or even if I didn't, she certainly did. I don't regret her, and I don't regret that we parted ways, but I regret wasting so much of her time."

She nodded. "So why did you?"

"You are straightforward."

"I am curious, and I must know," she said firmly.

She heard him inhale deeply and looked up to find him staring ahead, not seeing their younger sisters but rather simply ... staring. "I thought I loved her. My father adored my mother, and she him, in a way I desired. He always said it was love at first sight—and that after that, nothing could cause him to forsake her. I didn't want to be any less than my father. No man does. I felt that I must marry her after that first moment, or that first evening, when I found her so attractive. But I've since ... I've since moved away from the idea that love must rule a marriage." He glanced sideways at her, and she felt the hesitation in him before he even spoke his next words. "I'm not looking for a love match, Miss Hilton. I don't think I'm suited for it, and I'm afraid that it causes far too many complications. Yet I am ready and willing to commit to a woman, to pledge her my loyalty, come what may. I will not hesitate again."

"I see." She dropped her eyes, unable to look at him, unable to do anything but look straight at the path in front of her and think as hard as she could. There was no thought of prayer in this moment—she wasn't sure she had time to beseech the Lord. *No, that's not right.* Yet that's how she felt, as if her thoughts were spiraling so fast that she had best avoid the wise slowing-down that was recommended through prayer.

And here I told Patrick I was the wiser one.

Perhaps she wasn't, but she certainly got more done than Patrick ever would. Was that a flaw or a strength in her character?

"Miss Hilton, I won't bother you. Not for long, if you don't want me to. I'll back off—I don't want to lead anyone on. But if we could talk a few more times—if you could consider ..." He paused, and she felt the muscles of his arm jerk under her hand. "I know we've only just met, but I admit, the idea of keeping things simple and practical appeals to me. If that means marrying and then supporting my wife's plans until such a time as she is ready to undertake other tasks—such as motherhood or helping my sisters—I would be more than amiable."

Surprised, she looked up at him suddenly, having an idea her mouth was formed in a rather stupid *O*. "Truly?"

"Yes." He cleared his throat and looked away from her, but there was honesty, even in his red-faced embarrassment. "Truly."

"Hmm. That's interesting."

Ahead, their sisters had paused at a fountain at the crux of several paths in the park. Winnie had jumped up on the rim and was dancing around in a reckless way while Aubrey's sisters stood more sedately and spoke with her in those "are you sure you should be doing that?" tones.

"Of course," Lorelei mumbled, "there are complications for me. That's one of them."

"She's high-spirited," Mr. Montgomery replied generously. "And young."

"Not *that* young," Lorelei replied, but she was grateful for his good-naturedness. Not all English gentlemen would have been as willing to accept Winnie's occasional eccentricities. Though to be fair, he hadn't seen the half of it. "I shall want her to stay with me, if I can work it out in any way. Technically, she's under my father's control until she turns twenty-one—as am I, but he will not prevent me from marrying anyone with money, if I may be so crude. Winnie ... I believe he won't care about her for a few more years, nor will my mother."

"I see." He nodded. "Three girls is about the same as two."

She laughed. "That's one way of putting it." Then she walked forward and shouted at Winnie to hop down. Once her sister reluctantly agreed, at the promise of ducks in a pond a few more minutes down the path, Lorelei returned to Mr. Montgomery, leaving the girls to a giggling conversation about the merits of ducklings versus chicks. "She is more than high-spirited. She will try to convince you to keep dozens of pets. She has two dogs as it is—Potato and Mars. She'll want them to come with her. She'll want a horse to ride, and she'll ride it with recklessness. I may have a hard time convincing her not to wander into my bedchamber at all hours of the night, if I'm honest, which may be the one that affects you most deeply, if my understanding of marriage is accurate."

"Are you trying to talk me out of it?"

"I think, in the absence of any greater feelings, that is exactly what one ought to do," Lorelei said gravely. She understood love to be a powerful force—it was what Patrick and Cassie shared, she believed, and what had allowed them to wed, after all the obstacles that stood in their path, including both of their parents steadfastly disapproving of their marriage to this day. But Lorelei didn't want that, or need that, and therefore, every obstacle must be considered as what it was—a true obstacle, a reason why they shouldn't do this.

If the obstacles were too great without love, why marry?

"Yet truly, any two adults could have a decent enough marriage if they simply agree to, can't they?" Mr. Montgomery postulated. "You wouldn't deny that two intelligent human beings are more than capable of choosing to get along and finding ways to overcome obstacles in a mature way, if they decide to do so."

"Oh, but I'm not mature. I'm hardly out of the nursery," she murmured archly.

"Don't joke. I mean it."

"You are perhaps right," she admitted. But that didn't mean diving in with little wisdom was intelligent. In fact, it was anything but. "I want to be … cautious."

He nodded. "As do I. But that doesn't mean constantly talking yourself out of every potential opportunity for forward movement …" As they approached the pond, he dropped his hand to allow her to draw away from him, but something about his eyes on her kept her at his side. "That's what I did, you know. I found every reason why I shouldn't act. I won't do that any longer."

"Yet you must admit, there are serious obstacles—"

"Yes," he said, his unusual interruption silencing her at once, "there are obstacles. There will always be obstacles. I'm not proposing marriage this instant, for goodness' sake. I'm addressing difficulties. Are our respective ages a great impediment to you?"

She shook her head. "Not in the slightest." If anything, it was a point in his favor. She would've married a man much older than him—she appreciated maturity and stability above all else—yet it was nice that he wasn't truly so aged as to live in a realm entirely beyond her experience.

"What of our connection through your sister-in-law? Would you worry about our relationship? Would you feel you were only her replacement? Because that would not be the case—not in the slightest."

Lorelei thought for a moment, watching her sister almost fall into the pond in her eagerness to view the rapidly scattering ducks. "No. I would not feel threatened by Cassie. We are too different as women, as people. I believe she loves my brother ... and I believe you when you say you do not love her anymore. Besides, I think we'd offer different things to you. If you marry me, I'm sure you'll come to understand that I am nothing like her, and it would be foolish to be jealous of what time she had in her life when ... when I am not her."

"Indeed," he said, sounding amused by her assessment.

"What of the Hilton Shipping Company?" She paused and put a hand on his arm, then turned him to face her. "My husband will be granted a stake in the company. Despite being English, you will still have access to significant assets—and the option to take an active part, if you wish. I would like to be the one who manages that 'active part,' if you will. I want to establish a branch of the Hilton Shipping Company here in England and expand the business. I want to make it a stable and lasting empire. I want to travel occasionally, after I am settled—and yes, that could be after my children are grown—and manage our other locations. Father is managing the empire by himself right now ... and this is after Patrick expanded it. Father can't do that forever. He will need help, and he will have to admit it. I would appreciate some aid from my husband, in the sense that I would like a man to stand between me and any difficulties I may experience as a woman running such a corporation. Other than that, I don't need my husband to understand the business. In an ideal world, he would be open-minded enough to stand back and let me do what I was bred to do with the employees I specially choose."

He was silent for a long moment before he nodded. "Yes. I see that that would be important to you. I would not begrudge my wife, were she to have such an interest and engage in it."

"Good. Good." She paused, hands clasped in front of her, and thought while she tried to summon further words. In every way, it did seem that they would suit. Personalities, tastes, preferences, and even the heart of the man himself, she did not care about. She simply needed someone willing to achieve goals. But did that justify rushing into things? Especially with a man who shared a history with her own sister-in-law? She wasn't sure. Especially since Cassie might have had a different reason for refusing to wed Aubrey Montgomery than the simple one Lorelei had heard. *At least their stories match, though.* "Mr. Montgomery, may I contact you later—soon, but later—once I have given the matters we have discussed further thought?"

"Of course."

At least he gave her that.

She purposefully approached his sisters after that, speaking to them for the rest of their outing rather than to Mr. Montgomery himself. They seemed nice, well-adjusted girls, if a little dull, and they certainly adored their brother. Lorelei was more inclined to trust a man who had adoring sisters, having so much experience with that perspective herself.

Yet what if she were wrong in her estimation? She could bear almost anything but did not like to think of herself marrying a cruel man or a weak man or a liar. His sisters' admiration said much ... but did it say enough?

CHAPTER SIX

THE NEXT MORNING, AUBREY received a message from Lorelei. It was written in a simple but feminine script that he took to be her own hand—somehow, it seemed like her. The words themselves, however, were anything but simple.

Dear Mr. Montgomery,

I prayed last night, but I have never received words from God in the way I've heard other people describe. Have you? I often wonder if they make it up, for I don't feel anything. I pray and I pray, but I don't have any idea of an answer and then I make a decision. I don't know any other way. Perhaps, if we do pursue this relationship, you will be the leader of the home and teach your wife to do better. What say you to that? I know you're a Christian, but there's more to it than that, I think.

At any rate, I have not made a decision. I am sorry. I sometimes need more time than I thought. But we must speak again before I can set myself in a specific direction. I know how to use a sextant. Have you ever used one? Patrick learned and then taught Gwendolyn and me both. I remembered. Of course, there is no practical use for it—for a woman such as myself—but I have often thought of how difficult it was to learn to use it and how I still sometimes cannot do so with any real accuracy and how perhaps taking our direction from God is the same. What do you think?

Yet does that mean that I cannot sail at all until I learn how to do so, so competently that I never make a mistake? That seems ridiculous to me. I cannot accept that. I must move forward.

I am not a well-written woman. I consider myself fairly well-spoken. Therefore, I would like to meet with you and speak. My sister would like to meet with Francesca and Constance once more tomorrow. If this would suit, and if you could come during teatime, I could see that we have time to speak.

Perhaps you are tired of this entire issue by now and would like to seek a different partner, which would make my decision so much easier. If that is the case, no response is necessary. I will find myself another option in three days if you are disinterested, but I would prefer not to have wasted my time.

Your move.
Miss Lorelei Anne Hilton

This letter only served to frustrate Aubrey when he had hoped it would give him needed elucidation. It only served to make him less sure of her intentions, her wishes.

His wishes were becoming abundantly clear, however. Lorelei Hilton, from her own description, wanted what was essentially an arranged marriage, only without the unnecessary interference of parents. Despite being too young to legally make this decision, if they could convince her mother to give her consent—which with his wealth, Aubrey hoped they could—they could agree to terms and be married without much need for the more complicated elements of matrimony.

Marriages had been performed in similar ways for thousands of years. They were returning to traditionality, in a manner of speaking. If so many probable millions of couples had made marriages work in a similar fashion, who were they to say that they would be the one couple who couldn't?

They *had* met. It had been common practice, from his understanding, for women and men to marry without knowing each other first—and certainly with less in common than he had with Lorelei Hilton.

He liked her, too. That was certainly a point in her favor. She was intelligent and witty, practical and plainspoken, and he knew she could do all he asked of her with no difficulties ... and he might even be able to make her happy in a friendly way.

So he sent back a simple note saying he would love to attend tea at the Knights' the following day and then he barely did anything but think about what she might say to him—and what he might say to her—and how they might arrive at a life-changing conclusion—and how finally, finally something good might be coming into his life, something he could control, something that could be lovely in every way.

After a sleepless night, Aubrey was ready for the visit by early morning. Waiting until the afternoon—and then waiting for his sisters to prepare themselves and get in the carriage—was pure torture. His nerves were on edge in a way they hadn't been in years. He wasn't even sure he'd been this nervous about proposing to Cassie.

Honestly, at that point, he'd been less than enamored with her already. He hadn't known it, but all the feelings that had marked their early relationship had faded. Despite the fact that Aubrey knew this was technically common among all couples, he now believed that, in true love, some of the feelings didn't fade. Now Aubrey wouldn't have to worry about finding that love. If he convinced Lorelei Hilton that he was the man who could fit into her plan, he could abandon the confusing game his father and mother had played, that he had been so sure he must play, too, and he could accept himself as he was ... with the hope, of course, that Miss Hilton would do the same.

For Aubrey was a simple man, a stoic man, not a man capable of reading subtle emotional cues and responding to them. He wasn't capable of loving a woman well.

But respect? Honor? Perhaps even a deep friendship? Didn't he have that with his sisters? How difficult could it be to offer that to a wife, especially if the physical actions that proved these points were bound up in a contract, a gentleman and gentlewoman's agreement to the terms provided?

Yes, it was altogether perfect and entirely more reasonable than the ridiculous façade of courtship. How anyone navigated such things at all, he was not sure. It was certainly not something he was capable of, unfortunately, much as he wished he'd been born smooth and suave.

It wasn't that he wanted to be an unrepentant rake like Gibson Ashfield. No, the idea filled him with loathing. He had spent most of his life trying to convince Ashfield there was a better way to engage in romance ... if that's even what Ashfield was seeking. More and more, Aubrey felt he didn't understand his friend.

But there surely was a better way. Some people might not be blessed enough to know how to love without damaging, without hurting, without causing unnecessary entanglements ... and all the while, in a respectful way that failed to disobey any of God's laws, for those were important to Aubrey. So important, in fact, that nothing Ashfield had ever said had tempted Aubrey down the same road his friend had taken—not in the slightest. Though to be fair, his ineptness when it came to showing a woman how he felt—that, even, he wanted her—was a contributing factor to that.

He wondered if Lorelei could understand that and not feel he must break off his longtime friendship with Gibson Ashfield to marry her. But at this point ... Aubrey wasn't sure he ought to continue as Ashfield's friend.

Certainly it was something to consider. But he'd circle around to that after he understood whether it was to be a part of Lorelei's agreement with him now. If he had to make his own decision, he'd have to make his own decision.

But if the "contract" could simplify everything, all the better.

They arrived at the Knight town house at precisely the right time, despite his worries due to his sisters' delays. Perhaps he had been overly concerned.

Lorelei Hilton was as pretty and as quietly firm as he remembered. Sitting across from her at the tea table—with her mother, her sister, his sisters, and Mrs. Knight—proved a difficult experience for Aubrey, partly because he couldn't take his eyes off her.

It wasn't so much that she was inordinately beautiful or that he was wildly attracted to her—though he certainly was, at that. It was that he wanted to see if he could catch some hint of her thoughts in her facial expressions as she spoke.

All he was able to catch was that she was amused with his lack of suaveness and that her mother had caught on to his attention and was somewhat subtly finding out more about him and his family.

What was his relation to the Knight family?

He managed to answer that one in a way that avoided all mention of Cassie but still made it clear that he was available and interested in marital pursuits.

Had he been in London long? Did he come for every Season? Who were his family connections?

All subjects he had proper and, in fact, encouraging answers for, thankfully.

He managed to work in a mention of his estate, Montgomery Place, in Dorset and that it was the result of old money. Oh, and that he was often busy with business pursuits, or meeting with solicitors who ran his many business pursuits. That seemed to pacify Mrs. Hilton, for now. He knew there would be more official interrogation if he continued things with Lorelei. There would be papers drawn up about whatever financial and legal concerns there were to be considered. He'd have to have a meeting with a lawyer and discuss what it might look like to marry an American woman whose father owned a significant fortune and wanted to involve his future son-in-law in his even more significant business.

My, Aubrey had chosen the oddest and strangest situation to become involved in, but he couldn't find himself too bothered when he looked across the table into Miss Lorelei Hilton's laughing gray eyes.

Maybe this wasn't as practically driven as he wanted to think.

Toward the end of the tea, Miss Hilton rose and offered to take him to see the small garden behind the Knights' house. Of course he accepted.

Mrs. Knight and Mrs. Hilton both watched them go with what he could only interpret to be warning gazes, but they would be within sight of the windows, entirely in public, but able to speak without the listening ears of every woman in their lives.

The garden was similar to every patch of grass and shrubbery and flowers at the back of nearly every London town house owned by an upper-class family, only it was slightly larger than the average one. She took a seat on a stone bench and patted the place beside her.

He cautiously sat at the far edge and turned slightly to face her. "I am here."

"Yes." Miss Hilton inclined her head. "You are indeed. I have given it much thought, as you heard, and I cannot make a decision. Therefore, I must act."

"I see." Of course he didn't. However, he wasn't about to admit that to her.

"I realized that there is no real possibility of me mastering the decision-making process behind marriage in a timely manner. Therefore, it makes sense to simply move forward and hope that a dedication to the relationship will be enough to further my pursuits. We should marry each other, with full understanding of what we both expect, and have done. What do you think?" Then she waited as if she hadn't just proposed marriage but rather something far more casual.

Aubrey might not know many things about how marriages were supposed to work, but he did know it was not normal for the woman to propose.

"Well?" She expected an answer from him, didn't she?

Aubrey swallowed. "I—" *I wanted to be the one to propose. I wanted to ask you, honestly and bravely, after a period of courtship. I wanted to prove to myself that I could do that.* "I agree that there is definite potential in our relationship. I believe you are everything I would wish for in a wife, and I certainly find you appealing. But surely there's more to it than that."

"Yet what is that something?" Miss Hilton persisted, a frown sliding across her face. "I don't know. I'm not at all sure you do either. The truth is, I am in a tight situation. If I do not marry someone in the next month or so, while I am in London, I will return to Boston—and I will marry a young man named William Pent. I like Billy—I do. It's just that once that happens, my life will be over. I won't be a part of the Hilton Shipping Company. I won't be a part of anything. I understand that I must be a society wife—I do. I accept that. Further, I accept that I must be a mother—in the right time. But I cannot accept marrying a man who cares more for my father's good opinion than for mine, I cannot accept watching my husband be treated the way my father treated my brother, and I cannot accept taking no active part in the company I was raised to understand the inner workings of. I need someone to be my partner on this, Mr. Montgomery. It could be you. I'd like it to be you." Then she looked down suddenly, as if embarrassed. It wasn't like her to be embarrassed—already, he knew that—and it made him wildly curious.

"Why me?" Aubrey wasn't sure what made him lower his voice as if speaking to a startled animal, but he did it. He swallowed. He had a weak spot for women with pretty eyes who needed his help. "Was it because I was the first man you met? At that ball? It could have been anyone. That can't be enough reason to bind yourself to one man for the rest of your life." *Because that is not enough for me to bind myself to one woman for the rest of my life. Because I like you, and I find you attractive.* What if she never gave him even that? What if she was always cool and levelheaded while he began to lose his heart? It was a terrifying proposition.

"No," she said. "It is not that. Your convenience feels almost God-sent, but it's that you care about your sisters and that you are not ... you are not trying to control me at every moment. You are kind when you don't need to be. You let me speak freely, and that is to be respected in a man."

He swallowed. Perhaps that was enough. After all, his mother had always said a woman could not respect what she did not love. That said, the late Mrs. Montgomery had never met Lorelei Hilton, and he felt it would have given the poor woman an education. "I like that you feel willing to speak freely," he said. It was a good thing, not a flaw in her character. "I want you to continue doing so. It removes the mysticism that I often feel with women and allows me to ... to move forward. I wondered with ... with your sister-in-law. I often wondered. But with you, everything feels so clear."

She nodded. "Yes. I fear other men—or fail to respect them completely.

I don't experience that with you."

"We've known each other all of three days, though." Aubrey knew it wasn't wise to marry someone after knowing them three days. "I cannot ... I cannot marry you after only that."

"All right. I accept that." She rose.

So that was it, then? He wasn't willing to bind himself for life to a woman after having known her all of seventy-two hours, and for that, she would refuse him? Or rather, she would view it as refusal on his part. He, too, stood and watched as she started back toward the house without another word.

Perhaps she was not as simple to understand as he had hoped.

"That's it, then? I know you said you could find another man in three days, but ..." He trailed off in a mix of confusion and disappointment.

"Ah." She stopped and turned. "I thought we understood each other. Thank you for letting me know. I'm sorry—perhaps I did not verbalize my thoughts. I told you that I am not good at writing. All I meant about another man in three days was that was how long it would be until I moved on if you didn't reply. Not that it would only take me three days to select someone else. No, I make no such promises. I assumed our conversation is over for now because you need more time to get to know me. As it stands now, we ought to be plainer—you are right. How long would it take you to decide if I am a proper match for you or not?"

Oh. So she wasn't ready to abandon him yet. Should he be relieved or frightened? "I'm not sure. It's not ... it's not something we can just *decide*, is it?"

"One thing I will tell you, Mr. Montgomery, is that I prefer to live my life with a set of solid goals. Goals are not goals unless they have a limit attached to them. Two weeks? Three? I'm not sure I can go much over four, as I will have to return to America, but I will see what I can do. Perhaps three weeks, though, for you to court me?"

Aubrey swallowed. Impossible woman. "I ... I think four weeks ... and then if I am not ready to commit then, we can part ways."

Her forehead wrinkled as she considered this. "So then I am to put all my eggs in your basket, if you will. Oh, you know what I mean."

"No, I don't."

She laughed. "Thank you for telling me. What I mean is, I cannot secure a match in whatever time, if any, I have left after those four weeks are up. I shall have to trust the Lord to let me marry you if you are the person I'm supposed to marry. If I do not marry you at the end of those four weeks, I must marry Billy Pent. At least that is simple—and easy for the Lord to work with. God helps those who help themselves and all that." That wasn't quite right, but he didn't interrupt her. "Can I make a counteroffer?"

A counteroffer? *Lord, what am I getting myself into?* "Yes, you may," he said in spite of himself.

"We will announce our engagement today, and the banns will begin to be read. If I understand how English marital laws work, the last of the banns will then be read at the same time our limit is up. During that time, you can court me to your pleasure. If you feel, at the end of those four weeks, that we are ill-suited, or if you have any reservations at all, sensical or non-sensical, I will break the engagement and release you. Lady's prerogative, isn't it?" She shrugged. "If you think we are suited, we'll simply wed. I'm sure it won't hurt anything for us to prepare a wedding even if we don't go through with it. I think it'll be great fun, in fact, and your honor will be intact."

He raised his eyebrows. As if that could ever be consequence-free! Why, how would it affect his sisters to have a brother who had had two separate broken engagements—or practically? "Don't you rather think that—"

"It's the best option." She grinned, seeming to grow excited by her own suggestion. "Don't you *think* so, Mr. Montgomery? I promise I'll spread around some gossip about how my father wanted me to wed an American for money, I was a gold digger, and there was no fault on your behalf. That way, your reputation won't be injured, I'm sure. How would that do?"

She was clinically insane. That was the only reasonable explanation.

"I would be grateful forever for this service. It's so much better than relying on fate, to take destiny by the horns like a Minoan bull-leaper. What say you? Leap—or be mauled?"

"Those," he said in a voice he generally reserved for Fran and Connie, "are not the only two options."

"Hmm." She shrugged. "Whatever. Will you do it?"

He stared at her, her slim form and her dark hair and her gray eyes, the rosy blush lingering about her cheeks that proved she was not as unaffected by her boldness as she pretended. He wanted to win *her*, not the practical side of her but the side of her that must exist somewhere, that believed they could make a good match. Even if no feelings were involved, surely there was room for that, wasn't there?

"I'll do it," he said.

CHAPTER SEVEN

A UBREY MONTGOMERY WANTED TO court her, and Lorelei had to allow him, even if she found it exasperating.

Most of their time was spent with Francesca, Constance, and Winnie, so it wasn't as if Lorelei had to bear much romanticism. There was only so much a man could do in front of three young girls. The rest of the time, they were in the company of the Knights or even Mrs. Hilton, which offered even less opportunities for doting, which was the last thing she needed right now.

Honestly, she wasn't sure what he wanted at all. The decision had been made. What use was courtship? She wasn't going anywhere. He had brought her a ring that was a family heirloom, and she wore it on her left hand—it was a rhodolite garnet, a "rose stone." He'd told her it was his mother's favorite from the collection—not her own engagement ring, as that was tucked away at the estate, but one she had worn on occasion. Aubrey talked about his mother little, but she could tell he'd loved the late Mrs. Montgomery.

Aubrey had grown up with the unheard benefit of loving parents. That meant he probably knew how to love children—which meant he would love *their* children—which meant that *that* concern of Lorelei's was taken care of.

After all, she would be a poor mother, so her children would need love.

Or child, if she had anything to say about it—she didn't intend to have many, though perhaps it would depend on Aubrey. After all, he would be the one who was obligated to love any babies they had. She was perfectly willing to bring them into the world—it was the raising part she wasn't sure about.

Lorelei sat on a park bench in a quiet spot in London and watched Aubrey with his sisters and Winnie. A nearby pond contained a number of rather noisy ducks. He had brought bread along and was handing it out so the demanding fowl could be fed. Winnie loved this, with her insane fascination with every animal in existence, and Constance and Francesca seemed amused.

Next year, when it came near to Francesca's Season, Lorelei would have to get to know the girl—a little. Just enough to make sure whatever requirements Aubrey had in regard to finding his sister a match were fulfilled. Lorelei would be busy for a bit, if she had her way—with the Hilton Shipping Co.

Aubrey walked over and took the seat next to her.

"I'm glad they get along," he commented. "Connie and Fran bicker less now—your sister is good for them. I think she keeps things light, yes, but there's also a charming quality to her. It draws people together."

Lorelei nodded. Both Patrick and Winnie had that element in their nature, and Lorelei never quite knew what to make of it. After all, she had received none of their desire to placate, to make friends, or to keep the peace. She caused more problems than she solved.

Weren't people who had been raised in families like her own supposed to learn to settle in, sit back, and pretend everything was well? To not fight? To get along with people?

No, because Lorelei was foolish, like her mother before her. She never learned, and she never would.

"I'm glad you're not like her, though." Aubrey's voice was quiet but even. Had he sensed her thoughts? Was he placating her? But there was nothing in his tone to indicate it. "I don't think I need someone who will allow me to do nothing. It's good that you're a challenge."

She turned to him, probably a little wide-eyed, and then laughed. "That's quite the compliment."

"I ... I'm not sure I said that right." His voice sounded a little shocked, as if he weren't at all sure what he'd said, and he frowned. "I didn't mean it as an insult. Everyone is a challenge in their own way. I meant—" Then he paused.

With mixed amusement and delight, Lorelei decided to put him out of his misery. "It's all right." *The poor dear.* "We're not romantically involved. You don't have to compliment me, and I know I'm a challenge, so don't go on."

For a moment, Aubrey sat still, then he nodded. "I know you feel that way, but I want you to know that I'm not ... *indifferent* toward you. I can't help but feel like you're treating our engagement more like a business transaction than a relationship, which I suppose is the intention, but I am not sure I shall always be able to. Especially once—" Then he stopped again.

Hmm. "Especially once" what? But she didn't press him, as she was unsure she wanted to know what invisible curtain would have to drop before he would *"especially"* be unable to remain indifferent toward her.

Still, it was an empty promise. Aubrey Montgomery might believe that now—but as they spent time together, as they were bound by marriage, as they lived in the same household, he would feel differently. She could not offer him anything in return, and though Lorelei was the furthest thing from a romantic, she understood that the pain of unrequited love could be quite piercing. She didn't wish it on anyone, and given that she could not "requite" him in any way, shape, or form, he would have to suffer if he let himself slip.

There was little danger of that, however, given that *she* was *herself.*

"Courting you is a matter of tradition. I want to see that we suit, but I also believe that a man should love his wife."

She stilled. That was a belief he could not possibly uphold. Hadn't she made it clear how their relationship ought to proceed? "Aubrey, you know—"

He raised his hand. "Even if it is not a romantic love, we ought to have friendship and respect." Turning to her on the bench, he reached for her as if he wanted to touch her—but Lorelei didn't reach for him in return, and he withdrew, flushing slightly.

Did he even want to touch her? He'd been careful about that, but she wouldn't have minded holding hands, a brief embrace, or a few kisses if those things would please him as much as she was sure they would please her. He was not an unattractive man, and they *were* engaged, if only recently.

Still, Aubrey Montgomery was a man of *morality*, and she wasn't sure how much men of *morality* touched their fiancées. Perhaps not at all. It was not something she had ever considered, truly. Aubrey and she would be married in a month, so all those concerns ought to be put to bed then. She smirked to herself, which he didn't seem to notice, thankfully, for she felt no need to explain that particular thought.

At last, he spoke once more. "I will never make any grand gestures—I promise. I'm not sure I know how to be romantic. But there's a big difference between that sort of thing and being caring and tender toward someone."

Lorelei carefully schooled her features; she couldn't let him know what she was thinking—that she had little need for care or tenderness, especially from him. Instead, she trained her eyes on the girls, who had fed the last crumbs to the ducks and were now walking along the pond.

They were still within sight, though far enough away that they would have no idea of the conversation or even some of the actions of the couple they were supposedly chaperoning. Not that it mattered; Lorelei trusted herself and was near to trusting Aubrey Montgomery, if only because she didn't think he had the courage to do anything he oughtn't. Not in public and probably not even in private.

She tried to decide what it could be that would drive him to say such insane things, when she had made their position more than clear. *What could it be?* She eyed him with her peripheral vision. He had turned stoic, as if not wanting to let on that he had meant what he said. *But he does mean it, doesn't he?* Aubrey Montgomery was not a liar—if nothing else, she was sure of that.

Lust. That had to be the difference between him caring for her and not caring for her. Men had *lust* for women, didn't they? Did he think if he wooed her, if he pretended love for her benefit, Lorelei would be more likely to do as she was supposed to once they were married? Her thoughts whirled, playing with this idea.

Of course, there was a different side of those things, too, she supposed. Even if Aubrey didn't want to touch her, there was a possibility he also craved comfort, like an embrace or the squeeze of a familiar hand. Lorelei had often heard people express similar concepts. Winnie, in particular, was terrible at maintaining proper boundaries in a platonic sense—she flopped all over Lorelei and called it "affection." But why would one want to hug one's sister? Or one's fiancé, for that matter?

Still, she was unsure, and she hated to be unsure.

Lorelei turned to him once more, determination shoring her up. She placed a hand on his arm and looked him in the eyes. Her next words were chosen carefully. "You care for me?"

"Yes." The words stumbled out of his mouth, and his eyes were on her hand, not on her. "I do. I want us to be friends."

Hmm. A good start. "You want to become more?"

After a moment of consideration, he shook his head. "If we are to be married, certainly, I assume ... But no. I want to be as you want us to be."

Fair enough. She dipped her chin in acquiescence, then fixed her gaze on him. He had the prettiest blue eyes—better on a woman than a man, but she could accept them on him—and she made her eye contact deliberate—and held it. For a moment, she lowered her gaze, then brought it back up to his—and leaned in.

Aubrey Montgomery seemed like he had taken the bait. But then he swiftly rose. "We ought to find our sisters. They're wandering too far."

She rolled her eyes, accepted his hand, and rose. *So he doesn't want to kiss me? Then what on earth does he want!* Curiouser and curiouser. "Right. Let's go catch them."

He had almost admitted how badly he wanted to touch her, and she had perhaps wanted to kiss him. *I think.* Aubrey wasn't sure, having never had a woman attempt to kiss him before, let alone want to, but there had been a frozen moment, a lowering of her eyelashes over cheeks as she glanced down—toward the region where his mouth was—and then a quick look up as she leaned toward him.

But he had not taken advantage of the moment. He hadn't, even when he'd had a bizarre impulse to take her hands and press them, to hold on to them, to make her meet his eyes with sincerity rather than her normal sardonic bites.

Aubrey had never wanted to hold anyone's hand before. Even as a child, he'd walked on his own, reluctant to so much as accept help from a nanny or governess. When he'd courted Lady Mary, he had thought it respectful to keep a distance. When he had grown closer to her, she was the one who had occasionally pressed his arm as they walked or stepped into his embrace, usually without him particularly meaning to embrace her. When they had kissed, it had been performative. After all, kissing was confusing, impractical, and unsanitary. Aubrey hated confusing, impractical, unsanitary things.

Except Lorelei Hilton. Who was confusing. But he wouldn't have minded kissing her. Not one bit.

But that was not right. Not yet. It would be one thing if they were in love, he had courted her properly, and she had agreed, willingly and enthusiastically, to his proposal. That would be all right—if both parties were in agreement and it did not in any way go against their personal convictions on the subject.

However, in the situation they presently found themselves in, he wasn't sure. Aubrey didn't usually do things until he was very, *very* sure.

Another way in which Lorelei Hilton was proving incredibly confusing. She was making him question his sanity, and that didn't sit right with him.

Yet what was he to do?

Taking a deep breath, he led her along the path to catch up to their sisters.

CHAPTER EIGHT

TWO WEEKS LATER, LORELEI was happy to say she'd seen Aubrey Montgomery many more times and spent days with his sisters, too. She did feel like she had a better scope of the man. Further, she had reason to hope that he was somewhat attached to her—even if it was, like the man, a quiet and respectful attachment.

Today, Aubrey and she sat in the Knights' library, watching his sisters giggle over a romance novel and talking quietly about Lorelei's understanding of the Hilton Shipping Company, to which Aubrey was able to add much. In the last two weeks, he had done his research. She was impressed by that. Many men wouldn't have bothered.

"Oh, Aubrey, Winnie wants to take us upstairs and show us her own books. Can we go?" Francesca asked eagerly, rising from the sofa.

Constance nodded her agreement.

As always when they were left semi-alone, Aubrey stiffened but nodded. "Yes. Yes, that'd be fine. But hurry back. We can't stay much longer without pressing on the Knights' hospitality."

Lorelei watched the girls go with a grin. She had another experiment to perform, another reason why she might want to be with Aubrey Montgomery *or not*—for though she'd claimed her decision was made, Lorelei knew she must *test* him. It was the only way to be sure.

Lorelei had experimented with Aubrey's good nature more than once in these last two weeks, especially since she'd realized the wisdom of doing so at the duck pond. She'd been later than planned to a ball, intentionally. Not that there was a set arrival time for balls—that was not how London society worked—but that she'd promised him seven and arrived at seven thirty. No reaction, no obvious annoyance. The truth was, Lorelei was never late unless she intended to be; she had frequently abandoned Winnie for that reason. She'd broken her façade to tell Aubrey so, and he seemed relieved by this and had then admitted promptness did mean something to him, when it could be managed. Fair enough.

Then Lorelei had let Winnie test his impatience time and time again, as Winnie so professionally did. Lorelei's sister could probably make a living weeding out the patient, kind men from the impatient and the unsympathetic simply by being herself. For once, Lorelei was grateful for this. Aubrey remained consistently kind to her sister—and to his own sisters—when lesser men would have given in to annoyance.

As to his behavior toward Lorelei, he was circumspect. He always pulled away, stepped back, gave her plenty of space. He *always* acted the gentleman.

The purpose of these next five minutes would be to see if he could be … a *little* less so. For Lorelei did not intend to spend her entire marriage being constrained, even if she spent most of her engagement period being so, whether it was because her betrothed had convictions—or was scared stiff.

She plainly wasn't sure which was true, but she intended to find out.

Regardless of his feelings on the matter, she liked to be kissed—she was not above admitting this—and she wanted a husband who could kiss her well.

So without hinting as she had previously, Lorelei simply turned to him, moved along the sofa where they both sat, and pressed her lips to his.

It would've been a pleasant experience if he hadn't hastily quitted his seat, almost falling over in his haste to escape her.

"What are you doing?" he asked, looking far too shocked for a red-blooded man who was courting a red-blooded woman.

Narrowly avoiding a pout, Lorelei took a deep breath and glanced about before she responded. "I was going to kiss you, but you moved away, making it impossible. So now I am trying to think why you wouldn't want to kiss me—given that in the eyes of everyone concerned, we are engaged."

"But ... but ..." He sputtered off, staring at her as if she'd suddenly grown horns. "But we are not engaged."

"No, we are engaged."

"Semantics," he muttered, using her favorite word.

She grinned. "In this case, it's not. Sit back down and kiss me. I'm not asking you to ravish me in the library where anyone could walk in—and *no*, not because anyone could walk in. I want to do this right and honorably; I believe God must have made the rules about fornication for a reason. But kissing is not fornication, believe it or not, and I don't think we will be led to sin by anything but a lack of self-control. I have self-control, maybe enough for both of us, so you needn't worry, truly. For heaven's sake, you've kissed a girl before, haven't you? You've probably kissed my sister-in-law. Don't be a goose about it."

"A goose!" he protested, his face now red.

She laughed. "Or a gander. Sit!"

He did not sit. He paced to the window, mumbling under his breath about her American impertinence. Which she didn't mind, as long as he eventually spoke honestly with her. Which he did.

"I don't think we should kiss until we ... until we're truly *sure* we're going to marry," he said at last. "It is vital to me that I do not take something that is not mine to take. It's not because I don't want to. It's because I'd rather be sure."

"So these last two weeks have not made you any surer?" she asked pensively. "I had thought they would, and kissing would help us be surer. It's one of the reasons I didn't want to marry Billy Pent, you know. He kisses with a lack of competence—"

"You kissed Billy Pent?" Aubrey exclaimed, turning from the window. "Why?"

"Because he was courting me," she said patiently, despite the fact that

Billy had not been the first boy she kissed. That felt unhelpful to reveal in this particular moment, nor was it exactly a point of pride with her. The niggle in her conscience at Aubrey's obvious hurt frustrated her, but she kept it to herself. "Again, you have kissed Cassie."

A long beat of silence. "Yes. But not … but not …"

"Not passionately? You think I was suggesting we go further than a few kisses? Anything that leads to greater ardor would be inappropriate. Even *I* know that. You're saying I would be willing to do so?"

"No! I wasn't suggesting … *You* were suggesting," he said firmly, despite the fact that Lorelei had certainly not defined what she meant by "kissing" in the slightest.

"Further," Lorelei said, enjoying herself greatly, "you're also implying that *that's* what I did with Billy Pent, therefore negating whatever physical touch you shared with Cassie as purer and insinuating my character is not as stalwart as your own. That's rather a low blow, don't you think?"

Aubrey was silent. That generally happened whenever she'd rattled on to the point where he felt either confused or defensive. As always, he took a moment or two to think and then he replied quietly and sensibly. An aspect of his personality Lorelei preferred greatly to Winnie's whining or her brother's jocularity until pressed into nearly cruel shut-downs. "I did kiss Cassie—but mostly on the cheek. I wasn't eager to take things too far with her physically. I believe boundaries and self-control are necessary aspects of any relationship. Further, I do not judge you for kissing Billy Pent—I was simply surprised, as you made it sound as if you barely knew him. You can hold your own convictions on that front, and I will understand that. But I regret what I shared with Cassie, and I'm sure she does, too. I've seen the ruin of a man who has lost himself in the arms of too many women who probably are equally as lost; I want to be cautious about anything that could lead toward those types of situations. I don't want you to have regrets about me."

"That's sweet of you." Unnecessary, though. He was the furthest thing from Gibson Ashfield—or she assumed that was who he meant; he had so few friends. She patted the sofa beside her. "Come kiss me. You'll have to be quick about it now."

He frowned. "But—"

"Did I say you had a choice?"

For a moment, he watched her with half-closed eyes, as if he wasn't sure what to make of her, then he crossed the room, bent over, cupped her chin with his hand, and kissed her.

Aubrey was careful in his kissing, Lorelei discovered—as if afraid to hurt her by pressing her lips too roughly or even by following what she believed to be natural instincts—nor was he lacking in confidence. No, he was gentle but thorough. She liked that.

If she was breathless when he drew away from her, she believed she hid it well. For his part, he said nothing; simply returned to sitting beside her, at a decorous distance.

"That's it for now," he said after a long beat of silence. "Maybe until we're married."

"Very well."

Their sisters returned, and Aubrey told them they had to leave.

But as he brushed past Lorelei in the doorway, his sisters ahead of him on their way to the carriage, he squeezed her hand. "Thank you."

"You're welcome," she said, despite the fact that she, not him, had insisted on the kiss. "I liked that."

He nodded. "I did, too."

He left quickly, embarrassed, she thought.

It's a good first, though.

Lorelei could stake a lot of hope on a good "first."

Of course, Aubrey was not the only confused person as to Lorelei's recent actions. Her mother had been causing a bit of a fuss. She had at first accepted the "engagement" and the reading of the banns, agreeing that there was no real reason why Lorelei should not marry the wealthy Englishman. In fact, there was a hard glint in Mother's eyes that said she knew very well that her husband would prefer an American for his daughter.

Father, however, had not protested, nor had he come scurrying to England to view the wedding proceedings. In response to Lorelei's informative note, he'd sent back a telegram that simply read, "Sending N. Hastings to oversee procedures." There was no congratulations, but Lorelei took the lack of threats as a good sign. Nathan Hastings was one of his more upper-level staff, an unmarried man in his mid forties who could go and come as Father pleased. He would draw up the papers and such to see any assets were properly handled to assure that the Hilton legacy remained intact—and that Lorelei's future was tied up irrevocably with the company.

At that message, Mother stopped asking Lorelei any questions at all. She had grown bored with England and spoke of returning home to America as soon as the wedding was over. When Lorelei suggested that Winnie stay on with her for a few months, Mother waved her hand and went off to take a nap.

Lorelei felt sorry for her mother, in a way. She would return to Boston without her daughters—and even if she was a poor mother, certainly a great deal of her time had been dedicated to them for the last nineteen years.

Yet her mother seemed to be suffering from a mighty case of ennui. Ever since Patrick left, Lynnie Hilton had become a shell of herself. Lorelei had hoped that it was remorse, but she was more inclined to believe it was a kind of exhaustion. Her mother barely existed as a woman. She did a few things she was supposed to do—walked and talked and ate, dragged her children about from party to party as needed—and then retired to her room for the remainder of the time. In Boston, Lorelei knew, she would fall into a rhythm of empty conversations at lavish parties, and the rest of the time, she would "rest."

Mother slept more and more these days. If Lorelei didn't have her own problems to deal with, she'd suggest her mother see a doctor. She couldn't be well—though it wasn't as if she were physically failing. No, it was as if she'd given up ... and Lorelei wasn't sure any doctor of medicine could fix that.

Today, Mr. Nathan Hastings had arrived in London and immediately made an appointment with Aubrey's lawyers. Aubrey would be present, but they had not intended to include Lorelei—until Aubrey insisted upon it.

Lorelei became suddenly convinced that she'd made the right choice.

So at ten o'clock on a Monday morning, with only a few sips of coffee in her stomach, Lorelei met Mr. Nathan Hastings and Mr. Aubrey Montgomery in the foyer of the Knights' house. Behind her trailed a reluctant Harriet—her chosen chaperone, as her sister would've asked too many questions and her mother didn't care to listen at all. But Lorelei could trust Harriet to listen and remember what details she herself could not.

"Mr. Hastings." Lorelei walked forward and warmly took the older man's hand. "It has been too long. The last time we spoke was when my brother had me review our inheritance documents together—but all that has changed now."

Mr. Hastings, for his part, smiled at her, and shook her hand rather than kissing or bowing over it. For this, she was grateful. "Miss Hilton. Indeed, things have changed. But I am glad to be here for a happy occasion, for once." He had always had a sweet spot for her, Lorelei thought, and she was glad that her father had sent him over.

They made their way to the carriage and climbed in together. Harriet remained silent while Mr. Hastings quietly laid out a few details to Lorelei.

"I think the primary thing to understand, Miss Hilton," Mr. Hastings said with a sideways look at Aubrey, "is that anything that might have been yours in America—that might have been held in trust for you, that might have been separated from your husband's assets—will now belong to Mr. Montgomery."

Lorelei nodded. She had expected that. "I understand."

"You ... you will be unable to take any ... vested interest. In proceedings, I mean."

"Yes." Also something she understood. "This is acceptable to me. Mr. Montgomery and I have had a few conversations to this point, and we understand how the Hilton Shipping Company must be managed."

"I see." Mr. Hastings again glanced at Aubrey, who continued to say nothing. "There are several ways this could be set up, and I have been granted arbitrator rights. If Mr. Montgomery would like to take an active interest in the company, this could be arranged. If I may speak plainly, Miss Hilton, how much ... how much a husband and wife involve each other in their individual pursuits is the decision of the couple themselves, not of the law of the land."

"That is exactly what we've discussed, Hastings." Lorelei said. "A question for you. Would you be comfortable discussing our own personal agreements at this meeting? Would your lawyers understand?"

Aubrey turned to her and raised his eyebrows. "You would want to discuss that among others than ourselves?"

"I would prefer it."

"Very well then." He inclined his head. "We'll do as you say."

"Excellent."

Before another word could be said, the carriage slowed to a stop, and the four stepped out.

The offices of Wilson & Sons were expansive and elegant. Lorelei soon found herself seated at a table with Aubrey, Mr. Hastings, and two other men, supposedly both Wilsons of some variety, while Harriet took a seat on the back wall to wait. Of course, the Wilsons were shocked to see her there, but she said nothing and ignored their odd looks.

Legal papers were brought forth from both Hastings and the Wilsons. They spoke back and forth for some time, and Lorelei carefully tracked their conversation but said little—after all, there was no point in revealing how much of it she understood. That was something better discussed with Hastings at a later time.

As Lorelei had known, Aubrey was more than willing to take an active role in the company—and Hastings could remain in England to help them transfer the Hilton Shipping Company's assets to Aubrey's land in Dorset, which included a system of docks, as it were. They would simply have to be expanded and repurposed, as they had had little purpose for the Montgomerys other than as a fishing port.

Hastings was more than up for the challenge.

Papers were drawn up. Of course, it wasn't the complete control that Lorelei wanted. Nothing could be. But it was something, some fragile hold on the world, the life, the company she would have had if she were only a man—and surely that was something.

With Mr. Hastings casting her reassuring glances and Aubrey looking at ease with all the plans, she grew more confident and asked a few quiet but firm questions. Hastings answered them, and before the look of shock had faded from the eyes of the Wilsons, Lorelei considered herself well in possession of all the facts.

"Before we go," Aubrey said after they had concluded the official business, "I wanted to discuss a verbal and written but nonlegal agreement that Miss Hilton and I have assented to adhere to throughout the course of our marriage. Would that suit?"

If the Wilson men had looked shocked before, now they looked positively sick. Lorelei had to reroute all her energy toward not grinning at them.

"Lorelei," Aubrey said, turning to her slightly, "I believe you had prepared a list."

She nodded and reached into the pocket of her dress, where the carefully folded piece of paper rested. "And you?"

"Yes." He nodded. "I'd like us to discuss what we have on these lists, arrive at a verbal agreement, and then I would like it typed up and delivered to my house, as well as a copy given to Mr. Hastings and to the Messrs. Wilson. I know this is irregular, but it is important to both of us—especially to Miss Hilton."

"Mr. Montgomery," said one of the Wilsons, looking flabbergasted, "you realize that you cannot enter a legal agreement with your wife. Legally speaking, once she becomes Mrs. Aubrey Montgomery, she will no longer be a separate entity. Why, entering any type of agreement would simply be ... be an agreement with *yourself*, sir."

"Exactly. A resolution. You are not above making resolutions yourself, are you, Mr. Wilson?" Aubrey glanced around the table. "Surely all of us have decided to do something with the primary motivating factor being our own desire to do so. I involve my wife as she will be my primary companion of life and the one who my actions impact the most. Is that clear?"

Perhaps not knowing what to say or being too confused to say what they thought, the Wilsons quieted down, and Lorelei handed her paper to Mr. Hastings. Aubrey flipped open a leather binder he'd withdrawn from a briefcase and removed a few papers, which he also passed to Hastings, and the man sat down to read the lists.

Lorelei had focused primarily on guidelines for her involvement in the shipping company itself, made a notation about the possibility of future children, and laid out terms for her involvement with his sisters' debuts into society. While Aubrey had briefly touched upon the shipping company and his sisters' debuts, Lorelei got her first glimpse at his priorities—and she found she rather liked them.

He wanted a child—singular if the first child were a son and two if the first child were not a son, but ending at two regardless of the gender of the second—and he had further noted that this was if both parties were capable. He wanted to begin attempting to have that first child in two years but had no requirements of her before that time except that she would take an active part of Francesca's debut next spring and then Constance's when she was of age. He also indicated that Lorelei had equal decision-making power and financial independence as she wished even as concerned aspects of their life and his properties not related directly to the Hilton Shipping Co.

He wanted her time, her presence. He wanted her to agree to see him regularly, and for them to remain in the same house. The fact that he'd written that down—in plain black and white—and allowed it to be read aloud at a table in a room full of business-minded men ... Well. She wasn't sure Patrick would've allowed that. It was like announcing "I am lonely," and what man wanted to admit that?

Aubrey could have been cautious, but he was being generous. Though there was no legal binding to this, she knew he would keep his word.

The Wilsons blustered a bit—this was irregular, unheard of, and certainly not in any way legally binding, which again, had not been a concern, but Lorelei decided not to remind them of this fact. But they agreed to have the terms combined and copies distributed along with the other legal papers, and after some discussion, Lorelei was able to depart their offices feeling as if she'd more than accomplished her goals.

Aubrey said little on the carriage ride back, but after they'd parted ways with Mr. Hastings, they made their farewells in the foyer.

"I'm glad we did that," he said in an undertone as Harriet scampered off to prepare Lorelei's dinner dress. "I think it will set us off on a right note."

Then he kissed her—gently but thoroughly—before the footsteps of the butler were heard, and they hastily appeared to be doing nothing but speaking about the wedding arrangements. She realized suddenly that she was going to be married to this man ... and he wanted to wait two years to have children. Knowing Aubrey Montgomery, that would mean, to him, separate bedchambers.

How on earth am I going to fix that?

Chapter Nine

August 1884

Aubrey—and most men, as far as he knew or suspected—had never so much imagined his wedding day as the rest of his life to follow. However, if he had thought of it, he'd always felt resigned. It would be extravagant, and he would suffer from it.

But that was not the case. It was almost too good to be true—none of the fuss, none of the nonsense. Ashfield stood to his left—incredibly skeptical of proceedings, especially as Aubrey had only briefly introduced him to Lorelei—and Gwendolyn Hilton was opposite him. Aubrey's sisters, Mr. and Mrs. Knight, Mrs. Hilton, and a few family friends of the Montgomerys were seated on the pews.

At her own choice—Mr. Knight had offered to do the job in her father's stead—Lorelei walked down the aisle alone. Somehow, they'd gotten together a white dress trimmed with orange embroidery at the last minute, and it was lovely. Aubrey honestly did think she was the most beautiful woman he'd ever seen; he wasn't sure she'd appreciate hearing it. She was surely too practical to enjoy such compliments.

Perhaps over the course of their life, he would find a way to tell her through his actions. Though he wasn't supposed to be romancing Lorelei Hilton—or Lorelei Montgomery—or *any* version of Lorelei.

He was supposed to marry her and keep up his end of their agreement, but he was *not* supposed to love her. That was precisely what this arrangement was supposed to avoid. Love was an impossibility, a kind of wild stupidity that Aubrey was not mature enough, perhaps not man enough, to handle.

But if anyone should be loved, surely it was one's wife ... He was convicted to tenderly care for her, cherish her. Even if she hated it, that was nonnegotiable. He would be good to her.

So back and forth he went, feeling almost distracted as he took Lorelei's hands and repeated his vows. The Church of England ceremony was simple but formal—including a number of embarrassing lines, especially for a couple who was not going to have an average marriage. Even the vows were difficult to get through—he meant every word, but there was something far too sacred about them, and it made him squirm. But then there were the words he spoke to her as he slid one of the family rings onto her finger: "with my body, I thee worship." Surely that was too intimate for the relationship they were to share?

If Lorelei noticed anything, she didn't let on. She was solemn and serious during the entire ceremony—more bored than she was weighing the significance of the moment, he thought. That was Lorelei, and Aubrey was Aubrey. He was terrified by the significance of the moment.

The wedding breakfast was a blur, despite the fact that two hours seemed to crawl by at a snail's pace. It was a hazy, awkward blur, with him not knowing what to do or say. He didn't think he ate a bite.

Before they left, while Lorelei was presumably changing out of her wedding gown and into something she could travel in, he managed to speak briefly with his sisters, who were both tearful but congratulatory. Since Mrs. Hilton would be leaving a day after the wedding, Gwendolyn would be moving into the Montgomery town house—and Francesca and Constance were happy to have her company while Aubrey and Lorelei traveled to Montgomery Place in Dorset. The newlyweds would send for the girls, presumably after a few weeks. It was no honeymoon, certainly, but some privacy—and some time to adjust.

Much of the journey could be taken by train, and Lorelei was silent as they took a carriage from the Knights' house, where their wedding breakfast took place, to the train station.

Once they were seated in their first-class compartment, chugging southwest, Lorelei pulled a book out of her bag—and remained silent.

Aubrey didn't know what to say, so he stared out the window.

It was nearly one hundred miles to Dorset, but these days, they flew along the tracks, and it wouldn't be more than a four-hour trip. He thought about telling Lorelei all about Stirling Single, but he felt like she wouldn't care to hear about the train, so he simply ran through the facts in his mind. He'd been so fascinated by steam engines as a boy ... and though the fascination had faded, replaced by more serious or more relevant pursuits, he still admitted that train travel was interesting to him.

But women didn't like trains.

At last, they reached their stop in Dorset, and there was the hustle and bustle of moving from the train carriage to the Montgomery carriage, which they'd telegraphed ahead to have meet them. Lorelei was still quiet, though she did greet his carriage driver with a small smile and an acknowledgement when he wished her well and congratulated Aubrey.

Well wishes for the bride, congratulations for the groom. All the traditional things, but Aubrey didn't feel married. *Was* he really married, in the technical sense of the institution? That bothered him. In fact, it'd been bothering him for days, since they discussed their arrangement ... and since she'd agreed to wait two years to try for their first child.

There was an *implication*, an implication that there was no practical need for them to share a bed. Granted, the servants had probably prepared the master suite so they could easily sleep separately, but Aubrey regretted not asking for her to be his partner in that particular aspect of marriage.

Of course, maybe being lovers was too romantic a notion for a woman like Lorelei Hilton—er, Montgomery. He wasn't sure. He wouldn't know until he asked her.

As they began the final thirty-minute carriage ride along the seaside road to Montgomery Place, Lorelei's eyes were directed out the window, watching the coastline. Aubrey grew his courage—and spoke.

"Lorelei," he said, testing out her name on his tongue with a smile he couldn't quite hide, "when we arrive, it'll be past teatime. I thought we could have a small meal, if you'd like, in our rooms and rest for the remainder of the evening. The grand tour can wait."

She turned from the window—and grinned. "So, 'rooms'? Plural?"

"The master suite. The rooms are attached. I can always move my things—"

"No. You should stay with me tonight. You must, as a gentleman." She raised an eyebrow—yes, singular, somehow. This woman was truly an otherworldly marvel.

Ah. She must mean ... only, she couldn't mean ... but what other meaning could there possibly be? As he sat staring at her in befuddlement, she took mercy on him.

"We will be lovers," she said in a tone usually reserved for children. "All right?"

"All right," he said weakly. He was many things, but not an absolute fool, and if she said he would stay, he would stay.

She was gracious to not hold him to the word of the arrangement.

"I will come to you about two hours after we arrive. Will that suit?" It would give him time to make sure they were not disturbed for the rest of the evening, for he did not want to be bothered, and perhaps to bathe and prepare himself.

And maybe to pray. To pray a lot. He'd need it.

"That is more than enough time."

He nodded and opened his mouth to say more and then closed it.

The rest of the carriage ride was conducted in silence.

Aubrey wasn't sure there was a nervous bone in the body of Lorelei Hilton—Lorelei Montgomery now. Yet he was all nerves. He should be the one with experience, perhaps. He was a man, older than she, and had seen more of the world.

Yet he had not seen *everything*, much less done everything.

Lord, let me please my wife. If You want us to have a healthy relationship … help me.

He also acknowledged that Lorelei was a beautiful woman. Her gray eyes stood out so starkly against her dark hair, and she had rosy cheeks and pink lips and in every way was so ridiculously *feminine* in her form that it made him shaky.

The dueling desires to touch her and to preserve her were maddening. He *wanted* her in his embrace and he *wanted* her safe and he *wanted* to believe that these two things could be achieved simultaneously.

But was she so practical that everything they did together must be about duty? Or could she allow herself—and him—to have something sacred that couldn't be touched by the hard reality of their agreement?

Aubrey checked his heart at the thought. If he started wanting this—really *wanting* this—his natural honesty would make him inclined to tell her how he felt.

Yet he was faced with a quandary. Could the sacrament of marriage be entirely practical, or was there something otherworldly about it?

He at last entered her bedroom to find Lorelei sitting on the edge of the bed, wearing a nightgown under her dressing gown, with her hands neatly folded on her lap.

"Aubrey." She inclined her head. "How do we start?"

"How do we start *what*?" Surely she couldn't mean—?

She shrugged. "I don't have a good word for it—that I want to say aloud, I mean. I know the basics, but if you could take the lead, I would appreciate it. I'm inexperienced here."

"As am I!" he protested.

Her brow furrowed. "Yes, but don't men talk about these things?"

"In my experience, not nearly as much as women." Ashfield did have a propensity toward crude jokes, but Aubrey had always ignored them. "What do you know?"

To his surprise, rather than offering a vague reply, she gave him a brief but pointed explanation. Then she raised her eyebrows. "Did you hear about the same?"

Hot in the face, he nodded. "I had heard about the same." From an entirely different perspective, though. His conversations on the subject had begun and ended with his father when he was an adolescent. Lorelei's knowledge was mechanical whereas his was largely subject to his father's romanticized, yet biblical, explanations. The talks they'd had had been focused on morality more than practicality. Though Aubrey had long ago discovered where all the theoretical explanations led, he was surprised Lorelei's information was so practical.

Yet honestly, he *shouldn't* be surprised, knowing her.

"You know." He rubbed the back of his neck, regarding her with a sense of unease. *If only she wasn't so beautiful.* It would be easier to focus, to have a conversation. "We can wait until we … until we want children. When we know each other better."

"I'll get my monthly in about a week, so children are not a concern—I can tell you all about females, if you like. Later." She cocked her head. "Aren't you curious about what it would be like? I can feel you overthinking, but I'm quite certain nothing we do here will truly be wrong, as long as we are both committed to it." She shrugged as if it were the easiest thing in the world. "I'm attracted to you, you know, if that helps."

"I don't want to hurt you," Aubrey said in an undertone. "Surely you can understand—"

"Yes, I understand your motives." Lorelei stood and walked to him; she took his hand and pressed it. She had small, cool hands, drawing him back to the moment and away from the shakiness in his bones. "I promise that it will be all right. If you want, you can go to your own room right after, if the problem is sharing a bed."

Right, because that's definitely what I'm worried about. He stared at her hands in his and swallowed. "Do you want me to stay?"

"That seems like a decision we could make later—together. Aubrey, it'll be all right. I trust you."

She trusted him?

With a sigh, he gave up and began kissing her—because one thing he was quickly realizing was that if Lorelei Hilton Montgomery wanted something, she was going to get it. She tasted like coffee and a hint of vanilla.

As it turned out, she did prefer that he stayed with her—in fact, that she liked his arm around her and her body tucked against his and his face pressed into the softness of her hair.

And Aubrey realized that he was probably in love with his hurricane of a wife.

Oh, God, help me.

CHAPTER TEN

L ORELEI LET AUBREY HOLD her hand the next morning, and she wasn't sure why.

She could blame it on any number of ridiculous emotions that had no basis in reality, but she wasn't ready to analyze it. Not yet. There ought to be a honeymoon period, after all, oughtn't there? Lorelei was willing to be delusional for a week—no, five days—before she settled into a routine.

He led her into the main hall. It was a large area—one she'd not taken the full vantage of the evening before—and she appreciated the grandeur. Below, the servants had assembled to greet them. She was introduced to Mr. Gooden, the butler, and Mrs. Emmett, the housekeeper, who she immediately made a point of getting on her team.

She'd read any number of horrid romances with evil housekeepers, and Lorelei found them ridiculous. The key to getting the housekeeper on one's side was to respect her in everything yet be entirely competent at everything, both of which Lorelei could easily do.

"Mrs. Emmett, we will have to speak again later so you can catch me up on things around here," Lorelei said, keeping her tone level and respectful but lacking any subservience. "But first, Mr. Montgomery insists I get the lay of the land, and I think he is wise to suggest it."

Her deference to her husband was what caused the first softening in Mrs. Emmett's face—and Lorelei smiled for two reasons, one relevant and one an irrelevant honeymoon feeling. The first was because she had earned a small part of Mrs. Emmett's approval and would likely earn the rest soon. The second was because it meant that Aubrey was well-respected by his staff, which meant her decision had been the right one.

Aubrey looked amused, but she forgave him. He would see how well it worked in time. Besides, Lorelei was in a good mood—coffee in bed did that to a woman.

Her hand was still in her husband's somehow, as she followed him out the front door a few minutes later. "The gardens first—"

"Then the docks," Lorelei said. "I hope Hastings comes soon and gets things organized. Of course, we can assemble workers."

Aubrey chuckled, drawing her a little closer as they walked along a stone path that curled around the front of the large red-brick mansion with its white pillars. She could smell the sea air, despite the mile or so between them and the water, and she was eager to make her way down to truly experience what the Dorset coastline was like and if it were truly a good fit for the Hilton Shipping Company's new headquarters.

"Do you ever think of anything but the next task at hand?" Aubrey asked, leading her in an easterly direction, around the side of the house, and toward the gardens, which sat at the north of the mansion—likely, she supposed, because the big house offered something of a wind block.

Not that Lorelei disliked the wind. No, a sea breeze was stirring to her in a way few things were. There was something about it that made her happy, and so little was capable of giving Lorelei moments of joy.

A slow smile. Of course Aubrey had been added to that list.

Ignoring whatever rhetorical question he'd asked her, for she'd barely heeded it, she said, "I will never mention this again, as it was only my due, and I feel I should not offer excessive gratitude for what belongs to me, but thank you for last night. I believe men have this concept that they *must* be experienced in such matters, as if God called premarital intimacy a sin for no reason. Of course He knows best—I can acknowledge that fact—and 'tis far better to find a willing pupil than a graduate who was never properly tested. Don't you think?"

Instead of answering, he coughed and changed the subject, asking her what she thought of the grounds. It was a cloudy day for August—and cold for summer, too—but the gardens were extravagant.

Still, she'd given him a great compliment. What man wouldn't want to hear that? Perhaps she had not explained her meaning well. That might be for the best. She didn't want him to develop an ego.

"Come on, I'll show you my favorite place," he said, picking up his place slightly. His tone had lightened, and there was a slight spring in his step that had never been there before.

He loves it here, Lorelei realized. Perhaps that was a good thing—it would make him more motivated to improve his property with the docks and all the other aspects that would need to go into that.

He led her to a hidden nook, where a circle of trees and a series of ornamental hedges around a small fountain, edged by flowerbeds overflowing with roses, created a more private atmosphere. "This was my mother's favorite spot," he said, leading her to a bench. "She'd come sit here and read for hours, and I'd come with her sometimes, when I was quite young. I'd make a lot of noise playing, and she'd tolerate it quite well."

"I can't imagine you as a noisy little boy," Lorelei commented. If anything, she imagined him as a sedate, serious child who never had any fun—the kind she would've teased relentlessly.

"Oh, I had my moments. Granted, I had to be the mature older brother once my sisters came along, but of course I was an only child for a long while. After my father died, I had to step up." He shrugged. "It was my responsibility to be the man of the house before I was a man."

No. She didn't say that instinctive reaction aloud. After all, it had been his responsibility. Who was she to protest? But a part of Lorelei wanted to tell Aubrey that it was never the responsibility of a child to take the place of a parent.

That was irrelevant to their current discussion, however. After all, the past was meant to be disregarded, if it had its flaws. She wasn't able to change anything about his childhood, let alone her own; therefore, what was the point of going over it?

So instead, she said, "That makes sense."

"You had much the same problem, I imagine," he said, his voice taking on an overly serious tone that she longed to rattle out of him. Now was not the time to be serious. She was being delusional for five days—how dare he drag her back to reality? His hand took hers. "You are mature for your age ... I mean, you practically act as if you must be a mother to your own sister."

Lorelei laughed. "I would be a poor mother to anyone, Aubrey, let alone Winnie."

"She's not your child. Your natural feelings toward her are that of a sister."

"I suppose." She withdrew her hand. He couldn't be under any delusions in regards to her motherly capabilities. Perhaps he thought by the time their two years were up and they had a child, Lorelei would change, but she seriously doubted she could be any kind of mother, so he'd have to be a stupendous father.

"Should we walk down to the docks now? It's a bit of a jaunt, but I don't mind a good walk in the morning, if you don't." When she didn't reply, too caught up in her thoughts to form a response, he said, "Lori?"

Oh, right. That drew her out of her reverie. "You called me that last night, and I ... I didn't know what to think of it. I thought it wasn't the moment to correct you, but I do find it strange. No one calls me that—I'd never even considered it as an option. I've always been 'Lore.'"

He paused for a minute, then nodded. "All the more reason for me to."

"My brother calls me Lore—and my sister. My mother started it. She also called Patrick 'Trick' and Gwendolyn 'Win.' Did you know that *lore* means 'learning'?" She was rambling and coming dangerously close to admitting a secret hurt that she wasn't even ready to think about herself, but she did so anyway. "Or 'to teach." Etymology is not my best subject, but my mother enjoys it. *Folklore* comes from similar roots."

"'The learning of common people'?"

"Oh, did you study it?"

Very gravely, he said, "I may look stupid, but I promise, I am not. It's rather easy to piece together."

"It is." She shrugged. "I find it interesting. My mother certainly learned a lot with me."

He cocked his head. "Your mother felt it had ... a meaning?"

"Yes. She made that abundantly clear." She ducked her head and faked a laugh, as if it were a funny story instead of something she'd mulled over again and again, torturing herself with on nights when she couldn't sleep. "Lorelei is a German siren who sits on a cliff about the Rhine and lures men to their deaths. The name comes from that—I think it refers to the location; Patrick told me. But my mother viewed me as another lesson taught to her the hard way—another lesson of her own foolishness, of the failure of her marriage, of the cruelty of the world. Another reason to give up the fight. But I fight, don't I, Aubrey? I wake up fighting, and I go to sleep fighting, and I never stop. I'm the albatross, the bird that never roosts. Because I'm not going to give in like she did." She turned to him then and held his blue gaze, which was stoic enough that she felt she could keep talking. "I can't give in to bitterness and make everyone miserable and have no earthly use beyond the ornamental and fight with my husband and torture my children, but being soft isn't exactly a relevant option either, is it? There's no real option for a woman like me but to not suffer. So I don't. I keep on going. Sometimes I do wonder how I'm going to keep it up, but when you're out of options, you 'learn' or you die. You know?" She had said as much as she felt capable of, at least for now, so she waited for his reaction.

He stood and held his hand out to her. She took it and rose.

"I will call you 'Lori,'" he said quietly.

Then he led her back up the path toward the south— and the sea.

Maybe she could find peace there.

Aubrey thought the first week of his marriage had gone along fairly well, or as well as could be expected. Lorelei had revealed little bits of herself to him—honestly, due to how stoic she could be, he hadn't expected that much. But the other part of it was the gloriousness of holding hands and sharing kisses and walking together and sleeping together at night.

But if Aubrey knew anything, it was that all good things must come to an end, and now the honeymoon was over. He went in the carriage to meet his sisters and Gwendolyn from the train station and listened to their excited ramblings all the way back.

Lorelei hadn't wanted to come along. "I am too busy at the docks," she'd said firmly, "to leave, even for an hour. I'm sorry."

She hadn't meant the "I'm sorry," but she'd wasted air on saying it. That was progress, Aubrey thought.

Because he had decided he was going to try to win her heart. If he didn't succeed, he'd be right back where he'd started. But if he did succeed ...

A memory of his father's words about the sacredness of marriage, about the beauty of love, about the necessity to honor one's wife wholly without wish of return flashed through his mind. He could do that, but it would be so much easier if she liked him a little, too.

Aubrey was no good at courting anyone, but if anyone was worthy of being courted, it was Lorelei Hilton Montgomery. He wanted to give her the opportunity to be pursued—he wanted her to like it, and he wanted her to like that it was *him* doing the pursuing.

"Can we stop by the docks on our way to the house?" Gwendolyn asked eagerly, shaking Aubrey from his absent thoughts.

Apparently, the sisters had something in common—from the moment docks were suggested, they both wanted to visit. It was an odd obsession, but he was willing to indulge it.

"Yes, we can stop by and see Lorelei, unless you're too tired—"

"We are not too tired," Constance said, a thread of eagerness in her tone. "Are we, Fran?"

Francesca shook her head. "Not in the slightest. I'd love to see how Miss—I mean, how Lorelei is getting on. It'll be interesting to see a shipping business starting up in our own back yard."

The obsession was catching. Before he knew it, they'd all be mumbling about pilings and proper water depths and acceptably vast warehouses in their sleep like his wife was. He tapped on the carriage roof and, after the conveyance slowed to a stop, leaned out to alert the driver to the change of directions.

Lorelei had gone down to the docks at dawn that morning, Aubrey at her side, but she was unwilling to leave. It was as if she'd begun pouring her whole soul into the Hilton Shipping Co.

There was nothing left for Aubrey, though to be fair, she was also pushing herself rather hard in addition to the fact that her menses had started, leaving her in rather a lot of pain—which she steadfastly refuted. The exhausted look in her eyes, the frazzled nature, the slight stiffness of her walk, a permanent "pre-coffee" frown on her face as if she never quite woke up.

Still, she worked, but Lorelei was Lorelei, and she'd do what she wanted. Even if it just about killed her, which was what Aubrey feared. His guarded protestation that first day, when he'd doubted her ability to walk, had been met with a glare that could melt glass. He hadn't said anything after that.

The carriage rumbled through the village that stretched out along the harbor. The harbor itself was deep and wide, sheltered but not so removed from the sea to make it impossible to access. Indeed, it was perfect for Lorelei's purpose, especially if she meant it to be more of a resting stop on the way to London or a place for her to gather goods and store them in the large warehouses that would soon be built.

Aubrey took a deep breath as he saw the workmen scattered about the large docks and then toward the west, where empty land would allow for further building. Lorelei and Hastings had certainly let no grass grow under their feet.

Even as he helped his sisters and Gwendolyn down from the carriage, he scanned the crowd of men for Lorelei. At last, he found her, standing next to Mr. Hastings with what looked like a map of some sort stretched out between them. Lorelei was gesticulating wildly with one hand while clinging to the edge of the paper with the other. Mr. Hastings nodded but appeared to have the sense not to argue with her—smart man.

"There's Lore!" Gwendolyn squealed and took off down the wooden dock toward Lorelei.

Lorelei glanced up at her sister's various noises of delight and handed the map back to Hastings, dismissing him with a careless wave of her hand, then accepted her sister's tempestuous embrace with what looked like utter defeat.

Even Lorelei was no match for Gwendolyn's exuberance.

His sisters were starting to lose their sedate edge the more time they spent with Gwendolyn. He ought to be thankful for it, honestly; they could do with a little livening up, as could he. Of course, Lorelei had already livened him up plenty, he felt, but it didn't hurt anything to keep seeking more joy—or more happiness, even if it weren't anything abiding.

His sisters followed Gwendolyn down the dock, and he watched Lorelei greet them with what he took to be affection. Oh, it wasn't exactly what one wanted for familial relationships, but he believed that would come. Lorelei would become comfortable with them. After all, she was not the most immediately nurturing woman, but with people she loved, surely ...

Though she had said not to expect her to be too much of a mother, it was hard for Aubrey to take that too seriously. His own mother had always spoken of a kind of maternal instinct that took over when a woman had her first child and never quite let her go.

He wondered what Lorelei would be like when that happened to her. He had two years to wait, so he'd have to wait and see. Until then, he could only speculate.

He wasn't sure what he expected from Lorelei after a brief absence, but a civil nod made sense, he decided. He wondered if, were he gone for a few weeks or a few months, she would greet him with more sentiment, with perhaps an embrace or even a kiss.

He felt his face grow warm. Better not to worry about that. It might never happen, after all, as he intended to stay close to Lorelei for a long time to come, if not for the rest of his natural life. Honestly, he wasn't much of a traveler, and if he traveled, surely it would be with her.

Still, that provided little opportunity for him to satisfy his curiosity about what her greeting would be.

"I'll see you in my office, Aubrey," Lorelei said.

As usual, she could find a way to surprise him.

"For what reason?" Aubrey raised his eyebrows. "I'd only intended to stay for a few minutes, then get the girls home and settled in. Is it important?"

"Of course it's important." She gave him one of those "how could you be so foolish; you should know better" looks. "I've set myself up in a room at the back of the warehouse that stands over there." She nodded to the building that had formerly been used to store fishing equipment but could probably house a considerable amount of goods, if that was what she had in mind. "Come along."

With a sigh, he left his sisters and Gwendolyn to talk things over with Mr. Hastings and followed Lorelei to her office.

It was full of neatly stacked papers and a few books, and there was a file cabinet in the back corner that had come from who knew where. The desk, he thought, was stolen from the house. There were enough unused rooms in that mansion that she could have stripped one and no one would have noticed for at least a week.

However, she plainly hadn't, for the office was barren and smelled of dust and mildew, and the floorboards creaked.

He frowned. He knew she wouldn't think of it until her operations were built up, but he wanted her to have a better workspace than two rickety chairs set around an old desk.

"You should have a better place to work if you're to be down here all day," he said in a tone that he hoped bridged no argument.

Of course, she did argue. "The men don't have lavish offices, yet they're managing to work. So will I."

"Lori ..."

"Aubrey." Her eyes held a silvery glint that he didn't quite like.

He sighed. That was something he'd argue with her about later. Or just take care of it and not ask for her permission at all. "What did you want to discuss with me?"

"We have to write to my father and ask for the employees I need. I have men in particular I want—who I specifically have decided would be the best fits for this project. Men I can trust to travel for me until I am ready to do so. Further, men who can run operations seamlessly here or in London if I myself need to travel. Plus, there's the matter of the dogs."

Having hardly tracked what she was saying about the employees she needed—after all, wouldn't it be better to hire men who already lived in England than to send for Americans?—he was flabbergasted by what dog-related matters she was referring to. "'The dogs'?"

"Winnie's dogs," she said with a tone of great patience, as if they'd discussed this many times and he was forgetting once again.

He was quite sure they had not, and he had not. "Oh," he said nonetheless. "I see."

"Yes, she'll want Mars and Potato if she's to stay here for any length of time—which I hope you will allow. I refuse to have a horse shipped over here, though, so she will have to do without."

He blinked. That had even been an option that was on the table? "We have horses here."

"Precisely." She smiled. "So you see my point."

What point?

She sat at the desk on her tiny, rickety chair—which looked dreadfully uncomfortable—and withdrew a sheet of paper and a pen. "You'll have to sit, too, and write, so it's in your hand. But I'll dictate."

Oh, she would, would she? So his first official correspondence—his introduction, even—to her father would all be her words?

Grand. Just grand.

"So here's what you'll say." She cleared her throat as she nudged the paper toward him. "'Dear Mr. Hilton'—I think it's better than anything informal, or more formal, for that matter. Simple is best, Aubrey. It's always best when it comes to my father—remember that. 'Dear Mr. Hilton'—Actually, on second thought, perhaps it would be better ... No, no, I'll not overthink this part. 'Dear Mr. Hilton'—"

Aubrey sat down with a sigh and picked up the sheet of paper. "So I should say it thrice?"

She glared. "Don't joke."

"I was asking a clarifying question."

"No questions. Just write. 'Dear Mr. Hilton'—"

"*Four* times?"

"Just once, please. Now. Anyway, continue with, 'Thank you for granting me the inordinate blessing of marrying your beautiful and talented and intelligent daughter Lorelei.'"

He wrote 'Dear Mr. Hilton' while he hid his grin before raising his eyes to her face. "I'm not writing that."

"Why?" She arched her eyebrows. "Isn't it true?"

"It's true, but don't you think he'll start to catch on that it's you who is writing this letter?"

She rolled her eyes. "Very well. Instead, continue with something like … Hmm. 'Since we are unable to meet in person, I thought it wise to introduce myself in the only method available to me.' Very good."

"What's the 'very good' for?"

"You're worse than my brother. 'You will be pleased to hear that rapid progress is being made in establishing the Hilton Shipping Company in England. Ideally, it will only take us a few months to reach a state of readiness. However, it is worth noting that we could do with more talented employees. At the suggestion of Mr. Hastings, who has provided invaluable insight to our operations thus far, I have compiled a list of names, men who work in your company presently but who would be of great help to me as I establish our interests in this new area. With the help of Mr. Hastings, I have carefully outlined who they are, the duties they will undertake, and who might be a suitable replacement in the event that you cannot spare anyone from their current duties. This is in addition to the employees Mr. Hastings has already seen fit to—'"

"Slow down," Aubrey grunted. "Let me see. 'At the suggestion of Mr. Hastings …'"

Lorelei groaned. "I need a real secretary."

"It would not be odd for you to engage one and simply dictate to them," Aubrey said hopefully, rotating his already sore wrist. "After all, I am a busy man, and most busy men have secretaries."

Lorelei shook her head. "Later, yes, but for now, I think a handwritten note will prove more effectual. I will engage a secretary. In fact, there's one on the list."

"Where is this list?" Aubrey asked patiently.

"In Mr. Hastings's possession," Lorelei answered. "He is the one who would know far better than I what is truly needed—though of course, I did weigh in."

"Of course you did," Aubrey mumbled as he scanned over the words he had already written. In every way, they were Lorelei—so practical, so stern, so straight to business. It would be better for his heart when she had a secretary to write these words for her.

"I want men who will be loyal and who will accept me as their leader," Lorelei continued, as if he'd said nothing. She paced away from her chair and about the small, dark room as if it were a grand office and she, the mistress of something far more impressive than this dusty place. "I know that is a hard mark to reach. Most men would not accept a woman as a leader. That is why I am impressed by you."

Now, wait a moment there. "I do not think of you as my leader."

She waved her hand. "You so often give in to me, though. This is greatly appreciated, as I am convinced I know better."

It had not been his intention, however, especially as he believed a man to be the natural head of a household. "Do you not believe in the biblical command of wifely submission?"

Lorelei blinked. "Perhaps. In a safe and loving marriage ... in an *actual* marriage. But this is more of an arrangement, and there's nothing about my womanhood that makes me less qualified to lead in my areas than you in yours. You are in charge of the estate—and of your sisters—and of the household. But I rule here. Surely you see that's for the best."

He had agreed to have her run this. He supposed it wouldn't be fair to imply that he wanted anything different now, after having made those guarantees in their arrangement. Though he certainly hadn't said he would submit to her. No, that went against the Bible. Men led—lovingly and cautiously, but they *led*.

What about when there were children? They would need to see a biblical chain of command reflected in the household. On the other hand, Lorelei had told him before that she wasn't much of a nurturer, so it would be no great surprise if she did not intend to be involved at all.

"Aubrey." Lorelei's amused tone told him she'd said his name several times.

With an air of embarrassment, he caught up the pen once more and bent his head forward, ready to continue the dictation. He would address the issue of submission later. It wasn't as if he could force her—but he could reason with her and he could act as a man, and that would have to be enough.

Lord, make it enough. Show me how to do this. I want to follow You. Help me stand up to her when it counts.

In another twenty minutes, the letter was written and signed and ready to be addressed and sent off.

"Thank you, Aubrey," she said as she set the letter out to dry the ink. "I am most grateful. I'll see you tonight. I'll try to be up in time for dinner."

"*Try.*" He rolled his eyes to the heavens, wondering once more what he'd gotten himself into ... but in truth, there was no fighting with Lorelei Hilton Montgomery. In time, yes, as they settled into their relationship more, he might find some sensible ways to get on with her. Unfortunately, not now.

"Very well, Lori," he said gently. He walked around the desk, put his arm around her, and gave her a kiss.

She stilled, perhaps surprised by the invasion of her personal space, but she quickly rallied, wrapped her arms around his neck, and kissed him back.

Strange, strange woman. Would he ever know what to expect from her? He'd have thought she'd be eager to get the obligatory affection out of the way and *him* on his way back to Montgomery Place with his sisters, leaving her to her workday.

Instead, she'd melted into him.

A throat cleared, and he jerked back, though Lorelei made no similar startled reaction.

She simply raised a brow. "Hastings?"

Aubrey glanced at the doorway to see Mr. Hastings.

Mr. Hastings shuffled from foot to foot. "I need your opinion on something, Mrs. Montgomery, but I'm sorry to be interrupting—"

"Oh, no. Mr. Montgomery was just leaving." She bustled around the desk. "We've finished our letter. Goodbye, Aubrey. I'll see you tonight."

Aubrey nodded, trying to shake the fuzziness from his head as he ambled out of the office behind his wife.

CHAPTER ELEVEN

"ALL WORK AND NO play makes Jack a dull boy" went the old saying—but Lorelei was not Jack, and she could not be made a "dull boy." She had been born female, like it or not, and there would be no boyishness.

Yet she understood the point of the quote. That didn't mean she intended to embrace it, especially as she'd only been working for a little over a week—granted, with little rest, but Lorelei needed little rest when there was coffee always available, and she'd made sure there was coffee always available.

No, the problem was not the lack of rest, and it was not Lorelei becoming a dull boy—or even a dull girl. It was the interruptions from her family.

They were her family, too. Winnie, of course, but also Francesca and Constance—who Lorelei reluctantly admitted she ought to get to know; she had put out no efforts there so far. The only thing she'd noticed was that they were both dreadfully dull themselves—whether they worked *or* played, and she wasn't sure she'd seen them do much of either—and she didn't really think she would've gotten to know them if it weren't for the fact that she owed it to Aubrey.

But surely he would forgive her that given that she was in the midst of building up a new branch of a business.

All the same, an unfamiliar pang of guilt entered her chest when the four arrived at the docks one afternoon, having ridden down together. Apparently, Aubrey had furnished Winnie with a horse. They entered Lorelei's office, where she was up to her nose in research as she was determined to increase her knowledge to a point of competence unlike any other, and beheld them all in their riding habits, looking dreadfully cheerful.

Of course, Aubrey looked quite handsome, but she didn't say anything about it, despite the fact that his breeches were …

Not worth commenting on.

What was wrong with her anyway?

"We're going to walk along the coast," Aubrey said. "Why don't you take a moment and come along? See a little more of it."

Lorelei frowned. She'd seen more of the coastline of Dorset than Aubrey had in all the years he had lived here.

He seemed to anticipate her thought. "I know, but see it with the eyes of someone appreciating its beauty." He smiled softly, but there was an edge of teasing in his tone, and she realized he knew she wouldn't have seen anything in an inch of the terrain but how well it would suit for one purpose or another.

But beauty was so useless.

Yet Aubrey held eye contact even after she didn't reply, so she gave him what she hoped was her most withering "leave me alone" glare, and Lorelei hated it when people—particularly men—didn't back down easily.

Maybe it wasn't backing down. Maybe it was being the bigger person. Yes, that would make it more palatable, something she could sink her teeth into—something she could make a competition with herself, a competition she must win, would always win, as there was no other way. No other way she would *admit* to.

She gave him a regal bow of her head and stood. "We'll go at once." She liked his answering grin—liked the way it made him look so much more boyish, so much less imposing. Not that Aubrey was imposing to her—or ever had been, and she would never admit it if he had—but that there was an austerity to him that she only saw disappear in a few frail moments. She treasured those beautiful accidents when the mask slipped.

She wondered if she had mask-slipping moments. She hoped not. That was a dreadfully vulnerable position to be in—not removing the mask but having it slide off one's face, imperfect, admitting both that there was something underneath and that one had wanted the mask on in the first place.

She placed her hand into the crook of Aubrey's arm and let him lead her down the already existing docks, which would need repairs. Out over the water, she could see workmen on the more expansive, larger pilings she was having installed for larger ships—the massive ones, the ones with plenty of space for cargo and people. The kind her father owned.

Matching up to her father's standards would be near impossible, perhaps improbable, but she would do it. She would. With this little harbor, with these men, with her own know-how and ingenuity, she would do it.

If only she weren't so frequently interrupted in the midst of her research. Lorelei hadn't dreamed until the last year or so that she would have such a position—and her knowledge was not that of years of experience but of reading—and reading—and reading. She had more still to read; though Mr. Hastings had proven invaluable, she wanted to understand everything he said to her.

"I think it's coming along nicely," Aubrey commented. "You've done a good job."

But not a complete job, which was the only kind Lorelei would accept. That would take a while. Nevertheless, she accepted the compliment graciously. "Of course I have."

"Hmm." The sound was made low in the back of his throat, the same sound he made whenever she said something that amused him. However, his amusement was none of her concern. Her primary concern was getting back to her occupation so she could keep receiving praise—and so that praise would actually be valid. Because right now, she hadn't done enough. She must do enough; she must meet and then exceed expectations. She knew no other way.

Ahead of them, Constance was babbling—did Constance often babble? Was that a character trait Lorelei could identify her by?—while Francesca walked serenely at her side and Winnie danced ahead of them. Though she would always be all of three years old to Lorelei, it occurred to her that perhaps her big-sistering had her missing Winnie's growing up, for she had a womanly form now, and her expressions and speech all indicated a near adult. She was seventeen, after all. That was probably old enough to behave more seriously, but that wasn't in Winnie's nature. She was happy—and should Lorelei squash it?

Should she wish it squashed, as it had been in herself? Was that the goal? Was it admirable to have no joy, to be stuck ever on "adult" considerations—more than that, considerations not even assigned to one's age and gender in average situations?

She shook her head to remove these wonderings. Aubrey placed his hand briefly over hers, as if sensing her unrest.

Ridiculous. She must keep a tighter hold of her thoughts if they were springing out onto her face or some such.

Perhaps once she was settled, in three or four years, she might provide Aubrey with affection, for he certainly had chosen, for whatever inscrutable reasons, to provide her with some. It was almost like loving, and though he didn't love her—no one did—he did seem to regard her highly.

Perhaps that was how all men acted when they were attracted to a woman. Lorelei frowned, not quite liking the idea. But she couldn't think about that now. It was insufferable of her to worry about what was actually good in her life. In a rush of emotion, she leaned her head lightly, *slightly*, into Aubrey's upper arm for a moment—reminding herself that he was there and strong and steady—before swiftly straightening and continuing her walk.

If he'd noticed, he said nothing.

They walked along the rippling waves toward the end of the dock, where the three sisters now stood, chatting about some novel they'd all read—the sort of conversation Lorelei doubted she'd have time for again. Reading fiction wasn't exactly high on her list of priorities though, she admitted, she rather missed it.

Perhaps that was what made her feel so strange about Aubrey. It was the absence of those romantic novels Winnie liked—they must have been succoring some womanly part of her that was now neglected, and she was instead relying on her husband for those sorts of feelings. But their relationship, like those books, was a cleverly contrived fantasy—nothing else.

No one had mentioned that marriage could be complicated and full of different feelings that had no name when there wasn't love in the arrangement. The idea of a "loveless marriage" was either constant fighting, like her parents, or utter indifference, as Lorelei had hoped to have. She had neither.

She cared. She *cared* about this stupid, overly serious Englishman and his traditional viewpoints and his cloudy estate and his probably-dull-as-dishwater sisters.

But no, it was self-concern. It must be. What affected him affected her. That was all. She didn't like him; she didn't harbor ideas of romance. It was desire and companionship and self-interest. That was all. She could handle that.

If she cared too much, she would have something to fight about, and she didn't want to fight. No, fighting was the last thing she wanted ...

Winnie turned to Lorelei with a grin.

Lorelei dropped Aubrey's arm and drew up beside her sister at the end of the dock.

"Isn't it beautiful, Lore? I think the water is prettier in England."

Lorelei glanced down at the rippling water, barely creating waves in its soft splashing against the pier. It was a fairly calm day—she preferred storms. "I suppose."

"There's nothing like the seaside," Winnie continued. "I'll have to come down here more often. Especially with the workmen around."

Lorelei hummed at the back of her throat, not particularly liking the direction this conversation was going but having no way to stop it.

Winnie's eyes were wandering over the expanse of the harbor. "You've picked some handsome ones," she commented blithely. "What I wouldn't give to have a pair of arms like some of them have wrapped around *me*."

That's why I don't talk to you except to scold. "You'll shock the Montgomerys."

Winnie laughed. "Connie and Fran have heard me talking like this a thousand times by now, Lore—and surely the idea of a woman being held in a man's arms won't shock Aubrey at this point." The little devil winked.

Lorelei stood still for a moment, considering this comment, then nodded to herself and pushed her sister off the dock into the murky waves.

"*Lorelei!*" Aubrey's tone held a heavy degree of censure—*wait, toward me? What have I done wrong?* "She'll drown!"

Lorelei turned toward her husband, who was kneeling at the edge of the dock with a hand out. "She swims. Like a fish. We both do. But I'll warn you, you'll regret helping her." Even now, Winnie appeared, sputtering, in the water and was kicking with enough enthusiasm to seem stable enough, despite the many heavy layers she was in. Patrick had taken to tossing them into the water from the time they could walk, and they had learned to float and then to paddle, even fully clothed. There was no danger.

Yet Aubrey paid no attention to Lorelei's warning. He grasped Winnie's hand—and was pulled into the water with her.

Lorelei sighed and rolled her eyes toward the heavens. "Will no one *listen* to me—"

Winnie's laughter rose above the waves as Aubrey also sputtered. For his part, he swam all right, which was the only thing Lorelei had been concerned about. There was a lot more thrashing, but thrashing was a sign of "not drowning," actually.

Eventually, Aubrey hauled himself onto the dock and pulled Winnie with him.

Lorelei tsked and clucked her tongue. "Such foolishness. Not even in your swimming clothes. Aubrey, I can understand Winnie's impetuousness, but you—!"

"You keep quiet," he mumbled, but there was a flash of humor in his eyes, she thought.

For her part, she stood well back from the edge of the dock, near his tittering sisters who she was not above taking hostage if the battle turned ugly.

Thankfully, he simply removed his drenched coat and loosened his tie. His hat had disappeared—perhaps never to be recovered. But he should have thought of that before he dove into the water, now, shouldn't he have?

CHAPTER TWELVE

AUBREY WAS ACCUSTOMED TO Ashfield appearing at his estate at various times of the year—usually on the way to or from some entertainment off season. This time, he sent a note the day before that he had been attending a hunting party in the area and would be at Montgomery Place by the following evening.

Before, Aubrey hadn't particularly minded the man's presence in his life—he'd made his feelings on Ashfield's relationships with women clear but not felt a need to end their friendship over it. Even when Ashfield had fallen out with the woman he had been pursuing, who was now Mrs. Alice Strauss, he'd given Ashfield the benefit of the doubt and not taken Lady Mary's word over his lifelong friend's. Ashfield had insisted there were extenuating circumstances—that though things with Miss Alice Knight had not ended as well as he'd have liked, it was not entirely his fault. Perhaps foolishly, Aubrey had believed that Ashfield was correct in assuming Lady Mary was overly loyal.

Aubrey had felt he wasn't condoning Ashfield's actions; he simply was choosing not to let them stop him from witnessing to him. Whether or not it was true that Aubrey had a positive impact on his friend was up for debate, but he hoped he did.

However, from the moment Mr. Gibson Ashfield walked into the house this time, Aubrey felt ill at ease.

Maybe it was because he had four women in his household now instead of two young girls who scarcely left the nursery. Maybe it was because his mother wasn't there providing an air of respectability and preaching the gospel to Ashfield at every opportunity. Maybe it was because his relationship with Lorelei was making him rethink everything about his life, from simple habits that had seemed so ingrained to friendships he'd cherished for years.

If he were honest, part of it was that Ashfield had something legitimate to tease Aubrey about for the first time in years. He found that Ashfield flinging innuendos about his marriage irritated him more than he'd imagined. It wasn't something he wanted to discuss, yet it seemed to be a subject of fascination with Ashfield.

They wandered around the garden before tea, talking about this and that—well, mostly Ashfield talked and Aubrey listened. But one particularly impertinent comment finally pushed Aubrey over the edge.

"I don't wish to discuss it," he snapped. "If you keep speaking on these subjects, I don't think we can have a conversation."

Ashfield paused in his walk and stood, hands shoved in the pockets of his overcoat, regarding Aubrey with cocked head and inquisitive eyes. "But, Monty—"

"No. I'm serious. What I have with her is private, and I'd like to keep it that way." He took a deep breath, surprised at the catch in his chest. Did he care this much about that? Ashfield was only joking. Yet somehow, it mattered. "Marriage is sacred, holy before God, and the same applies to the marriage bed. The way you talk about it is degrading and inappropriate."

Ashfield arched an eyebrow. He reminded Aubrey of Lorelei in that moment—ever skeptical of whatever Aubrey cared about enough to fight for. "You know, I never will understand why you married her."

That was unexpected. "What do you mean?"

"She's not the type of woman you have ever pursued in the past. Granted, I haven't spent much time with her, but from what I can see, she's forceful and independent. This whole business with her family's company ..." Ashfield shook his head. "If I had a wife, I wouldn't care what she did—but you're going to care. You do already." He smirked. "Does she know you're infatuated with her?"

Rather than replying, Aubrey sighed and turned his face toward the mansion. Beyond it were the meadows that led to the coastline. Lorelei would hopefully come home in time for tea tonight—but nothing could be guaranteed. Perhaps he ought to send for her—he'd like another adult to be around, just in case ... He wasn't sure why, but it made sense to have more eyes than normal on the girls today.

"Even if you won't admit you care about her, you have to see how ill-suited you are."

"I think we're well-suited." He swallowed, and without quite knowing why, he told Ashfield what he could barely admit to himself. "I think God knew that she was more suited for me than any other woman possibly could be. We seem created for each other." It was more than that, too. The bond he felt to Lorelei ran to the deepest part of him. "I think she could be the making of me."

Ashfield made a quiet but vehement sound of disagreement. However, he'd finally learned to close his mouth—for Aubrey would not have appreciated any insulting comments at that present moment. "We all have to fall someday," Ashfield said after a long moment of silence.

Aubrey smiled in spite of himself. Ashfield's sardonic, bitter tone was not unfamiliar to him, but somehow, today it struck him as oddly comedic. He did care about Ashfield, but Aubrey disapproved of his friend's behavior. He always had.

Perhaps that had reached a critical point.

They made their way around the mansion only to see the Montgomery carriage pulling up to the house. Lorelei descended a moment later, a bundle of files in her arms, and spoke to the footman briefly before starting toward the house.

"Lori!" Aubrey called.

She paused and glanced over her shoulder.

He picked up his pace, leaving Ashfield behind, and hurried to her side. "I think I mentioned Gibson Ashfield would be here. Will you come speak with him?" He wanted the two of them to meet now, to talk, when before he had been fiercely shielded Lorelei as if Gibson might somehow corrupt her. Perhaps he was not as rational as he wanted to pretend he was.

"Mm-hmm." She handed him her papers. "Hold."

He tucked the files under his arm and turned to Ashfield, who was slowly approaching them. "Ash, you've met my wife, Mrs. Lorelei Montgomery."

"Mrs. Montgomery, always a pleasure," Ashfield said smoothly. He jogged the last few steps, as if suddenly eager to greet Lorelei, took her hand, and kissed it.

Aubrey felt every muscle in his body tighten, but he shook off the wave of possessiveness. She was trustworthy, if only because he wasn't sure she'd ever acknowledged a man who wasn't in some way affiliated with the Hilton Shipping Co. It wouldn't suit her interests to encourage Ashfield's flirtations.

Lorelei withdrew her hand gently but regally, like a queen being forced to engage with a pauper. Her look was that of cool disdain.

Interesting.

"Mr. Ashfield," she said. "So you've come to visit. I hope you intend to behave yourself in my house. I can't say I've heard good things about you."

"I can't say there are good things to hear." Ashfield grinned.

Aubrey restrained himself from making an annoyed sound or rolling his eyes.

Lorelei turned to him, effectively dismissing Ashfield, and Aubrey resisted giving in to the swell of pride in his chest. "You're not doing anything until teatime, I presume. Will you file those in your office? They need to be restored here. I'll change for tea, all right?"

Aubrey nodded. "I'll do that. Thank you for coming up." He should have known she'd be early if she actually intended to come at all; that was how she was.

"Mm. Well. Old friends and all that." She glanced at Ashfield again, then went into the house.

Ashfield was smirking now, and after Lorelei disappeared, he turned to

Aubrey. "Hmm."

"What is it?"

Ashfield's hazel eyes swept him up and down, lingering on the papers tucked under his arm. "I see you've been promoted to secretary."

Aubrey frowned. "I'm trying to be helpful." It was what Lorelei valued, so he had adapted his treatment of her to prioritize offering competent assistance in any way he could. It was one of the few things that brought a light to her eyes—he treasured that light.

Ashfield laughed. "I'm sure you're being helpful, but then, so is a well-trained dog. Before you know it, you'll find yourself collared, leashed, and sleeping at the foot of her bed."

Aubrey blinked. He didn't like *that* one bit. There it was again—that clear indication that perhaps he ought to be taking a more active role in his marriage. No, not even that—it was more that he ought to be *leading* his marriage; instead, he was following along, a forlorn pup trying to please his sometimes uncaring mistress.

It wasn't as bad as all that, but there were definitely some areas where he felt disrespected and talked down to—and he didn't like that. Aubrey was sure his wife would decry any attempt of his to explain this as hurt feelings and wounded pride. But he did want to feel that he was a part of their relationship—not her sidelined worse half, a burden she must bear for the greater good of her true love, the Hilton Shipping Co.

When Aubrey said nothing, Ashfield spoke again. "You need to take her in hand. I'd never suggest that you need to control her every moment, but some women need bullied, especially the strong-willed ones, if you're to have your way with them."

Aubrey flinched. "That's incredibly disrespectful, Ash, not to mention cruel."

"Wouldn't you say, as a sex, that women are incredibly disrespectful, not to mention cruel?" Ashfield grinned and cocked his head, as if daring Aubrey to challenge him.

Sometimes, Aubrey let it drop, let Ashfield's harmful rambles remain. Today, he couldn't. "I wouldn't say that at all. Men and women are different, yes, but no less equal. We're all heirs to the Kingdom of God. No one 'needs' to be bullied, much less women—women deserve respect and care. There's a quote in 1 Peter about it: 'Likewise, ye husbands, dwell with them'—your wives—'according to knowledge, giving honour unto the wife, as unto the weaker vessel, and as being heirs together of the grace of life; that your prayers be not hindered.' I'd say women need a staunch defense against evil in their lives—not for their own husbands to become that evil."

Ashfield looked decidedly uncomfortable, shifting from foot to foot, but he kept his tone light as he responded. "I'm not unfamiliar with the Bible, Monty. 'Wives, submit yourselves unto your own husbands' is another verse. You wouldn't say she's doing that, would you?"

"No." Aubrey could admit that. "Not yet. However, it's not the husband's job to 'bully' his wife into submission. I could do better as a leader—that's true—but no decent leader would harm or abuse the very creature he has been commanded to protect and cherish. It'd be like a general turning on his own troops and massacring them."

Ashfield arched his brows. "I'm sure no general would lead his troops without a firm hand."

"Maybe so, but it's not a perfect simile. Women are not soldiers." Aubrey swallowed, his thoughts flying as they perhaps never had before. He was so unused to defending himself. He preferred time and quiet to consider his thoughts before stating them—but it felt urgent to tell them to Gibson now. "As we both grow in Christ, I'd like to have the final say, and I'd like to be respected and seen as the man of the family, but don't think for a moment that I don't trust my wife to make her own decisions or that I intend to be anything but caring toward her. That's how my parents' marriage worked. Do you remember them together, Ash? Have you ever known a more content couple? They consulted each other in all things, and both treated the other with equal respect, but you would never say my mother failed to submit to my father, not in the things that mattered."

Ashfield hesitated, his eyes darting about rapidly as if searching for an escape, but even he couldn't insult Aubrey's mother. "No, I would not.

But your mother was a saint."

Aubrey shook his head. "She was not. None of us are—not in the way you mean. She had flaws, sins, but she dedicated her life to Christ, and a part of that was her marriage to my father. Marriage is supposed to be refining to the couple in question—maybe Lorelei is so suited to me because she forces me to act." Marriage mattered too much to be reduced to a few lines in a contract, but Aubrey didn't say that to Ashfield. He was sure his friend wouldn't understand.

There was so much about him that his friend didn't understand.

After a moment, Ashfield shrugged. "Whatever makes you happy, Monty," he mumbled before brushing past Aubrey into the house.

Aubrey closed his eyes for a moment and uttered a silent prayer for guidance. It was going to be a long few days until Ashfield left.

CHAPTER THIRTEEN

L ORELEI DIDN'T LIKE GIBSON Ashfield.

Call it woman's intuition—not a concept she believed in—or a gut feeling, but she didn't like that he was in her house.

Was she going to protest? No. He was Aubrey's friend. Aubrey was an adult, this was his home, and if he wanted Mr. Ashfield here, he could have him here.

Lorelei didn't have to like it, but then, how much time did she spend at the manor house anyway? Very little. The docks were her domain—as it should be. She was no more a homing pigeon than an albatross.

Even so, she watched him across the table with a wary gaze as he chatted and flirted with Winnie, Francesca, and Constance. Lorelei was polite—somewhat—when he engaged her but ignored him otherwise, keeping her focus on the mushroom soup before her.

She was not usually empathetic, but she could *feel* the tension rolling off of Aubrey, even from the opposite end of the table. Something had been said between his friend and him that he was stewing over while pretending fastidiously not to stew—and he didn't seem to like Ashfield's flirting either.

Fair enough. Aubrey seemed to have a clear code of moral conduct that ruled his every move, and flirting with a friend's younger sisters or sister-in-law was apparently outside the presumably unstated code.

Ashfield complimented Winnie on her "very pretty" hair, she blushed and giggled, and Aubrey's fingers tightened around the spoon he held as his eyes burned.

Oh.

Some instinct in Lorelei, born from years of catering to her father's temper, arose, and without particularly thinking about what she intended to do, she rushed to smooth things over. "How long will you be staying with us, Mr. Ashfield?"

The man had the decency to flicker his eyes to Aubrey. "I'm not sure yet."

Not long, if Aubrey had the gumption to say anything, Lorelei guessed. "I see. You grew up with my husband. Or so I'm told."

"Yes, Mrs. Montgomery. I did. We've known each other since our school days."

"Mm." She took a sip of her wine. "I wonder that he was not a better influence on you. I think he's a good influence on me." A bone she could throw Aubrey, for his gentleness and caring were so unlike anything she'd ever experienced before, and it didn't hurt for him to know it.

"Perhaps he is. I am not easily influenced."

"More's the pity." She set down her glass. "He's worth being influenced by."

Out of the corner of her eyes, she caught the flush on her husband's cheeks and narrowly avoided smirking, but she would not behave so in front of Mr. Ashfield—in her mind, a stranger. Aubrey might claim they were friends, but a friend would treat him with far more respect than Mr. Ashfield seemed to.

Not that you treat him any better, a voice seemed to whisper in her ear, but Lorelei ignored. One thing at a time.

"Those must be the kind of comments that have Monty so thoroughly under your spell." Ashfield smirked. "I've never seen him so horsewhipped. Not even with the ineffable Lady Mary, who I daresay was more suited to him than you are. But you're the woman who would take him, for better or for worse, for richer or for poorer ... certainly for richer."

Lorelei felt Aubrey stiffen, and a silence descended on the table; even her sister stilled momentarily.

"Ashfield." Aubrey's voice held a warning—a soft warning, but a warning.

"Oh, don't bother, Monty." Ashfield's eyes had a dangerous light in them, a cruel light. Lorelei had never seen him looking anything but jocular and insincere, and she feared his next words—for Aubrey's sake, not her own. "I've seen her type before, though more often in the dregs of society. A common fishwife has the same tone, and a madam the same business sense, but you don't often see it in the more polite—"

Aubrey jerked to his feet, the tableware rattling as he did so. "Get out."

Lorelei's eyes flickering rapidly between her husband and Mr. Ashfield, whose mouth hung open in shock.

"I want you on the first train in the morning, and I hope you'll never think to darken my door again."

"Aubrey." Lorelei glanced to her husband, not particularly liking this side of him. She didn't like angry men in general, and though she knew his fervor was protective, perhaps even what could be called *safe*—as a castle must be strong and intimidating to defend the weak, so must sometimes a man—her stomach clenched. "It's all right. I'm—"

"No. He will not sit there at my table and speak of you, of *us*, in that way. Get out." He tossed his napkin onto his plate. "I hope you'll have the decency to keep to your room tonight, Ashfield. You can go there now and stay there until dawn, but after this, if I see hide or hair of you around my house or my family, I will have you forcibly removed."

Ashfield slowly rose, his eyes pinned to Aubrey. "Monty—"

"No. I don't want to talk about it." Aubrey turned and left the room. Ashfield followed him.

Lorelei took a sip of her wine. "Winnie, please close your mouth. You'll catch flies."

"Monty!"

Ashfield's voice followed Aubrey through the house, but Aubrey didn't heed him. He strode into his study and slammed the door behind him.

How *dare* he?

It was one thing for Ashfield to pick at him, in any way he saw fit. Aubrey didn't care about that. But to insult his wife, in his own house, was unacceptable in every way. Not to mention, it was blatantly untrue and cruel.

He would talk to Lorelei about it later, but for now, he needed to calm down, to allow his blood to cool. Knowing her, she was probably less affected than he was, but he would still make sure she had not taken a word of Ashfield's vitriol to heart.

The door opened, and Ashfield entered. "Monty." He frowned. "You cannot mean it. After twenty years of friendship, to end it over a comment like that! Look, I'm sorry. I didn't mean it. I'll apologize to the girl if you want."

"I don't care for your apologies. This is the straw that broke the camel's back, Gibson. You're a rake and a bully," Aubrey gritted out. "Having you around the women in my life is no longer acceptable—and I can't stand to look at you. Do you have any idea of the lives you destroy, the worlds you crumble? Do you care that you're selling your soul, your chance at salvation, for a momentary pleasure, for a sick, twisted desire to corrupt? You're not the man you should be, Ash. God help you, but I cannot." He paused and shook his head, sadness replacing anger for the first time. "I can't in good conscience associate with a man of your character."

"Do you think I don't know that? Do you think I want to be this way?" His voice rose with every desperate word. "I am my father's son. All right? I am. This is bred into me. I tried to be decent—I did, Monty. I courted the girl, I asked her to marry me, but I wasn't good enough for her, and how did I react? I hurt her. I was angry, and I pushed her. She could have been killed because of me—if she'd hit her head harder, if she'd fallen in a different way." He sucked in a harsh breath. "I will never be anything more than that man, and if you cannot accept that, it is good that we part ways."

Aubrey stilled, his eyes on his friend's face, waiting for a sign that Ashfield was being dramatic, as he often was—for surely, it could not be that bad. But Ashfield just stood there, panting as if from the effort of the confession, and realization crashed over Aubrey like a thunderstorm.

Lady Mary had not exaggerated Ashfield's sins. She had not been overly defensive of her friend and spread whatever lies she was told, and her delay must have been from fear—not from pettiness or lack of confidence in her conclusion.

Because Lady Mary had feared Aubrey's reaction. Had known that Aubrey would not protect her from his own friend.

She had been right to leave him, for he was a weak fool, risking what was most precious in his life for a friendship that could only corrupt.

"Get out," Aubrey said, his voice rougher than he'd anticipated, cracking around the edges. "Get out of my house."

"I'll gather my things and be out in a quarter of an hour. There's a tavern in the village I'll make use of for the night." Ashfield turned on his heel and stormed out of the room.

Aubrey sank onto the armchair by the fireplace and dropped his face in his hands.

Oh, God, forgive my foolishness and allow me to make amends.

Lorelei saw the girls settled before making her way to the master suite that night. She wasn't sure why—just that it seemed right to briefly speak with Winnie about how the evening had gone, and somehow, Francesca and Constance had been there, too. Shy and quiet, but present, listening to Winnie's rambles about how "shocking" it had all been.

Once the girls were settled, Lorelei went to her room. Aubrey was already there, lying on his back on the bed, fully clothed, staring at the ceiling.

"That was exciting." She went to the bellpull and rang for Harriet. "I ought to thank you for coming to my defense. I wasn't much offended—any woman who entered a man's arena should expect any number of accusations; I've accepted that from the start—but I understand why you did it."

"It was overdue," Aubrey said. "He needed to be gone."

"Yes. I think so, too."

"I found out tonight that he'd abused a woman I would never have wanted harmed. He's not welcome in this house, in our life." Aubrey pressed his hands to his face. "I was a fool, Lori. I refused to heed the warnings of those who knew better than me." He dropped his hands and sat up. "I don't know what to think. I'm not sure I'm the man I thought I was."

Lorelei glanced at him. There was guilt written all over his face. "Why don't we talk about it after we're settled for the night? You can tell me, if you want. I don't mind." In some ways, she was starting to like their chats in the evenings after everyone else was tucked away in bed. They had begun when she had her monthly. Now, she liked to have him stroke her hair and to eventually transition from talking to whispering to kissing. It was effortless, somehow, as if they had always done so. He had a nice voice—low and quiet, gentle but not without substance—and she appreciated his willingness to discuss all things with her.

Even though she didn't always give him the same consideration. She ought to, though, truly especially if, well, he was going to be *defending* her.

Filled with a sudden rush of an unnamed emotion, she added, "Make sure to wash your face! Everything feels better with a freshly clean face."

That was the most she could offer in terms of caring, for now.

He gave her a bemused look but went off to his dressing room.

After Harriet had come and gone, Lorelei settled into bed with an account ledger and waited for her husband. He arrived a few minutes later and climbed under the blankets next to her. She set aside the book and slipped into his arms. She felt he held her a little tighter than he might have otherwise.

As she lay there in his arms, he told her about Gibson Ashfield and the former Alice Knight, about his disbelief of Cassie's vague reports as to how their relationship had ended, and about his relationship with Ashfield—how Aubrey had not felt he could dismiss a lifelong friend so easily, how his loyalty had blinded him to the truth.

"But you did realize the truth today," Lorelei protested. "You did realize it, and you acted on it. That's all anyone could ask of you, to do what is right *now*. What does the past matter?"

"The fact that it took me so long means I am not the man I thought I was," Aubrey said solemnly. "Ashfield was right. I am weak."

"No. You're not." Slow to act, and at times easily confused, but not weak. "And even if you are, what is the point of living if you don't grow? You have heroism in you—you must choose to embrace it. Perhaps it's a matter of being ... *godly*. In all facets of your life. Protector and provider and all that." She was shaky on some aspects of manhood, not being one herself, but she knew that being a man of God was a good thing.

"Yes." He nodded and pressed a kiss to her forehead. "I have only to grow closer to Him, to submit myself and my failings to the One Who will redeem me. That's a good reminder."

She hadn't known it was, so she simply shrugged and snuggled closer to him.

"I do ... I do want our marriage to be godly, Lori."

Hmm. "What about it isn't?"

"I know that in certain aspects, you are taking the lead, such as with the business, but I ... I do believe that the male leadership is important in any marriage, regardless of how ... how businesslike it is. In my way of seeing it, there is no other way it works."

She stiffened before forcing herself to relax and consider his words. In theory, yes, but men were so unpredictable, and life was even more unpredictable. How could she submit, if that's what he was asking of her, when she wasn't entirely sure she could trust him? Oh, it wasn't personal. At this point, she wasn't sure she could trust anyone at all, herself included.

She drew back slightly and met his eyes. They were a soft sort of blue, a morning blue—and beseeching now, asking her to see his side of things, to follow him into a new territory, where perhaps their marriage would become a little more real.

She wasn't ready for that.

Yet she nodded. Inexplicably, she nodded. "You're right. I want to ... I want us to do what is right. I ... I can't promise it'll be easy, though. I am not a quick learner when it comes to certain things, and there are ... there are reasons I have always been careful ..." Not to trust. Not to let people in. Not to allow anyone or anything to have a hold on her, to have authority over the deepest parts of her, to be trusted with her weakest, softest places.

"I have a lot to learn, too," he said. "But maybe we can learn together and help each other along the way. You can tell me when I fail you. I will listen."

Lorelei pressed her lips together, unsure she could believe him. Men might say such things, might pretend that they did not desire, at their basest, to press down those who were weaker than them, but who could resist the draw of power and control? Oh, but she *wanted* to trust him. "I'll try," she murmured at last. "I'll try. But please be patient. We're both new to this, Aubrey, and I ... I mean, it would be easier if ..." If he loved her. But she didn't believe in love—not for herself. "Let's take things one step at a time."

"Right." He smiled then. "That's more than fair. But I will tell you that in future, I would appreciate a little respect."

Also more than fair. She nodded to that, too.

Perhaps, perhaps everything would be all right. They had to stick to the plan.

She could respect him if that was what he needed from her—treat him with deference, try to listen to him on matters of import, consult him on the bigger decisions. After all, having a business partner wasn't a bad thing—and it was *illegal* not to consult your business partner on major decisions.

It was a matter of common law.

Of course, there was something between them other than legality. Even she wasn't fool enough to pretend that he had his arms around her now because of marriage contracts and written agreements. Maybe after a few years, she would have time to love Aubrey, in her own way. But her love was not a prize worth winning—and never had she been more cognizant of that than when faced with her husband's overwhelming loyalty.

He would die for her.

She wasn't even sure she could live for him.

CHAPTER FOURTEEN

November 1884

T HE MONTHS HAD RUSHED by, every day feeling more hectic than the last. The docks were coming along nicely, and though Lorelei wasn't sure they'd be officially up and running until the spring, most of the big pieces were in place. To accomplish this, she would have to push herself to do better.

Which was why it was not the time to be ill.

Though she knew she wasn't ill—not really. She did. It was inconvenient to think about alternatives for the exhaustion, the nausea, the dizziness that had appeared and then progressively worsened in the last month or so.

There was a doctor in the nearby village, and after delaying as long as she could without raising suspicion from her husband—who was concerned about her symptoms—she took a carriage and went to see the man of medicine ... before heading down to the docks. She rarely missed a day there if she could help it—and she was always more than capable of helping it.

Of course this has to be the thing I've lost control of.

For she soon found herself ushered into the doctor's private office by a flustered maid. The maid looked confused, but Lorelei didn't mind confusing people—notwithstanding the fact that she knew that no proper lady, in England or America, would go to the doctor.

No, the doctors came to them and visited with their maids present. But this wasn't something Lorelei wanted Harriet to know about yet—and once the doctor was in the Montgomery household, everyone (including her husband and their three sisters) would know he'd been there and draw the logical conclusion. The one Lorelei didn't *want* to draw but was going to have to. Because what illness did a healthy, hearty nineteen-year-old who had recently married have?

She almost laughed at herself as she waited for the doctor to join her. Even now, her head throbbed, which she hated as it usually hurt worse when she was bleeding, and she wasn't, which meant something was certainly going on with her body and had been for some time.

"Maybe I am deathly ill," she mumbled to herself, drumming her fingers along the embroidered arm of the chair she sat on. "Maybe I'll be dead in a week." It might be better than the humiliation of admitting she'd been foolish.

The doctor entered then. He was young—perhaps in his early thirties—and not unattractive, but not attractive enough to be a bad doctor. Lorelei was of the opinion that too handsome a man could be distracting and indicate that he didn't know what he was doing.

"Mrs. Montgomery." He bowed to her, and deciding not to rise, she inclined her head. He came to sit across from her. "I'm Dr. Burton. I am surprised to see you here."

At least he was honest.

"I wanted privacy, and I cannot get it at my own house. But I think I'm pregnant—or else terribly ill with some female ailment."

He blinked at her, that same expression on his face that often inhabited her husband's. "I see. What reason have you to believe so?"

She briefly outlined her symptoms and gave him the dates he requested, and he nodded gravely.

"There is no reason to believe you might not be with child?"

She disliked "with child" as a description. "Pregnant" was more clinical. Nonetheless, she shook her head. "None."

"Would you allow me to complete a physical examination?"

She quirked an eyebrow. "How much of one?"

This made him uncomfortable for some reason, despite the fact that he was the doctor and she the patient. *Doctors under the age of fifty shouldn't be tolerated,* she thought, though they had to get to fifty somehow.

Yet he responded, after a beat of silence, "I would need to palpate your abdomen, which would prove difficult in your current state of dress. This is why most ladies prefer to be examined in their own home."

"I see." She frowned. Well, it would get out sooner or later. "Then will you come to my house this evening? My husband's house, I should say. It's the rather large one on the hill."

"I know where you live, Mrs. Montgomery."

"How frightening." She rose. "But you will come?"

"Yes. I will. At what time?"

She stilled and gave it a moment of thought. "I must work today—and I have much to do. But I can attempt to be back shortly after dinner. Shall we say nine?"

He hesitated—she wondered if he had a wife and children who he wanted to be home with—then nodded. "If that suits you."

It did suit her, so she went to work.

That evening, she arrived back at Montgomery Place in the middle of dinner—and dealt with Aubrey's inevitable inability to scold her while also wanting to scold her for staying alone in the dark with about a hundred men, notwithstanding the fact that there was nothing they could do to her without losing their jobs.

Perhaps she ought to be happy he was concerned, but she wondered why he said nothing. Her brother would have berated her. She knew what she was doing held risk; the men in her life should acknowledge that. Yet it was unreasonable to expect Aubrey to do what she had not voiced, and she was not about to tell him she knew she was taking risks, especially now, when he would inevitably begin to think of her as more valuable.

With a sigh, she asked for coffee to be sent up to her room and left the other members of her family to protest her lack of dinner-eating.

She was hungry, in truth, which was another strange symptom, but she'd rather have food sent up later, and besides, eating meant more nausea probably, which she didn't want. It came and went, but she couldn't be bothered by nausea if she had nothing to lose, in the most literal sense, could she?

In the hallway, she met a footman and told him about Dr. Burton's imminent arrival. She asked the footman to send him up to her room and have him avoid the rest of the family, if possible. With raised eyebrows, the young man agreed.

At least that was taken care of. She went to her room and changed into her nightclothes.

Half an hour later, Dr. Burton was ushered into the room by a wide-eyed Harriett.

"Your maid will stay?" He held himself confidently as he set his bag on her nightstand, but there was an air of unease about him that indicated he was not at all sure she *would* have her maid stay—and he was uncomfortable with the concept of facing her husband later and explaining that he had seen her alone in her bedchamber without much of an introduction.

Fair enough. Not that Aubrey would do anything but sigh in that particular way of his and move on, but the doctor didn't know that.

She inclined her head to Harriet, who scurried over to her side. "He's going to palpate my abdomen," Lorelei explained, to which Harriet, accustomed to her mistress not explaining anything that was not pertinent, simply nodded.

"Does your husband know I am here, Mrs. Montgomery?" He reached into his bag and withdrew a small cloth pouch and a green glass bottle with a label in a sloping feminine hand. Both were set on Lorelei's bedside table.

"No, he does not, but you can explain that when you talk to him after." Lorelei stood, undid the tie at her waist, and draped her robe over the edge of the bed.

To his credit, Dr. Burton didn't flinch at this proclamation or at her partial disrobing. "You do not wish to tell him yourself?"

"No." She didn't even want to think about it, much less have an awkward conversation with Aubrey where he was sure to be both apologetic and thrilled—even if he initially tried to hide it. She couldn't bear that. Maybe tomorrow. Things always seemed brighter in the morning and all that. "Let's get on with it."

So she was poked and prodded, and the doctor agreed that there was indeed some swelling of her womb, subtle though it might be, and there was no earthly reason to believe she wasn't "with child."

Lorelei corrected him to "pregnant."

"So you'll tell my husband on the way out," she said, she said, putting her robe back on and avoiding Harriet's eyes.

"I will. But one more thing." He went to the bedside table and collected the items he had deposited there earlier. "My wife always sends these with me when I visit a new female patient, particularly one in a delicate condition. You can choose whether or not you utilize them; I'm not convinced they have any real usage." He held out the pouch. "This is lavender and a scattering of other herbs. She swears, placed in a bath, they help with headaches—but it has a pleasant aroma."

Lorelei took the pouch. "I'll give it some thought. And the bottle?"

"It's ginger, more lavender, and—well, a number of other things. She wrote the label on the bottle." This, too, he passed over to her. "She explains it better than I would, but it's for nausea. It may not prove helpful, but it's harmless."

Lorelei turned the bottle over, briefly casting an eye over the ingredients and directions. "She's claimed you," she said with a soft chuckle. "She's said to every woman you visit 'here's my tag on him. Don't you dare touch my man.'"

For the first time, Dr. Burton flushed slightly. "I don't see it as such."

Lorelei rolled her eyes. "You wouldn't. But tell her the message is received—not that you were ever at risk. But one doesn't send a young husband anywhere women are present without wondering. I can't understand it, but I can respect it. Thank her for me, will you?"

He nodded. "I will." He picked up his bag and left Lorelei alone with Harriet.

"Mrs. Montgomery—"

"I'd ... I'd rather not talk about it tonight, Harriet. You're dismissed."

"But—"

"Harriet." She picked up the accounting book she'd been working her way through. "I'd prefer to have an evening by myself."

Harriet left, and Lorelei sat on the chair by the window and looked over the numbers—but time and again, they grew blurry, and she was obliged to run a hand across her eyes. Eventually, it grew so distracting that she marched to the bedside table and withdrew a handkerchief.

She felt miserable. The nausea was rising again, but she didn't feel like rubbing Mrs. Burton's potion on her stomach, as directed, nor did she have much in her stomach but coffee. Of course, the annoying sobs that kept coming out of nowhere were not helping her feel better, and she found herself retching into a chamber pot.

She rose after a time, wiped her mouth, and went to bed, where she lay down.

I'll feel sorry for myself for one night, then I'll get up. That's it. I'll let Aubrey comfort me when he comes up—but I won't let it happen more than one night.

One night was enough time to recover from all her plans suddenly being tossed away, wasn't it?

The air in Aubrey's office was thick and still, as it was every evening. He sat in front of the fire and swirled a glass of brandy that he probably wouldn't finish drinking and wondered how long it would be until he could acceptably go up to Lorelei.

She probably wanted to be alone, based on her lack of interest in sitting for dinner with the family—he should make sure someone had sent up food for her; she couldn't possibly survive on the amount of nourishment she consumed, at least in his presence.

But even if Lorelei wanted to be alone, there was only so much of it Aubrey could take, and now that his sisters and Gwendolyn had gone upstairs for the evening, he was abominably lonely again.

One would think marriage would fix that, but apparently not.

They'd made an agreement, and he was trying to be respectful of that. So he sat and looked around the mahogany-themed office. The room, adorned with heavy velvet curtains and antique furniture, was comfortable for him—but there was little that could put him at ease other than sitting with Lorelei ... or better yet, holding her, though she would only allow it in certain circumstances. Namely, utter exhaustion.

She'd been tired a lot lately, and it had brought out a side of her that cuddled up to him as she drifted off to sleep. He rather liked that side of her, though he was under no delusion that it would last. Aubrey had come to expect nothing with her—for it would only lead to disappointment.

There was a knock at the door. "Mr. Montgomery?" It was the butler. "Yes?"

The door opened. "Dr. Burton is requesting an audience with you."

Aubrey raised his eyebrows. "Dr. Burton?"

"Yes. He was up to see Mrs. Montgomery—"

Aubrey lurched to his feet, nearly spilling his glass. "What?"

"Yes. He would like to speak with you, if this is a good time."

Speechless, Aubrey simply nodded and gestured nonsensically—this time, he did slosh his drink, and mumbling under his breath, he hurried over to the table and found a cloth with which to wipe his hand.

Dr. Burton entered the room and introduced himself. He was older than Aubrey by perhaps only a few years—still young and certainly not an unattractive man, objectively speaking.

For some reason, it irritated Aubrey that this man was allowed to interrupt his wife's evening—even though he knew the only emotion he should feel was concern. Surely, if she'd called a doctor, something was wrong.

"Mr. Montgomery, I've just come from visiting your wife." The doctor seemed ill at ease with this pronouncement—which meant that Lorelei had been her typical self. Aubrey wasn't sure if it was Americanism or some unique aspect of Lorelei's personality, but she tended to make Englishmen rather uncomfortable. "Congratulations are in order. You're to be a father."

It was a good thing he'd set down his drink already, for he would have spilled it again. "She's with child?"

"Yes." Dr. Burton paused, then cocked his head. "Surely that can't be too much of a surprise."

"Why ... why do you ask?" Aubrey was stalling, but he wasn't sure what his response ought to be—let alone what it was.

"Mrs. Montgomery did not seem ... typically pleased." Dr. Burton shifted his bag to his other hand. "However, that could simply be natural nerves or apprehension. Many women experience that at first."

But Lorelei would continue "experiencing" it because she doesn't want my baby. He couldn't say that to the doctor, so he simply nodded. "That's ... excellent news." What else did one say? How was he supposed to act? He'd been given no script for this, no indication of what behavior was proper and what would be unacceptable.

Yet his heart was thudding because he was going to have a child—and though he dreaded Lorelei's reaction, and her not telling him herself didn't bode well, he couldn't help the sparkles of joy that threatened to make him do something truly foolish, like laugh or grin.

Dr. Burton nodded, a faint smile playing on his lips. "Indeed, sir. Mrs. Montgomery is in good health, from what I can tell, and if her estimations are correct, we can expect the little one at the end of May or June."

May or June. Not long after Lorelei's twentieth birthday. Though Lorelei had proved her maturity in some aspects of life, it suddenly seemed too young to ask a woman to be a mother. *But she hasn't any choice. We haven't any choice.*

"Thank you, Dr. Burton. Your visit is appreciated." Aubrey cleared his throat. "I understand she is not feeling too well, or she wouldn't have called you."

"Her symptoms are typical—nothing to worry about. But she ought to rest." Dr. Burton clasped his hands behind his back, his expression grave. "Before I take my leave, Mr. Montgomery, there's something I must impress upon you. The health of both mother and child is paramount, and I trust you'll ensure Mrs. Montgomery is well cared for, that she takes the rest she needs."

Aubrey nodded, his brow furrowing. Getting Lorelei to rest—or eat or sleep or do anything else—was going to be near impossible, but he would try. "Of course. We'll do everything necessary for her well-being and for the baby's."

Dr. Burton nodded. "Please call on me if there are any concerns. It's important that she eats plenty of nutritious food, but it also may be impossible for her to keep anything down for the first several months. This could lead to fainting spells and exhaustion—she may become dehydrated, and she may lose weight. I would recommend keeping a close eye on her."

As if I can do anything like that. As if she'll let me ... Aubrey simply nodded. "I'll do that."

After Dr. Burton took his leave, Aubrey collapsed on his chair by the fire. *I'm going to be a father.* He'd desired that, yes, but he'd no idea of it happening any time soon. He hadn't meant to trap Lorelei into an arrangement she didn't desire. They'd agreed not to start having babies—or one baby, if it were a boy—for years.

How would she take this?

But how could Aubrey *not* be happy?

He left his study behind and made his way upstairs to the master chambers—but outside the door of Lorelei's bedroom, he paused.

Would she want him right now? Even for comfort?

No. Not Lorelei Hilton Montgomery.

With a sigh, he retired to his own rarely used chamber and settled between the cold sheets with a shudder.

CHAPTER FIFTEEN

THE HOURS TICKED AWAY, and Aubrey didn't come to her bedroom as he normally did. Lorelei had stopped crying and washed her face a while ago, but that didn't mean she wanted to be alone with her own thoughts, nor did it make it any less irritating that Aubrey hadn't deigned to provide her with his presence.

Especially since this was arguably all his fault.

Well ...

At least as much as it was hers.

When she could bear the silence of her bedchamber no longer, she stood and caught up her robe. Wrapping it around herself, she marched across the room and flung open the adjoining door to his bedroom.

"Aubrey." She snapped out the word into the dark room.

She saw him move on the bed in the waning moonlight. He'd avoided her completely—gone to bed without even speaking to her, without acknowledging what the doctor had told him?

She nearly screeched with fury. She felt so ... so ... *so much*. But instead of expressing any of it, she slammed the door, marched across the room, and slid onto the bed beside him.

"I'm pregnant," she said, so there could be no doubt.

He sat up at once. "Dr. Burton told me that. I ... I hope you're feeling all right." His voice was unsure enough that she felt a bit of pity for him—*a bit.*

"I'm not feeling well at all." She scooted close to him—it was freezing in this room; no one had prepared it, probably expecting Aubrey to share her bed as he always did.

Now she felt melancholy. Wonderful. Was this going to be how she was her entire pregnancy? One moment full of a deep, hot anger and the next, sadness?

She placed her palm on his chest. "I didn't want this," she said, even though Aubrey knew this.

Aubrey was silent for a long while before he replied. "I should have known better," he murmured. He made no move; she wished he would stroke her hair or rub her back or something, but it occurred to her that she had never given any indication that she would like that. "Even though I want the baby, this is unfair to you."

Lorelei frowned. She had not referred to *It* as a baby yet, and that irritated her, bringing a rush of irritation that prompted her next words. "You're not in my bed tonight because the job is done."

He had been still before, but now she felt him stiffen beside her. "*No.* It's *not* that. I thought you wouldn't want me there now. I knew a child was possible, but I was reluctant ..." He paused. "I should have done better by you."

"Yes, well, a man has needs," Lorelei mumbled. Unfair to him and un-true to the situation? Oh, *decidedly*, but he *wasn't* pregnant right now, so she decided being *unfair* to *him* was the only *fair* thing she could do.

He didn't reply for a long moment. When he did, his voice was soft and grave. "Yes. Maybe you're right." He said the words as if he were not quite sure he did have needs.

With no explanation that she could think of, she felt she *hated* this man so much that she was not quite convinced she wouldn't rather try widowhood. Who would convict her, an innocent mother-to-be?

She took a deep breath and fought to tame the spiraling thoughts. The last thing Lorelei wanted was to be accused of hysteria—that was the worst thing that could happen to a woman, in her view. "You're being hysterical" was a condescending and unclear way of saying, "I will not take you seriously no matter how logical your arguments happen to be." "What's done is done, but it's your ... *yours*."

"My baby?" Aubrey suggested.

Lorelei frowned but nodded, staring up at the darkened ceiling. "Yes. That. I don't want *It*, but since you do, you must tend to your responsibilities."

"What do you mean?" Good, he was confused again—his natural state.

"You've got your child. So take care of me." She rolled over to face him. "No leaving."

"I only went to my own bedroom—" he started patiently, but she stopped his mouth with a kiss.

"No arguing with me," she said firmly after she withdrew. "None whatsoever. Just put your arm around me and keep me warm tonight."

"But what—"

"Tomorrow." The exhaustion of the day overtook her, and she allowed herself to cuddle into him. She felt repentant then for her harshness and even her cruelty in the face of what must be, for him, a most joyous revelation. But she didn't say sorry. She said, "Please."

With another sigh, though perhaps not as irritated as she'd feared, he pulled her close and dropped his head in hair. "I'm sorry," he murmured. "Truly."

Why should he apologize when he has only done his best to care for me? "You can't do anything. Let's not worry about it."

Not for now. It was too late to think about the fact that her life was over—that she would never have a single thing of her own—that she was but a vessel for the Montgomery heir, like hundreds of women had been before her.

There would be no Lorelei Hilton Montgomery, mistress of the Hilton Shipping Co. Father would catch on to the fact that she had been managing things as aspects of her branch went neglected or simply never came to be in the first place, and he would find a way to undo the contracts. Or it would fail on its own—whether or not she liked it. Or her father would send men to manage it for her.

She was losing control again, and after only three months of freedom, that felt so unfair that she wanted to cry and scream and throw a tantrum like an errant two-year-old.

Instead, she ducked her head against her husband's shoulder and tried to go to sleep.

"Lorelei?"

The soft female voice called Lorelei away from the breakfast she was falling asleep over. Aubrey had insisted she take a tray in bed—and further, ordered even lighter, more flavorless repast for her, in hopes she'd be able to keep some down. So far, Lorelei had only managed to sip coffee and stare at the distasteful toast and egg whites. There had been a threat of broth, but none had been brought up.

Thankfully, she felt less sick this morning—she was just tired. A good thing, too, for Francesca Montgomery stood in the doorway of Lorelei's bedroom, and Lorelei didn't want to appear at a disadvantage to her sister-in-law.

"Francesca," Lorelei said and gestured to the chair near her bed. "Would you like some cold toast?"

A little smile flickered across the girl's pale lips, and she shook her head. "I have already eaten. Thank you." She took the seat Lorelei had offered. "I was told congratulations are in order."

Ah. So Aubrey had told his sisters. *I wonder if he's mentioned it to Winnie.* Probably not, as Winnie often slept in, and if she'd heard a whiff of it, she'd have pounced on Lorelei with a thousand questions. "Perhaps a little prematurely—we'll see how *It* turns out." She gave what she hoped was a carefree grin. "I was told May or June. Probably June, if I can count at all. You can see then if *It* is worth congratulations." Poor *It* didn't deserve Lorelei's skepticism, and she felt a little bad for *It*, but despite the fact that *It* couldn't help *It*s circumstances ... neither could Lorelei help hers. She never had been able to. That was the way of the world, she was learning. There were so few controllable elements.

Francesca ducked her chin in a pretty, delicate nod. "I'm sure I will love my niece or nephew very much."

"Niece or nephew" made *It* sound so real, though, and Lorelei didn't want to worry about *It* until she had to. She must eventually decide how *It* could have a better childhood than she'd had. *It* should be happy and healthy and beloved. But she wasn't the person to provide that, probably. She couldn't be a mother. But when she had more energy, she'd solve the problem for *It*. That was the least she could do.

Aubrey would give his love, she thought, and his protection, his guidance, his time. Lorelei could offer a plan and pray that others would pick up where she would inevitably fail.

But that was making her want to cry, and she had cried enough. One evening of self-pity—that was all she deserved, and even that had been extravagant. From now on, she must simply set her face toward the sunset and move.

The sunset of my all too brief life.

Three. Short. Months.

To Francesca, she offered a tight smile and said, "I'm sure you will be an excellent aunt, for which I am grateful."

"You will be an excellent mother."

Why don't you stab a knife through my heart? This butter knife would do. After all, it's quite dull and will take a while to kill me dead, which I presume is what you intended after that comment. "Perhaps I will," she said aloud. Her voice had a squeak to it she didn't like.

"No, I ... I mean it." Francesca raised her blue eyes—so like her brother's—to Lorelei's face with a surprising determination. Lorelei realized that perhaps this was the first conversation she'd had with her sister-in-law, and she had no idea what kind of person this young woman was. "One of the things that makes a good mother is secure boundaries. You can provide that. Besides, a baby is always a joyous thing. It'll be good to have a child in this house—if nothing else, it'll be good for Aubrey to have something to focus on. It will be so good to see him happy. Not that you haven't made him happy, because you have—but this is something I think he's wanted for a long time."

It was probably the pregnancy, but Lorelei was unexpectedly touched. Francesca wasn't right, but it was still nice of her. "Aubrey and I had always intended to have a child. You must know this wasn't the timing we had agreed upon, but this is what's happening, and there's no way around it." No *moral* way. She wasn't naïve enough to not know that there were poisons one could take or "procedures" one could go through with a discreet doctor or understanding midwife. There had been whispers about such situations, when a child was conceived out of wedlock or an affair would become obvious due to timing issues unless the "mistake" was taken care of. However, *It* might be little, and *It* might be dependent, but *It* was still a small human, and Lorelei wasn't stupid enough to risk her life to murder an innocent.

"I intend to do my best." Her best would involve not dying during childbirth, which was the epitome of her goals at this point, and then creating a safety net for *It*; beyond that, she could not be responsible for what happened.

"I'm sure." Francesca smiled. "I do love babies, so I'm not nearly as apprehensive as you seem to be, but then, it will not be my baby."

Hmm. Perhaps now was a good time to find out a little more about what Francesca wanted—kill two birds with one conversation. "Would you like your own?"

"Yes. When I'm married." She flushed. "Of course, that may happen next year—but I'm guessing we'll delay my debut. I couldn't imagine a better reason."

Ah. Right. Lorelei would be rather incapacitated when the London Season began. Another reason why the timing wasn't the best. "Will you be too disappointed?"

"No—and anyway, we could always go to London off season. I don't need any of the specific events or entertainments. I'm simply happy to meet people."

"To meet a man, you mean?" Lorelei clarified, for she wasn't about to drag the girl around to socialize. All things should be done to a purpose, and though Lorelei knew some socialization was necessary for making business connections and such, she wasn't about to endure hours of operas and balls so her sister-in-law could have a bit of fun.

"Yes." Francesca nodded. "I don't expect you to spend long on me either. I understand that it was part of your ... your *agreement* with Aubrey. He told me a little, but I assume not all. He's always so vague. I already have ideas of who I would be interested in receiving calls from."

"Ah." Lorelei cocked her head and played with the eggs on the tray. "Don't go telling me you have a secret lover." She doubted Francesca did, especially at her age, but it never hurt to check, and her expression would tell Lorelei everything.

Francesca blushed but didn't drop her eyes. "Of course not. But I know men who have expressed a slight interest—who I like very much, too."

"Hmm." Not exactly what Lorelei had expected—she'd assumed a girl-hood crush or two, but not an actual indication that there was interest. That wasn't allowed before a young woman "debuted," was it? Lorelei's parents had never held the leash that tightly, so she wasn't sure, but she understood that girls were specifically off-limits until it was made clear that they were "out." "I hope that works out for you. I will do all I can to help."

"Because of the agreement," Francesca said.

Lorelei was obliged to nod, though it seemed a little silly said aloud. But no, no, it wasn't silly—it was the agreement. The agreement was everything. But given that it'd already been broken, more or less, and due to her own folly at that, perhaps there wasn't much hope in keeping to the agreement.

"We'll have to reevaluate—after I'm sure how ... how everything will progress." Which was a stupid thing to say, as Lorelei knew *exactly* how things would go. But perhaps she'd be able to be more active than she at first supposed—perhaps she could keep up with ... everything.

That seemed reasonable. After all, she wasn't going to be a normal mother once *It* was here, so why be a normal mother before *It* got here?

"Connie is excited, too," Francesca commented. "But I told her not to come in and overwhelm you. She can be exuberant."

Lorelei doubted "Connie" even knew the meaning of the word *exuberant*, but she nodded nonetheless. "She can talk to me any time she wants to. I don't bite."

Francesca's eyebrows arched. "How were we to know that? We've not said ten words to you between us."

"At your choice," Lorelei said. "I have never asked you not to speak to me or said you shouldn't, nor have I cut you off." They couldn't blame her for not having spoken to her themselves. She had given the idea that she was too busy to be bothered, and she hadn't reached out to them. She was not the type to force her presence on those who may or may not appreciate said presence.

Francesca said nothing for a long moment. "You don't owe us anything—an explanation, a relationship. Winnie is such a good sister to us, you know, and I understand that you're busy. But in time, I think we would both like to be your friends."

"Friends." Hmm. Lorelei had never had a *friend* outside of Patrick and Winnie. But she supposed Aubrey was her *friend*, in a way, though perhaps that descriptor was even too emotional for what they shared. They were business partners.

No, you're more than that.

She pushed aside the thought with a toss of her head. Even if it was true, it wasn't relevant. Lorelei tried not to give too much heed to irrelevant thoughts—not if she could help it, for they were the things crushed hopes and broken dreams were made of.

"I'll leave you now," said Francesca, rising. "I appreciate you speaking with me, though. I do believe we could be friends—if you would let us be. I don't dislike you, you know. I don't want you to think that. I'm glad you're making Aubrey happy."

Lorelei would have laughed in Francesca's face if it weren't for the sincerity in her eyes. Because of that sincerity—or maybe because she wanted to believe it—she simply shook her head, the weakest form of denial. "Thank you for your congratulations, even if this is not ... a usual situation."

Perhaps it was good to be reminded that for some people, this type of thing was a joyous occasion. At any rate, she was getting Aubrey's obligatory child out of the way. That was something to be glad about, wasn't it?

Chapter Sixteen

I T WAS A WEEK later, perhaps, that Lorelei received a message from London. At first, she paid it little heed, having so much business correspondence to sort through, but the handwriting caught her eye and stilled her heart.

Trick.

She almost whispered her brother's pet name aloud as she snatched up the letter from the tray the butler had brought up to her that morning. She had taken to dealing with the first bits of her correspondence on her own bed, as there was little she could do anymore to function before ten or eleven in the morning. Hopefully Dr. Burton was right and the nausea would fade a few months into proceedings—and she could get down to the docks earlier once more. As it was, she didn't want to show signs of weakness in front of the men, who had still not been informed of her "delicate condition."

She ripped open the letter and scanned down the page, reading the only words her brother had written to her since her birthday—and the only unrestrained words she'd had from him in almost two years.

Lore,

Cassie and I are in London—after coming back from visiting her family in the countryside, by which I mean her sister and brother, as her parents and ours ought to form a club for hating one's own blood—and we received word upon reaching the Knights that you were in England. This included some other news that I had not previously noted—perhaps because we've been traveling, as it must've been in the papers.

What on earth are you doing? We need to talk.

Give Winnie our love.

Trick

She sat with the letter clutched in her hands for a long time after receiving it, frozen with a mix of relief and fear. Relief because she longed to hear from her brother—to see Cassie and him, and of course their little son—to have a relationship once more with the man who had been more a father to her than her own.

Yet there was fear, too, for she knew she had made a decision Patrick would not approve of. Aubrey's relationship with Cassie before Patrick and she had wed would assure that. Though Lorelei didn't believe there was any ill will between Cassie and Aubrey—or if there was, Aubrey didn't know of it and Cassie was too polite to mention it—Patrick might not be as kind. He was protective in the best of circumstances, impossible in the worst. Lorelei didn't doubt that despite the fact that he was never the type to push anyone around or be rude, he would make her suffer. Patrick was anything but a bully, but somehow he'd been born bossy when it came to his sisters.

She took a deep breath and let it out slowly—her only defense, at present, against the nausea. She hadn't tried Dr. Burton's wife's potion; if Lorelei kept growing weaker, perhaps she ought to meet the woman. These days, Lorelei was letting herself sleep longer and more often. Last week, there had been several days when she stopped by the docks for a few minutes—and then left Mr. Hastings and the workmen to take care of the rest.

Granted, a great deal of her work was simply research, which could easily be done at home. That didn't mean she'd given herself permission to stay away from the docks, but she could. She should, perhaps, if she wanted to hide the growing weakness.

How she hated weakness. How annoying and impossible it made the growth of the Hilton Shipping Co. But she couldn't stop. Managing the company was the only thing that would give her life meaning.

She wouldn't become her mother. She *wouldn't*. What third option was there? Either she would be an empty-minded socialite with a broken family and a string of regrets or a strong, capable woman who practically ran a shipping company. Certainly, she wasn't the type to be a mother—she argued that even her own mother had been more suited to that task than Lorelei was.

She ran her hand over her eyes. Her life wasn't going as she'd planned, but what else was new?

She set the letter aside and took a sip of her coffee. The taste had shifted slightly—there was an acidity to it that she didn't like—but she knew that not drinking it was not an option. She had terrible headaches as it was.

She'd been abusing caffeine until her hands were shaking by midmorning, but no, she wouldn't think about that now. She'd consider it later, when she had more time to consider the ramifications of drinking less of her primary source of nourishment.

She wouldn't turn to the leaf water. She wouldn't. England could only do so much to her, and that was not one of those things. If Lorelei resisted nothing else in this life, she would resist becoming a tea drinker.

At last, with a heavy sigh, she set her breakfast aside and called for Harriet, who was in the other room, selecting Lorelei's outfit for the day. She fought against the dizziness that threatened to upend her and allowed Harriet to dress her and arrange her hair for the day.

"I'll have another cup of coffee in the library—I want to reply to some correspondence there. Please let someone know. But I'm going to speak with my husband first." She returned to the bed and caught up her brother's response. "Have you seen Mr. Montgomery, Harriet?"

"No, ma'am. Wasn't he ...?"

"He was with me last night, yes, but disappeared by the time I woke up. I think he takes the girls riding early in the morning—those that make their way out of bed, that is." She doubted Winnie was frequently a part of that, but perhaps she was wrong. Lorelei spoke to Winnie as infrequently as possible, especially since now her sister was agog with nursery details and baby names and all those other things that were simply too frivolous for Lorelei. She'd almost rather be poor where the biggest concern was making sure one had food for another mouth—at least, Lorelei would be more comfortable with such a discussion. However, that was not a concern here, and therefore, all the talk was about bonnets and blankets. She'd given her sisters-in-law and Winnie free reign over the nursery and all the items required there, and the girls seemed to consider this a great boon.

Lorelei was grateful to be excluded.

She left her room behind and went to hunt down her husband. It was far past breakfast, and she honestly had no idea what he did throughout his days. He told her, but she didn't have much of a memory of exactly what it had entailed. Estate management tasks, she imagined, but how did that vary from running, for instance, a company?

She found him in the private library, looking through estate books with a man who must be an employee of some sort. Upon seeing Lorelei, he told the man he addressed as Jeffries that he'd be back in a moment and led her to the drawing room.

He must've known instantly that she had something to say, must have read it on her face. *Oh, the terrifying ordeal of being known.*

She could only be comforted by the fact that he didn't know too much. Couldn't, she thought. She played her cards close to her chest, where they could not be stolen.

"How are you today?" he asked upon being alone with her, which was the furthest thing from a relevant issue. It mattered little how she was—except that she was up and walking. "How are you today?" was a question for an invalid, not a woman who had complete control of her faculties. Which, Lorelei insisted stringently, she did.

"I'm fine. I hope you're fine as well, but I didn't come to discuss that."

There was a softness in his eyes she didn't particularly like as he replied, "I know that." He gestured for her to sit down. "Tell me what you've come to discuss."

She watched his face as she sat down, looking for signs he was mocking her—Patrick would have been—but saw none. "My brother and his wife are in England. Meaning, I would like to invite them here—to stay a few days. There are things I would like to discuss with Patrick, but I understand that could be awkward for you." Her personal take was that he ought to bear through the awkwardness, if there was any after all this time, but she didn't say that as she might have ... well, with Patrick. Something had been keeping her from being as transparent with Aubrey lately as she might have otherwise been.

It was wildly irritating.

"I see." But other than saying those words in a casual tone, Aubrey gave no indication of his feelings on the matter.

But what do I care about his feelings?

"It would be for the best, for all concerned, if we got this meeting out of the way and realized that we are, like it or not, family. As we had discussed before we married," she prompted. Perhaps he needed the situation laid out for him so he could offer his thoughts—which, Lorelei hoped, would simply be, "Of course, you are so right, and we'll do exactly as you have said."

"I see." He nodded. "Yes. They ought to come."

"Do you wish ..." Then she stopped, confused. What did it matter? He could hide in the library—it was *she* who must see Patrick, speak to him, perhaps pick his brain on matters relating to the shipping industry. The rest hardly mattered. Aubrey could avoid eye contact and go silent and taciturn for the entirety of their stay, for all Lorelei cared. She didn't need him to be polite—just to not start any brawls. That was more than enough for her.

A slow smile, almost mocking, spread across Aubrey's face. She didn't like *that*. "Would you truly heed me if I protested?"

"I'm not sure," she said. If nothing else, he was owed her honesty. "I would like to."

He sighed. "I'm fine with them being here, and I'm sure it's the right thing to do." He stood. "I'll leave you, then, to mail the letter you've presumably already written."

A part of her was wounded by his assertion, strangely enough, though Aubrey had no reason to believe it wasn't true. After all, that was in character for Lorelei. She could hardly fault him for what was perfectly within the realms of both possibility and believability.

Yet she wanted to clarify that she had not done so, even though it was a needless distinction. "I came to you first," she said. "I thought you would want to know, and it changes how one writes the letter, you know, if you have the permission of the estate's owner or not."

Aubrey cocked his head, then gestured around the drawing room with its slightly outdated mid-century decorations. "All of this is yours, too, as you surely know. You've not been shy about utilizing any assets at your disposal."

"That's different. I was told to do so. This is your home."

"It's your—"

But Lorelei couldn't even let him say that. "It's not my home. I don't have or need a home. Have you ever heard of an albatross?"

"Of course." He gave her that "I'm not an idiot" look.

"They spend most of their lives at sea. They don't need a nest. They're wanderers. I've considered myself much the same." Ever adrift, floating with the tides.

He frowned. "I'm not convinced that's entirely accurate, and even if it is, they always return to their breeding sites. The same ones they came from, I believe."

His knowledge of bird life irritated her. "Yes. Well. That's true. My point was that I am not nearly so tied to this house as you are, and I think it's worth acknowledging that you deserve to say what goes on within these walls." She, too, stood and marched out, casting the words "I'll write the letter now!" over her shoulder.

She was not out of hearing when she heard him begin to quote "The Rime of the Ancient Mariner."

'God save thee, ancient Mariner!

From the fiends, that plague thee thus!—
Why look'st thou so?'—With my cross-bow
I shot the albatross.

If he was trying to bait her, it wasn't working.

The wait for Patrick and Cassie's arrival seemed like forever rather than a few days. She was sent a brief note with a train's arrival time and promised in return to send a carriage to collect them.

At last, the day arrived.

The first hint of Patrick's arrival was the chaotic barking of the dogs, Mars and Potato. Potato had a high-pitched bark, and Mars, a throaty one, and together, they caused enough cacophony to make Lorelei's head throb.

Grand.

Then a third bark answered—a short, deep response, a warning—and Lorelei's heart tightened.

Bell.

She left the entryway, where she had been lingering, too impatient to work, and walked outside to where the carriage had stopped. Winnie, who had waited on the driveway, rushed forward as the door opened. After a sleek black dog leaped out, so did Lorelei's brother.

Patrick pulled Winnie into a fierce hug that, somehow, Lorelei felt. She wasn't sure how—it was a fanciful idea—but she was sure of it.

He released Winnie slowly, smiling and laughing at her rambling. Lorelei thought he had tears in his eyes and that perhaps Winnie was talking to keep herself from crying, yet instead of stepping forward, Lorelei stood back, suddenly feeling awkward, as if this wasn't her life anymore.

Perhaps it wasn't. The truth was, she didn't know what her life was anymore.

"Trick," she whispered, but she didn't say it very loudly. She had asked them not to line up the servants and greet their guests in true formality—and she had encouraged Aubrey to wait to meet them until dinner.

She wanted to hear a little about what Patrick was thinking before she committed to letting him in the same room with Aubrey. Like it or not, she now arguably needed this man alive—to be a father, not for any other reason—so scoping out her brother's mood seemed wise.

Cassie stepped down, looking as pretty and blushy as ever. She was pale, as many redheads were, but there were freckles dancing across her cheeks, and any cold turned them pink.

It was a cold day, after all. Perhaps Lorelei should usher them in.

But Winnie was embracing Cassie and getting introduced to the little man she held, and there was a lot of chatter, a lot of voices strained by emotion, and Lorelei didn't want to be a part of that.

She certainly wasn't going to cry.

At last, Patrick broke away, leaving his wife and child in Winnie's clutches and the dogs to chase each other around the lawn—even Bell had gained puppy energy upon meeting her own son again—and walked toward Lorelei.

Oh, and there was caution on his face. Patrick was often nervous, though usually he hid it under a light, polite charm. But not for her. He couldn't, Lorelei thought. She would see.

And she did see—the strain behind his eyes and the pinch of his lips.

"Lore," he said as one might speak to a spooked animal, "you look pale."

She laughed. She supposed she did—she felt pale—but still. "What a way to greet your sister."

He stepped closer, reached as if to touch her, then shuffled back. Was he mad? Diseased? Was he truly angry at her? Suddenly, what had been a slight but passing worry seemed rather large.

He hates me. He hates what I've done, and he won't help me. I have lost my brother, the only person who loves me unconditionally, because I could not be bothered to wait for a second option.

She wanted to scream. *No. Not Trick. Anyone, anything, but him.*

Yet she must put on a brave face. She summoned her strength. "It's cold. We should go inside."

His eyes flickered about. "Oh, should we? Into Montgomery Place? Goodness. To think, this might have been Cass's home."

Oh, he was going to play dirty, then? Fine. She'd played in the mud with him before. "Oh, you know, like a true middle child, I am content with what others would throw away." She turned to the door. "A footman will show you to your rooms—and I'll see you at dinner."

"Lore, wait." She heard his two steps to catch her, and then he spun her around. "I don't know what to say, but I know it's wrong of me to say it now. Here." He yanked her close for one of his interminable hugs, which, granted, usually only lasted a few seconds, but he hugged too tight, she never knew what to do with her hands, and she hated that she actually found this annoying creature comforting when she ought to be self-sufficient.

Of course, Aubrey's embraces were neither awkward nor boring—which made sense, come to think of it. 'Twas a different relationship. Still, Lorelei had no problems being comforted by Aubrey, though she might not name it such—with Patrick, it tasted of pity and innocence and childhood.

How she *hated* pity and innocence and childhood.

She wrenched away from him. "We'll talk later." Her words were too harsh, she knew, but she felt harsh—and she wasn't sure why, for she'd been looking forward to seeing him. Yes, Patrick could be stern with her, but she'd not believed he would have the nerve to truly be angry this time. She thought he'd be intimidated by the situation she'd found herself in—and settle in to helping her with little protestation.

Cassie walked to her then, with Winnie at her side. Winnie held the small fellow who must be Aidan, and Cassie was largely preoccupied with making sure Winnie provided the proper support. However, she took time to smile at Lorelei. If she were aware of the tension between her sister-in-law and her husband, she gave no sign of it.

"Lorelei," she said in that soft, even voice. "We've missed you. Thank you for letting us come to see you—I know it must be an inconvenience, but I don't think either of us could bear to leave England without seeing you and Winnie. It was too good an opportunity to miss."

Lorelei nodded but said nothing. If she'd been the blushing type of woman, she'd have blushed at the sight of Cassie. As it was, she simply dealt with the lump in her throat and the heaviness in her chest with what she hoped was little outward sign. For the first time, she seriously considered the fact that she now had the life Cassie would have had. Only Cassie would have been a better wife—and certainly a better mother—than Lorelei could ever hope to be.

This is not fair to Aubrey.

Having Patrick and Cassie here with their child was sure to remind Aubrey of what he could have had—and how poor Lorelei was as a consolation prize! Oh, they had their agreement, and they would have their child sooner than anticipated. But at the least, Cassie would have offered Aubrey the life he probably wanted, even if he claimed that what Lorelei and he had was sufficient.

How could Lorelei be *sufficient* when it came to wifehood?

But, she reminded herself firmly as she instructed the servants to take Cassie and Patrick's luggage upstairs, she didn't want to be sufficient as a wife.

No, no, that didn't matter. She wouldn't let it. After Patrick and Cassie were gone, her guilt would subside, and she would get back to work.

CHAPTER SEVENTEEN

AUBREY HADN'T EXPECTED LORELEI to be the one who was nervous. He'd expected her to be typically unflappable. He'd expected her to be enjoying her brother and sister-in-law's company. He'd expected her to be irritated in any lapse of perfect behavior that he himself demonstrated. But whether it was due to the exhaustion her lack of sleep and poor eating habits had caused combined with her delicate condition, or if she'd had some conversation with Patrick that Aubrey hadn't heard of, she wasn't in the best mood. She was taciturn during dinner, picking at her food.

If Aubrey weren't so worried about her, he would have, in truth, felt a little awkward about Patrick Hilton and the former Lady Mary Cassidy O'Connell's presence. Lady Mary had meant a lot to him, briefly—and Patrick Hilton was probably the reason why Lady Mary had made the final decision not to marry Aubrey. Not that he blamed her.

However, as it was, he was too concerned about Lorelei to pay attention to much else. He kept up a polite stream of conversation with the Hiltons, as he had been trained to do, asking questions about Patrick's work and their home in Philadelphia and what they were doing in England. Mary said little—though he supposed everyone referred to her as Cassie, and perhaps he ought to as well. However, it didn't seem right. In truth, unless told to do otherwise, he should refer to her as Mrs. Hilton.

Meanwhile, Patrick seemed at ease. The affection between Gwendolyn and him was clear, and he also engaged Aubrey's sisters. He must be as frustrated with the situation as Aubrey was, but he gave no indication of it, and Aubrey followed the younger man's example. After all, no reason to make things any more awkward than they already were.

Besides, Patrick and Aubrey were both very consumed with trying to get Lorelei to take a part in the conversation despite the fact that their attempts only seemed to distress her.

Lovely.

Does Patrick have any idea what's going on with her? Aubrey hoped so, for he was at a loss. Though there'd been an unspoken restraint between Lorelei and him since they found out about the baby, he'd thought that seeing her family would help rather than bring forth an even more silent side of her.

With dinner over, he was given the opportunity to send the ladies off and have a drink with Patrick—instead of finding a way out of it, as Aubrey had hoped to do, he seized the opportunity.

I have to know if he had any idea what she's thinking.

He could only hope that Patrick knew more of his sister than Aubrey knew of his wife.

Over a glass of brandy in the dim but cozy study, Aubrey was not even obligated to speak.

"I don't blame you, you know. Lore is hard to turn away once she has an idea in her head. I haven't talked to her well enough to understand her motivations, but I do know there is little you could do once she had it in her head that she'd be marrying you." Patrick shrugged and took a sip of his drink. "I was surprised, however. I knew she wanted to marry—and I suspected she would try to find a situation that gave her a bit more freedom. But England is the last place on earth she should have been able to find it. Cassie's friend got it from her mother that Lore has reached some ... some *agreement* with you." Patrick said *agreement* like it was a dirty word.

Aubrey nodded. "She wanted my assurance that I would allow her to take on aspects of your father's company—it made sense to lay out the exact details, even if it cannot be legally binding."

"So I gathered." Patrick's slightly arched eyebrows and twisted mouth indicated he didn't approve. "She is an adult, more or less, so I suppose she has the right to make such decisions. I have no right to tell her what to do, but I do wish she had thought to wait. Marriage is not an institution to be entered into hastily. I know Lore would probably say she doesn't even want an actual marriage ... but Cassie thought it a strange choice for you. She felt you were different."

For a man taking such a light tone, that was quite the accusation.

"I wasn't sure of Lorelei's offer when she broached it the first time—you must know, she was the one who brought this idea up first. She could do nothing less. But she is ... unique. I felt we would get on well—and in many ways, we have." Until she realized that she would be having a child, at least. But if Lorelei hadn't told Patrick about this yet, Aubrey wouldn't be the one to break her confidence. "We are in some ways very suited, and she picked up on this with astonishing speed."

Patrick hesitated, then nodded. "She can be insightful, when she chooses to be."

"Exactly. But I hope you know, I didn't ... I didn't urge her to marry me. Quite the opposite. I laid out the possible struggles, and she fully understood them at the time of our marriage. I've told you we get on well, and she seems happy working at the docks. I've done all I could to assure her comfort." *Other than keep my hands off her,* but that didn't seem a thought to share with her older brother. He had an idea it would not be appreciated.

After a moment, Patrick shrugged. "I'm sure you have. I still think it foolishness—but it's not as if she eloped with a circus acrobat or something. She has a home and a family and a place for herself. That's more than she might have had if she'd simply married the man my father had for her. Billy Pent is a good boy, but he was never going to be anything more than a boy. No, not when he was fifty." He shook his head. "It's good that Lore found her own place. That said, the family ... connections ... I'm glad we're allowed here. I wondered."

Aubrey smiled. That much was simple. "Lorelei cares for you. Of course you had to come."

"At present, she won't speak to me—I'm afraid I got off on the wrong foot with her. But I'll regain my ground. I need to sit down and tell her that I don't resent her. I think she presumed my ... less than suave greeting was an indication that I harbored more anger toward her than I truly do."

Aubrey shrugged. Accidentally upsetting Lorelei over something that should've been nothing was a feeling he'd become rapidly familiar with over the last few weeks. "She's sensitive just now. I'm sure it'll fade—and it's for a good cause."

Patrick, who had gone to set his glass down on the sideboard, turned as Aubrey realized the ambiguity of what he'd said—and the obvious conclusion any sane person would draw. "She's pregnant?" Patrick said. "She didn't tell me."

Aubrey hated to lie, so he simply nodded. "You've only been here a day. I shouldn't have let on—I'm sure she'd want to tell you."

"I'm quite sure she'd rather have kept it from me and written a single letter when the baby comes. She's never wanted children—she made that abundantly clear. I assumed that part of your arrangement would be ..." Patrick paused and shook his head. "I was wrong."

Had Patrick assumed Aubrey had sacrificed children for Lorelei? "We hadn't intended ... It doesn't matter now."

"You hadn't intended to get her pregnant?" Patrick's incredulous voice, which didn't accurately finish Aubrey's unsaid thought, rose. "I'd think a man of your age would have an idea of how that happened and be able to avoid it."

Aubrey felt heat flush his face, but he chose to ignore it. Instead, he debated his options. After all, he couldn't remind Lorelei's brother that it took two; neither could he admit that neither of them had intended to spend more than a few nights together, but it had gotten out of hand.

Simply put, it was stupidity—and somehow, despite the fact that it was Lorelei who had declared such activities stupidity, he was the one who should've left her room. But he hadn't. He still hadn't.

What sane man would remove himself from the only situation where he got to hold his wife, no matter how briefly?

At last, Aubrey settled on saying, "Regardless of our intentions—which are a private matter and do not need to be explained to you or anyone else—it has happened. Perhaps we ought to join the ladies."

Patrick stiffened, then seemed to force his shoulders to relax. "You're correct. It isn't my business. I only care about my sister's well-being—but I'm sure she'll adjust. Thank you for humoring my concerns in the first place." He started toward the door.

Hmm. Perhaps Aubrey shouldn't have driven him off so soon. After all, he did want to benefit from the man's superior knowledge of Lorelei. "Could I ask you one question?"

Patrick paused. "Of course."

Then Aubrey froze, for he wasn't at all sure what, of all the many pressing questions about Lorelei he had, was the most important. At last, he settled on "How can I make her happy?"

Patrick cocked his head. "You'll find that out on your own, I suspect. She'll tell you."

Aubrey doubted that anymore, as she had been increasingly quiet these days, but he nodded, nonetheless. "Perhaps. But if you had to guess ..."

Patrick seemed to take a deep breath, his eyes absently staring into nothing, as he took a moment before he made his response. "I would say, be truthful with her and say what you want and allow her to come to you. She's not an easy woman to deal with, at times. She considers so many feminine things to be weakness. My mother never listened to her, and any protestation was labeled as 'hysterics' by both our parents. She won't shake that easily—but I would like her to. She shouldn't be made to feel that way. Not by anyone. I hope you'll encourage her to confide in you. I haven't always known how to myself."

"I will attempt to." Not with any certainty, but it did help to know that Lorelei had been so sternly rebuked for any reaction. It explained a lot about her—though not her honesty. That was a mystery. Most people would learn to lie under such circumstances. Aubrey wondered if Patrick was the cause of Lorelei still speaking truth even in the face of such treatment, but it seemed too much to ask his brother-in-law to reveal a portion of his relationship with Lorelei to a man who was nearly a stranger and almost an enemy, so he didn't ask. He followed Patrick to the parlor where the women sat.

Mrs. Hilton had won the affections of all the ladies. She was good like that—always knew how to talk to any young woman, especially if they were in need of guidance.

Lorelei had disappeared, something he shouldn't be surprised about.

Aubrey sat in the corner and watched the crowd talk and made the occasional comment. But mostly, he thought—about himself, about Mrs. Hilton, and about Lorelei.

After a time, Connie left and Fran was consumed in a conversation with Patrick and Gwendolyn. It was then that Mrs. Hilton broke off and came to sit nearer to him.

"I want to talk to you." She adjusted her skirts, pale hands fluttering about in a nervous sort of way. "I must go upstairs to check on my son soon, and I shall probably retire afterward, but I didn't want to wait. To speak to you, I mean."

"Go ahead." He kept his tone even and light. They hadn't had a conversation since her rejection of his proposal—and though he applauded her bravery, he wasn't sure he was on equal footing with her.

It wasn't that he regretted her or wished things had turned out differently, but rather that he didn't know how she viewed him. Had he become a villain to her? He hoped not. He'd hate to be a villain to anyone. But with the way he had disregarded everything she told him, perhaps he ought to be viewed as a villain.

"I'm sorry things ended badly between us—though I'm not sad about the results. I did the right thing in refusing your proposal, but I should have broken things off earlier. In fact, I never should have let myself fall so easily into my parents' trap. They do not have my best interests in mind, and in such an important decision as who I would spend the rest of my life with, allowing them to rule me was foolish. I will say, I was young. I'm sure some seventeen-year-olds are more than capable of judging their own feelings—but I thought what I felt for you was more than puppy love, and I let things drag on believing it must've been ... It hardly matters now. I'm glad you found Lorelei."

He nodded. "Thank you. There was so much I should've done better. I never attempted to understand you, and I'm sorry for that. More than that, I should have listened to you when you told me about Gibson Ashfield. He was not a good man, and I know that now; he won't be associating with my family anymore. But I'm sure Lorelei and I shall get along well."

Mrs. Hilton nodded. "I'm sure you shall." She started to rise, then stilled. "Mr. Montgomery, why can you never pick a woman who will stay home?" she mused. "Lorelei isn't home often, from what I understand from your sisters, but you must have known that would be the case before you married her, and I think that's fine. You didn't know it about me, but I like to be moving. Patrick jokes that I spend more time with the Strausses or the Baldwins than at our own home when I'm in Philadelphia—and I think you'd have been unhappy with that. I think I'm unusual in comparison to most women. Patrick and I will travel a lot throughout our life, as long as he works for Baldwin & Sons—that's the shipping business he works for." Mrs. Hilton hesitated. "But I worry for you and Lorelei."

Aubrey could see her point, but as she'd said, he'd known that about Lorelei. "I think it would have strained me with you because I wouldn't have expected it. I think you've a wandering soul, and you've found the man who can embrace that. But it's not that Lorelei is wandering, exactly. I think she needs a home; she's simply slow to accept that she needs to roost here." Perhaps that was fanciful, but he'd been mulling over albatrosses for days.

"Perhaps you are right. You've spent more time than I have with her, altogether, and I'm sure she's shared more of herself with you." Mrs. Hilton smiled, though it was tight. "I want you both to be happy—but especially Lorelei. Patrick loves her so, and I've come to care for her, too. She's a good girl. A little lost, but perhaps you're right. Being lost means finding a place to rest and settle down, and you could certainly provide that for her." She rose. "I must see to my son. I want you to meet Aidan at some point—though even if he were to wake now, he'd be in a foul mood. I promise he's a charmer, when he's not at a disadvantage. Tomorrow, I hope."

Aubrey nodded. "That'd be fine." Children were always such a tension breaker. He hoped his child with Lorelei would serve a similar purpose.

Mrs. Hilton paused once more. "I think perhaps Lorelei must grieve a little before she can fight—and she doesn't know that. Help her however you can, all right?"

Aubrey agreed hastily, but he wasn't entirely sure how to interpret those words. After all, Lorelei wasn't fighting anything—and what did she have to grieve?

Just more things for him to puzzle out when it came to his wife.

Chapter Eighteen

Lorelei knew Patrick was an early riser, so she became one the next morning—which just about killed her. Once she managed to make it outside and get a breath or two of fresh air, she was able to stand without wobbling, which was good enough for her. As long as she could keep moving forward, surely she wouldn't collapse to the ground.

After a brief walk, which was more an excuse to wander about and gain her bearings, she made her way to the breakfast room, where she wasn't perhaps the earliest riser after all. Aubrey, Patrick, and Cassie were already seated at the table, Cassie with Aidan on her lap.

Glad they're getting along. Without me.

But she didn't feel much like getting along with anyone that morning; she simply collected a piece of toast and a cup of coffee and slouched down on her seat.

She felt Patrick side-eyeing her, but he refrained from his usual "Lore, you need to eat something" this once. Which was funny because normally—well, before he'd been banished—he would talk of nothing else but how she ought to force herself to eat until she gained an appetite, she couldn't survive on coffee alone until whenever it was that she got around to eating something decent, and on and on while she vainly told him to mind his own business.

Nonsense. She'd been doing it for years. In normal circumstances, she felt fine.

"How are you feeling, Lorelei?" Cassie said as she adjusted the sleeping Aidan to her other arm.

Lorelei wondered why she'd brought him down just to sleep—couldn't babies stay alone in a room? Or was that not possible? She frankly didn't know—and she had not intended to care. "Well enough. How are—" Then she stopped, for there was something like empathy in Cassie's eyes that she didn't like. She turned to Aubrey. "Did you tell them?"

Aubrey paused midway through a bite of scrambled eggs and squirmed. "I may have let it slip. I don't know if your brother—"

"He told me," Cassie said swiftly. "I'm sorry it wasn't on your timing, Lore, but I'm happy to know. Congratulations."

Lorelei hadn't intended to tell them at all, timing or no timing, but she simply nodded and gave a half-hearted, "Thank you."

"We can talk later, if you like."

"Perhaps." Probably not. She didn't want to talk about it, and for now, she'd been managing everything quite fine. Granted, she was getting sicker and sicker every day and had no idea how to ease it, but it wasn't as if she would admit such weakness, so she must find a way to cope.

It would be all right. It must be, for there was no other way to manage this than to be "all right." She couldn't turn back the clock and give herself a larger dose of self-control. She could move forward in a wiser, more staid way. That was all. Anything else was a foolish wish that could never come into fruition.

"Lore, after breakfast, will you show me what you're doing here?" Patrick asked. "I'd like to see your operations—unofficially, I mean. As you know, I work for Baldwin & Sons, so we should both be cautious, as much as we can be. My employer is aware I am here—they were kind enough to encourage Cassie and me to see our families while we are in England, knowing how distanced we have been. They have entrusted me with much, and I could never break that confidence."

Lorelei nodded. She had suspected that would be the case—after all, what Patrick did, he did with excellence. Of course, the Baldwins wouldn't fail to realize this. That said, she could still find use for Patrick. She was sure of it.

They took the carriage down to the dock a few minutes later and got out to walk along the coastline. Lorelei pointed out a few of the buildings going up and the rapid progress of the docks now stretching out into the bay, and Patrick said little. He simply shoved his hands into his pockets and nodded and tried to change the subject at every turn.

She'd known for years that men were frustrating, but she'd never expected Patrick to start acting like a man.

At last, she stopped rambling about the business workings for a few minutes, and they walked in silence.

"I'm proud of you, Lore. You've done so well here," Patrick said softly.

Eagerness bubbled up in her chest. "Perhaps I could take you to the offices and show you my plans. I—"

"*Lore.*" Despite his quick rebuttal, there was laughter in his tone—and in his face, for that matter. "You know I can't do that. It'd be bad for both the Hiltons and the Baldwins. I don't want even a hint of inappropriate behavior."

Lorelei frowned in annoyance. "But all I want—"

"I can't. The Baldwins have done so much for me. They took me in when they shouldn't have trusted me—the son of Clarence Hilton—anywhere near their business, and they've treated me like a son and Cassie like a daughter. They're more family to me than Mother and Father ever will be. I will never forget that."

Lorelei turned her face to the sea. How annoying to have Patrick's infernal loyalty get in the way of her interests instead of being the only thing in her favor, as it always had been before. "But, Patrick—"

"I know you feel differently, but you must understand my position. Legally, as well. I couldn't do anything to benefit the Hilton Shipping Company." She felt Patrick shrug as he stepped closer to her, leaning against her as if to offer comfort—or a wind block, which was more appreciated, given the breeze. "I'd rather hear about your life. Your marriage. Your child. Honestly, Lore, what is the business, the shipping company, *anything*, to that?"

Of course. Patrick was an enamored family man now; he wasn't one to care about business and all those other worldly pursuits.

She rolled her eyes. "I know you better than that."

"Maybe I've changed." There was a bit of an edge to his voice, as if he both wanted her to believe him and knew she would not. "But that doesn't matter. I'm worried about you. I don't have the words to discuss this, so you'll have to try a little, but all I know is, I can't bear to think you hopped out of the frying pan and into the fire. This is all so ... sudden. So unexpected."

"*Right.*" There was sarcasm in her tone, though. Patrick would say that. He never made any decision with any speed. It took him ages for his stubborn brain to come around to a new way of thinking. He must have changed; she had perhaps known he would as soon as she'd watched his eyes find Cassie again and again in the Knights' gardens. Patrick had never looked at a woman that way before—including the woman their parents had chosen to be his wife, though Lorelei couldn't fault him for not being terribly attracted to Blanche Linden. Lorelei had decided Blanche was a fast woman.

Patrick's attraction to Cassie had heralded a change—and a rising tide lifted all the boats in the harbor, hers included. Patrick should've known that his shifting seas wouldn't leave his sisters unaffected. In fact, he *had* known, when he left—had he deceived himself, as he ran off and lived the life only a man could hope to run off and live? Or had he simply forgotten that Lorelei had few options outside of marrying until she turned twenty-one?

She couldn't wait that long. Not with Billy Pent and her father attempting to trap her.

When she said nothing, Patrick spoke again. "I want you to be happy, Lore. That's what I've always wanted. I know I might not do a good job of showing it, but I love you. A lot. I'd been begging God to show me a way to get you and Winnie out, but He never gave me one. I'm a little upset He didn't let me save you. I thought I'd given the idea up, but I couldn't help praying for it. If you'd come to me ..."

"What would you have done? Father was my legal guardian; he still is Winnie's. If he found out you were here, he'd be furious." Lorelei sighed and wrapped her arms around herself. "I was unprepared for marriage in some ways. That much is true—I'll not pretend I knew exactly what I was doing. But with the exception of this little interlude"—she gestured toward her still relatively flat abdomen, hidden though it was under layers of warm clothes—"we have done very well. He has been kind to me, supported me in everything, and more than upheld his end of the bargain."

"Yet he obviously wasn't as restrained in some matters."

Lorelei laughed, surprised. She wondered if he had intended to speak that thought. "Trick, neither was I."

"But—"

She scoffed, interrupting whatever nonsensical tirade he was about to start on. As far as she was concerned, he could be disillusioned as to her innocence now, and then they'd be done with this ridiculous conversation that neither of them needed to have. "How would you like it if Cassie's brother came along and implied that you were at fault for Aidan's existence and, further, that it was some great burden to her, some lack of restraint on your part?"

"*That*"—he snapped out the word—"was not what I implied. I didn't mean to—I'm sorry. All I am saying is that he wants a child and you do not."

"But I wanted *him!*" Her voice rose, and even as she began her next sentence, she lowered it again, glancing around to make sure she had not been overheard. "Is that what you want me to admit to you, Trick? That sometimes I want to feel something other than fear and worry? You can call me whatever you want—" She slashed a hand across her eyes, which had suddenly become damp with angry tears. How she hated that he could make her cry so easily. Few others had that power over her. "You can call me any name that pops into your mind for a woman who acts as I did. *I knew better.* But even if it's counterfeit love, maybe I'm willing to lower myself, to sink—" She couldn't continue.

Patrick stared at her and said nothing. After a moment, he made a strangled noise at the back of his throat and walked away, obviously as frustrated as she was with the turn of the conversation, but then he paced back and took her arm. His grip was firm but gentle—he didn't squeeze, but she could feel him trembling. "Lorelei Anne Hilton, what did I say to make you think like that?"

She ignored his use of her maiden name. It ought to be corrected, but she understood the meaning of the emphasis. To Patrick, "Lorelei Anne Hilton" would probably always be her full name. "You didn't have to say anything. I watched our parents and saw passion for myself—and decided I'd have none of it. But I'm becoming Mother, aren't I? You got out—you're not anything like Clarence Hilton—but I'm becoming *her*. I'll be jealous of him, won't I, Trick? Isn't that the way this goes? When he loses interest, after *It* is born perhaps, I'll be furious, and I'll take it out on anyone near me ... and then he'll turn to me in cruelty, punishing me for challenging his neglect. Oh yes, I hope I've learned my lesson, but we Hilton women never learn, do we?" Lorelei shook her head. "Mother never learned to stop fighting with him. To give up. To not care what he did. She couldn't help but push, but be cruel, but give into hysterics, and then she'd be punished for it. Over and over again." She shook her head, blinking back more tears, and tried to pull away.

Patrick was the troublesome brother; he didn't let her. He grabbed her arm and held her steady, not hugging her but not releasing her either. "None of that is true. Not a word of it. You've built it up in your mind, but not a word of that has any place in the real world. I promise you. Come on. Let's go sit on the end of the dock."

He half dragged, half led her there and made her sit on the damp, cool wood so that their feet dangled over the edge. Her breathing had gotten frantic, like a caged animal's, and she took a moment to compose herself.

"Let's talk about this," Patrick said. "Tell me if I miss a point. First of all, you're afraid of becoming Mother. Perfectly logical in some ways. I follow the train of thought. I'm terrified of becoming Father, and you're right—with the help of godly mentors and always listening to every word

Cassie tells me about myself, I can hope to avoid that. I won't be cruel to Aidan, and I'll love him regardless of anything he does or does not do. He'll never be a tool to me, nor an inconvenience, nor a means to an end. But to address your concerns about being Mother … I know what they might be, but could you tell me specifically?"

Lorelei frowned. "You know what Mother was like."

"I do, but what do you fear imitating most?"

"I told you. She is miserable, and she makes everyone around her equally as miserable. She hates Father. She hates *us*. Sometimes I think she hates that she has to keep living and breathing. Honestly, I think she'd have run off west with a circus or something years ago if it weren't for us—and though she claims her children are what hold her to her marriage, she neglected us; she treated us with spite and dislike; she showed nothing but contempt for us."

"All right." He wrapped his arm around her shoulders; she didn't shove him off, though only for his sake. Patrick liked to feel like he was offering comfort. "You won't hate anyone, Lore. Not Aubrey Montgomery and not the child you carry. You might be indifferent, if you force yourself to be, but if you hated him the way Mother hates Father … I mean, I'd have seen it. They can't last an hour without quarreling over something. You share a room with the man. Willingly."

That was true. But … "Presumably, Mother and Father have shared a room at some point or another in their marriage. We had to come about some way, as my little *It* did."

He cleared his throat and shifted uneasily, but his tone was even and quiet. "I wonder if you shouldn't have a chat with Cassie about these feelings. I don't know if I can give you advice myself, but you and Mr. Montgomery belong to each other. It's a Biblical concept. You shouldn't feel shame about that."

Lorelei swallowed. She wasn't about to admit to her brother how tentative her relationship with God felt these days, especially after she'd always prided herself on rigid adherence to Christian ethics.

Perhaps Patrick would understand. After all, it wasn't as if he'd always had the deepest relationship with Christ—in fact, in the two years leading up to him leaving, he'd noticeably struggled with his faith. Though Lorelei knew this to be true, she was also afraid to tell him—for it seemed insanity to admit to Patrick how much she doubted these days.

Oh, not that God existed or that everything in the Bible was true—but that she was capable of having that personal relationship that Cassie and he spoke of. Knowing about the love and care of God and experiencing it were two different things entirely.

"I think you should talk to Cassie," Patrick said in a tone that indicated that not only did he "think" she ought to talk to Cassie but he was going to do everything in his power to make sure she did.

"What would we discuss?" She wanted to laugh at the absurdity of the situation. "I'm fine, Patrick. I truly am."

He shook his head but said nothing for a long moment. "It's cold. We ought to head back."

"Right."

With his help, she stood and plodded up the dock.

CHAPTER NINETEEN

LORELEI STAYED FOR DINNER—AUBREY suspected primarily because her brother insisted upon it—and then went upstairs right afterward to lie down. Therefore, Aubrey forced himself to stay still, to not bother her, to be well-behaved for about an hour ... and then made his excuses. He wanted to be alone with her—to make sure she was all right, to comfort her if she needed it, to tell her that this couldn't possibly go on forever and she would feel better and have her energy back and all would be well.

Perhaps. He didn't know much about this sort of thing, but he suspected that not every woman who had a child was permanently incapacitated.

They had made the decision—or Lorelei had; he wasn't sure—to spend their nights in the mistress's chamber once more. Lorelei was set up there, which at present meant an endless supply of pillows and a ready chamber pot.

Poor thing.

Now she was lying on her side in her nightgown while her maid bustled about, straightening things up. Her hair was damp from a bath—he was glad she'd taken some time to relax, for that was one of her comforts these days—and she was staring at the grate across the room, but she glanced up when he appeared.

"Aubrey." She nodded to him and started to sit up then stopped. Her eyes remained on his face, and she smiled. "I actually feel all right, but I'm exhausted."

"Ah." His concern must have shown on his face. "Good. I mean, I'm not glad you're exhausted, but ..."

"I understand. Harriet, you can leave. I think we're set for the evening. Don't rush us out of bed tomorrow."

Once her maid had scurried off, and Aubrey took a moment to contemplate the niceness of "us" over "me," he went to his dressing room, prepared for bed, came back, and lay down beside her.

She scooted up to him and tucked in his arms with a soft sigh that he was becoming accustomed to—not accustomed enough to fail to see its novelty and beauty, but enough that he understood the sign of her contentment.

"My shoulders hurt," she commented. "That's about it, though, which is irritating. I wish I could have one night where I didn't feel miserable. I was reading most of the afternoon, you know—all about accounting. I'm not much at math—*maths*, if you will—but I'm determined to understand it in case I ever have a crooked employee. I'd like to catch it if I'm being ill-treated." Here, she flopped away from him, onto her stomach, and dropped her face into her folded arms. "I don't want to talk about that now, though. I should stop."

Aubrey placed his hands on her shoulders and gently rubbed there until she arched into him and moaned. He withdrew, a little startled at himself for having reached for her in the first place, which was not the right decision given her annoyed look.

"You'd think by now you would have learned what I do when I don't want you to stop," she mumbled. "Men are untrainable."

Aubrey swallowed. "I apologize. I don't ever know—"

"I know you don't," she snapped, then she stilled and sighed. "I'm sorry. I'm so tired, and I hurt. That's no excuse to act in an irrational manner. I shall attempt to do better."

Aubrey swallowed and thought. "Lori."

"Hmm?"

"It's all right to be irrational. Especially now. I'm not going to go anywhere if you snipe at me a bit."

She stilled then, and her breath was soft and even, as if she had started thinking about the way she was breathing and was measuring every intake and exhale.

"I understand I'm not the most feeling man, and though you might say you are not the most feeling woman, you do have a heart, like anyone, and I understand that everything has been difficult lately. I'm not going anywhere if you are a little harsher with me than is warranted—and honestly, you don't offend me." She confused him, but he was never *offended* by that confusion. "I like being with you. The truth is, I like being with you an awful lot."

If she had been still before, now she was stiff. He swallowed, heart pounding. Perhaps he'd said too much—this wasn't supposed to be anything but a pleasant enough arrangement, and with the child, he'd already tried his luck far too much. To specifically go against her wishes, to admit to a greater feeling ...

Yet something within Aubrey said that perhaps it wasn't time to hold back from his natural inclinations. He loved her, and he wanted to tell her that he loved her. Was that so insane? It was the natural inclination of any man, he supposed, to want to tell the woman one loved of greater feelings.

"Lorelei, I'm in love with you," he murmured, lowering himself onto the pillow beside her and placing a hand on her back. "I think I have been for a while."

"You shouldn't say that. Especially if you're just saying it because you got me pregnant." Her voice was tight, and she turned with her back to him, spine still stiff. "I don't need your pity. It's fine, Aubrey. I'm ... I'm going to come to peace with it, and it's going to be fine. You don't have to—"

"I know I don't have to. But I also feel that it's unfair of you to ask me not to speak the truth—to ask me to keep this to myself, to not love you." He reached for her and, when she didn't tug away again, drew her close, into the curve of his body, and settled his arm around her. "Let me tell you about it a bit. See if you can tolerate my wooing you."

Lorelei scoffed. She couldn't help it; she believed "wooing" was more of a courtship-stage term—and that was nothing a married couple should have to engage in.

It shouldn't happen many months into marriage, after the lady was already won. It certainly shouldn't happen when the lady was pale and wan, likely to sink into another round of sickness at any moment, her hair damp and tangled. That was not the kind of woman a man made wooed.

Indeed, a wise man would have stayed away, but Aubrey's words and actions proved he was not wise. His arms were around her, his hand stroking her hair. When she didn't raise a protest beyond the single sound at the back of her throat—which she had thought indicated her disgust at the notion—his lips were near her ear, and he whispered that he loved her again and that she was ... well, everything she wasn't.

Beautiful, treasured, cherished.

She swore on her life that the words he was saying, barely perceptible due to her own misery and exhaustion, were love-making, courtship words.

Like anyone could be romantic in such a situation. Perhaps she was delirious. She must be. It was the only logical conclusion, truly.

Lorelei placed her hands over his, cupped over her abdomen where the barely perceptible swelling indicated the growth of their child, and she cried.

She tried to stop herself, but he shushed and murmured and *encouraged* her, the stupid man, and she gave in, turned to him, dropped her face onto his shoulder and sobbed. She'd thought she'd gotten this out of her system with one night of self-pity, one night of screaming to the ceiling that this was unfair.

But perhaps this wasn't about *It*. She wasn't sure what the crying was about, but she'd had to think about *It* consciously, to assign the reason for her crying to *It*. Rather, she felt a mix of elation and fear, neither of which made sense and together were not the most logical combination of emotions.

In time, she quieted but remained close to Aubrey, enjoying his warmth and the strength of his arms—not that he had unusually muscular arms, but he probably didn't sit in his office all day either.

"I would like to spend a day with you sometime," she commented.

"Why?"

"To see what you're doing."

"Oh."

Lorelei grinned and gave his arm a little squeeze. "Good."

"What?"

"You're confused again." She giggled, which was also unlike her, and tipped her face up to his. "You should always be confused. It's so funny."

"Oh, is it?" A sardonic edge teased his tone. "I'm always happy to be entertaining."

"I appreciate your sacrifice." She sat up and reached into the bedside table's drawer to snatch up a handkerchief. After wiping her face and energetically blowing her nose, she set the handkerchief aside and turned to him. "I shall make sure to spend a day with you when I next have some freedom. I must work when I can—and I also have to speak with Cassie—but I'll let you know when I am next free."

"What do you have to speak with Mrs. Hilton about?" he asked, sitting up himself and straightening the bedclothes.

"Us, a little, I think. She's Cassie, after all. Everything she says makes sense to me. I thought maybe she could help me understand marriage better."

He nodded. "All right." But his eyes were on her in a searching way, a way that she disliked greatly. "What is it that you want to understand more about? Let me be a part of that." Though Aubrey's voice was level, she caught the pleading side.

He wants to be a part of my life. The thought was unexpected but rang with truth. "Can I tell you later?" She didn't have the energy tonight. "It's nothing specific." She simply had a general idea that she knew nothing about love or relationships—and would never be able to have a healthy one.

"All right." He kissed her forehead and turned out the light.

As it turned out, avoiding a conversation with Cassie was not an option. Directly after breakfast, Patrick suggested Cassie and Lorelei go for a walk. Cassie sent him a patiently beseeching look, whereas Lorelei simply sighed in exhausted submission, but there was no getting around it, especially as neither Cassie nor Lorelei was determined to be stubborn about it.

"I'll take Aidan. Get him some fresh air while the sun is out," Cassie said. "That way you can focus on the girls."

Patrick agreed with this, and in no time, Cassie and Lorelei were marching along through the fields that rolled out to the ocean. They were above the bay, which offered a spectacular view and a little too much wind, but it was tolerable, and if Aidan, tucked safely in Cassie's shawl, noticed, he said nothing—simply napped contentedly in his mother's arms.

At least Patrick and Cassie had a good baby. That must be nice. Maybe Lorelei would have a good baby, too, though she rather doubted it.

"Patrick said I should talk to you about marriage," Cassie said, "but I don't have to talk to you about anything. Not if you don't want to."

Lorelei tossed her hand carelessly. "It's all right, Cassie. Go ahead."

"I don't know what to say. I'm not long married, Lorelei, and besides, I can't say I'm the best at being married. Other women are surely less stubborn and more patient. Patrick and I have fought. We have been selfish. We have deliberately stepped outside our roles, we have pushed each other to the brink of insanity, and we have spoken harsh words. But that's a part of being human. We're learning to love each other better; Patrick is learning not to overreact when we fight, whereas I am learning to not draw into myself and pretend it never happened. But even if it's imperfect, having him in my life is such a gift from God. For every mistake, there are many beautiful things that give us the strength to push through and give ourselves over to God." Here, she paused and glanced at Lorelei. "You must keep God at the center of your marriage. If He's not at the crux of all you say and do to each other and every step you make, well, I don't know how couples survive without that ... that spiritual backbone."

"Right."

"Patrick said that perhaps you didn't understand the difference between lust and desire, too. Should I talk about that, or will you be embarrassed?"

"If you don't relate it to anything to do with Patrick, I will not be embarrassed."

Cassie chuckled. "I think I can safely avoid that. I ... I don't know why he couldn't say this to you." She shook her head. "He's funny, isn't he?"

"I think our conversation had already taken far too many turns he was not expecting," Lorelei mumbled wryly. "He was not eager to continue said problem."

"Lust is simply selfish, perverted desire. But you know that, don't you? It removes the couple and God's will for the couple, but that doesn't mean desiring your spouse is wrong. Have you ever read Song of Solomon? It's blushworthy, but it shows you a simple truth: you cannot parcel out any one aspect of marriage and leave the rest unaffected. It doesn't work that way. Every aspect of the marital relationship bleeds together—and that's good. It's incredible, actually, like magic. But it means, as much as desire is important, that when passion fades, love carries you through. Does that make sense?"

Lorelei shrugged. She was fairly sure her cheeks were red, which was such an unusual situation for her to find herself in that she didn't even want to talk.

"Do you truly believe that what Aubrey offers you—the understanding, the comfort, the care that even I can see so plainly in the few interactions

I've viewed—doesn't hold a degree of love, whether he intended it to or not? I don't know how you view it, and I certainly don't know what happens behind closed doors, but I'd say he loves you. Or he treats you in a loving way, which is what matters." Cassie paused and gestured down the path a ways to a log, a fallen tree offering them a seat that looked out over the sea. "Let's sit."

Lorelei sat when they reached the impromptu bench. "He did tell me he loved me."

Cassie transferred Aidan to her other arm. "You don't believe him?"

"No, I do. But I don't love him, at least not ..." Not enough. Not in the way a woman ought to, probably. She wasn't even sure she could—or should. There was too much of her mother's blood in her. "He wasn't supposed to love me."

"Yet how could he not?"

Lorelei chuckled sardonically. "I am not so loveable as all that."

"No, but you're married." Cassie's free hand reached out and took one of Lorelei's. "In doing the right thing, he showed you love. Is it so strange that his heart would follow? Perhaps if you were to try—"

"I can't." Lorelei shook her head, swallowing frantically around the sudden lump in her throat. "I can't."

"Why not?"

"Because ... nothing is going well." Nothing at all.

Cassie drew back slightly, nodded. "Patrick mentioned that you were disappointed that the child is coming along so quickly. But that can be good, too. I mean, we loved having Aidan so early on. I wouldn't trade him for the world. I promise, once you hold your baby, everything will change. I wanted Aidan, but I had no idea of the depth of feeling I was capable of until he arrived—and I was also unprepared and terrified. These have been some of the hardest months of my life, but they've also been so good. I love him more than I thought possible, but there are things I wasn't expecting, things that have made it a challenge to be Aidan's mother. I think it's the same for all women."

Lorelei shook her head empathically. "All women but my mother. All women but *me*."

"But you won't be like your mother, Lorelei! You're nothing like her. Why—"

"I can't do this, Cassie." Lorelei dropped her face into her hands. "I *can't* do this. Don't talk to me as if I will when you must know I will not. I am going to abandon *It* to a nanny. Aubrey will raise *It*. I will do what I can to make *It* happy, but that is the most I can do. I cannot ... I *will* not take an active part in destroying the life of another human being."

Cassie stared out over the water and patted Aidan's back and hummed softly in a soothing way—and as Lorelei's breath slowed to a reasonable rate, Cassie spoke. "I want you to know that for the first few weeks, I was overwhelmed by anger and fear every time I looked at this little fellow. The first few weeks, I cried every day. He made me think of my childhood. I'm angry and disappointed that my mother never loved me as I love my own child. Then when I went to see my sister and saw her happy, healthy children and observed how different she is as a mother, I was ... You don't move on from the childhood our parents gave us overnight, darling. You don't forget, or your heart doesn't. You carry it with you. But that doesn't mean you will be a bad mother yourself. In fact, I think ... I think you need this baby."

Lorelei scoffed. "Like I need a shot in the head."

Cassie smiled. "I think raising a child is one of the most healing things some women can do. Especially one who has experienced mistreatment from a parent. It can crush some, but I don't think you will let it crush you. I think it feels like being torn apart ... but it's not Aidan who was making me cry, and it's not the baby that has you so terrified. It's all right to have these feelings and to struggle with them and to not be perfect. Goodness, we'll never be perfect! But we can still give whatever we have left to our children—and know that God will make it enough. We can choose to heal and to grieve and to still strive to improve, to make the most of every day we are given. We can choose to let God work in us and through us, especially in our brokenness."

Lorelei stiffened. "I am not broken. I haven't let them break me—I haven't."

Cassie shifted Aidan to her lap and adjusted the blanket around him despite his flailing arms. "We're all a little broken. That's sin. But that's good because then God has room to work. Oh, Lorelei, when you hold your baby for the first time, all you've suffered will be worth it. You'll see! You'll love 'It,' as you put it, so much. It's a heady, incredible, intense, awful, wonderful, terrifying feeling. It's not even like what I feel for Patrick—or what you feel for Aubrey."

"Again, Aubrey and I have—"

"I know, an agreement." Cassie sounded less than convinced, which irritated Lorelei. "It's why he can't keep his eyes or hands off you in a way he never acted with me—why he hangs on your every word—why he follows you around like a lost puppy."

"I don't do any of that," Lorelei pointed out.

"You're less demonstrative, true. But you show it in little ways, I think." She rolled her eyes. "Aubrey, demonstrative?"

"More than you, when it comes to his wife. He was not so with me, and he isn't with his sisters."

"Right." Yet there was a part of her that doubted even that. Cassie seemed to be seeing what she wanted to see. "I understand your point."

"If nothing else, have the baby for him."

"I'm going to have the baby."

Cassie was quiet for a long moment, then she nodded. "I know that, but I wonder if you wouldn't consider taking better care of yourself. Eat more. Rest. Don't be out of the house from dawn until dusk. That's what Francesca and Constance say your life has consisted of lately—and I don't doubt you intend to return to the same as soon as we're gone, even if you risk injuring yourself by doing so. Please, think of the baby. I know you don't want 'It,' but I know you wish him or her no ill will. You don't have it in you."

"I'll do what I can," she said and rose. "We ought to head back."

"All right," Cassie agreed. "If I talk about pregnancy and childbirth on the way back, will you be mad?"

With a sigh, Lorelei resigned herself to this. Besides, it might be nice to know a little more than she did, if this was going to happen whether she wanted it to or not. She was reluctantly given a stomach-wrenching education.

CHAPTER TWENTY

T HE PARLOR OF THE estate was bathed in the warm glow of candlelight, casting eerie shadows on the ornately patterned wallpaper. Lorelei leaned back on her armchair and watched the gathering unfold, but she was disinterested in participating.

After all, she was so tired these days, and she didn't feel like she fit in anymore in this happy, carefree group. Patrick was in rare form—he was in such good spirits that she almost didn't know him—and Winnie was egged on by his merriment.

Patrick sat cross-legged on the plush rug, Winnie giggling beside him, with Francesca and Constance across from them, also seated, though perhaps with a touch more decorum.

"Let's play proverbs and phrases," Patrick suggested, grinning as the girls exchanged glances. "Come on, it's fun. We played it with Cassie's family last month—or I did; Cassie was a stick-in-the-mud—and I was fantastic at it."

Winnie clapped her hands. "Yes! Though I'll beat you at it, Trick; you know I will."

Lorelei rolled her eyes. Winnie always thought she was good at parlor games, but in truth, Patrick had been prone to letting her win in the past. Lorelei hoped that would no longer be the case.

From a nearby sofa, with Aidan cradled in her arms, Cassie laughed.

"Patrick, you know very well I don't have any interest in playing when you were all being so wildly competitive. Anyway, you and Freddy made a good team. But I will say, girls, that he lost every time."

"Cassie's sister and her husband cheat," Patrick said, his tone full of casual disdain.

Lorelei hid her grin. That sounded like Patrick—playing hard and still failing to win. He might be competitive, but he always held back at the last, his killer drive never quite what it should be.

"They don't cheat; they know each other well," Cassie protested. "What about you and Freddy? Mouthing the words to each other." She shook her head in disapproval, but she was smiling.

"We were not! If you wanted to prove to us how it could be done, perhaps you could have played it." Patrick patted the rug beside him. "Come on over and prove your mettle, Mrs. Hilton."

"Nonsense, I don't play with cheaters. I never liked playing with my sister and her husband; Catie and Stuart do seem to know how to read each other's mind." She adjusted her son in her arms so the half-asleep baby could see the proceedings. "Aidan and I will watch."

Patrick rolled his eyes and turned back to the girls. "All right, are we ready?"

The girls nodded.

Patrick's fingers were already tracing invisible words in the air. "Very well, I'll start. We won't play on teams. It's like charades, only every term is a proverb or a phrase. A cliché, if you will. Same rules—no *mouthing*, certainly. Ahem."

Clearing his throat dramatically, Patrick began to mime out a series of actions, his movements exaggerated and animated. Winnie and the other girls watched intently, exchanging whispered guesses.

Which, from Lorelei's angle, were indecipherable indeed. Patrick was enthusiastic at charades but bad at it, and this was no different.

"Um, is it ... 'A rolling stone gathers no moss'?" Francesca ventured, her brow furrowed in concentration.

Patrick shook his head. "Not quite, Francesca. Try again."

"Not supposed to speak, even to confirm," Cassie murmured to Lorelei. Lorelei snorted and nodded in agreement.

Constance raised her hand eagerly. "Ooh, I think I know! Is it 'Actions speak louder than words'?"

Delighted, Winnie clapped her hands. "Yes, that's got to be it, Connie!"

Patrick chuckled. "Well done, Constance! That's right. Your turn next. We'll go around the circle and then divide into teams." He paused and glanced over his shoulder. "Lore, join us."

"No, that's fine. I'll watch. You know I hate this kind of thing." Parlor games inevitably made the player appear ridiculous, and Lorelei hated to appear ridiculous. "You go on and have fun. I'm tired anyway."

Patrick's expression softened with understanding, though a hint of disappointment flickered across his features. "Rest, then."

Lorelei watched her brother and the others with a pang of guilt tugging at her heart. She ought to make an effort for Patrick's sake, since he would not be here much longer, but the fatigue and nausea made it difficult to summon the energy.

She couldn't shake the feeling that she was letting him down—that she was always letting him down these days, that she was not what he would have expected of a member of the Hilton family. She wasn't sure she could bear that, much as she claimed complete independence. She wanted Patrick's approval again. It had always been so readily available to her; it was the only consistent thing she'd ever had in her childhood.

She rose from her seat and came to rest next to Patrick.

He glanced at her, smiled, and nudged her. "Playing after all?"

"Yes." She paused, then scowled at him. "Don't comment on it."

He held up his hands. "I wasn't about to. I think we've all got the hang of it; why don't we say Lore and I on one team, you three on another?"

Winnie narrowed her eyes. "So you'll win?"

"That is the point of a competition, rather," Lorelei said drolly. "Let's start."

The game was indeed won by Patrick and Lorelei, the winning point being for "The early bird catches the worm."

Flushed with pride, she rose. Winnie wanted another round, but Lorelei wasn't about to lose her winning streak, such as it was.

"Lore, why don't you come sit with me while I put Aidan to bed?" Cassie stood, the baby still in her arms. "He likes to be held for a long time, but from what I've found, he doesn't mind any amount of sound, so we can chat. I don't like to be alone if I can have company."

"Cassie's always taking him over to Caroline Webster's house—or wherever she ends up—so I think he's gotten used to napping wherever he is," Patrick observed, a trace of amusement in his voice. "Go, why don't you, Lore? I'll stay here and play another round. Winnie, will you be on my team?"

Winnie eagerly consented, and Cassie gestured for Lorelei to follow her—which she did, reluctantly.

What does she want from me now?

After having struggled her way through the too-long conversation about pregnancy and childbirth, Lorelei found herself wary of future conversations with her sister-in-law. However, like it or not, she admired Cassie—perhaps even wished, in some ways, that she could be more like her. More ... womanly, if that was even the quality Lorelei saw in her sister-in-law.

There was something missing in Lorelei, certainly. Something broken and little, something she had to either embrace by stuffing down what should be her natural instincts or hide behind gaiety.

Nevertheless, Lorelei sat opposite her sister-in-law in the dark, firelit room as she clucked and hummed to her baby. As Aidan settled, Cassie began asking Lorelei questions—casual ones like "What do you do all day?" and "Have you read anything interesting lately?" The sort of questions meant to loosen her tethers, perhaps.

Only, I'm too far gone now to be loosened.

"Lorelei." Cassie's soft voice broke through Lorelei's ruminations. "What about God?"

"What about Him?" Lorelei replied in a light tone that she immediately regretted. Even if she wasn't the most reverent person on earth, she understood that some lines ought not to be crossed—and doing or saying anything to offend the Creator of the world was a step too far even for her.

"Hmm," was all Cassie said, more for her infant than to respond to her sister-in-law's sauce, but somehow, Lorelei still felt it in her soul. Cassie's disapproval crushed her in a way that Patrick's didn't—or in a different way.

After a long silence, Cassie spoke again. "You profess to be a Christian, don't you, Lore?"

"I do." Lorelei had been raised Christian. She knew all the tenets of the faith. She'd been taught to repeat back verses and concepts, and she'd believed them to be true. She still did. But ... "I don't know if I'm a good Christian."

"That misses the point, doesn't it?" Cassie smiled. "To be a good Christian is an oxymoron, much as is being a good person. We come to Christ in our failures, and He loves us and redeems us even so. His power is made perfect in our weakness."

Lorelei looked away to the fire flickering in the grate as she mumbled, "'Therefore I take pleasure in infirmities, in reproaches, in necessities, in persecutions, in distresses for Christ's sake: for when I am weak, then am I strong.'"

"Exactly," Cassie replied. The smile was still in her voice, though Lorelei didn't look to her. "We must trust the Lord most in the places where we are weakest or where we suffer the most. It seems backward, I know—but we must overcome our self-reliance and submit to Him. It feels dangerous at first, like flinging ourselves into the air without hope of being caught, but He is always a step before us, cleansing us of our sins and giving us His Spirit. He only wants your heart."

Lorelei laughed at that. "I've never understood that concept. I mean, I do from a ... a theoretical standpoint. The heart is desperately wicked; He died on the cross for that sin; He cleanses us and makes us whole. It's nice, but sometimes even so ..."

Then she stopped, for she didn't want to say that. That no one—not even God—wanted her heart. Not if the whole story was known, from the depths of her own selfishness to the battering she'd received over the years to the way she'd hardened herself in response.

Cassie rocked her baby and clucked her tongue. Perhaps she had known what Lorelei meant—that her heart was not worth claiming.

"I wonder if what you need is to understand the true nature of God a little better." Cassie rose and walked to a basketlike thing in the corner, where she set the baby. For a moment, she stood, smoothing a blanket or whatever she was doing, before turning back to Lorelei. "Let's go into the next room—it's Winnie's, I think, but she won't be up for hours."

Lorelei rose and followed Cassie. A fire had been lit in Winnie's chamber, but other than that, it was clear the servants couldn't keep up with her sister, for clothes were strewn about everywhere, along with a book or two and some other personal effects.

They sat on the bed, which had been made at some point during the day.

"This feels a little like being girls again," Cassie commented. "I remember sitting up late into the night with a friend, chatting about this and that."

"But we are neither of us girls anymore," Lorelei said solemnly.

"Mm." A trace of a smile slid about Cassie's lips, then she shook her head. "No, you are right. We are not. But that doesn't mean we don't need Christian women in our lives to sit on a bed with us and talk about whatever comes to mind. In fact, that's what we need most—companionship, encouragement. A reminder of how much God loves us, perhaps. You know the verses. 'For I am persuaded, that neither death, nor life, nor angels, nor principalities, nor powers, nor things present, nor things to come, nor height, nor depth, nor any other creature, shall be able to separate us from the love of God, which is in Christ Jesus our Lord.' It's a love we can trust and abide in, and it's not a love that leaves us where we are; it's a love that changes us."

Lorelei drew her knees to her chest. Though she refused to drop her face forward, to allow herself to surrender in such a complete way, she could feel the slump in her shoulders and knew the churning in her stomach was not from *It* but rather from the effect those words had on her soul. "I ..." She cleared her throat when a tightening made that single word sound pitiful. "I know I should be changed, but I am not. I don't know what it looks like to surrender myself."

Cassie nodded. "It's an ongoing journey, certainly, but we Christians can be assured that Christ is strong enough to carry us, if we allow Him to. From 2 Corinthians 13:5, we have 'Examine yourselves, whether ye be in the faith; prove your own selves. Know ye not your own selves, how that Jesus Christ is in you, except ye be reprobates?' But it cannot be done without a surrender, as you well know. 'I am crucified with Christ: nevertheless I live; yet not I, but Christ liveth in me: and the life which I now live in the flesh I live by the faith of the Son of God, who loved me, and gave himself for me.'"

"'I do not frustrate the grace of God: for if righteousness come by the law, then Christ is dead in vain,'" Lorelei mumbled. Yes, she knew the verses—the theology—the tradition. She desired that forgiveness that was offered, and she'd thought she'd become a Christian years ago, as a child.

But somehow, there was something wrong with her. She hadn't allowed Christ to change her. She was not as good as other Christians.

Honestly, she wasn't even sure what *Lorelei, the Dedicated Christian* would look like.

As if anticipating this thought somehow, Cassie's voice broke through her thoughts. "If you could let go of yourself, of even your concept of who you are, and embrace God and *His* concept of who you are, you'd be better off. I had no idea who I was, let alone what I was supposed to be doing, until I submitted myself to God and let Him make the decisions. Then the self God created emerges—and I know the Lorelei God created is a wondrous creature." Cassie reached over and took her sister-in-law's hand. "Oh, not that I don't love you now. Of course I do; Patrick and I both do. But we're going to love you no matter what."

"A lovely sentiment." Lorelei shifted on the bed and then made a big show of yawning. "I ought to be getting off to bed. I am so weary—even you said that was normal, Cass."

Cassie nodded. "I won't keep you, then. But can I pray for you before you go?"

Lorelei couldn't stop that, and in truth, she didn't want to. She needed all the prayers she could get. "I would like that."

As if on cue, there was a rap at the door, and Patrick poked his head in. "There you are."

Cassie leaned back against the bedpost. "Where are the girls?"

He grinned, perhaps too jauntily for a man who had never won a game of anything without a sister or two assisting him. "All scattered in defeat. Winnie is searching for Potato who has somehow disappeared, I believe the Montgomery girls have gone to bed, and I think your Mr. Montgomery has gone to bed, too, Lore."

She didn't protest "your Mr. Montgomery." She was truly too tired to fight it.

"We were about to pray," Cassie said, making a half-hearted shooing motion. "Then I'll come join you."

"I could stay," Patrick said, though it was more of a question than a statement. "I could pray, too."

Cassie's soft chuckle answered almost before he finished speaking. "I am aware you're capable of prayer, darling, but perhaps it's better—"

"No, let him stay," Lorelei said. "I don't mind him hearing what we've spoken of, and I assume that's why you're requesting privacy."

Patrick would hear it one way or another anyway. He might as well know the extent of her shame.

Patrick crossed the room and perched awkwardly on the edge of the bed, but he relaxed when Cassie put a hand on his arm. He took her hand. "I'll start, if that's all right."

Cassie nodded and bowed her head, and and Lorelei imitated her despite the fact that surely Patrick understood less of what she was experiencing than Cassie did. Lorelei hesitated when Patrick's hand extended to her, too, but then she took it. Her own foolishness, her own grief, her own confusion shouldn't affect him. It was unfair to treat Patrick differently because there was something wrong with *her*.

"Dear God," Patrick said in the soft but even voice he always used when praying, "thank You for this time we've had with the Montgomerys—and particularly, with my sisters—after such a long separation. It is only through Your mercy that we can hope for redemptions in any of the sin-soaked situations we find ourselves in. I pray for both of my sisters, but especially my Lore, that she would grow close to You, that You would give her healing and peace, that You would help her walk the path You've laid out for her, whatever that may look like. Give her the strength to follow You even if You lead her in directions she was not expecting—and would not have chosen for herself. Your ways are best, even if they do not seem to be at first." He paused. "We all know that sometimes the most unexpected blessings are the ones most worth embracing, but that doesn't make it easy, especially when our own expectations can cause us so much grief—can even blind us to what is right in front of our faces."

The pause was longer this time, as he seemed to consider his next words. Perhaps it was that his natural instinct was to push in harder, to give Lorelei the scolding she probably deserved. But he didn't. He cleared his throat and continued.

"Please help Lore embrace the holiness of marriage and grow her relationship with Aubrey Montgomery in whatever ways it needs to be grown. Help her know when sacrifices should be made—and when she must stand firm. Most of all, help her know You. Your love, Your hope, Your grace, Your healing. In Jesus's name, I pray, amen."

They sat in silence, and Lorelei was not sure if Cassie intended to pray, too, or if they were done—and she could leave. She wanted to leave, for she was crying, and it seemed unfair that Patrick should see her in another moment of vulnerability.

Then she was enfolded in a tight hug, and Patrick was rubbing her back.

"I'm sorry," she panted out, burying her face in the rough fabric of his waistcoat. Her throat was tight, her chest heaving. She hated this feeling, but it couldn't be helped. "I'm sorry. I'm sorry."

"You have nothing to be sorry for, you hear me?" Patrick said. There was a fierce edge to his voice Lorelei had never heard before. "Nothing at all. Not to me. I'm proud of you, all right, Lore? I'm proud of you, and

I love you. I know you are going to find your way in life, and God loves you more than I or anyone else ever has, and He has a plan for you. He doesn't promise immediate healing, but His ways are best. He's not going to take our pain and suffering away—not every time—but He will sustain us through it."

Lorelei nodded, because what else could she do other than work on calming her breathing? She badly wanted to believe what Patrick said, but her flailing mind couldn't process anything but a need to breathe. So she breathed until he let her go, and she went back to her room and lay in her husband's arms and dueled with insomnia until sickness woke her early in the morning.

And she wondered why a God Who loved her would persist in punishing her.

And she knew that she deserved every moment of that punishment.

CHAPTER TWENTY-ONE

C ASSIE AND PATRICK LEFT after only one short week at Montgomery Place, needing to get home to Philadelphia before the worst of the winter weather set in.

Though they'd not been there long, Lorelei missed them. It eliminated the distraction and meant she must begin to move forward with living her life—even if her life was not exactly as she would like it to be.

Today, she woke up sicker than what had become her new normal, which was bizarre, given that she was supposed to be past the point of illness. Even Dr. Burton had said Lorelei should start to feel stronger now. Added to concealing her illness from the men at the docks—though she was fairly sure Mr. Hastings had caught on and simply said nothing—she was forced to wear loose coats or a shawl at all times to hide the slight swelling that had appeared in the last week or so, a testament to the fact that, whether she liked this or not, it was real.

Poor It, *with such an awful mother.* If only she could transfer the baby over to someone more caring, more loving, who would take good care of *It*, provide *It* with the love and care *It* needed.

But no, Aubrey would have to do—and his sisters and hers—if *It* was to have affection. Lorelei didn't know how. She struggled to talk to near grown children; how could she become acquainted with a baby? Such was madness—impossible madness. Lorelei was many things, but she hoped "mad" was not one of them.

After dragging herself out of bed, through a bit of breakfast (which she did not hold on to for long), and then back to bed for half an hour to hopefully sleep it off (she did not), she finally dressed and took the carriage down to the docks.

She felt weak. Her hands were shaking, and her head had that odd "full but also light" feeling that she disliked greatly. She'd stayed home most of the day yesterday, though she'd read a great deal, and another day absent from the company she was trying, albeit unsuccessfully, to run could not be tolerated.

The builders were working on a new headquarters, but for now, she hurried from the carriage into her tiny office in the warehouse. She sidestepped piles of building materials and tables full of plans to the cold, dark back room, where she lit a lamp and stripped off her gloves.

For a moment, she braced herself against the desk and caught her breath. That was another problem—she struggled to breathe now, her chest never expanding fast enough to take in the oxygen she needed. Lightheaded, she sank onto her seat and dropped her face into her hands.

"Mrs. Montgomery?"

At Mr. Hastings's voice, she jerked to her feet—a mistake, as a wave of dizziness assaulted her, and she was forced to sink back where she'd been before. "Mr. Hastings," she said through gritted teeth. She had nothing in her stomach, but she felt like retching still. A maddening position to be in.

I think I'm going to die, she noted to herself as she met her employee's eyes across the small desk.

"Mrs. Montgomery, are you well?" There was genuine concern in the stoic man's eyes, and that only served to make Lorelei feel sicker. After all, it must be obvious if even those who had seemed so determined to ignore that something was wrong—which it wasn't exactly, but that was beside the point—had noted it. "You seem ... ill."

She was, but she shook her head. "I'm fine. What is it, Hastings?"

He came to stand in front of her desk and launched into some little speech about the progress that had been made on building. He must now go to London and ... do something. She only half heard him, as her head was now throbbing in an alarming way, and keeping herself from sinking to the floor was about all she could focus on, seat or no seat.

He paused. "Mrs. Montgomery?" His words sounded echoey, bouncing about the corners of her mind and telling her that something was wrong. "Mrs. Montgomery?"

Was his voice even fuzzier than last time? Could a voice be fuzzy? She wasn't sure. Suddenly, he wasn't where she'd last seen him—he was around the desk, with his hand on her arm as if supporting her, which was when she realized she'd started to slip off the seat.

He lowered her to the floor and said her name again, but she didn't reply because first, she wasn't sure what to say, and second, she wasn't sure she was understanding properly because there was this odd ringing sound and around her vision, black circles that closed in, getting dangerously closer and closer to consuming her ... then there was nothing. Nothing at all.

Aubrey paced up and down in the hallway outside the master chambers, sweat dampening his brow, his hands shaking. He'd never felt more wretched, more concerned. A long line of what-ifs ran through his head.

What if I lose her? What if we lose the baby? What if she hates me for bringing this on her?

Aubrey knew he'd only been married to her for a few months, but he felt as if she were as necessary as breathing. He'd told her weeks ago that he loved her—and though she'd not returned the favor, he hadn't expected her to.

He'd expected to be allowed a lot more time to love her.

Suddenly it felt like there was more left unsaid than he had believed.

Oh, he wasn't sure what exactly, only that he would need a lifetime to say everything he wanted to say to her.

Plus, there was so much unfinished business between them.

Perhaps he was being melodramatic. That was within the realm of possibility. In truth, he'd never felt so strongly about anyone or anything as he did about Lorelei Hilton Montgomery, and he wasn't sure what to do about it—but he knew he could certainly not live without her.

But even if he hadn't felt that way about Lorelei, even if he weren't worried about her because he cared about her, she was his wife, and he didn't think anyone could blame him for being concerned about his wife. It was disconcerting at the least to have the woman one had pledged one's life to brought back home unconscious, to have a doctor examining her, to fear that her collapse at her office meant she was seriously ill. That was reasonable, even if one didn't have tender feelings for said wife.

Which he did, but with Lorelei's general antagonism toward his feelings for her—if she took the time to think about them at all—he felt a need to justify his own worry.

He stopped, placed a hand against the wall, and ducked his head. "Lord," he murmured, "keep her safe. Please don't take her or the child from me. Let this be a passing thing."

The door opened, and Dr. Burton stepped out and closed it behind him. He looked solemn. "Mr. Montgomery."

"How is she?" Aubrey would've been embarrassed in the past to be so eager, but he couldn't help it in this case. He was eager. He wanted to know that she was all right, even if it meant showing a depth of feeling he generally wouldn't publicly display.

"Mrs. Montgomery seems to be recovering. She woke up for a few minutes and seemed to recall what had happened; she's resting now, with my wife tending to her. This is not to say I'm not concerned, Mr. Montgomery, but the immediate danger seems past."

Aubrey swallowed. Thank God for that. "The child?"

"It's hard to tell at this stage. There was ..." The doctor hesitated as if unsure how to proceed. "She has lost some blood—not much. She says she doesn't have any pain, which is a good sign. This early on, it could mean nothing ... but it could also mean she is miscarrying. She is at a stage where she might begin to feel the child move—but she says she has not, not discernibly, and I am worried about that."

"I see." So they might lose the child. Aubrey pressed his lips together. That seemed so unfair, that God might take that little life so early on, yet in some ways, it was probably exactly what Lorelei would wish for if she could get out of it unharmed. That bitter thought had him raising his eyes to the doctor. "Will she survive it, if there is ... is a miscarriage?"

"In all likelihood. At this stage, there are more risks. It's not as simple. There's also some risk if ... It's too early to discuss that. I am by no means saying that it is certain that she'll lose the child. There is still hope. Some bleeding at this stage is not altogether unusual, and a woman's first child will often take some time to make itself known, so the lack of movement is not alarming." Dr. Burton shook his head. "She is an unusual patient, though."

Aubrey sighed. He already knew he was about to be told something ridiculous. "What did she say?"

"She said that you must know she didn't do this on purpose. She said I should tell you as soon as I see you."

Aubrey nodded. He had known that. Even Lorelei wouldn't do anything to purposefully cause a child harm. She might refer to their baby as "It" and insist upon the term "pregnancy" rather than the more proper, more humanizing "with child"—despite the fact that he ignored her wishes. But she had said she would give him this child—and she would if it lay within her power.

"What is the next step?" he asked. "What can we do for her?"

"Bed rest, I should think. At least for a few weeks."

She wouldn't like that. "I see."

"I will also write up a list for your cook—she needs more nurturing foods than she has been getting, at least according to her maid. My wife will also have recommendations." The doctor might have rolled his eyes, but he couldn't be sure. "She always does, when it comes to such things."

"I see. Thank you. Should I go see her?" He wanted to, if only to sit at her bedside. He was anxious to hear her talk, to learn if she was upset or if she was taking this in her stride, and he wanted to know how she felt, for Aubrey believed Lorelei capable of lying—especially to a doctor—to get her way.

She must know that bed rest would be recommended. In her mind, it might be in her best interests to lower the chances of an extended stay in bed. However, Aubrey was going to make sure she stayed put. Even if she didn't realize it, her own health was at risk, alongside their child's. He would never forgive himself if something happened to either of them that could possibly have been avoided through better care.

"If you don't disturb her. I think my wife would like to stay on hand until she wakes up again, to give instructions, but I'll collect my things and return for her in the evening, if that is acceptable. She does mean well."

Aubrey tried not to raise his eyebrows at this phrasing. Instead, he simply nodded and thanked the doctor.

Soon, he found himself seated beside Lorelei's bed, watching her restless sleep—which could be due to it being the middle of the day, but she wasn't waking yet. She could probably use the rest. There were dark circles under her eyes, and she seemed too pale.

I should have stopped her from going down to the docks weeks ago. But it seemed unfair to restrain an adult woman from doing what she wanted, especially given their agreement. It felt like breaking a promise, and Aubrey hated to break promises.

But on this, he must hold firm. He knew he couldn't control her life or death—that was in God's hands, whether Aubrey liked it or not—but he could insist she take necessary precautions. Though he doubted Lorelei was keen on collapsing in her office a second time. Even she had her limits, and doubtless she'd internalized some nonsense about seeming weak in front of "her men," as she called them. If only she could have a little more grace for herself, but that seemed almost too much to ask.

For now, that would have to wait. His biggest priority was seeing her awake and alert. As he sat there, Mrs. Burton—a somewhat curvy woman who spoke with the barest trace of a French accent, to his surprise, though he didn't dare question it for fear of being seen as impolite—knitted in the corner. She'd spoken a few words to him, more comforting by far than her husband's, and certainly warmer, but otherwise kept to herself.

Perhaps she realized how on edge he was. She must, as a doctor's wife, see many anxious or grieving people, and he was grateful for her silence. He wasn't even sure he'd been coherent when speaking to the doctor, though he'd tried his best to control himself. After all, Lorelei was at risk—and it was as if that thought had consumed all others.

Lorelei woke again slowly, her body and especially her head feeling so dreadfully heavy. She heard Aubrey say her name, and this obligated her to respond in some manner.

"What time is it?" she asked without opening her eyes.

"About two o'clock."

"In the afternoon?"

"Yes."

Ah, she hadn't slept as long as she thought. She opened her eyes to see the dim room, as lights had been lowered and it was a cloudy, near snowy day. The fire in the grate provided a flickering, inconsistent glow that cast shadows on her husband's face.

My, he looks worried.

"Good afternoon, then," she mumbled. "How long have you been sitting there watching me sleep?"

He shifted slightly, as he always did when he was contemplating telling a half-truth. He did not, based on his relaxed expression; he was not a good liar. "A few hours. Since the doctor left."

"Ah." Her eyes swiftly swept the room. There was Mrs. Burton in the corner, knitting on some project. She was French—or had been before she married Dr. Burton and moved here—and lively, which Lorelei had been amused by yet had little patience for at the moment.

"How do you feel?" Aubrey asked, taking her hand.

She withdrew it. Now was not the time for affection—not any more than any other time, and she did not wish to show obvious regard for him in front of Mrs. Burton. After all, that was misrepresenting herself, surely. "I feel fine. I think the doctor was overreacting—" She glanced at the doctor's wife. "No offense to your husband, Mrs. Burton, but I don't believe most men know what they're talking about. You can't expect me to view him as an exception."

Mrs. Burton nodded and said, "I agree with you. I do not view him as the exception either."

Lorelei heard Aubrey sigh beside her. "So you think he was overreacting?"

"I think a lot of women become ill while they are pregnant without becoming wilting flowers. I do not think it is without danger, but neither is your child cancerous." Mrs. Burton rose and put her knitting in a bag that rested beside the chair she had occupied. "There are things to make this easier for you, though. I believe every woman should know what she can do to help her body."

Lorelei grinned and cocked her head. "Oh, do you?"

Sincerity clear in Mrs. Burton's brown eyes, she nodded. "*Oui.*"

"Hmm." Lorelei glanced sideways at Aubrey, who looked more frustrated than anything—but that was often the case. "I remember those potions you gave me earlier." She gestured toward the bedside table. "I didn't use them. Is that what you mean?"

"Naturally! But you must also eat and sleep and get fresh air. Even my husband would agree with that. I sent him to you with herbs to be placed in the bath; that will help with your headaches and promote relaxation." She stepped over to the bedside, wiggled around Aubrey—who started back, much to Lorelei's amusement—and withdrew the bag and the bottle.

"The tonic is to be taken in the morning to help you feel less ill."

"I see." Perhaps it was worth trying. "You won't convince me to do everything, but within reason, I will hear you out."

Mrs. Burton inclined her head. "That is the most I can expect from a near stranger. Though we can become friends, if you will call me Aimée. That is my name."

That seemed perfectly reasonable. "Then you will call me Lorelei." That settled, she turned toward Aubrey. "Have you spoken to my sister?"

"Briefly. Just to tell her that we didn't know much and you are all right."

Lorelei grinned. "Oh, she'll have been suffering all day. Excellent. You should put her out of her misery—run along and tell her, why don't you?"

Aubrey hesitated, then nodded.

As soon as he was gone, Aimée turned to her with slightly raised eyebrows. "Did you want him gone?" Her playful tone made Lorelei smile.

"My sister can let herself become a bit of a tortured soul if left to her own devices. I'm sure she was already mourning my loss and considering how long she can manage to turn wearing black into her personality." She picked at the comforter with a forefinger. She had also wanted Aubrey out of the room so she could ask a few relevant questions. "May I have some water? How long have you been married?"

"Of course, to the first question—and about two years, to the second question." Aimée crossed the room and picked up a pitcher from the side table. The doctor had given her a glass before, but already Lorelei's mouth was dry again. Something about sleeping in the middle of the day seemed to do that to her.

"I suppose you have followed your husband about some, assisted him with cases such as mine."

Aimée nodded and handed Lorelei a glass of water. "Yes. I like to go where I can with my husband. I am interested in babies. I have one of my own."

Lorelei contemplated this as she sipped at her water. That was a surprise. Aimée didn't appear much of the motherly type. Oh, she had the figure for it, Lorelei supposed, in all the ways Lorelei noticeably didn't, but "motherly types," to Lorelei, were overly tender and serious. Aimée was neither. "What is it?"

"A girl. Louise is with her nanny today, though. She says three words now—all French. You would find her charming. Everyone does." Aimée sat on the edge of the bed and folded her hands neatly on her lap. "Why do you ask about my life? I do not mind, you understand, but I can understand people easily—it is my talent. It's hard to believe you care."

Smart of her to see that. "It was polite to ask about your child, but no, I'm not particularly interested. I do not like children, though I'm sure yours is sweet. Let me ask you a more relevant question. When you see situations like mine, where there has been a little bleeding that stopped quickly and no pain, does the pregnancy usually continue? What are the chances?"

It should have been an easy out, to miscarry and no longer be pregnant at no fault of her own, but Lorelei found herself holding her breath. She wanted *It* to be fine, to be still growing and thriving. Besides, there would be a little body, no matter how miniscule, and as much as Lorelei wasn't particularly looking forward to any aspect of motherhood, she especially did not want to be a grieving mother. If she was going to have a baby, it had better be a living, healthy, breathing baby—not a helpless little fellow that wouldn't even get a proper Christian burial.

She wondered if they'd be able to tell if *It* were male or female, or was it too soon, leaving them without even the attachment of a set identity to mourn?

Oh, but she wouldn't mourn, surely ...

Something tells me I would.

She ignored that thought, instead listening to Aimée tell her that it was likely the baby was still alive, but caution was necessary.

"The bleeding is inconsequential, and as for the baby needing to move, my husband is correct that some women will experience the quickening at this point—but it is early. In two or three weeks, it would be more alarming. It may have happened now, and you may not have noticed." Aimée nodded her head toward Lorelei's stomach area. "It is like the fluttering of butterfly wings, perhaps, or a bubble popping at the start. It cannot be felt from the outside, so it is your secret to hold. But you will know when it is a kick more readily as the baby grows."

Lorelei shrugged. "I think I would have noticed, even if it's not easily discernible." Probably. It sounded strange, to be sure, and Lorelei tended to notice strange things. "But we shall see."

"*Oui.*"

For a moment, they sat in silence, then Aimée spoke again.

"I am concerned that you are unhappy. I know I do not know you well, but I worry to see any woman in such a state when they are with child."

Lorelei raised her eyebrows. "Why do you worry?"

"Because I have seen too many women who have struggled before and after their child's birth with … malaise. That is the word." She nodded emphatically. "Now we are friends, and I will do all I can to help you. I may not be able to fix everything, but I can do something. That is what any friend can do."

Lorelei laughed softly and took another sip of her water, finishing it off. Though she was not the type to have a *friend* of any type, perhaps having the doctor's wife around would be amusing. That was the basis of a friendship, after all, wasn't it? "I suppose so."

"May I ask why you are apprehensive?"

"I am busy." Too busy to be a mother. "I hate to be slowed down, and I am saddened that *It* will not see much of me. I didn't see much of my own mother, and I feel as if I'm forcing someone else to feel the weight of neglect. But I have my husband and my sister and his sisters, and they will love the baby—so you needn't worry."

Aimée nodded, seeming to take these thoughts in. "I see."

"You do not believe me?" Lorelei asked.

"Yes and no. I believe you are sincere. I wonder if you will not love your child when you see him or her for the first time. I am not above confessing that I was not at all sure how I would feel about Louise until I had the pleasure of meeting her." Here, Aimée paused and smiled. I wanted a baby with Alexandre—that is my husband; you would say Alexander.

Fortunately, I am an excellent mother, aided greatly by an excellent nanny."
She winked. "The same will be true of you."

Perhaps. Lorelei thought it would probably be truer that she would find
an excellent nanny than that she would become an excellent mother, but
that was not worth explaining. She shrugged, and Aubrey reappeared, so
for now, the subject was dropped.

Chapter Twenty-Two

December 1884

T HE DAYS SLIPPED BY into December in a sad, slow way that filled Lorelei with a mix of vague apprehension and constant fear. Aubrey fussed; his sisters visited and politely asked how she was; and Winnie was inconsolable at the thought that Lorelei might die, the baby might die, or *anyone* might die.

Aimée came by often, sometimes with her husband and sometimes without him. She insisted Lorelei take various tonics, and whether it was because she was resting and eating or because of Aimée's help, Lorelei was beginning to improve. Of course, she'd far rather attribute this to the progress of her pregnancy, as supposedly she was far past the days of "morning sickness"—a misnomer, she thought; it had been all day and even all night, too. But there was no more bleeding, and the doctor believed she showed no signs of miscarriage. Of course, they wouldn't know for sure until the quickening.

What a horrible thing to put anyone through.

One cold morning, as Lorelei sipped her hot chocolate—a compromise, as the doctor had insisted Lorelei "take a break" from coffee since it "seemed to increase her heart rate to a dangerous point" or some such nonsense—Aimée appeared in her room with a smile.

Lorelei tilted her cup toward Aimée in sardonic greeting. "You've turned my maid against me."

Aimée removed her muffler and coat and laid them over the chair in the corner. "She only cares for your health, as I do."

"Harriet never cared about my health before you became a part of my life."

Harriet, who was laying out Lorelei's clothes for the day, turned with a betrayed expression toward the bed. "Mrs. Montgomery—"

Lorelei waved her away with a flip of her hand. "Never mind it, Harriet. I understand that your salary comes from my husband, and your heart is in the right place. Though I do believe Dr. Burton's Coffee Act of 1884 may cause a riot if it continues. But I won't be dumping coffee beans into that harbor; I can promise you that."

Aimée clucked her tongue as she rummaged through that infernal bag of hers. "After the child is safe, in a month or so, you can have whatever you want in moderation."

"Oh, right, 'in moderation.' Tyranny, I say. *Vive la révolution.*"

Aimée rolled her eyes and withdrew what looked to be another fearsome bottle of some herb that had been beaten into a liquid. "You must let me teach you to speak French."

Lorelei shook her head. "As I have said before, I speak Italian badly, and I can usually read German. French is beyond me, though. I cannot begin with it."

"Oh, we can change that," Aimée said.

Lorelei laughed. This was not the first time Aimée had tried to convince her to learn the language Lorelei had suffered over for several years before switching to Italian. "Did anyone ever tell you you're annoying?"

Aimée shrugged. "My husband, many times. He does not mean it, though; he could not live a day without me. But you must speak French. It is a beautiful language—and not so different from Italian."

Aimée wasn't wrong there, but the pronunciations were what froze Lorelei in her place. "Every French cognate in English makes the language even more abysmal."

"As if Celtic languages are better!"

Lorelei shrugged. "Perhaps every language has its quirks. But I am familiar with my own—and Italian made some sense to me, though yes, it does have its strangenesses, too."

"If you learned French, you could assist me in turning my child against my husband," Aimée said helpfully. "That is all I want in life, to make her detest the English language and then use her French against him. His is passable, at best; once she can speak it fluently, he will not match her."

"A noble cause, I'm sure, but I'm afraid I cannot help you there," Lorelei said with a grin. "What's her name again?"

"Louise."

"Ah yes, Louise." Lorelei nodded. Her head cocked as she regarded her new "friend," if this was what friendship was. "You love her."

"*Oui*. She is the most charming child who has ever lived." Aimée's voice held an easy confidence that brushed away all deniability. "You must meet her someday."

"Perhaps." So far, Lorelei had been able to put her off every time she brought it up. "Maybe when I am out of bed—I hope that will be soon."

Aimée inclined her head. "At least for Christmas, but I doubt my husband or yours will want you down at the docks any time soon."

"Don't remind me." Lorelei's time away from the docks was nothing short of torture; every day, she was reminded of the work she was missing, the changes she wasn't observing. She'd been allowed to sit in the parlor for a few hours once and speak with Mr. Hastings, which had helped her catch up some. Though he claimed everything was going smoothly—and due to the time of the year, progress must be halted slightly anyway—Lorelei wasn't sure she believed him. She wanted to see for herself. She wanted to make sure everything was under control, because it was under *her* control.

"Wouldn't you rather be with that little girl than with me?"

Aimée paused in the middle of mixing two of her potions together. "Is that your gentle way of insinuating I am not wanted here?" Yet her eyes twinkled with amusement, denying the offense she'd forced into her tone.

"You are rather frequently here."

"I will not be forever, but I have taken an interest in you," Aimée said firmly, dousing a cloth with the liquid she held. "Pull up your nightgown. This needs to be rubbed into your lower abdomen."

Lorelei grinned. "Now that's what a woman wants to hear."

Aimée ignored her and proceeded with the treatment.

"What is it?" Lorelei asked.

"Olive oil and lavender, as last time, but I have added clary sage since I came upon some a few weeks ago and finally am satisfied with my fermentation. You need not worry—my husband says it can not cause any harm. This is his highest praise for anything of this sort I do. He does not believe there is any benefit in it, but he lets me continue."

Lorelei nodded. "That's about the same as my husband. Of course, he is currently *not* letting me do what I want to do." Against the terms of their arrangement, too—though to be fair, Lorelei had put up very little fight. She might believe in pushing oneself as hard as possible, but there was a limit, and that limit was the risk of death—for anyone, *It* included. "Did your husband know about your nonsense tonics before he married you?"

"*Bien sûr.*" Aimée corked the bottle and returned it to her bag. "He knew."

"He did not object then?"

"*Non.*" She washed her hands in the bowl on the table. "He is my husband, but like all Englishmen, he loves devotedly. At the end of the day"—she snapped her fingers—"he is weak in my hands."

"Is that so?" Lorelei said with a grin.

"*Mais oui.* I had hesitated to marry an Englishman. But they are such trainable sorts. You think they cannot be made to do anything, but then you, as their wife, find that they feel they are obligated to do so. Ah, there are boundaries, but they are not as inflexible as you think."

Lorelei cast a glance around the room; Harriet had slipped out. Good. This seemed a conversation that would embarrass the maid, who was staunchly traditional and probably respected Aubrey more than Lorelei did, which was an honest shame, but Lorelei wasn't sure how to change that. "I don't think Englishmen are trainable. At least, mine is not."

"Ah, he did not give you pleasure?"

Lorelei paused, then shook her head with a wry laugh. "I didn't think that was what we were talking about; my mind must be purer than yours. As you can see, I'm more concerned with trying to stay alive." Having Aubrey in her bed had stopped being a matter of passion and started being a matter of comfort months ago.

Aimée quirked an eyebrow. "But before?"

That, Lorelei would admit to. "He took good care of me before."

"Exactly! It's as I said—they try. That's all one wants in a man—consistent effort—in every area of marriage. But then, as a woman, you must give the opportunity to practice."

"That is true."

Aimée took up her bag. "I must go now, but I will come back and see you in a few days. Christmas is just around the corner, so I will be busy—I do have my Louise at home, and she's delightful around the holidays."

Lorelei nodded, thanked Aimée, and took up her now cooled beverage—*cold* chocolate, she supposed. Wrinkling her nose, she set it aside and called for Harriet.

Christmas was just around the corner. She supposed she'd better send her maid to collect presents this year.

Aubrey loved Christmastime.

He had a scattering of ill memories surrounding the season, but most had been overshadowed by other events. He'd often felt alone during the holidays—for years, it had been his parents and him, and then his sisters had never been the most entertaining playmates as he grew up. That had changed now. Then there was the matter of Mrs. Hilton's rejection of him, which had taken place on Christmas Eve. But that was a faded memory.

Today, a few hours before their traditional Christmas Eve celebrations began, he stood in his office, staring at the bundle of wrapping paper before him that had somehow managed to morph into something he had not originally intended. The scent of pine from the boughs his sisters and Gwendolyn had interspersed through the house mingled with the subtle aroma of burning wood. He took up the scissors once more and cut the ribbons that precariously drew the brown paper against this intended gift.

Aubrey dropped the paper onto the growing pile on the floor. He might as well start anew—after all, he wanted this to actually resemble the other presents that were tucked away, courtesy of Lorelei, her maid, and a small added effort on his part. He had no doubt his sisters and Gwendolyn would also add to the abundance on their own, one way or another.

He keenly remembered being tucked beneath a blanket on his mother's lap and hearing the annual Christmas Eve telling of the Biblical nativity story as if it were once more the first time. How he missed his parents, wished either of them had lived to meet the child that would arrive next year or simply to meet Lorelei, for that matter. He wasn't sure they would have liked her at first, but they certainly would have come to love her.

As I did.

Aubrey measured out the paper and snipped through it. He hoped Lorelei would appreciate this. Though he'd sent to London for a gift he thought she'd enjoy, and though he'd asked his valet to see that some of the family jewels were put aside and wrapped for her, he wanted to do this one himself. His father had made a tradition of passing down one of his childhood toys and then eventually other family heirlooms to Aubrey every year—and he wished to continue that tradition for his child. So he'd scrounged through the nursery until he'd found one he thought Lorelei would like—for it would be years before their child would care about such things, and at the moment, all that mattered was her regard.

He folded the paper more carefully this time and tied the ribbon with more care. It still appeared lopsided to him, but with a sigh, he admitted defeat. This was the best it was going to get—and it was better than nothing.

He was looking forward to the next Christmas and the ones to follow. It had been a long time since there was a child at Montgomery Place.

He couldn't help but smile to himself at the thought as he tucked the gift under his arm and left his study behind. Already, the girls were surrounding the large Christmas tree in the hall, arguing over the placement of ornaments.

Lorelei would come down and sit by the fire that evening. He'd read the nativity story from Luke—and he'd give her the gift.

"What's that?" Connie asked, grinning as she turned from the tree. "A gift for me?"

He laughed. "Not for you, no. This looks splendid."

"It's not done yet," Fran said firmly. "We've more work to do."

"Oh, have you?" The poor evergreen looked full to the brim. "How much more can you decorate it before it topples over?"

"*Plenty* more!" Gwendolyn exclaimed cheerfully. She was balanced on top of a ladder, held by a terrified footman.

Aubrey set the package down on a side table. "Get down from there. I'll help you reach whatever you need to."

Reluctantly, Gwendolyn clambered off the ladder. The footman took what was probably his first deep breath of the day, and the decorating proceeded as planned.

"Perhaps I should have brought Lorelei down," he commented as he placed the final ornament.

Gwendolyn laughed. "Lore doesn't care too much about such things, Aubrey. I wouldn't worry about it."

"Perhaps." But he felt as if he should have included her, nonetheless. "I think I'll go see to her."

He picked up the parcel from the sideboard and made his way up the stairs to Lorelei's bedroom. She was lying on her side, her eyes directed out the window opposite—the one that faced the sea. There was such a darkness about her now, as if the frantic energy of her ambition had given away to something more sinister. Even if it were not something serious,

Aubrey didn't like to see his wife living under a perpetual rain cloud.

She turned and ran her eyes over him. "It's Christmas Eve, isn't it?" she said in a flat, quiet tone.

"Yes. It is. I thought you would come down and sit—have dinner with us. My family always reads the nativity story from the Bible, and we'll have popcorn balls, I think."

"Hmm. All right." She sighed. "Will you call Harriet? I might need some help getting my dress sorted. I think I'll wear the green one—more festive and whatnot. Winnie will like that."

He smiled, pleased. Any effort on her part was appreciated, and he always liked it when she showed any regard for her sister. It meant she cared about something; not all things and persons were alike to her, tools to be used or disregarded. She had a heart.

Convincing her of that fact proved impossible, but he knew, even if she didn't.

"I think that would be nice. But first I have something for you."

"That was the other reason I asked if it was Christmas Eve. I was afraid I'd slept the day away." She arched an eyebrow but accepted the package. "This is the sort of thing one does tomorrow, isn't it? Or have I been celebrating all wrong?"

"No, you haven't. Unwrap it, and I'll explain."

Aubrey watched as she unwound the paper. She was fastidious, but even that couldn't make the package look any more appealing. His only consolation was that it hadn't been wrapped long.

She withdrew the small wooden ship, crafted with meticulous detail, and frowned. Though it was certainly accurate to ships of yore, there was a sturdiness to it that made it clear it was meant to be a toy. The shadow that always lay across her features these days darkened. "Aubrey, it's too early for gifts of—of that sort." She spat out the words, her brow wrinkled. "You should have saved this for next Christmas or simply tucked it away somewhere until it was time. It's too early."

Aubrey sighed. "Lori—"

"No. Why would you give this to me? It's like a slap in the face. You know I don't—" Then she stopped herself, calmed whatever anger she felt at his gesture, pushed it back somewhere to that place inside her where she seemed to hide her deepest emotions. "I know you meant well. If I were normal, this would be the furthest thing from an insult. I'm sorry."

Aubrey took a moment before responding. "I wanted to continue a tradition. Christmas Eve gifts for our little one, as my parents did for my sisters and me. They would always give us something of their own—a toy one of them had owned as a child. That's where my watch is from—and almost any jewelry you see my sisters wearing. I thought our baby would appreciate that, too."

"I see." She nodded, her features carefully sculpted, her eyes blank of any feeling. "Thank you. I'm sure this is lovely." But she swiftly placed the ship on the bedside table, as if holding it burned her fingers. Her hands were shaking.

"What is it?" he whispered. "Tell me what you're thinking."

"I cannot." She shook her head and took a deep breath. "I'm sorry, but I cannot. I don't know what I'm thinking. I just know that ... that I'm sorry I'm not normal. You deserve normal."

Aubrey cocked his head. "I'm not sure anyone has normal, Lori."

"I'm sure they do. Patrick has normal. Probably most married couples have normal. I'm quite sure Dr. Burton doesn't get yelled at by his wife when he gives her a present for their daughter. But then there's me—*not normal*."

He took her hand. "You hardly yelled."

"I wanted to. I wanted to scream. I still do." She took a deep breath. "Oh, Aubrey, Christmases are so hard!"

"Are they?" he asked. "Could you tell me why?" *Let me in. Let me see a little part of you. Anything, any scrap of who you are; I want to see it. Please.*

"My parents didn't celebrate Christmas. My father was quite literally Ebenezer Scrooge—granted, he didn't stop others from celebrating, but he didn't even take the day off work. He used it as a catch-up day for paperwork. Patrick was the only nonexempt employee. Reverse nepotism, if you will." Lorelei shrugged. "I didn't mind. It was nice to have Father gone. My mother usually grew exhausted halfway through the evening, if she participated at all. We had no other family, so it was me, Trick, if he could slip away, and Winnie. We would sit around the fireplace and exchange gifts and laugh and joke far into the night. It was *something*. I enjoyed it. I looked forward to it, to a degree. But it was also a reminder that our lives were not what I wanted them to be." She pressed her lips together. "I always thought, if I had to have a child at all, that their life would be different."

"It will be," Aubrey said, squeezing her hand. "It will be."

"Perhaps. Perhaps. I sometimes wonder if I am not a necessary part of *It*s life. It is better to have no mother than a mother such as myself."

Aubrey frowned. "I wish you wouldn't say that."

"Why?" She lifted her eyes to his. There were tears there, and he hated them—yet at the same time, he welcomed any expression of her emotions. "Why, Aubrey, truly? Because tradition demands you must or because you truly believe it? You haven't seen me with a child. I'm awkward and withdrawn around them."

"You might not be with your own," he suggested. After all, he was not the best with children, though he wanted to be; that said, he was sure that his love for his own child or children would overcome that. "Perhaps once you have your own baby—"

She held up her hand. "Nothing will change. You'll have to love *It* enough for both of us. I hope you understand that."

"Honestly, I hope you will feel differently when you meet the child."

"I know I will not." Her voice was sharp again, but she swiftly regained her composure. "I know I will not because I know myself. I know the way I was raised, and I know what I have within me to give. I am not stingy about whatever energy I possess—I'll hand that over to anyone who wants it. But that doesn't mean that what I have contains a motherly impulse. I'm not that way." Her breath was coming fast now, and he drew back.

"I'm sorry if—"

"Aubrey, if you don't know that I would not be much of a mother, why did you—" Her strained voice cut off mid-sentence. Her hand flew her to her side, and she gasped.

Everything in him stilled. "Lori?"

She shook her head and waved her other hand at him.

"Lorelei. Are you all right? Is there any pain?" He shouldn't have upset her. What if … what if …? *Lord, please. Not the baby.* "Lorelei!"

"No, I'm fine," she mumbled. "I think … I think *It* doesn't like us … talking to each other like that."

"Why?"

"Because *It* did a little tumbling routine for me." She relaxed slightly. "Not sure how I feel about that. Goodness. That's so strange. Aimée was right—it is like bubbles."

The air stilled between them as they stared at each other. Aubrey, for one, had no idea what to say. In his mind, he ran over the same two words: *Thank God.* "Do you think I could … feel?" he managed after a moment.

"Probably not," she said. "You can try, but I think the doctor said that might be later on."

Still, he wanted to touch—so with her permission given, he settled a palm over their child. She was right—no movement—but he was still delighted. He smiled but managed to restrain anything odd, like a joyous laugh, and simply sat still for a long time.

He looked up to find her watching him with an amused look settled across her face. "You are a trifle strange, Mr. Montgomery," she said.

"You're the one who's strange, to not love this," he countered, then thought better of it. "But no, you're not abnormal, Lori. You're different. I love you. I hope someday you'll realize that love can be safe, but I understand why it isn't for you, and I can respect that."

She frowned. "I don't like how reasonable that sounds. Take it back. I'd rather fight."

Aubrey did laugh then—and shook his head at her stubbornness. "I'll ring Harriet, and you can get dressed. We'll have to tell the girls."

"And have Winnie crawling all over me? No, thank you. Besides, thinking I'm on death's door has made them all so well-behaved. I can milk this for a few more years."

Despite her protestations, there was certainly a lightening in her tone. Aubrey felt she was as awash with relief as he was—to know that in all likelihood, their baby was all right, was healthy, was strong, and was growing.

What more could they possibly ask for as a Christmas gift?

He rang for Harriet and went downstairs—and yes, he would tell the girls the good news, whether Lorelei liked it or not. With another grin, he thought that perhaps it would be good for her to tolerate their happy questions.

CHAPTER TWENTY-THREE

THE CHRISTMAS SEASON PASSED in a blur, and the New Year took its place. Lorelei was allowed up more often now but was largely confined to the house except for the occasional carriage ride or brief walk when the snow was not too thick. She was not allowed to visit the docks except when accompanied, and even then, she was not able to work—simply to visit, to hear from Hastings how things were doing.

With every day seeming to bring new growth in the stomach region, she doubted she would be allowed to work ... ever.

If January had been difficult, February proved its own torture. There were still months left until her "confinement," as Dr. Burton delicately referred to the upcoming travails of labor and then recovery, which Aimée said was also an irritating part of the process. Of course, Lorelei was already confined, but the doctor ignored her when she told him so and continued to recommend rest and relaxation.

Lorelei was particularly bad at engaging in rest and relaxation.

Aubrey had promised to visit the docks a few times a week, to see that all was running well, but that couldn't be enough. No, especially in these early stages, and then especially as spring came, Lorelei would be needed there.

But with *It* being so obviously present now, and with the conclusive recommendation of the doctor, that would be impossible.

She wanted to wail and scream with the unfairness of it all, but she had not been raised to wail and scream. She hadn't been "raised" much at all; she had simply become, through the cruelty that had formed her like a rock beat by the tide. Lorelei hadn't become a sandy beach; she'd become a strange lone pillar out in the midst of the waves, gradually wearing down more and more as the weather battered it.

She wasn't sure being formed into a sandy beach was the ideal position to be in, anyway. It sounded a rather lackluster proposal, to be trodden upon by so many feet, used as a vacation spot, viewed as nothing more than another sight to be seen.

But perhaps that was unreasonable; perhaps she was going a little insane.

The rhythmic patter of the rain against the library's windows created a melancholic backdrop as Lorelei sat on a plush armchair. She stared out into the cold, wet landscape and tried not to become too discouraged.

How she hated rain.

Yes, a thunderstorm was nice—exciting—and a crashing storm exhilarating. But she was tired of the continuous dripping.

After a moment, she stood and slammed her book down onto the table in the corner. She didn't throw it—the book didn't deserve her fit of pique—but she wanted to do something. There was an ache in her bones, not exhaustion but rather nervousness. She disliked the sensation.

Her shoulders felt heavy, too. Oh, the invisible weight of too many concerns! Concerns about the Hilton Shipping Co. and the docks and everything related to them loomed so large that they threatened to choke out whatever was left of her. The business was supposed to be her passion, the only real thing she ever offered this earth. The business would prove her worth, her capabilities.

Instead, the impending arrival of *It* had displaced her. No, she wasn't angry at the rain. Rain had nothing against her, nor she against it, truly. By June, the rain might have stopped, but unfortunately, so would have her life.

The creak of the door drew her attention, and she turned to face her husband. There was worry etched across Aubrey's face, his blue eyes seeming almost liquid with his care. She hated that, too—how without trying, she had won his heart and now would hurt him, without meaning to, again and again.

If only he'd held back, restrained himself, as she had. They would both be happier if there was no love between them. Still, she didn't turn him out of her bedroom—still, she clung to him like her only anchor in the storm.

Foolish and weak. A deadly combination. Especially for a woman.

"Are you all right?" he said. "You've been ..." He struggled for a word, then settled on "distant."

"I'm worried about the docks," she said. "The snow has melted, and though it's raining, the men ought to be hard at work again. I want to be prepared as soon as the spring comes. Instead, I'm stuck here." She gestured around the room, though she meant the entire house. "I feel as if it'll take me years to catch up from these months of being away."

Aubrey nodded, his brow furrowed. "Why don't we go down together this afternoon? We'll take a look at things, and you can tell me how I've been doing."

Lorelei nodded. It'd been a few weeks since he'd allowed her that, but Hastings had not been there at the time, having been attending to business in London, which had made it difficult to discern exactly what was happening. "I'll get my coat, and we can go."

In no time, they were rolling through the cobblestone streets of the nearby village and then out to the docks. Her thoughts were a tempest—greatly preferable to this pattering rain, so gentle, so thought-provoking. She hated having her thoughts provoked; she preferred to have them on her own time.

The activity of the bustling waterfront became apparent as soon as they arrived. Crates were being loaded and unloaded onto the smaller boats Hastings had running to and from London. There was the sound of shipbuilders' hammers echoing through the damp air and the shouts of the men and the scents of salt air and dead fish.

The atmosphere, alive with an industrious energy and the cleanness of the sea, now felt distant and foreign—of some world Lorelei was no longer a part of.

The carriage rolled to a stop, and Hastings came over as if he'd been expecting them, a plan of some sort tucked under his arm. He didn't show it to Lorelei.

At first, Hastings addressed her, but she had nothing to say to him, so she simply murmured a greeting and sat back. With a sideways glance at her, Aubrey confidently turned to Hastings and engaged in a conversation full of educated questions. The exchange between the two men seemed seamless—and it grated at her nerves.

She had built this place from the ground up. She should be the one who possessed this knowledge. Yet as she listened to their efficient discussion, discussing the merits of one business move or another that she no longer understood the significance of, a gnawing fear took root.

This work had been stolen out from under her without anyone, Aubrey included, really intending that to happen.

She might never reclaim it.

If she were a different woman, this would make her cry. Instead, she simply asked Aubrey to take her back home, which he did.

As they rolled back toward Montgomery Place, *It* decided to pitch a fit of some sort—*It* liked to throw little kicking parties these days. "What did I do now?" she mumbled to herself, much to Aubrey's concern (she ignored him). She placed her hand over her stomach—the kicks were strong now, nothing like the "bubbles" of early days. She was going to sign the child up for whatever sport England had that involved kicking as soon as *It* arrived.

Another strong kick—this time, the sensation prompted a rush of anger.

She would never be at the helm of the Hilton Shipping Co. Not truly. *It* had stolen that from her, taken her dreams and crushed them, just when they were within the reach of her grasping hands. The docks, once a haven of purpose, felt strange now, a world she didn't belong to.

How unfair. How marvelously unfair.

It was a paradoxical storm that whirled angrily about her gut—a longing for the life she once knew and the daunting prospect of a future that seemed to demand the sacrifice of her ambitions.

Could one go back after months of uselessness and steal away what was being confidently handled by others?

Did she even want that anymore? Did she even care?

Lorelei took hot chocolate in her room after they got back. Aubrey had asked her what was wrong, but she had declined to tell him, saying she needed to be alone—which wasn't true, exactly. It was more that she expected herself to be alone, that she didn't believe there was an alternative. Not without inconveniencing someone, forcing onto them problems and emotions that were best dealt with on her own. As she always had.

The rain outside had settled into a soft drizzle, casting a muted gray haze over the estate as she sat by the window. It was then that she saw a small black carriage pull up to the house—and Aimée stepped out.

Thank God. A distraction.

In five minutes, Aimée was settling onto the cushioned armchair across from Lorelei. More hot chocolate was brought up, and they sipped together.

"You seem ... upset." Aimée cast her eyes furtively in Lorelei's direction before looking away. "Is everything all right?"

"I'm not sure," Lorelei said pensively, setting her cup down and sighing. "Everything is different. I'm not sure if that's all right or not. I don't think it is, but I am not the only person in the world. Perhaps it's all right if my happiness is not considered."

"Everything is different," Aimée agreed, her voice soft, less carefree than Lorelei had heard it. "Is it the baby?"

"Yes. And other things. This sensation of nothing being the same as it once was or how I would have it be. Yet I must bear up." Lorelei swallowed that irritating lump rising in her throat as it so often did. "There's no other way. I don't know how to be a mother, but I can't ... Well. I'm afraid going back to the shipping company may not be an option for me. If it isn't ... what does that leave me with?"

Aimée reached across the small table, placing a reassuring hand on

Lorelei's. "You are not alone in feeling that way. No one expects you to know how to do everything all at once. Why, when Louise was born, I was certain I would surely grow bored with her sooner or later, and what then? I was determined to have her, for my husband—and perhaps I shall give him another someday. But it was insane to think I could forget her. I never could. She is too much a part of me. Your child will be a part of you."

Lorelei managed a weak smile. "Perhaps you are right." She wasn't, but Lorelei had come to like Aimée, and Lorelei was growing shy about correcting her as they grew closer.

"You should meet my Louise. I think she would adore you, and it would be good for you to see how sweet a child can be. Louise, after all, is perfection," Aimée said "No child has ever or will ever be so charming."

Lorelei laughed. "The more you say that, the more I am sure she will be a little troll. She's too good to be true."

"She sounds too good to be true, but that doesn't mean she is!" Aimée exclaimed. "You must meet her. Can I bring her up?"

"Oh, I don't know." Lorelei drummed her fingers along the arm of the chair. "I'm sure the girls would like to meet her, but I am not good with children. She won't like me; they never do. I mean, my nephew was here for a week, and I never held him despite the fact that every other female in the household was head over heels in love. I'm not like that. About anyone." Babies, children ... adult men.

"Nonsense! Louise is not a normal child. Even though other children may not like you, she will—and vice versa, I am sure."

Reluctantly, Lorelei agreed to meet Louise the next day, though a knot of apprehension lingered within her.

She only hoped Aimée wouldn't be too disappointed.

The morning sun struggled to pierce through the lingering clouds the next day. Aimée arrived not so long after breakfast, her daughter Louise in tow.

She was a sweet child, with Aimée's brown eyes and flyaway golden-brown hair. Aimée had said she would be two in a few months, but she seemed more serious than a child of that age ought to be, her inquisitive gaze taking in everything around her. She was certainly a pretty little girl, and the few words she said, all in French, were to the point—demands, Lorelei thought. She couldn't help but grin at the forcefulness such a small voice could hold.

But it didn't mean she liked the child. She greeted Louise in English—a simple "hello"—and the child replied with "*bonjour*." The single word was perfect—Aimée had absolutely coached her for hours on that.

Lorelei continued grinning, but she stepped back after a moment and allowed her sisters-in-law and Winnie to have at the child—for of course they must.

So Lorelei perched in the sitting room, observing the scene unfolding before her. Aimée introduced Louise to the three girls, who swiftly became fast friends, based on the sound of Louise's laughter as Winnie teased her and Connie joined in. Francesca had discovered a box of old toys in the nursery and had brought them down, and the three young women were excitedly introducing each toy to Louise, who proved delighted by each one. Francesca apparently spoke a fair amount of French, and she took to teaching words to Louise—the toy dog was *le chien*, the cow *la vache*.

As Lorelei had guessed, Aimée had been wrong. This only served to remind Lorelei of the hard truth—that *It* would be mothered by her sister, by her sisters-in-law, rather than by herself, if *It* received any feminine, motherly love. She had accepted this—why did it still hurt?

Louise ran giggling to her mother's arms and buried her face in Aimée's shoulder—somewhere between overwhelmed and delighted by the abundance of attention, if Lorelei understood the interaction. Her heart squeezed because she would never ... No, she could never ... It *wouldn't* ever come to pass. There could be none of that. No kisses pressed to *Its* neck—no warm embrace—no soft whispers of reassurance before sending her back to learn and grow with her new friends.

Lorelei's role, it seemed, was destined to be more of an observer than an active participant. Could that be the rest of her life?

The door to the sitting room opened, and Aubrey appeared. At first, his eyes went to Lorelei—questioning—but Louise came darting away from the girls sitting on the floor and offering her their full attention and went straight to him.

As Lorelei had expected, his eyes softened when he saw the child. Of course they did—he was a normal human being, and normal human beings liked children. He knelt and received her as she crashed into him with a giggle.

"Louise," Aimée called. "*S'il vous plaît, faites attention.*"

Louise glanced back at her mother with a cheeky grin, then back up to Aubrey. "*Bonjour,*" she said in a serious voice.

"*Bonjour,*" Aubrey replied softly.

Aimée laughed. "This is my Louise, Mr. Montgomery."

"Does she understand French, then?" Aubrey asked, reaching down to tug at a loose curl.

"Some," Aimée said with a shrug.

"*Comment allez-vous, Mademoiselle* Louise?" Aubrey asked.

Louise giggled and glanced back at her mother before running off into Francesca's arms with no response given.

"She can say '*bonjour*' and '*non,*' and we have a '*chatte*' named *Chaussettes*, whom she has learned many words for— '*La chatte grise est folle. La chatte n'aime pas qu'on lui tire la queue.*' Oh, and she can ask for sweets, though please do not bring it up." Aimée rolled her eyes toward the heavens. "But she is learning English at a rapid rate, Lorelei. I told you I would fight it, but I cannot. Her nanny is English—and my husband refuses to let me hire someone French or to insist the nanny learn French and only speak it with her. I shall fail most tragically in my quest."

Lorelei chuckled. "Though I am sympathetic, I cannot help but feel it is for the best, both for your daughter and your marriage."

With a dramatic sigh, Aimée shrugged.

Aubrey went to sit beside his sisters, and there was something strange in Lorelei's chest as she watched him offer a wooden *"cheval"* to the child; it was accepted, and Aubrey had Louise learning new words in description of the horse in minutes—all in French.

Will he be so sweet, so earnest, with It? *How could he say he is not good with children? He is, obviously.* A strange mix of delight and jealousy swelled in Lorelei's soul as she watched.

If only that could be how I am, too.

But it was not to be.

Chapter Twenty-Four

Four Months Later

June 1885

F INISHED. AT LAST.

A shriek of displeasure split the air as Dr. Burton scooped *It* up, and the screams continued as *It* was severed from her—and that was done, then, too.

It wasn't a part of Lorelei anymore. And they both appeared to be alive. She had done it—the one aspect of motherhood she'd promised herself had been performed.

She reached up to brush sweat-soaked strands of hair from her eyes, but before she could, Aimée smoothed them back with a practiced hand.

"Ah, *chérie*. We shall bathe you shortly, but you must hold your little girl first."

Lorelei's heart dropped. *Ah. It* was female. "Oh, a girl?" she asked, even though it was not debatable.

"*Oui*. I am sorry you do not have your son, as you wanted, but you will love her. For now, you rest and enjoy holding her. All right?"

Lorelei shook her head and straightened herself—to her disappointment, she felt weak, practically faint against the pillow, not to mention she still hurt, a lot. The relief had been immense at first, but she was certain she was still having contractions, and though not on the same level of unbearability, she was having a hard time keeping her head straight—especially since she was so *tired* all of a sudden. But she forced her next words out. "That's all right. Could you fetch Harriet, and we can begin cleaning me? I don't want to hold her. I feel awful, Aimée."

"I know," Aimée tutted sympathetically. "But when you hold your daughter—"

Lorelei cast a side-eye to where Dr. Burton and his nurse were performing an examination and perhaps cleaning up *It*. "Just shine *It* up some and bring *It* to my husband. He's dying to see *It*, and he'll take care of *It*. I know infants need love to thrive. I want *It* to have that, and I would rather that happen sooner rather than later. I'm afraid *It* will begin to fail if you keep *It* with me." Perhaps Lorelei had been neglected when she was born, and that was why she was so strange and unwomanly now. If Patrick had been older, or even one of her parents attended to her with love, she might not be the person she was today. Aubrey could make the difference for *It*. He must.

"Please hold her for a moment," Aimée said. "Then we will bathe you. Please, Lorelei. Even if she is a slight achievement to you, you grew an entire human. Surely that is an accomplishment worth admiring—a blessing from the Lord, too."

Lorelei sighed. "If Dr. Burton brings *It* over, I will hold *It* while you fetch Harriet."

At last, Aimée agreed, and in moments, the bundle was placed beside Lorelei. She let *It* have *It*s head against her arm but let a carefully placed pillow take the brunt of the slight weight.

It was not a pretty baby. Red, wrinkled, funny-looking in the oddest way ... and *It* didn't know what was best for *It*. *It* couldn't, for *It* immediately stopped fussing and curled into Lorelei.

Aimée had promised to go immediately, but she lingered at Lorelei's side and pressed a handkerchief to her cheeks.

"I'm crying?" Lorelei said, followed by a sniffle of a childish nature. "Why?"

"The rush," Aimee said as if this were the most logical explanation in the world. "It is intense."

Lorelei nodded. *Intense* was right. She didn't know what kind of intensity, for she did not swiftly identify her own emotions at times, but she couldn't take her eyes off the ugly little thing. She wanted to memorize *It*, from the puckered lips to the heavily lidded eyes to the twitching nose to the wrinkled forehead.

Protectiveness swelled deep in her chest, and she frowned. "Maybe Aubrey should come to me. I can tell him ... tell him to take care of *It*." It was more vital than ever that *It* was happy and healthy. Loved. Aubrey would love *It* so much. Even now, she could envision how perfectly cared for, how adored, how wanted *It* would be in Aubrey's care. He would be an excellent father, provide everything *It* needed both physically and emotionally.

Yes, Aubrey must come to her so Lorelei could give her instructions. He might do it without her ordering him to, but she wanted to impress upon him how very much work she had put into *It*, and how he simply couldn't let that go to waste.

It stirred and fussed, and Lorelei stiffened. "Aimée, please," she said urgently. "I'm hurting her."

Her. It. *Whatever.*

Aimée came and placed a hand on Lorelei's arm. "There, there. You are not hurting her. Babies make noises—they make a lot of noises, actually—and that is not a 'hurt' sound. She would let you know. Relax—she's stiffening up because you are."

But for reasons she couldn't identify, Lorelei was still crying, and she at last convinced Aimée to take the baby away from her.

It was a whole baby, after all. Perhaps *"It"* was worthy of being a "she."

The nurse helped the doctor with Lorelei—she had been warned about the afterbirth but not enough to have truly prepared herself, and she found the whole affair distasteful and exhausting. The nurse rubbed her stomach at some point in the process, too, which made Lorelei see stars—it hurt far too much.

Harriet was there, then, and they did help Lorelei get cleaned up. Even when that was all done, she was still hurting—*why, why, why am I still hurting?*—and Aimée told her gently that she might feel like this for a while, and Lorelei felt that familiar sensation that she was beginning to realize was "wanting to be hysterical but knowing that it would only make things worse."

Instead, she cried—big tears rolling down her cheeks and into her ears, sobs shaking despite the fact that they only increased the pain.

At last, feeling so alone despite the dual comforts of the concerned but helpless faces of Aimée and Harriet, Lorelei begged for Aubrey. The nurse had brought the baby to him—but he could put the baby down long enough to come see Lorelei. She needed to look into his eyes and hear him tell her she'd done well at this one thing—that the baby was what he wanted.

That was all she needed.

Aubrey's nerves had been on edge since the beginning of Lorelei's pregnancy, and today, they were much worse. Fran and Connie and Gwendolyn sat with him, which was the only reason he wasn't frantically pacing instead of tapping his foot to the rhythm of the grandfather clock.

At least his sisters and Gwendolyn seemed to know better than to interrupt his brooding. Honestly, he was trying to pray, because he felt that was the right thing to do, but his mind kept getting distracted by his fear.

Lorelei had been stoic when he saw her last. He'd been allowed to visit her for a few minutes, to wish her luck and offer the frail hope that it wouldn't be too much longer, which she hadn't appreciated much. A sharp gasp at one point had been the only sign of her pain—and he'd been ushered out of the room shortly afterward.

If she had cried or moaned or screamed, the echoing halls of the house had hidden it from him, carrying the sound elsewhere, away from the silence of his study.

It also meant he likely wouldn't hear his child's first cries, but he thought he might lose his mind if he were forced to attune to every sound of the birthing chamber, so he had ended up here, with his sisters, who apparently didn't want to hear anything either.

There was a soft knock at the door, followed by the appearance of Dr. Burton.

Aubrey jerked to his feet. "Doctor?"

"Mrs. Montgomery is safely delivered. You have a daughter."

Aubrey nearly collapsed with relief. "My wife is safe?"

"Yes, the birth proceeded normally, and she did quite well. Better than many first-time mothers. I have asked the midwife to bring the child to you as soon as possible."

Aubrey's brow wrinkled. "Can I not go to her?"

For a moment, a shadow crossed the doctor's face. "I can ask Mrs. Montgomery if she would like to see you."

Oh. Of course. She probably wanted to be left alone—he was not much of a comfort to his wife, after all. "Oh, never mind. I would like to see my daughter, though." A little girl! Lorelei might be disappointed, for she had so desperately wanted to "get an heir out of the way," but Aubrey didn't care. He was delighted to have a child regardless of her gender.

Fifteen minutes later, Aubrey was ushered into his own bedroom, where the nurse introduced him to a tiny baby who made a series of soft grunting sounds. He wasn't quite sure what her noises meant yet, but as he sat on the edge of his bed and stared down at his daughter's tiny face, he promised he would learn—and quickly.

Irritatingly enough, after only allowing him five minutes or so to memorize everything about his baby, the nurse interrupted his series of epiphanies concerning life and what really mattered to ask him a lot of questions and update him on a lot of things.

They would need a wet nurse. Had one been sought out? Oh, good. She should be here soon and be able to settle in with the baby. It would be ideal if Mrs. Montgomery could breastfeed the baby for a few days, but she was not sure Mrs. Montgomery would agree to do so—and the feeding would induce further lactation, which would make transitioning to the wet nurse more painful for Mrs. Montgomery. The nursery had been prepared, yes, but the staff were not fully in place. That must be taken care of at once. Oh, and what was the child's name to be? He wasn't sure? There was time yet before the christening to make that decision, but it is something to consider.

Then the door opened, and Aimée entered the room.

"Mr. Montgomery, she wants you."

Aubrey immediately rose, the baby still clutched in his arms, and crossed the room to Aimée. For now, he surrendered his child to her, then went into the adjoining room.

Lorelei, pale and wan, lay on the bed. Her cheeks were marked with tears, her eyes red with crying, and she silently held a hand out to him.

He rushed over and took it. "Lori," he whispered. "Darling. What is it?"

"Everything ... h-hurts." She struggled to get those two words out. "I ... I can't do this again. Aubrey, I can't. It was so much harder than I thought it would be. I *didn't* take it in my stride; I don't know what's wrong with me; I *should* have taken it in my stride! But I still feel awful. I don't know what to do."

"Shh, shh," he murmured, and he put his arms around her and leaned awkwardly onto the bed as she clung to him. "It's all right. Go ahead and cry. I'm sorry. I don't know what to say—except thank you. Thank you for our baby, Lorelei. She's perfect."

She nodded sharply. "I feel so shaky. I hate it."

He glanced at Aimée, willing her to tell him, somehow, how his wife was, if she was truly ill—if any of this was normal.

She seemed to sense his distress, as she came to the other side of the bed and sat down on the edge, the baby still tucked into the crook of her arm. "You need to drink and eat, Lorelei, and breathe."

Aubrey nodded. "Yes, please, Lori. Do as Aimée says."

Lorelei jerked her head in what might have been a nod, and Harriet came over. When water was brought to her lips, Lorelei sipped it—and when soup was spooned into her mouth, she took a few obedient swallows. She started to calm down, and Aubrey took the baby and sat beside Lorelei, more relaxed now, as she laid her head back against the pillows and closed her eyes.

"I did think she looked all right," she admitted. "The baby, I mean. She can't be perfect, but she's close to it. What are you calling her? Does she have a name?"

She. Not "*It.*" *She.* "I haven't decided. I thought you might like to help name her."

"I think you should name her something you'd like to say every day," Lorelei said softly. "I think you should name her something you associate with ... with good things."

"I see." He wasn't at all sure what that was. "I could name her for you."

"Don't be silly. She should have her own name," Lorelei said in a tone that held so much disapproval that he didn't dare defy her.

"*Good things.*" Hmm. "I want to give it some thought," he said. "Think through what is the best name for her."

"Good," Lorelei murmured. "She deserves pondering."

He stared at his daughter's little face and smiled. "She looks so peaceful."

"Peace," Lorelei murmured, "is not going to be our child's name."

He grinned. "That wasn't what I was thinking. Though I will say, I do associate peace with good things. There's a verse about it: 'Peace I leave with you, my peace I give unto you: not as the world giveth, give I unto you. Let not your heart be troubled, neither let it be afraid.'"

Lorelei rolled her eyes. "I'm not going to name my child 'Peace.' I think it would launch us both back in time and onto the Mayflower, and I refuse to ignore years of progress. There are better ways to cross the Atlantic now."

Aubrey furrowed his brow, then nodded, unsure if she were babbling madly but willing to accept it if she was. "Very well."

"You should name her Serenity or something like that. Serena." Lorelei paused, and he glanced at her to find her staring at the baby. He shifted so she had a better view, which caused her to immediately look away.

"Maybe you should hold her for a minute. Tell me if she's a Serena," he whispered.

"Well—" Already, she was withdrawing, pulling away, her eyes flickering about in search of an escape route, and he couldn't have that.

"Please." He reached his free hand out and took hers. "For me? You know how indecisive I can be, even if something feels right."

Lorelei nodded—and he transferred the baby into her arms with only a little fussing as she settled back in. Did Lorelei realize how naturally she shifted her arms to hold their child? How her hand came up to caress the baby's cheek with a new gentleness? The look in her eyes was anything but disinterested. "I think," she whispered a little breathlessly, "that Serena is a good name for her. It's pretty. Will you name her after your mother? Serena Francesca? That was her name, wasn't it?"

There wasn't a chance he'd allow that, but he felt that outright denial had no place here, in this room. "How about Serena Lorelei?"

"No." The firm edge hadn't left her voice. "You know what that name means."

He sighed. "No, it doesn't. Your mother doesn't get to make that decision for you for the rest of your life—she doesn't. But Serena Anne?"

"If you like—I don't care." She turned her face away, whatever spark that had flamed to life having flickered out. "You should take her. I don't want her to fade."

"In her mother's arms?" he chanced. Perhaps now was the time, if there ever was one, to take risks with her—to say what he felt, what he believed to be the truth. "You think she doesn't recognize you—your heartbeat, your voice—to mean safety and warmth? She certainly doesn't seem to be 'fading.'"

"I don't feel well," Lorelei whispered faintly. "Please, Aubrey. Take her."

"Here." Aimée approached and held out her arms. "I'll take Serena. Mr. Montgomery, please get her to eat a few more bites of stew, then sleep."

Aubrey nodded and did as he was told—and Lorelei was passive, quiet, as he helped her eat and then tucked her into bed.

Aimée returned and told Aubrey she had set up the cradle in the other room and that she would stay the night until they could get a nurse settled.

"Will the baby be all right?" Aubrey asked anxiously.

"Until tomorrow. We will make sure all is well." She slipped to the side of the bed and placed her hand on Lorelei's shoulder. "Lorelei, please do not worry. Your daughter is healthy and safe and loved. You can rest."

Lorelei nodded and sighed, and Aubrey wished he'd sensed that Lorelei needed to hear that. Not that he hadn't said some variation at some point throughout the night, he thought, but he wanted to keep saying those kinds of things. He wanted her to know he believed it; he wanted her to know he hoped she would believe it someday, too.

But maybe it wasn't in Aubrey's control to help her. Maybe God would have to make the difference in his wife's life.

Lord, help me know what to do—and where I must let You do Your work.

CHAPTER TWENTY-FIVE

T HE NEXT FEW DAYS weren't what could be called fun, but Lorelei coped as well as she could. She ate when she was fed. She slept a lot. She held Serena when Aubrey placed the baby in her arms but was always happy to pass her back to him or to one of the girls.

She met the wet nurse—Leolyn was her rather fanciful name—and told her to take good care of Serena. Leolyn agreed to do so, and Lorelei felt she would, though she wanted to make sure Serena spent plenty of time outside the nursery. She was concerned that after the novelty wore off, the girls and Aubrey might not love Serena enough.

Serena needed a lot of love. Lorelei was certain of this. She needed love and maybe even an edge of spoiling. It was the only way.

But that was a concern for another day. For now, it was all Lorelei could do to perform for a few hours a day—eat, listen to her sister, nod to whatever her sisters-in-law were saying, then spend perhaps ten minutes holding Serena and being unnerved by the way Aubrey looked at her.

For his eyes said "I love you" in a way they hadn't before. He had gone from a romantic interest to something somehow deeper than romance. Oh, perhaps he had loved her before, but now …

Oh, she could destroy him, perhaps permanently, and she was terri-fied of doing so. She tried to be gentle, but she didn't know how—and that wasn't what Aubrey wanted. Somehow, gentleness was not in great demand, as it should have been, but her honesty was. Oh, and Lorelei was honest—about what she understood—but Aubrey wanted something more from her. Something she wasn't sure either of them could put a name to.

Vulnerability, perhaps. The exposing of whatever soft underbelly she had. Lorelei didn't want that to happen. Ever.

Therefore, their relationship was ... well, it was what it had always been. He was tender and took care of her—even though she didn't want to be taken care of. If she'd had her way, Lorelei would like to be alone, but duty held her to the simple responsibilities she'd forced upon herself. Then she slept. Nothing sounded interesting for some reason, and when she was awake and not distracted, her thoughts spiraled.

But Aubrey was a problem. For one, she wasn't sure they could ever be lovers again. She had told him she couldn't have another baby, and she'd meant it.

But she'd worry about that problem later. In fact, she wasn't sure she would ever have the energy again to give that—or anything—serious thought. Aimée said that Lorelei's mind might begin to clear in the next few weeks, but Lorelei wasn't convinced that would be a good thing.

Everything felt so odd now. *She* felt so odd now. *Offish* was the only word that made sense, as if everything that made her up had changed irrevocably, and there was nothing she could do about it—so she tried not to do anything at all.

Aimée came by nearly every day. Lorelei wasn't sure why—why her eyes were so worried, her manner so gentle when formerly it had been playful. Lorelei wasn't broken—she *wasn't*—and being treated like cracked china wasn't helping because she was completely whole.

So the days passed, some better than others but also coated in a gray sameness that denied the beautiful summer days everyone told her were beyond the windowpane.

Almost as if terrified of the silence, Aimée rambled a lot when she was there. Today, she was chattering on about how Serena might grow in the next several months. Apparently, sometime in the next four weeks or so,

Serena might begin to smile. Lorelei didn't expect to see that, but Aimée spoke about it as if it were something she should care about, so she nodded along.

"Of course," Aimée added, "Louise smiled much earlier. Six weeks. Now, granted, this is not unusual, but the way in which she smiled was."

"Right." Lorelei picked at the edge of her blanket, her eyes fixated out the window at the line of blue sky she could see from where she lay.

"Of course, you'll have to get up and see her." Aimée's meaningful side-eye as she rummaged through her bag reminded Lorelei of the olden days, before her friend had become convinced that Lorelei was about to shatter into a thousand pieces. "Though I am not, in general, the type to complain about a woman resting after giving birth, I wonder if perhaps a bit more activity may help in your case."

Oh good. They'd arrived at the *honesty* portion of their relationship. Perhaps that was better than being a chipped teacup. "I do intend to get up, but ..." But once she did, Lorelei would remember all the things that felt so unimportant now. Serena was better off in the hands of her wet nurse, her father, her aunts. The Hilton Shipping Company seemed to be getting along quite well without her—at least, she had not heard anything to the contrary. Without intending to, Lorelei was living her mother's life.

Aimée cocked her head. "I thought I would be begging you to rest rather than running down to the docks as soon as Serena was born. Instead, I almost wish you would go down now—to see some life in you."

No, because I ruined my own life. There was nothing left now—the world had passed her by, as it had passed her mother by. Lorelei had missed the boat and would now sink or swim on her own—and probably, given that her mother's blood ran in her veins, she'd sink. "I don't want to think about that right now" was all she could manage. There were dangerous tears hovering around the corner of her eyes, a dangerous fury directed entirely at herself tightening her chest. She had caused this—because she had been everything her mother before her had been—reckless, stupid, tossing away reason for little reward and then not even embracing what was given to her in return.

"Someday, you will have to think about it. About all of it," Aimée prompted. "What will you do then?"

"I don't know." Again, that was rather the point of not thinking about it. "Little will change. I will be alone. As I am now." The words were quiet, but they were said. "I will never have anything or anyone. I don't know any other way." There was no peace waiting for her around the corner. She would always be free to waste away on her bed, inactive but not at rest, to wilt like her mother did.

Perhaps if she didn't fight it, it would happen sooner. The pain wouldn't be prolonged—for herself or for those who must suffer her presence.

Yes, that made sense. It made more sense than anything had lately.

Aimée lowered herself onto the edge of the bed. "I think you are a foolish woman, aching and longing for what already is yours. You will not be alone. You have friends, family, people who care for you. Even if you did not, Aubrey belongs to you, Lorelei, whether you like it or not. He won't leave you. Let him comfort you."

Lorelei rolled her eyes because she didn't want Aimée to know how much her heart hurt. "Right. I should keep taking things from him. I already failed to give him a son—"

"As if he cares! As if it could be your fault!" Aimée exclaimed.

"Perhaps not," Lorelei murmured, "but it is my fault that I don't want to have another one. He'll want an heir eventually, and—"

"What if you gave him six daughters? There are no guarantees. Besides, surely that manner of thinking is old-fashioned. It's 1885, not the 1700s." Aimée scoffed. "If my husband were to even act as if Louise—"

"That's different." Lorelei had to make Aimée understand so she'd stop bothering her. "In our agreement, I promised to give him a second child if our first wasn't a boy. But I can't. I can't do this again. I feel as if—" There was a thickness in her throat that she didn't like, and she felt fairly certain a tear had slipped down her cheek like some pathetic Gothic heroine. She *was* pathetic, after all. Nothing like the woman she'd wanted to be. Endlessly becoming the evil she'd fought her whole life to get away from.

"Lorelei." Aimée took her hand. "Lorelei, Lorelei." She tsked and squeezed Lorelei's hand and smiled. "I have seen that man's face when he looks at you, and it doesn't matter to him. The agreement. A second child. None of it. You should ask him if he cares. You have prided yourself on honesty, so be honest with him!"

"I cannot!" The words burst from Lorelei. "I ... I ... I cannot." That was all she could say. With great effort, she turned her head away from Aimée. "Please leave me alone."

Aimée sighed and went to fuss about the room. She placed another of her tonics on the bedside table—Lorelei glimpsed this action out of her peripheral vision—and left.

Half an hour later, Lorelei roused herself, stood, and dressed.

Then she walked out of her room, through the halls, and out of the house. Her eyes flew about the empty grassy expanse, the sunshine screaming "Today is a happy day" at her. *How annoying.*

"Lore!"

With a sigh, she turned to face her sister and the two dogs trailing after her. "Win."

"You're up!" Winnie flew to her and gave her a hug. "I'm so glad! Where are you going?"

In a split second, Lorelei decided. "To the sea."

Winnie hesitated, scanning Lorelei up and down, then nodded. "We'll come with you."

Lorelei raised her eyebrows. No "May I come with you?" No "I would like to come with you." Just that she *would* be coming. That annoyed her. Where did Winnie get off, acting like it was her prerogative to join Lorelei on this walk? Not to mention that she felt a little unhinged and wanted to be alone. "I would rather—"

"Please, Lore." Winnie's eyes were wide. "You look a fright. Let me come."

Lorelei sighed, turned, and started down the path. She heard her sister's footsteps behind her. Ahead of her, Mars loped, his long strides eating up the terrain, and Potato barked at something. She ignored them all. Her primary focus was getting to the water.

She rambled off through the large field that stretched out interminably, the flower gardens eventually turning to meadows that turned into sand and seagrass. She could feel and smell the sea breeze, taste it in the air, hear the beating of the waves, and at last, she found her way to a cliffside, not a large one, but a small outcrop that overlooked a tucked-away cove Winnie and the girls often used for swimming.

She felt weak, and she stood, panting, holding her side, and watched the water play against the shore.

Winnie came up beside her, annoying in her lack of effort, her breathing imperceptible. What had practically destroyed Lorelei had failed to wind Winnie. Of course, the dogs had scattered off to investigate new smells.

Lorelei slowly sank into the sea grass. After a moment, Winnie joined her. Lorelei leaned forward, wrapping her arms around her knees, and dropped her face forward. The moderately damp sand was bother-some—she knew this skirt would be practically ruined by the time they walked back. Yet Winnie didn't seem to mind terribly. She simply sat, silent for once in her blessed life, next to Lorelei and allowed the sea to wash over them both.

"Could you tell me even a little bit? About why ... *why*, Lore?" Winnie murmured at last, her voice just loud enough to be caught by Lorelei before the wind found it and carried it away. "I ... I know you think I'm young and immature, but I might understand. I'm here, after all, aren't I? No one else is. Not Cass or Trick—even if they'd be the better confidantes, in your estimation."

Lorelei took a deep breath and let it out slowly. "Cassie said I would love my baby when she came. She said everything would change. She said my instincts would kick in, and I'd feel like a mother when I held her."

Winnie shifted next to her. "It didn't work?"

Lorelei shook her head, a laugh far too shaky for its own good escaping. "Part of the problem is that it did—I do love her. But that makes it worse. They bring her in to me every afternoon and I hold her and I feel like I'm going to hurt her. She's so delicate—so small—so in need of so many things that I can't ... I can't provide. I want to shove her back in her nanny's arms and run. I wonder if we were unloved—or if we were too much for a young woman, younger than me when Patrick came along, to ... to raise." She sucked in a deep breath. "But, Winnie, I don't want to be Mother. I keep thinking, even as I fight these thoughts because I know they can't be good, that Serena would be better off without me—without any mother at all. Irrationally, I think Aubrey would be better off without me, too. He could remarry. He could ... he could find another woman to raise Serena and have more children with. To give him a son." Her voice caught. "I don't want to resent that little girl for not being a boy, but God help me, I do."

"Oh." Winnie's wide eyes and circled lips told her what Lorelei had already known—she was losing her mind. "Does Aubrey know you feel like this?"

Lorelei shrugged. "I don't think so. Perhaps his perspective is more that I don't want the baby than anything. I wish ... I wish things ... But t hey *aren't* different. I wish Trick were here. He could get us all back on track."

Winnie squinted. "I don't think that's true."

"Maybe it's not. I don't know. I wish that someone would come along and take it all away and make ... make this all easier. Any part of it. I'm so tired all the time, and I don't know why. I wish I could sleep forever."

"Golly, Lore."

She winced. "It's not so bad."

"That sounds pretty bad."

"Yes, but it doesn't change anything."

"No," Winnie said after a moment, "it doesn't change anything. But I think it would help everyone understand. It never hurts for people to understand, Lore. Besides, you've always been so honest with Aubrey. It feels unfair to not tell him everything now."

Lorelei shrugged. "I'm not even sure I understand myself anymore. I feel odd. Like I'm not me anymore." She sniffled and was forced to wipe her eyes with her sleeve in a rather undignified manner. "After twenty years, one becomes accustomed to being oneself. Now I'm ... I'm nothing."

"That's not true!" Winnie exclaimed, turning to Lorelei. Out of the corner of her eye, Lorelei caught her sister's look. "You're Lore!"

"What does that mean, though?" Lorelei said with a shaky laugh. "I thought it meant a competent young woman who could make her own way in the world despite obstacles. I thought Lorelei Hilton would never give up. I expected more of myself—but here I am. I get pregnant, and from then on, my life spirals. I don't want to do anything anymore. I don't even want to be at the docks. I want to ... I don't want anything," she repeated, in awe of this realization. For when had she ever not *wanted*? No, craved. Begged and pleaded and then fought for the crumbs of love, of attention, and then of control and of power, to keep herself safe and give herself some anchor in the storm?

And now she wasn't satisfied. Instead, she was hollow. Like she'd been rattled around and emptied of the only thing she had left—*wanting more*.

Without that ... what was she?

"I see." Winnie scooted a little closer, and her shoulder hit Lorelei's.

She did Winnie the immense favor of not immediately moving away.

"You've got us both safe. We're *safe*. Did you ever think about that? Even Patrick couldn't do that, but Father hasn't even mentioned me coming home. I'm eighteen now, and I could leave—let myself be cut off—if I wanted. I won't—I'll probably wait it out until I'm twenty-one. They don't treat me that badly compared to how they treat you and Trick. I can handle it. But it's nice to have a break—to be here where we're safe and cared about." Winnie placed a hand on Lorelei's lower back, with a remarkably similar gesture to the way one might use when placating a frightened horse, which was within Winnie's experience, so that made sense—Lorelei could stand being comforted in a way that was familiar to the comforter, if it was well-meaning. "I'm so sorry you don't feel that way. But thank you for taking care of me—like you always have."

Lorelei frowned, not liking the pang in her heart, the welling of her eyes. "I'm glad you're happy."

"That's not the thing that matters, though it helps." There was a smile in her sister's voice. "God loves you as you are, Lore. You know that, don't you? That He loves you?"

Lorelei nodded because that was what one was supposed to do, not because she believed it. Oh yes, He loved her—but Lorelei hadn't done anything good, so she wasn't about to be rewarded by Him or anything. She didn't deserve blessings.

"He loves you a lot," Winnie continued, heedless of Lorelei's lack of interest in this topic. "So much so that He sent His Son to die for you, but it's more than that. It's that He longs to offer you comfort. I'm not exactly the most spiritually mature. I wish I were, but I'm not. But I know that He loves me and He knows me and He desires that I know Him. That *you* know Him, Lore. If you were to focus more on knowing Him, everything else would come into place. I feel sure of it."

A naïve thought, but Lorelei shrugged. "Perhaps." She didn't have the energy to know much about anyone, let alone the Lord. "Perhaps if He made it a little easier, I would be more inclined." She didn't have the mental energy to spend hours poring over the Bible, to pray until she ran out of words, to sing until her voice was hoarse. Those were the requirements, weren't they?

"Oh, Lore, it's not hard at all! It's—"

Lorelei cleared her throat. "I'm so tired, Winnie. Let's go home."

With a sigh, Winnie stumbled to her feet and held out her hand.

Lorelei accepted it, and they walked home together with Mars and Potato escorting them. Winnie didn't speak again. Perhaps she sensed Lorelei's mood had shifted to grouchy once more.

CHAPTER TWENTY-SIX

L ORELEI WAS EVIDENTLY IN an unusually bad mood that morning.

It'd started when Aubrey awoke to find her staring at the ceiling. He asked how long she'd been up—she said she wasn't sure she'd slept at all.

Not a good sign. Especially given that she seemed to need so much sleep lately. Only four weeks had passed since Serena arrived, and ever since, it was as if Lorelei's body was in permanent resting mode. Which was good—he wanted her to be comfortable, to feel like she need do nothing but *be*. In some ways, he wondered if it were healthy rest, if she were doing anything but hiding from reality, but that wasn't his decision to make.

"You didn't sleep?" he murmured, placing a tentative hand on her shoulder. "Are you feeling all right?"

Lorelei simply shrugged and sat up. "Oh, as well as I normally feel. I was thinking, though."

"Ah." He, too, sat up. "About what?"

"Oh, things. God. Serena. Will we see her today?"

"Yes." Usually he visited Serena shortly after rising, then he'd eat breakfast, then he'd bring her to Lorelei after both Serena and she were well-fed and fairly placid. "You could come see her with me now, if you like. I'll run and get dressed, then I'll be checking on her."

Lorelei glanced at him but shook her head. "No. But I think I'll go with you to the nursery, rather than having you bring her here. It seems strange to bring her to a room she doesn't recognize rather than going there myself."

Aubrey nodded. "All right." Whatever she wanted. At least it was a good sign that she was slowly becoming more and more willing to move about. Winnie had mentioned they'd gone on a walk yesterday while he was down at the docks. Maybe they could work back up to getting Lorelei to take an interest in something again. He didn't need her to do anything in particular, but he wanted her to feel as if she had a purpose, if that would make her happier.

He jumped out of bed and went to his room, where he hastily dressed, and then made his way to the nursery.

Leolyn was already up with Serena—she probably had been for several hours—but she looked more worn than usual.

"Was she up much?" Aubrey asked, scanning the sunken eyes and pale complexion.

"Yes, sir. Most of the night."

"Oh." Aubrey walked over to look down at his cheerful, gurgling daughter. "Perhaps you should rest today. I am happy to take her."

Leolyn's eyes widened. "Oh, sir, I couldn't—"

Aubrey held up his hand. "I'd rather not be argued with. I'll keep her with me for the day except when she absolutely needs you." Aubrey suspected the poor nanny was struggling to stay upright. "When did you feed her last?"

Leolyn gestured to the cradle. "About ten minutes ago. She should be all right for a few hours. She'll let you know when she's hungry."

"Thank you, Leolyn. Go lay down—I'll bring her, or someone will, in a few hours."

Leolyn agreed but insisted upon pointing out all the things Serena needed—clothes, nappies, et cetera—which Aubrey tried to understand. If it came to it, he was convinced he could learn to do everything Serena needed him to do—but to be fair, she was tiny. Hopefully he would rise to whatever occasion presented itself.

After Leolyn disappeared into the next room, Aubrey carefully picked Serena up and navigated her into the crook of his arm. Quite pleased with the smoothness of the motion, he smiled down at her and managed to adjust her blanket in what he thought was a cozy sort of way, which filled him with further pride.

He'd make a fine nanny himself, he thought.

Except for that he couldn't feed a baby, he'd only helped bathe her three or four times and had been wracked with anxiety throughout, and his ability to change nappies had yet to be firmly established. Also, he'd not spent the night with her, and babies were known for not being easy at nighttime.

"That's a career best left to the professionals until I've a little more experience," Aubrey informed Serena, who gurgled happily at this statement. "Here's what we shall do, Miss Montgomery. We'll have breakfast with your mother—and then we'll talk to her for a bit—and then we shall spend some time with your aunties—and then you shall have another feeding. Which I'm sure you will fuss for, as you are wont to do."

Serena's agreement was signaled by a flailing of a single chubby fist. She had dark hair, his Serena—a patch of it—and grayish eyes that occasionally crossed. (Dr. Burton said this would not be a permanent feature, in all likelihood.) Aubrey tucked her fist back under the blanket—it was a warm day, but he took no risks with her—and proceeded back to his wife's bedroom.

Lorelei, already nibbling at some toast, frowned at him when he appeared.

Wonderful. The mood had lingered.

"I thought we'd agreed I'd go to the nursery today," she said, the pinch in her brow and her voice indicating that, for some reason, this small change in routine had irritated her greatly.

"Yes, but Serena kept her wet nurse up most of the night," Aubrey said. "I thought it'd be nice if she had a little extra time to sleep. After all, we can't have Leolyn becoming ill." She was the key to his daughter's health, and he couldn't let anything happen to her—and though his motivation was selfish, he understood further that nursing a baby was tiring, especially as a job for a woman who already had a child of her own to care for, and she'd have to keep up her strength. Presumably.

"I see." Lorelei took a bite of toast, chewed, and swallowed. "Is she all right?"

"Leolyn?"

"No. I'm sure she'll be fine; she's an adult woman who has handled months of being a mother before today, what with her Johnny. I meant Serena."

"Yes. I think so." She had started to settle in, in his arms, heading rapidly toward another of her near constant naps.

"Wouldn't she be better off in the nursery? After all, Leolyn could be right on hand, and then you would have everything you needed if you insist upon remaining present while Leolyn rests." Lorelei raised an eyebrow. "I know you've grown accustomed to bringing her here, but I told you, that's no longer necessary."

"Oh." He frowned. After a moment, he sat on the edge of the bed, regarding his daughter with a touch of worry. "Why don't you want her here?"

Lorelei made a seemingly meaningless gesture with her hand—an upward and downward flutter that indicated the entire room was at fault somehow. "For one, it's my room, and I never wanted to be in my mother's room, I'll tell you that. Serena deserves to be somewhere that can provide her with love. Something I can't give her, as we've previously established."

"But your mother was ... not you." Aubrey gave his full attention to his wife. "You can choose to love Serena."

"Hmm." Lorelei shook her head and turned back to her breakfast.

Aubrey stayed. He had to, somehow—to prove how happy Serena was here. And indeed, she was sleeping in his arms with barely a twitch, peaceful, *serene* even, as her name indicated.

After a time, Lorelei finished her breakfast and sat on her bed, her eyes on him and presumably their daughter, and Aubrey asked her if she would like to hold Serena.

"No, I don't think so. I need to stop. It's giving her ideas—about how comfortable she should be with me. I'm afraid she will trust me and then it will wound her greatly when she begins to think for herself."

Aubrey raised his eyebrows. "She's a baby. All she knows is that she is safe and loved with you."

Lorelei rolled her eyes. "I won't hold her."

A few minutes of silence rolled past while Lorelei fidgeted and squirmed but decidedly did not get up or ring for Harriet or do anything that might indicate a desire to change the situation they were in. "I could hold her for a few minutes," she said at last.

Aubrey swiftly but carefully transferred Serena to Lorelei's arms.

As always, the move was unproblematic. Serena was a deep sleeper for a newborn.

They sat together while Serena napped and Lorelei stroked Serena's cheek and Aubrey watched them.

He was almost starting to hope they would be all right.

Lorelei had admitted to herself a while ago that her relationship with her own child—possibly now her only child—could not be businesslike. Not exactly. It could be distant, or it could be loving. She had felt that distant was the better option of the two, but apparently, such was not possible.

The problem was, Serena was perfect. If she'd been a little less perfect, Lorelei would've found it easy to dismiss her, another little baby who would someday be another little person in this wide world full of needy individuals, none of whom Lorelei could save, but this was *her* baby. Between the fear of hurting her and the desire to keep her close, Lorelei found herself torn in a battle she could not win.

She pressed her lips to her child's brown locks and clucked her tongue—the baby should have been blonde and pale with a hint of the neoclassical, not dark-haired and ruddy and possessing Lorelei's nose and possibly her ears.

In an ideal world, Serena would look like the Montgomery girls and act like a Montgomery girl, but when, in time, she stirred and looked up at Lorelei with eyes that seemed more silver-touched by the day, there was a spark there.

Perhaps Lorelei was losing her mind, for a baby of that age couldn't have the American grit Lorelei imagined, but she *thought* she'd seen that spark. If she had, what did that mean?

What kind of creature had she brought into the world, and what would she do if there was no way around her need to nurture that creature? What if she simply *had* to raise her daughter? What if she had no choice?

What if this meant more than the Hilton Shipping Company?

What if that torturous excuse for a corporation didn't mean anything at all?

Aubrey stood. "I'm going to go check in on the girls—it's been quiet today, and that scares me—and then we'll take her up to Leolyn for her next feeding before she gets angry at us. All right?"

Lorelei nodded, barely registering his words. She had too much to consider—Serena, the future, the company. Maybe even Aubrey, if time and feeling allowed for it.

Aubrey's steps retreated down the hall.

Serena's face crumpled, and she squawked.

Lorelei's chest collapsed in fear. What had she done wrong? Nothing. She'd done *nothing*. Was her existence enough to cause such a reaction in her daughter?

Serena's singular cry turned into a series of panicked shrieks as Lorelei adjusted her in her arms and felt a fair bit of panic herself. She didn't know what was wrong—how to help, how to fix this.

"What do you want from me?" she mumbled. She transferred Serena to her shoulder and patted her back. She felt sure she'd seen *someone* comfort a baby in this way, and it was worth a try.

After a moment, Serena's screams turned to a series of discontented grunts and whimpers, but her body relaxed against Lorelei's in a way that was rather nice.

Aubrey came in then and approached the bed. "I heard her cry," he said, a cheery smile on his face. "She must need to eat and be changed. Good you got her calmed down, though."

As if it were as simple as that.

Lorelei handed the baby off to Aubrey's waiting arms, picked up her wrap, and followed Aubrey to the nursery.

Leolyn took Serena back and prepared to feed her, and Aubrey excused himself, perhaps assuming Lorelei would want to return to her room.

She did not.

"Can I stay? I'd like to talk to you, Leolyn."

The nursemaid's eyes rose from the baby to Lorelei with an inquisitive expression, but she simply nodded.

So they were seated on chairs opposite each other, with Leolyn nursing Serena and Lorelei staring out the window at the bleak, slightly stormy day.

"What is it that you wanted to say to me, Mrs. Montgomery?" Leolyn chanced after a long moment. "If there is something you're concerned about, to do with Serena—"

Lorelei lifted her hand. "No, nothing like that. I wondered how she is doing. Overall. The doctor and his wife both assure me she is growing at the rate she ought, but you have your own child."

"Yes," Leolyn agreed, "Johnny."

"How is she—compared to … Johnny?"

"She's strong and healthy. About the size he was at this age." Leolyn smiled. "You've no need to worry for her, Mrs. Montgomery. She's a strong child. Never a day ill. She's a good baby, too. I don't think she's quite figured out how to smile yet, but she will soon—you can tell when she's happy."

"Can you?" Lorelei murmured. "Is it just when she's not screaming?"

"Oh, well, she mostly screams and sleeps," Leolyn said, "but she does have moments when she's content. She's alert more than most babies—and she makes those grunting sounds. But you shouldn't be upset, Mrs. Montgomery, if she doesn't take to you right away. She'll warm up to you. Just you see!"

Leolyn meant that to be reassuring, but Lorelei's eyes burned, and she was forced to turn her face away to hide the presumed crumpling that was happening there. Of course Serena wasn't used to her; she didn't find comfort in Lorelei's arms.

That was what Lorelei wanted, wasn't it? For Serena to view her as a distant creature that provided for her and was even proud of her—but wasn't capable of giving love.

A child wouldn't understand that, though, so she would view Lorelei as cold. Frightening, even.

That thought was more crushing than she'd imagined it would be.

Silence reigned as Lorelei struggled to get her emotions back under control. But there were tears trickling down her face, and she would have to lift her hand to wipe them at some point—and then Leolyn would know.

Lorelei was undone simply by hearing a few softened words of truth.

"Mrs. Montgomery?" Leolyn's voice was gentle. "It's all right. I know it's hard—especially at first. But it will get better—and make more sense. I promise."

"How do you know?" Lorelei whispered.

"I just know," Leolyn replied. "It got easier with Johnny—and it will get easier with your little one. You have to keep trying."

Lorelei shook her head. "I'm not supposed to be ..." She stopped and collected herself. "I'm not supposed to be trying at all. She's cared for. That's what matters. I'd ... I'd planned to give her up. To her father, her aunts ... to you. I'm not ... I'm not suited to be a mother, so I thought—" Her traitorous voice refused to go on without verging on that dreadful word.

Hysterical.

"Of course you're suited to be her mother!" Leolyn sounded indignant.

"You are, aren't you? She's yours, isn't she?"

"Any more than she is yours?" After all, Leolyn was the one who fed her, dressed her, cleaned her, cared for her.

"Pardon my impertinence, Mrs. Montgomery, but that doesn't make her *mine*. I think she's a sweet baby, but I have one of my own to care for—and in time, you'll have a nanny for her, and a governess, and she won't be *theirs* either. Surely you had a nanny and a governess; you knew they were not your mothers."

Lorelei shook her head. "I had a nanny, yes, and I did have governesses on and off. Mostly my brother raised me, though. He wasn't my mother, but he was something better than she ever would have been." Just *Trick*, with no need for a label. "I think I would've hated to have greater involvement from my own parents." *They would have destroyed me more than they already did.*

"But, Mrs. Montgomery, surely you could make different choices from the ones your parents made—and then Serena would never need to regret your involvement."

Lorelei looked at Leolyn, at the eyes softened with pity, at the child in her arms. She said nothing, for she had nothing to say. No rebuttal, no reason why she couldn't be better than what she believed she could be. Only that she assumed she was a wretch born without natural womanly emotions ... but was that true? Even if it were, did that mean she could not change? That there was not something inherently growth-oriented in the human nature, that could be reached by an all-knowing, loving, powerful God and altered through the power of His Spirit?

She had believed so once. Perhaps she did believe it—for others. But for herself? How could she?

Especially when Serena mattered so very much. Any misstep on Lorelei's part could cause some permanent damage—she knew that more than anyone. So how could she hope to be her mother?

"I'll put her down now, Mrs. Montgomery. She's fallen asleep."

"I could sit with her for a while. Hold her," Lorelei offered.

Leolyn nodded. "If that's what you want, ma'am."

"Yes." It was what she wanted, strangely enough. "But you'll be on hand?"

"Yes, ma'am. I'll be in the next room. You can call if you need anything at all."

"Very well."

So Lorelei accepted her daughter back into her arms—and watched her sleep.

CHAPTER TWENTY-SEVEN

T HE MUTED GLOW OF the lamps was casting dim shadows along the corridors by the time Aubrey emerged from his study that evening. He'd stopped briefly to eat dinner before returning to the accounting books, determined to finish before the end of the month.

He made his way up to his wife's bedroom—only to find the room empty. The bed was made—and the servants had cleaned and straightened the room, probably eager to take advantage of their mistress's unusual absence. However, instead of providing the sense of comfort an orderly bedroom might otherwise have, this put him on edge.

He didn't like the fact that there *wasn't* a sense of mussiness about her room—a blanket tossed here or a slipper there, as if her maid simply couldn't keep up, as if the other servants felt unable to breach her privacy. The fire was lit, but even its steady flickering failed to comfort him.

He frowned. Where had she gotten to?

Of course, Aubrey had left her in the nursery, but that had been hours ago, and by this time, Serena ought to be tucked away for the night.

Perhaps it was worth checking, though.

His footsteps hastily took him to the nursery's door. Inside, the room was dim, lit only by a singular lamp on a table in the corner and the hearth fire, though with the pastel-colored walls, it still felt cheerful and warm—in his opinion. A tray with two plates sat on the table—had Lorelei sat up here all afternoon and evening, taking her dinner with Leolyn? Well, perhaps she had, for even now, Lorelei sat on a cushioned chair by the window, cradling their daughter in her arms.

Honestly, he wouldn't have believed it himself if he hadn't seen it, but she was there, and she looked … almost content. Her focus was entirely on Serena—her eyes fixed on the baby's face, one hand stroking the baby's cheek. Leolyn was nowhere to be found.

Relief flooded him, though he was careful to temper it. After all, this might not be a permanent change. Lorelei had been a bit inconsistent with what he knew of her lately, and he wouldn't let himself hope …

That was a lie. He would *hope*. He would always hope, while there was any chance that someday Lorelei would feel as he did about Serena and that she would return his regard for her, too, but that seemed almost too much to ask.

He shifted, and the floor creaked.

Lorelei's eyes flew to him, but if she were startled, she did not so much as twitch. "There you are," she murmured. "I thought you'd come find me eventually."

"Yes," he said, keeping his voice low to match hers. "Are you all right?" Perhaps that was the wrong thing to say, but he had never known the right thing to say. That would have to be enough.

She seemed to pause before she answered, her eyes returning to Serena, a heaviness about her that he couldn't place his finger on—only, he felt, it was different than the darkness that had veiled her for months. "I'm better, I think," she said. "Come sit. Leolyn is sleeping—Serena was fussy and didn't want to lie down, but I wanted to hold her anyway. I said I would wake Leolyn when I needed to sleep myself, and we would find a way to get Serena to stay in her cradle—though part of it is that babies must cry. That's what Leolyn said, but I couldn't bear to hear her. Serena, I mean. She sounded so pitiful. I would feel differently if I had to mind her all the time, but just this once …" She shook her head. "I'm not creating bad habits in one night. That's impossible. Habits take time to form. So much can happen in three months—I asked, and Leolyn said that in three more months, she will hold up her head, and in another three months after that, she may begin to crawl. Johnny is. That's Leolyn's child."

"I see."

"Yes. Can I ask you a question?"

"Of course."

"How do you know if you're breaking apart in a good way or a bad way?"

He sat still for a long time, considering this, before he replied. "I think God has to be your guide on that."

Lorelei nodded. "I'd like that, but I don't know God as well as I thought I did, Aubrey. Winnie thinks I should get to know Him. I don't know where to start."

This, too, he considered. "The clearest verse that comes to mind is 'Be still, and know that I am God: I will be exalted among the heathen, I will be exalted in the earth.' Psalm 46, I believe, which starts out with, 'God is our refuge and strength, a very present help in trouble.' To me, that is worth clinging to. The entire Psalm describes how He is present and has great strength in our most desperate moments, in the times when it seems that the entire world is shattering around us. 'Though the waters thereof roar and be troubled, though the mountains shake with the swelling thereof.'"

"Right. I know that." There was a shakiness in her voice. He wondered if she knew it; he wasn't sure she would care if she did. "Do you think I'm having a nervous collapse?"

"I don't know. Maybe." He shifted and reached out a hand, then placed it on her shoulder. "Do you feel like you're having a nervous collapse?"

"I feel like I've had five this year," Lorelei said plainly. "I'm wondering if I'm nearing another one and if it's a good sort or a bad sort."

"I don't think there is such a thing as a good nervous collapse."

"I disagree. There must be, for people have breakdowns and turn down better paths all the time."

Aubrey raised his eyebrows. "Are you sure?"

"Yes. Think of Ebenezer Scrooge."

"I don't think—"

"What else could it be? Ghosts don't exist."

"That's fiction, Lori."

She rolled her eyes. "Here I was, looking for my Three Ghosts to wake me up and make me see the error of my ways. I know it's fiction, but all fiction has a little truth in it."

"You think the portion of *A Christmas Carol* that has a little truth in it is the ghost parts?" he said incredulously. "Or Spirits, rather?"

"No, the nervous collapse. I swear, sometimes it's like you don't even listen to me."

The concept of having multiple nervous collapses a year was ridiculous to him, as he'd think such a thing would rather halt life for the bearer thereof, and Lorelei's life hadn't slowed down much in the last year.

But there *was* an all-powerful God, and He *did* love Lorelei, and there *was* a reason for all that had happened, positive and negative. Even if Lorelei didn't immediately see it, perhaps she could be coaxed—perhaps, even, he could be a part of her growth, her accepting what was and must be true.

"I have not been in much of a position to take care of a baby," Lorelei said, breaking the silence that had fallen between them. "I'm sorry about that. Sorry I didn't even try. I put no effort into motherhood—I still haven't—but I'd like to ... I think I'd like to *try*."

"I think you will succeed," Aubrey said quickly. "I think you could be a splendid mother. Even if you're not at first, you will learn, as I am determined to learn how to be a splendid father, in time."

Lorelei nodded. "You are right. But ... there's also the company. I think you're managing it well, but frankly, it's hard for me to ... to want to support a company that is so ... I'm not sure I need to ... No, I'm not sure I *want* to cling to it. It would be better if I took a less active role."

"I see." Honestly, that was music to his ears, but he didn't want to strip her of that aspect of her life if it wasn't truly her choice. "You could easily do both, you know. When you're recovered, I mean—completely recovered. You could be a good mother to Serena and take an active role in the company, but you wouldn't have to be your father. You could work in moderation."

The little nod she gave indicated that he had been accurate in his assumptions of her thoughts. "Yes. I could."

"I would support you in it, whatever that meant."

She frowned at him, adjusting her hold on their daughter. "Why are you so good to me? You're too good to me, and I am a poor wife. I didn't give you a son, and I may not ever. I never love you back—with actions. We can't even enjoy physical relations right now, and I don't know how we will again, given that I seem to be rather on the fertile side but also not so good at managing the results of said fertility. So why?"

"I love you," he reminded her.

"Why?" she persisted. "Why me? Because I am your wife, you could say, but you didn't have to marry me, nor did you have to fall in love with me once you did. No, there was no obligation there. We agreed to not. There was more risk than reward there for you. So why?"

"Because ..." He struggled for words. "You are so perfect for me. Your fire, when you have it, and your need for comfort, for steadiness, when you don't. Your outspokenness, your stubbornness, the mix of grief and anger I see in moments of vulnerability, when your whole body tenses for a fight against your own emotions. You suit me so well. I am in love with the woman God created for me. I am convinced our marriage was meant to be, and I am convinced once we figure a few things out, we will be happy. I think we can only be happy together. I'm that idealistic." He offered a slight smile. There were tears trickling down her cheeks, but he didn't back down at the sight of them. "Mostly, I want to show you I can be a rock in the storm, or, if you'd rather, a harbor—a safe place where you can swim into rather than persisting in drowning. Because you don't have to keep fighting to be valuable. You can stop—you can stop anytime, Lori. I'll be here—loving you even if you never do anything else for the rest of your life."

She didn't say anything. He got out a handkerchief and offered it to her and then when she didn't acknowledge him, wiped her cheeks himself with it.

At last, she turned her face to the door and called for Leolyn, who appeared and took Serena. As the maid settled the baby, Aubrey was momentarily distracted—and when he looked around, he saw that Lorelei had disappeared.

They shared a room. It wasn't as if she could duck out and avoid a conversation.

He hurried down the stairs—but her bedroom was empty. He frowned and walked into his room, but he thought he caught a sliver of light through the window as he passed it—and going to it, he saw a female figure carrying a lantern disappear into the gardens.

He wouldn't have minded, but it was night and raining, and he couldn't bear the thought of her catching her death—or doing something foolish. The thought of that spiked an instant panic within, and he snatched up a coat before hastening downstairs and out the door.

She was sitting on the bench, in his mother's favorite spot. The lantern rested on the ground before her, but he could see her shadowed face well enough to tell she was still crying.

"Lori, you need to come in. It's raining." He took off his coat and draped it over her shoulders; she didn't protest. "I'm afraid you'll become ill."

"You know, I do wish for love, but since I struggle to return it, it seems so unfair to ask for it. Like pushing my luck too far." She shrugged. "Craving what I cannot give."

"Some people show love differently," he said softly. "You love your siblings. I think you love Serena, too."

"So I love my own blood? How touching." She shook her head. "What do I do for them? Winnie would be so much happier with Trick—I haven't seen him in months, and I constantly forget to write even though I could. I only spent more than an hour altogether with my daughter after she was already a month old. If this is the way I love, I might as well not love at all. You love me, and I'm foolish enough to believe you, but accepting it would be ... I almost feel better pretending I don't know. As if I'm not torturing you in that unique way that unrequited love tortures someone."

"I don't feel tortured," he reassured her, taking a seat on the bench. "I don't think I'd have been happy married to someone I couldn't like or love."

"But you gambled with that chance anyway," Lorelei observed.

"I liked you when we were married; I was already coming to love you. If nothing else, love is a choice. A gift from God, yes—that, too—but we choose what we do with our feelings, and nothing about them is uniquely fulfilling except what God gives us. That's what I think you need to know—that only God's love can fulfill you. It's the selflessness of His sacrifice for us that fuels our own love, the greatest reflection of Him we have to offer. I'm not selfless—but I want to be, for you. I'll never be perfect, but I must try, because I want you to be happy."

"That doesn't lie with you. My happiness, I mean."

"No." He took her hand. "It lies with God. Turn to Him. Do as Winnie says—open yourself to the possibility that He loves you regardless of your actions, that He exists to wipe clean our slate and give us new life."

Light flooded through the clouds, and Aubrey turned his face up to the nearly full moon before returning his attention to his wife.

Lorelei laughed shakily and wiped at the dampness on her face—a mix of tears and raindrops, he thought. "Do you believe in signs from God, Aubrey?"

Aubrey glanced back up at the rapidly clearing sky, stars peering down at them from above. "I wouldn't read too much into English weather, darling."

"But it could be," she persisted. "It could be a sign."

"Yes. It could be." It wasn't.

"Do you really believe ... do you really believe all I have to do is *be* and God will love me?"

"Yes. It's entirely true. I love you the same way. I'm not God, and I will be human and I will disappoint you—unlike Him."

Lorelei nodded, a thoughtful expression on her face as she watched the clouds. "Perhaps you are right," she said placidly. "I'll have to think on it."

He put his arm around her and hugged her damp body to him. She was shivering despite the extra warmth of his coat. "We should go inside," he murmured. "Change into dry clothes."

"We won't catch our deaths. That only happens in novels."

"Nonetheless—"

"Just be still for a moment. Be still with me."

So they sat for a long time and took deep breaths of the scent of the air after rain—fresh and new, hinting at flora around them, carrying a whiff of the sea to the south.

"It's not unselfish, Aubrey, so don't read anything into this—and I don't mean it in the romantic declaration way, as I've always felt such were more gestures than reality—but I do love you. Just not well." Her eyes flew to his face and then she smiled at whatever she saw there. "Now, don't look so shocked. It's nothing. As you said, I love Serena and Trick and Winnie—"

He kissed her to stop the tide of words for a moment and give him a chance to think. "You love me?" he whispered when he withdrew.

She held up her hand. "I'm not going to repeat it often either. Or at least—maybe I will someday. But not now. I'm a little wrung out—but I'm being honest, and I don't think I'm overwrought. Just tired."

He nodded, trying helplessly to process this announcement, to sort through what it meant for Lorelei Montgomery to say those words—if it meant anything at all.

Maybe it didn't matter. Maybe what mattered was that she was sitting beside him and the rain had stopped and the air smelled fresh and new.

She placed her hand into his without being asked, and he held it until she was ready to go inside and sleep.

CHAPTER TWENTY-EIGHT

August 1885

S ERENA WAS TWO MONTHS old now, and she had taken to smiling many times.

Lorelei did think it was a gift, but she hadn't had any marvelous epiphanies from it. It was a baby's smile—and though it was the best smile in the world, as Serena was the best baby in the world, it had yet to reveal anything particularly marvelous to Lorelei.

Leolyn had brought Serena out in what was apparently called "a pram," and Lorelei had joined her. She didn't want to push the thing, but apparently in this warm weather, it was all right for Serena to be exposed to fresh air—even to be taken from the carriage and placed on a blanket on the ground for a few minutes. So Lorelei sat next to Serena and watched her wiggle and squirm but not make much progress in any way. She lay on her stomach and repeatedly tried to raise her head.

When Lorelei had commented that if Serena had a more proportional head to her body size, her efforts would be easier, Leolyn said all babies were sized like that. Which was rather irritating, as Lorelei remembered enough to know that there had been a great deal of struggle surrounding the birthing of that head.

"Hasn't Eve left us with enough curses? It seems like it's not one but thirty or forty," she'd commented.

As if in response, Serena gurgled and attempted once more to make some form of movement with her head, which again was without success.

"Do you mind if I speak with her alone, Leolyn?" Lorelei asked.

"Of course not, Mrs. Montgomery. I think I'll go to the rose garden and come back in a few minutes."

If there was a tone of hilarity in Leolyn's voice, Lorelei ignored it this time. She talked to Serena a lot when no one was around, for she had words to say to her daughter that she didn't think anyone else would understand. She told Serena the safest, most sanitary bits about her childhood; about Patrick and Cassie, both of whom Serena must come to love some day and who would love her very much when she met them; about how she shouldn't trust her Auntie Winnie too much, though she would doubtless be an amusing aunt; and about how Lorelei hoped Serena would be when she was a woman. But there were more subjects to be discussed than that—endless subjects.

"I went down to the docks with your father today," Lorelei said. "I've spent so much time reading and walking about and visiting you, so it's not that I haven't gotten out, but I've not gone down there in a long time. Since ... months before you were born. It's entirely different. Docks and structures extend deeper into the harbor. They had to dredge the thing, you know, and that took up most of June—but now we're settled. Of course, it's not as if this will ever be a primary shipping port, but it'll function all right. I don't know that I ... that I even understand what's going on. Your father says there's an office at the docks for when I'm ready, if I'm ever ready ... Oh, he doesn't say that. You know him; he's being diplomatic. But I think he believes I'll not return to work there in the way I have been. Hastings is competent, and your father can step in where need be ... but I'm not sure I want to be that involved."

Serena made a series of frustrated noises that Lorelei immediately recognized as the start of a fit. She cautiously, awkwardly, picked her daughter up and adjusted her so she lay against her shoulder, her hand at the back of Serena's neck. Of course, she was getting sturdier, but as her attempts at lifting her head proved, she wasn't quite there.

"I can't believe you're so affected by this," Lorelei said softly. "I didn't know you cared so much for my career as a shipping magnate. Don't fuss. Did you know that if albatross chicks fall out of their nest, their mother lets them die? She can't rescue them, and she doesn't recognize them except by the house they live in. Isn't that an interesting fact? Don't cry."

Serena obligingly did not cry, though whether it was because of Lorelei's "fun facts about albatrosses" was yet to be determined.

She moved Serena to rest against her knees and gave her a serious look. "I'd do much to keep you safe in the nest, my chick."

"Lore!" Her sister's shout drew her away from Serena, and Lorelei turned to face Winnie, who was rapidly crossing the lawn toward her.

With a sigh, Lorelei gave Serena a secret look of annoyance before turning again to Winnie. "What is it?" Lorelei called back.

"Just got the post," Winnie replied, then came to flop down beside Lorelei. "Here." She dropped a sheet of paper next to Lorelei. "Read it, why don't you? It's from Mother. Can I hold Serena?"

Lorelei handed Serena over and picked up the letter. It was a short missive, threatening in a sickeningly sweet way, reminding Winnie that eventually she would have to return to Boston—sometime next year, Mother said. She intimated that she had already put Father off about it once, though it was more likely that they'd simply been arguing and Mother intended to bring Winnie home as a ritual sacrifice to appease him.

Lorelei set the letter down and turned to her sister. Winnie wasn't in tears or frantic, but Lorelei's chest was tight enough and her throat choked enough for both of them.

"You won't go back," Lorelei said in a tone that sounded dull and flat even to her.

"I don't have much of a choice, Lore." Winnie glanced up from Serena briefly before returning her eyes to her niece. "I don't mind. I'll be fine."

"What do you mean, 'you'll be fine?'" Heat rose before Lorelei's eyes. "After all we've gone through, Winnie? You'd throw away freedom? Why?"

"Well, Lore, I—"

"No!" The word came out more a screech than a word. "No! You will not go back to Boston. I will find a way to keep you here. They'll hurt you, Winnie. Don't you see—"

"Lore, I don't need you to sacrifice everything for me! I'll be fine."

But Lorelei couldn't hear it. She lurched to her feet, eyes filled with tears. Out of the corner of her eye, she saw Leolyn hurrying back across the lawn, perhaps having heard Lorelei's raised voice. "I'm going to talk to Aubrey about how we can get you out of going home," she said fiercely and marched off, heedless of Winnie's protestations.

Aubrey was in his office sorting through paperwork he had picked up from Hastings that morning when Lorelei burst in, eyes wild, tears staining her cheeks.

"Aubrey," she said, her voice full of tense fear, "I need your help."

He rose. She went to him willingly, stepping into his arms and letting herself be pulled close.

"It's Winnie," she whispered. "Mother wants her to come home to Boston, and I can't let her go. I can't. I know it won't be until next year—that's what Mother said; she can always change her mind—but it's still too soon. Winnie won't be able to bear up. I ... I need you to talk to my father or ... or something. Find a way to convince him to let Winnie stay here. Please, Aubrey. I'll do anything. Even ..." She paused. "I'll even give you another child."

"Shh ... slow down." He gave her a quick hug, then held her back, his hands on her shoulders. "That is not going to happen. I don't need bribes to help you. I'll do it regardless—but you need to take a deep breath first."

She shook her head; he heard the fast pace of her breathing. He led her to a seat and knelt before her as she released a series of sobs. Her hands were cold in his.

This had truly upset her that much?

"I ... can't ... can't let anything h-happen to Winnie," Lorelei managed eventually. "I can't. I can't bear it."

"I know. I know. But let's talk this through—after you're calm. For now, breathe, Lori. Breathe and know that I won't let anything happen to her or you. You're safe—she's safe. We'll figure it out."

"Maybe she sh-should have m-married someone here. Maybe she could still. But I didn't want that life for her. This was supposed to be a sacrifice on my part that saved her."

"I see," he murmured, not letting himself think about the fact that she viewed their marriage as a sacrifice—despite having said she loved him. "I'm sure we can figure something else out. If not, she'll be twenty-one and free in three years. Two, by the time she'd have to be with your parents."

"Well ... yes." She leaned forward against him. "I don't know what they want her for. They need a pawn to pass between them, to play with." She shook her head against his shoulder. "Oh, Aubrey, it's so awful how they treated us. How they treated me—and Patrick—and how badly they would treat Winnie. She never was exposed to them before. We always shielded her. They treated her like a spoiled daughter, but without me there to take the blame for everything, to stand between her and whatever might come, she'll be hurt. I know she will be."

"Perhaps."

"I ... I was ... an inconvenience, an 'albatross.' Another reason Mother couldn't run home to Virginia when the war was over, another reason Trick couldn't marry the woman he loved until it was almost too late. Winnie is about the only person to benefit from my presence, and if she loses that ... if *I* lose that ..." Her voice broke again, and she cried.

He wasn't sure what to do, and he felt rather awkward kneeling in front of the chair, so he didn't do anything. He held her while she wept, until her breathing slowed a bit, and she sniffled and reached into his coat pocket for a handkerchief.

After she had wiped her eyes and blown her nose, he examined her. She was embarrassed now, her eyes everywhere but on him.

"I didn't realize," he said slowly, "that when you said you were an albatross, you didn't mean you were some soaring, free, always-flying creature. I didn't know you thought you were an inconvenience. But I want you to know you are not an inconvenience to me—to me, you are everything. You are not an inconvenience to anyone, honestly. Winnie adores you. You're a big part of Serena's world, as we all must be right now."

Lorelei nodded succinctly. "Yes."

"Are you afraid of Winnie having to ... to marry without love ... as you did?" Aubrey murmured. "For that's what your parents wanted, wasn't it? The only reason you didn't take the man they wanted for you was because of the company, and Winnie won't care about that."

Lorelei shook her head. "I am happy with our situation ... but I fear Winnie may be put in a worse one."

"I see." He gave her one last squeeze. "I'm going to have the servants draw a bath for you and take you upstairs to our chambers. All right?"

"But I want to talk to Winnie. I left her, but ... I don't know. I was angry or something."

She'd been a little hysterical, but Aubrey didn't say that. She would think it was an insult—and he didn't mean it as one. He wanted her to have strong emotions. "How about I send her up to you?" Then Lorelei could talk to her while surrounded by water, which seemed to be one of the few things that kept her completely calm. "You should talk. Please, Lori. This is what I want you to do." *Do it for me. Be safe, be calm, be happy—for me.*

After a moment of hesitation, Lorelei nodded, and she let him help her to her feet and up the stairs.

When Winnie, looking concerned, entered her room about a quarter of an hour later, Lorelei was settled in a bath filled with herbs and scents and feeling considerably better. She'd taken care to wash her face so that her emotions might not be as easily discerned, but Winnie's eyes held consternation nonetheless.

Wonderful. Lorelei had worried her little sister.

"Take a seat." She gestured toward the chair on the other side of the room. "I need to talk to you."

"I know. You seemed upset."

"I was concerned."

"Whatever. It's practically the same with you," Winnie said, and Lorelei glanced over to see the tail end of an eye roll. "Lore, has it occurred to you that I'll be twenty-one in three years? That by the time I return to our parents next year, I'll be near to nineteen, which is how old you were when you married? They'll want me to wed, I think, but I don't mind. I *wouldn't*. I like most of those boys in Boston, and if they marry me off to one of them, fine—but I don't think they will. I think Mother wants someone to offer her a shield from Father. She ought to have that. She *deserves* that."

Lorelei frowned. "What are you talking about? Mother doesn't *deserve* anything from us after how she treated us all those years."

"Oh, Lore, but she's been so heartbroken!" Lorelei was surprised to see that Winnie's eyes were full of tears. "She regrets it. I know she does. She wants Patrick back, she's sorry about you, and she ... she wants to meet her grandchildren. I know it; I could see it in her eyes. She's always been nicer to me anyway."

"Because Trick and I have protected you," Lore insisted, picking up a bar of soap and turning it over and over until her hands were slippery with it. "Because we have kept you from the impact of our parents' actions. We have loved you, Winnie—they never had."

"I'm not an idiot, Lore. I see what they've done. But that doesn't mean that Mother doesn't need—"

"She doesn't need anything from us!" Lorelei snapped. "She's not been a mother to us. She's hardly noticed us. How can you even consider—"

"Because I've seen how sad she is! Mother is ... Mother is saveable. Maybe not Father. I don't think he cares about either of us—not at all—or anything but himself and the company. I think he'll ... he'll kill himself someday from it." Two tears trickled down her cheeks, but she kept talking. "But Mother wants things to be different. I'll go to her—and help her make them different. Maybe Trick would help her—if I was there, if he felt it helped me. It's worth finding out, surely."

Lorelei frowned and shook her head. "But—"

"It's my life." Winnie's voice held a firm note it never had before. "I must be allowed to direct my own life. I must. You shouldn't be the one to deny me that. Besides, what could you do? Bribe Father? He won't care. He wants me there to keep the peace with Mother or ... or something. Maybe because he's come up with a decent match for me."

Lorelei sat still for a long time. "You are becoming a woman; perhaps you should be allowed to make your own decisions. But I don't have to like it."

Winnie stood and started toward Lorelei, then stopped awkwardly. The bath had been a good choice; it stopped any unnecessary shows of affection. "I do appreciate it, Lore," Winnie said softly. "I'm sure you'll feel it necessary to offer all your advice, so I won't ever be without you. I love you."

"I love you, too," Lorelei mumbled half under her breath. "Now will you leave me alone? I have tragedies to contemplate, such as your insistence that Mother is a human being and not a screeching harpy."

Winnie laughed and started toward the door. "Lore?"

"Yes, Winnie?" Lorelei said. Her voice had let on more of her exhaustion than she cared to admit, but there was nothing she could do about that.

"Do you feel a little better now?"

"Yes. I do."

Winnie smiled before she disappeared through the door and pulled it click shut behind her.

Lorelei had taken her meal in her room, and Aubrey left her to her own devices, knowing sometimes giving her time to herself was the best medicine for any ills she had. However, after dinner and after making sure all the girls were settled for the evening, he made his way up to Lorelei's room.

She was sitting on the bed with a book, but she put it aside when she saw him. "I talked to Winnie," she said. "She is determined to go—and she reminded me that it would perhaps be unfair to control her actions. Therefore, she will walk into the lion's den next year unless something comes up in the meantime. We'll see." She drummed her fingers along the coverlet. "I don't like it, but I can't stop it."

Aubrey nodded. "That's probably for the best."

"It's made me think about our future, though. Come sit. I want to talk about it."

Trepidation flooded him, but he crossed the room and sat next to her. "What about our future did you want to discuss?" Surely she didn't want to back up, to be less intimate than they were now. He was starting to feel like they were in such a good place, and he wanted to keep moving along that path.

"I think we both need to back off at the Hilton Shipping Co.," she said. "I will acquiesce to you if you truly feel otherwise, but you need to focus on the estate, and I have things to focus on myself. Serena, of course, but also our sisters, the household ... I want to redecorate, actually. The south parlor is hideous, frankly speaking—forgive me, but your mother must have had little taste if the decorations and furniture were her decisions. Oh, and friends. I have a friend in Aimée, but I want to make more friends and do more and understand how this world works—this new world that I've barely been living in as your wife. I don't mind us maintaining what control we have of the company, and I think the docks were a good choice and will yield profits, but my father made a mistake I will not make; he could not trust anyone except Trick enough to delegate. I have no idea how Father is managing elsewhere in the world, but here in England, I trust Hastings. He's more than proven himself. I would like to review the books with him, especially since I did learn how to do it and I'm not going to let all that information go to waste, but I do not need to stand over him and manage his every movement."

A little speechless, Aubrey hastily nodded. "You are right. There is no sense in doing the work twice. Hastings is a good manager, and we can easily review documents, sign papers, and make the bigger decisions. Anything else is unnecessary interference that will only serve to slow down operations in the long run."

"Exactly." Lorelei extended a hand to him. "Come closer. I want to tell you the rest, but you can't be sitting practically across the country from me."

He moved across the bed and put his arm around her, despite the fact that he despised being on beds when fully dressed.

"I'll take all three of our sisters to London in the winter, if you think that is wise. I'd like to shop and prepare them to debut. Also, then we could introduce Serena to the Knights—I think Mrs. Knight would like to meet our daughter. I wrote and told her about Serena. I don't know anyone else we could show her off to in England, but I want to do that. What do you think?"

"I think that would be nice."

"Then, after the Season is over, or slightly before it is over, we can start trying for your heir," she finished, folding her hands on her lap. "What do you think?"

He hesitated. "I think we can ... discuss that." The last thing he wanted was to drag her through pregnancy and childbirth again when it clearly was so hard on her. "Maybe in a few more years, after Connie has debuted."

Lorelei shrugged. "I can't force you. I'm also not sure how things will go with a second baby, but I'm starting to think that ... Oh, it doesn't matter. You're right. We'll discuss it. Other decisions, I can pretend to make without you, but I can't even make believe when it comes to children that that's an independent effort." She smirked, and there was a light in her eyes that there hadn't been in a while. "But think how much fun we had with the first one."

"Lorelei." He kissed her forehead. "If you're ready to start talking about that, we can, but let's not worry about that now. We'll want to pray before we make any decisions. It's something we can figure out together, with God's guidance." *Together* was a lovely word.

She tucked her head under his chin. "I shall have to trust you to bring it up again and not pretend that only selfishness could lead you to me. I'm going to want you again someday."

"You are right," Aubrey said in a slow, firm voice. "I want our marriage to honor God in every aspect. But I'd like us to pray about this. We haven't talked about what our relationship would look like if we didn't have to worry about the agreement."

"I thought I'd made it clear I don't care about all that anymore," Lorelei mumbled, as if embarrassed by this admission. "It's not like it was legal anyway. It can be that simple."

Through his eyelashes, he regarded her with a mix of annoyance, amusement, and affection. "I don't think anything with you is going to be simple, but I don't know if I'm simple to live with either. I'm willing to dedicate the rest of my life toward pursuing the Lord with you. If you want to seek Him, consider me a willing classmate, for I need Him desperately, too. I love you, Lori."

"I love you, too," she whispered.

Aubrey nodded and sat, content, with his wife tucked into his side.

CHAPTER TWENTY-NINE

L ORELEI SENT A LETTER to London the following morning and then visited the docks by herself. She called Hastings into the small but professional office Aubrey had obviously put some thought into organizing. She didn't want to admit it, but she was touched by the commanding but ultimately plush chair he'd placed behind the desk, sized to her slightly-more-diminutive-than-the-average-businessman height.

Still, she could encourage Hastings to make more use of this office himself. It was certainly comfortable enough.

"Do you have a copy of the contract between myself and Mr. Montgomery at hand, Hastings?" she said as soon as they were both settled onto their respective seats—her behind the desk, him before it.

Hastings looked to her with surprise, then nodded. "Yes. Yes, Mrs. Montgomery—I have it here." He walked to a file cabinet, which he opened. After a moment of shuffling through papers, he withdrew a folder and handed it to her.

For the first time since her marriage nearly a year ago, Lorelei looked over the carefully typed words of the agreement. The agreement that she believed would hold her marriage and her life together—but that, perhaps, had done more to keep them apart. That was what she had wanted, after all, but no more. No, she would find a way to remove these obstacles, one by one.

Aubrey wanted a full marriage. Though it scared her to death, so did she.

Honestly, Lorelei was more likely to bear being scared—horrified, even—if she wrote down that she intended to "grin and bear it." Which she would. Somehow.

God would have to help her. That was the promise she had been made—that if she surrendered, He would help. It would be a big job, but He was a big God, or so she'd heard tell. It was madness to believe that the Creator of the world couldn't render a change of heart in a small woman. Besides, her heart was ready to be changed—weary and broken and *ready*. Surely the Lord would see that—and heal her.

"'The Lord is nigh unto them that are of a broken heart; and saveth such as be of a contrite spirit. Many are the afflictions of the righteous: but the Lord delivereth him out of them all. He keepeth all his bones: not one of them is broken,'" she mumbled under her breath.

"What is that, Mrs. Montgomery?" Hastings sounded more shocked to hear her quoting Bible verses than anything.

"Oh, nothing." She'd best focus on the task at hand or she'd frighten poor Hastings. Lorelei bent her head over the pages before her—she had a good memory and knew it word for word, nearly by heart. After all, Lorelei knew what she wanted—she always had.

But she wasn't thinking about what she wanted. No, as Hastings waited for her "review," she wasn't considering her options or trying to think how to better her own interests.

She was praying.

Lord, help me surrender. It was a weak prayer, she supposed, but she didn't know what else to pray. *Help me give my all to You—and then to my husband and my child and my family and my friends. I don't know how to do this. I thought it was beyond me. But I'm told You created me—and You don't make mistakes. Not even with me. I'm not a strong woman, as I thought I was, and I've always known I wasn't a pleasant one. If You could show me how to tell my husband that I am ready to be his wife, and that I'll listen if he leads, that'd be nice.*

There. That'd have to do.

Perhaps she'd better pray to pray better—she never had had the words before, and now it seemed even worse—but for now, she simply raised her head and looked Hastings in the eye.

"I have a few changes I need to make," she said. "I need you to help me make them, so when we review them, they make a little sense. I haven't much of a mind for how these things ought to be worded, you see."

"Very well, Mrs. Montgomery," said Hastings, taking her seriously as he ought to. That was the nice thing about Hastings; he always trusted her when no one else did. "This information could be settled between Mr. Montgomery and yourself."

"I know. But I think it would lend a certain legitimacy to have it reviewed by yourself and the Wilsons once more." Lorelei drummed her fingers on the table to keep them from doing something more harmful with their nervousness. "I wish to show my husband that I mean what I say."

"I see." Hastings cocked his head. "Is he not fulfilling some ... some aspect of the agreement as it stands? Legally, you have no recourse."

She shook her head. "Mr. Montgomery has been more than fair. It's me ... I haven't been as fair as I'd like. Mr. Montgomery's terms are too generous."

"I see." A slow smile spread over Hastings's face. "I think that is a wise thing for you to do, Mrs. Montgomery. Equal terms will benefit the arrangement greatly."

"Exactly my thought." She slid the papers across the desk and rose. "Take up a pen and help me make notes."

Agreeably, Hastings did so, jotting down all she said as she paced around the room and tried not to blush. It was most disagreeable to feel like blushing in a business meeting—but hopefully this would be the last time she ever had cause to feel so.

This agreement would last her quite a while, perhaps throughout her lifetime.

"'Til death us depart,'" she quoted sardonically aloud at this thought.

"Should I write that down, Mrs. Montgomery?"

"No, Hastings. Please do not."

Aubrey received a mysterious message from his lawyers announcing that they would be arriving a sennight hence for their "meeting," which made little sense, given that Aubrey had called for no such meeting, nor did he believe there was a matter that needed discussion. Further, he had never requested his lawyers come all the way down from London; he visited them there, when he happened to be in town.

Yet they were coming.

It occurred to Aubrey after a few minutes of staring at the paper in his hand that his wife was probably the cause of this. However, he had thought Lorelei had lost interest in business proceedings—and what could she want with the Messrs. Wilson, anyway?

When approached about the subject, Lorelei was evasive—she told him that discussing it at the meeting would be best. When Aubrey object-ed that perhaps it would be best for all parties to be consulted, Lorelei disagreed, insisting that, after all, his lawyers didn't know what they were coming for either.

This did not exactly comfort him, but he was glad she had taken interest in some business pursuit again, so he let it sit.

A week later, he was sitting in his office with a Mr. Wilson, Hastings, and Lorelei. Hastings handed everyone several papers, and Aubrey found himself looking at his agreement with Lorelei.

His eyes flew to her. "Why?" he asked quietly to disguise the pain in his heart. Did she want to remind him that things were supposed to be businesslike between them? That he had no place in her life, her heart, her bed? That seemed too cruel after the progress they had made, especially lately.

"Hastings will explain" was all Lorelei said, already sorting through the papers in front of her.

"Mrs. Montgomery called this meeting to discuss some needed revisions to the written agreement between Mr. and Mrs. Montgomery," Hastings said. "The first two papers are the arrangement as it now stands; however, Mrs. Montgomery and I have laid out a differing arrangement that we feel more accurately and fairly represents the interests and desires of both parties."

Aubrey hid a smile at the expression on Mr. Wilson's face when he realized that he had made the trip all the way out to Dorset for a matter this trifling. However, Aubrey didn't have long to savor the expression on the man's face as Hastings's words sank in.

He swiftly brushed aside the top two papers and pulled out the ones beneath. Taking a deep breath and ignoring the beginning of a tirade that was erupting from Mr. Wilson, Aubrey began to read.

This contract (referred to as "Agreement" throughout the remainder of this document) is entered into on the twentieth day of the month of August, in the Year of Our Lord, Eighteen Hundred and Eighty-Five, by Mr. Aubrey Montgomery of Montgomery Place in Dorset (referred to throughout the remainder of this document as "Party I") and Mrs. Lorelei Hilton Montgomery of Montgomery Place in Dorset (referred to throughout the remainder of this document as "Party II"). This agreement is not legal in nature but binding to both parties as a solemn promise between Party I and Party II to provide clear expectations during the length of their marriage, the parties having been bound in holy matrimony via the church of England on the twenty-eighth day of the month of August, in the Year of Our Lord, Eighteen Hundred and Eighty-Four. The alterations to this agreement will override and replace any previous terms set in the contract established previously between Mr. Aubrey Montgomery and Mrs. Lorelei Hilton Montgomery.

After this, the agreement was divided into multiple sections, each concerning a different aspect of their lives. When they had first written the agreement, it had all seemed so simple—terms of their lives written out in a way that was easy for both of them to understand. Now it felt wrought with peril to set such delicate things, the events of life and the movements of a relationship, to a contract. Yet as he skimmed the agreement, Aubrey found that it had moved further away from a traditional legal contract than it even had been before. Even the sections were different.

"I. Decisions" was the first section he read. Where before it had offered great power to Lorelei, now it did the opposite. Though there was still a notation about open discussion on any events that concerned both of them, now he had been named "executive," which amused him greatly. "If Party I wishes to override the decisions of Party II, Party II will yield in any matter that does not hold moral concern, and in any case, regardless of the area of concern, Party I will take the lead, whereas Party II will attempt to follow."

It went on to discuss a few options for solving conflicts as well as the somewhat sarcastic comment of "Party II will never be entirely content to be removed from the equation when it comes to matters of business, and this must be considered, even with considerable reduction of Party II's powers being made by this revised agreement."

He looked up to Lorelei, but she simply gestured back to the page. She, too, was ignoring Mr. Hastings and Mr. Wilson, who were now arguing, but all she said was "You can't be done."

"I'm not," he said. "But, darling—"

"You should finish before you decide if you want to sign it."

"I want to sign."

She laughed and shook her head. "Not until you read it all. It's wise to read before you sign."

He reached across his desk for a pen, grinning at her.

"No, *read*. Please—for me. Perhaps the power the first bit promises will not be so sweet when you read my full terms."

"It's not the power," Aubrey said. "It's that you'd do this at all."

She flushed, and Aubrey was grateful that Hastings and Wilson were so consumed.

He turned his eyes back to the contract and continued reading.

She'd discussed his sisters' debuts under "Social Responsibilities of the Parties," she'd termed it, which he was fairly sure was what was currently causing Wilson to see red. She'd discussed maintaining the household and hosting any needed events, both for business and pleasure, in addition to attending church in the village or in London—something she had not done in some time—and visiting with his tenants. He had a similar section, where it mentioned what aspects of society he might engage in, though from what he could tell, it was simply based on his weekly schedule with some fairly close guesses as to what he did when he was in London.

Aubrey realized then that she knew him better than he thought, which pleased him.

There was no amendment to the first paragraph in a section she had retitled "Antisocial Responsibilities of the Party," which concerned them remaining in the same household and seeing each other regularly. However, in the second paragraph, she had said they must share a room or suite of rooms at all times that it were possible and that they should attempt to resolve disagreements before the conclusion of their evening, "amicably enough that this should never not be the case."

It appeared Mr. Wilson hadn't gotten to that section, if he was even reading it at all at this point, for Aubrey was certain he would leave after reading that. Aubrey wanted to leave the room after reading that.

How had she looked Hastings in the eye and had him agree to type that up?

The third paragraph of this section indicated that they must spend time together every evening when they were together, and with their child or children, and that holidays were to be spent with other family members as much as was possible.

Honestly, at this point, Hastings was humoring her in whatever she wanted to say, but Aubrey didn't care. No one in their right mind would sign an agreement like this, for who could predict what life would look like?

But he must be out of his right mind, for he was going to sign it with a flourish as soon as she let him.

The next section was titled "Progeny." Here, most of the original lan-guage had been removed and replaced with provisions for their daughters monetarily with what had been put in trust for Lorelei herself. It occurred to Aubrey that she was right to be so specific here—and once Wilson calmed down, Aubrey would have to have an actual conversation with him about making sure everything was properly set up in a truly legal fashion for Serena and any child that came after her. Which was what the rest of the "Progeny" section concerned.

A yearly review will be made on the subject of children between Party I and Party II, with no outside influence rendered by any unrelated party or any legal advisement, though decisions may also be made throughout the year if it suits both parties. No legal (or moral) agreement need be made now, as perhaps the greatest agreement that can be reached is that Party I and Party II must have a deep trust between them, and a greater trust with their Creator, if any hope of a happy settlement is to be found.

That seemed more than fair to Aubrey. "I'll sign," he said, looking up to her.

"You didn't read the last section," she said, a hint of disappointment in her voice.

"How did you know?"

"You didn't react to it. You read about children and are happy I'm not insisting on starting on the second tomorrow now that I've got it on my mind." Lorelei frowned. "Read."

"This from the woman—oh, excuse me, the Party—who 'will yield in any matter that does not hold moral concern,'" he quoted wryly.

"It doesn't hurt for you to do what I say sometimes." She smirked. "It's an agreement. It's not legal. I can try to boss you around and not be guilty of breach of contract."

He shook his head but returned to the final section, "Choice."

Party I and Party II agree that they will turn their faces toward God, submit to His will, believe in His Son, and follow His commandments. As the Bible clearly indicates (see references provided at the end of this section for general guidance), it is the clear responsibility of Party I and Party II to offer each other love, for Party I to give himself up for Party II, and for Party II to submit herself to Party I. In the face of their occasional or perhaps constant inability to do so on their own power, they will turn to God, the Provider of strength and courage. 'And he said unto me, My grace is sufficient for thee: for my strength is made perfect in weakness. Most gladly therefore will I rather glory in my infirmities, that the power of Christ may rest upon me.' (2 Corinthians 12:9)

He looked up at her. "Lori."

"See, that's the reaction I was waiting for. Complete and utter exhaustion mixed with confusion mixed with what I think is a bit of affection. Isn't it?" She smiled once more, but it swiftly faded. "If you don't want—"

"No. You know that's exactly what I want."

"I wouldn't have been able to write it at all if you didn't want it. I'm not sure I have the strength, but I know you'd say that God does, wouldn't you?"

Aubrey glanced at Wilson, who was collecting his things, and Hastings, who was fastidiously ignoring them. "Yes, Lori. God does."

"So I don't need to," she said with a triumphant grin. "So you will sign?"

"Yes—and then I will put this away and never look at it again. If we want to be Biblical about it, darling, we don't need an agreement; we have a covenant."

"This is important to me," she said simply, rising from her seat. "It means something somehow. Perhaps it oughtn't to. But if I write my name down next to yours, I will do as I said I would—I will love you, and I will obey you, because I put my name to it. I only put my name to things I mean, Aubrey. But you're right that our real agreement is with God—if it's an agreement at all."

"It's more like a desperate plea for guidance," Aubrey admitted. "But the wondrous thing is that we are loved even though we are sinners—and we are offered so much grace."

"That's what I want. But this is my first step. You have to sign first, though, or it doesn't count."

Aubrey nodded despite the fact that it didn't matter in what order their names were signed. As Hastings slipped out of the room, perhaps to try to detain Mr. Wilson a few minutes and perhaps to give them privacy—Aubrey never could tell how discerning the man truly was—Lorelei walked around the table, leaned over him, and signed her name by his. Aubrey rose and put his arms around her.

"We should get Mr. Hastings back in here, and Mr. Wilson, and you should make Mr. Wilson set up a trust for Serena so she's protected in case you die tomorrow," Lorelei said.

He nodded. "I thought of that when I read the agreement. I should have known you didn't call him down for this."

"I would have, but I had other motives, too. I usually do," she said, with a quirk of her head. "I want our daughter to have security; I realized that I'd never worried about it before, but it's important." She shrugged. "The money needs to go somewhere. I was going to put it back into the docks, but it doesn't make any sense if I don't aim for rapid expansion, which at this point makes little sense."

"I know." They could talk about that later. "You're right that she is provided for, but there's more I could do. I think it's good that you are able to remind me."

"I'm glad, for I won't be able to help it. I also had a thought, while I was in the carriage the other day, about the management of the tenant farm that sits on the edge of the property—oh, I think it's the Joneses' or something; I asked the driver for the name, but he wasn't sure. Anyway, if you were to have them grow—"

"Lori."

"What? You said you liked to be reminded."

"I'm not going to have them change what they've been doing for probably centuries. Let the poor Joneses be. They like their farm the way it is and they keep up on their rents, and that's enough for me."

She grinned and stepped out of his arms. "What if it's better my way?"

"What if it's not?"

"That's a risk we may have to take. We'll talk about it when you come around. Just let me know when you're ready to see reason, and I'll explain mine." She took his hand and tugged him around the desk. "Come on, we've got to find Hastings and Wilson."

Aubrey dug in his heels—something he supposed might need to become a permanent feature of his nature if he were to survive the rest of his life with this woman—and pulled her back. "Thank you," he said, looking her in the eye. "We'll catch Hastings and Wilson in a minute—if nothing else, there's no train to London until the evening—but I want you to know this isn't something you've coerced me into. This is my choice, to love you."

She drew back once more. However, she stayed close to him, one hand on his arm, and regarded him pensively. "Certainly, I am not easy to catch, so you must know it was my choice to love you, too."

Aubrey nodded—there was a tightness in his throat that didn't allow for speaking—but he kept her at his side, and they stood, for a time, in the quiet of the office. For once, everything was right, and even if such a feeling were transient and such a reality in this fallen world impossible, he knew that there was a joy that transcended those things.

For once in his life, Aubrey was sure—of his next step, of his duties, of his primary focus—his priority being God and this woman and their family, all molded into one common calling. The clarity of that gave his step a lightness he'd never known before.

At last, Lorelei did step back, but they walked out of the office together, to face whatever might come next.

Epilogue

March 1890

T HE SPRING SUNSHINE DAPPLED through the oak tree under which Lorelei sat, trying to understand the books Hastings had brought to her yesterday. Since the merger, he'd been visiting less regularly, but whenever he did, she was fastidious in her review. It kept Hastings there a few days, and he would fuss about needing to get back to work. Lorelei thought he secretly enjoyed the little vacation and the chance to see the Montgomerys.

A little-boy giggle pierced the silence, and she looked up to see her son, Samuel, barreling through the bushes, his sister behind him.

Lorelei raised her eyebrows. "Serena, I thought I told you to keep Sammy on the front lawn until—"

"Mama, we found the bestest bug!" Serena ran, a big grin on her face, to Lorelei's side. Serena's hands were cupped in that way Lorelei hated most.

She loved being brought "gifts" from her children, if they were rocks or flowers or about anything else that was found in nature—as long as it wasn't alive in that particularly creepy-crawly way that required cupped hands.

"Why don't you bring it inside and show it to your father?" she murmured mildly, turning back to the ledger before her. "In five minutes, I'll be done. Then we can go for our walk. In fact, why don't you fetch your father—"

"I'm already here." Aubrey appeared after the children. "Let me see your bug, sweetheart."

To Lorelei's relief, her children dashed over to her husband, and Lorelei closed the book. So much for that. She'd have to finish this evening, if Aubrey let her. Truly, why had she believed the children would entertain themselves in a non-insect-related way if brought outside? Letting the nanny have a half day had been a mistake of monumental proportions. The woman was paid to work—she should work.

Aubrey had made a big show of whatever dangerous creature Serena had captured but also insisted that it ought to be released. After this feat was accomplished, he turned to Lorelei with a smile.

"Do you want to go on that walk now, Lori?"

"Yes. Let's go by the front door, and we can leave this with the butler."

After dropping off the ledger, Lorelei, Aubrey, and the two small monsters walked off toward the cliffs. It was Lorelei's favorite journey of an afternoon—off to see the ocean, to feel the wind, to hear the seagulls' cries—and the children seemed to enjoy it, too. Though she took the walk nearly daily with her children, she was loath to do it without the nanny, for fear someone would escape her and go tumbling off a cliff's edge—hence Aubrey's presence. She loved her children, but she worried about them constantly, too. Though she knew that in theory, they were content even when only she was around, and perhaps safer with her than with anyone else, too, old fears liked to resurface, taunting her, assuring her that she wasn't enough for her children, and also, that she was on the verge of accidentally getting them killed.

It wasn't true.

At two years old, Samuel was lagging by the time they reached the edge of one of the cliffs. Aubrey knelt and picked him up, and Samuel giggled and screeched in delight as he was lifted onto his father's shoulders.

Lorelei reached up to touch her son's chubby leg, steadying him, and found herself smiling into her husband's blue eyes. They were like Sammy's, much as Lorelei's were like Selena's. "Let's go down to the beach," Lorelei said after a moment. "If you like, I mean." She preferred to stretch out the days, to make more of them, when Aubrey came with them, to allow him to watch the children play and to play with them. She wasn't always the type of mother who engaged willingly in the games her children brought to her, though she tried to be a good sport, but Aubrey was that type of father, and watching him with their children filled a place in her that she hadn't known needed filled.

Down where the sand met the waves, she walked alongside Aubrey while he talked changes to the estate and his understanding of the year's figures with the shipping company. Serena and Samuel were playing their own game, letting the waves chase them, and usually Aubrey would have joined in, but he lingered at Lorelei's side, taking her hand and lacing her fingers with his.

She looked up at him, finding his eyes on her with concern. Right. She was preoccupied, and he'd known it at once—as he always seemed to understand her moods, to even anticipate them.

"I'm all right," she murmured, squeezing his hand in what she hoped was a comforting way. *Hoped* because Aubrey always acted like hand-squeezing was an act of great comfort, and Lorelei did it often in response. Plus, it had then begun to have a similar effect on her, in that she now found it comforting because she knew he did. It was funny how things with Aubrey worked like that. "I'm tired. That's all."

He smiled and bent to kiss her.

Samuel ran over, shrieking, "Mama!" and kicking up sand as he went, and threw his arms around her skirts. The soggy dirt on his fingers and clothes immediately began the process of transferring to her embroidered silk frock.

Lorelei smothered a laugh and affected sternness as she made a show of attempting to unwrap his clinging arms. "Get off me, child."

Giggling, Samuel increased his grip, and Lorelei was forced to tolerate it, as he was far too strong for his own good.

"Why doesn't he fear me?" Lorelei asked, half kneeling to hold him in place for a moment. He had long since passed the stage of regular clinginess, and she was ashamed to admit how much she missed it.

"You're not scary, darling," Aubrey said apologetically. "Not with him."

Lorelei frowned but stroked back her son's golden-brown curls so he would know she wasn't serious. "Sammy, you're this close to plummeting through the proverbial ice to your doom. This is embroidered silk." She bent to place a kiss on his forehead. "You're my boy, aren't you?"

Samuel laughed and let go, running off to catch his sister, who called to him that she'd found some interesting rocks.

Aubrey placed a hand on Lorelei's lower back. "You're the one who dresses like she's going to promenade through London while taking her children down to the coast. Of course they want to cover you in sand."

"I simply believe that one ought to look their best always." This was Aubrey's favorite dress, at least of the ones that were appropriate to wear for this type of outing. She wasn't about to march toward the ocean in a ball gown, but a walking dress that made her husband's eyes follow her at all times? Naturally.

"You do look lovely," he agreed. "Dirty, though."

She shook her head and brushed at the front of her skirts. "Children," she mumbled. "They ruin your clothes and steal your heart, neither of which I wanted. And to think, we're having another later this year."

Her husband stilled beside her. "We are?"

"Yes." She dropped her hands to her sides and turned to him. "Maybe I'm not right—I'd be a month gone is all. But I was right about Sammy. Seems to be about the same every time."

Then she was in his arms, and she tucked her head under his chin and stayed there.

"I'm so glad," he murmured, his voice all froggy. "Oh, Lori, I'm so glad." Then he held her back and looked into her eyes. "You're all right?"

"Yes. I'm all right. I'm ... I'm happy, I think." Or something like happy. Terribly frightened but also terribly glad. "I think Serena said she wanted a sister, so of course I feel it's imperative." She'd give Serena the moon and the stars, if she could lasso them herself. "Samuel shouldn't be the baby.

He's too spoiled as it is."

"Someone's got to be the baby someday," Aubrey observed practically, but he pulled her into another hug. She could feel his heart pounding, and it made her smile—how easily she could crush or make his world, how effortless love had made it to choose the latter, how the Lord had gifted that love to her when she'd been so resistant to it.

"But not for a while. Now, don't get me wrong, Aubrey, I don't want a dozen—but I want a few. I'm affectionate toward families of three children, though I suppose I would tolerate a fourth ... ah, ah, ah, I mean in the right circumstances. Don't get your hopes up. You're going to have to ask God to smack me around a little more."

He chuckled. "I think that's loving guidance, dear."

"Whatever." It felt like smacking, though she knew it was to a purpose.

"Mama! Papa!" Two little voices called them back to reality and out of their embrace. Of course, Samuel slammed into Aubrey's legs this time—he was forever slamming into things; Lorelei felt strongly that little boys were inherently more violent than little girls, for Serena never *slammed* anything. Serena slipped to Lorelei's side and presented her prize—a handful of pretty stones.

"Thank you," Lorelei said, gravely accepting this gift in the spirit it was given—for, after all, it did not crawl. She could tolerate wet, sandy stones. It was "gifts" with legs that she didn't like. "We ought to go back to the house now, Serena. It'll be time for tea."

Serena placed her small hand into Lorelei's. "I hope there are cakes," she said. "I should like that, Mama."

"Mm-hmm." The rocks were placed in Lorelei's pocket, to be added to a collection of similar ones in a box on her nightstand. "I think there might be some."

Holding her daughter's hand, with her other clutching her husband's arm, Lorelei started up the path away from the sea and toward the house she'd come to call home.

A Note from the Author

Dear Reader,

Thank you for taking the time to read Aubrey and Lorelei's story. This was a difficult one for me to write for many reasons. First, Lorelei is not an easy character to write. I'm still not sure I got the balance right! Second, the plot itself changed about three times on the way. What had started out as a somewhat comedic concept quickly became traumatic. (Story of my life, right there! Or rather, story of my writing!) However, months later than I had hoped, God finally gave me the words I needed and allowed this novel to be shared with you.

Of course, I have some thank-yous, as always ...

To Kara Swanson-Matsumoto, my friend and mentor, I offer my complete gratitude—and the dedication of this book. Your impact cannot be underestimated, and you never fail to inspire and encourage me.

A special thank-you to Aimee Simpson, for various contributions, including the accented version of your name. I let you marry Perry's grandson. This great blessing should ingratiate you to me for life. But seriously, thanks for letting me read aloud to you until I lost my voice.

I'd also like to give a big thank-you to Katja H. Labonté, French expert extraordinaire. Katja, you are always so kind to me, and having you check my few lines of this mysterious language for accuracy really helped. Any remaining errors are my own.

Of course, big round of applause to H.S. Kylian, M.C. Kennedy, Loretta Marchize, E.R. Ingraldi, Abigail Cleek, Jessica B. Brown, my alpha and beta readers. You helped me figure out if this story could work, which I didn't believe for a while, and for that, I am endlessly grateful.

As for what comes next, of course I'll be sharing book three in The Hilton Legacy, *Like Lightning in a Bottle*, soon. Winnie's story is going to be a lot of fun, especially if you love horses, fireflies, and ... the fake dating trope? But not really?

Until then, make sure to head over to my website and join my newsletter: kellynrothauthor.com. This is a great way to stay in contact with me and hear all the latest news!

TTFN!

~ Kellyn Roth ~

Also by the Author

The Chronicles of Alice & Ivy

The Dressmaker's Secret
Ivy Introspective
The Knights of Pearlbelle Park (novella)
Becoming Miss Knight (novella)
At Her Fingertips
Beyond Her Calling
A Prayer Unanswered
After Our Castle

The Hilton Legacy

Like a Ship on the Sea
Like the Air After Rain
Like a Storm Against the Cliffs

Kees & Colliers

Souls Astray
Goldfish Secrets (short story)
The Lady of the Vineyard
Flowers in Her Heart

Standalone Short Stories

Esther Ashton's New Dress
Kind: a Christmas short story of post-WWII Munich
Eddy & the Tidepools
Baby Mine

Anthologies

Springtime in Surrey
Novelists in November
Fingerprints in Frost
Voices of the Future: Stories of Courage & Compassion

A Free Novella for You

Interested in a free novella, available only for subscribers to my mailing list?

January 1944

June Halsted moved her son to Hearthstone Cottage to escape the memories of her failed marriage and estranged family. A struggling artist in the midst of one of the coldest winters in Yorkshire, she finds herself seeking solace at church ... only to meet Mark Hayes, a kindly farmer with a limp and a knack for cheering up her son.

Inspired by The Tenant of Wildfell Hall, *this novella is a sweet romance with Christian themes.*

Go to *kellynrothauthor.com/newsletter* and subscribe to my email list to receive your free story!